Flight

A NOVEL

GINGER STRAND

Simon & Schuster

NEW YORK · LONDON · TORONTO · SYDNEY

SIMON & SCHUSTER
Rockefeller Center
1230 Avenue of the Americas
New York, NY 10020

Copyright © 2005 by Ginger Strand

SIMON & SCHUSTER and colophon are registered trademarks
of Simon & Schuster, Inc.

For information about special discounts for bulk purchases
please contact Simon & Schuster Special Sales at
1-800-456-6798 or business@simonandschuster.com

Manufactured in the United States of America

1   3   5   7   9   10   8   6   4   2

Library of Congress Cataloging-in-Publication Data
Strand, Ginger Gail.
Flight : a novel / Ginger Strand.
p.   cm.
1. Air pilots—Family relationships—Fiction. 2. Parent and adult children—Fiction.
3. Fathers and daughters—Fiction. 4. Weddings—Fiction. I. Title.

PS3619.T7354F58 2005
813'.6—dc22   2004062572

ISBN 0-7432-6684-6

For Bob, who made it possible,
and Miranda, who made it worthwhile

one

THE THING TO UNDERSTAND ABOUT AIRPLANES, WILL always says, is that they want to fly. Diving, rolling, breaking to bits, plummeting to earth—those are things you have to make them do. When the girls were little, he would tell them to put their hands out the car windows and let them glide on the solid cushion of air. *Now angle it up,* he would say, and they would shriek with delight as their hands rose smoothly toward the sky. Margaret always rode behind the passenger seat. She had figured out that you see more from there, without the freeway median blocking your view. Also, being closer to the billboards gave her an advantage in the alphabet game. Leanne never seemed to mind.

A tiny raindrop lands on Will's face, sharp and precise as a pinprick. He looks down, surprised back into the present. The driveway asphalt twinkles up at him. What was he doing? More and more, he's developed the old person's habit of getting overtaken by his thoughts, contemplation swallowing his intentions until he stops, unsure how to move forward. Almost sixty. Almost entirely used up, at least as far as the FAA's concerned. He blinks. There's a large black emptiness in the center of his field of vision. It's from staring up, not at the sun, hidden behind a white scrim of clouds, but at the white sky. An airplane passing overhead, that was what made him stop and think about flying. Leanne is flying home today, arriving in Grand Rapids this morning, three days before her wedding. Absently, he wonders if the rain will slow things down at the airport. There's no reason it should, but like all small airports, Grand Rapids is hard to predict. Sometimes they keep it together, but a little weather can drive the tower wonky.

The spring rain is lasting so long this year. Usually by June in Michigan, you can count on the days being mostly sunny. The strawberries will suffer for it this year. They like a burst of sun at the last minute.

Actually, it's Margaret he's worried about. Leanne will be fine, gliding in on Continental, subject to minor delays perhaps, but safe. At least as long as nothing unnatural happens—he veers away from even thinking about that. Margaret and David are the ones to fear for, driving up from Evanston, where they both teach. That could be ugly if it starts raining hard. The Dan Ryan, slick with oil and water, crowded with speeding Chicago drivers. Or that section of I-94 near Gary, Indiana, where all the trucks seem to converge. Even when traffic thins out around Michigan City, it's still a fast road, given to construction barricades and narrow shoulders, tractor trailers jackknifing and minivans charging down on you from the right. He knows it well, knows every mile of it like a well-used garment. He's worn that highway like a coat for over thirty years, since he moved the family to Ryville, Michigan, and took on the two-and-a-half-hour commute to O'Hare. It's the bald midwesternness of I-94 that causes problems. The road is straight and flat and not as crowded as highways in the East or California, so people think there's nothing to fear. They put their feet on the gas and drive flat out, their thoughts elsewhere, eyes fixed and numb, like people awake but dreaming.

Will doesn't fly out of O'Hare anymore, but when he did, he would check the highway on the approach. From the east, the approach to O'Hare sweeps over southern Michigan, following the path of I-94, the only major east-west road in the lower third of the state. It was easy to tick off Michigan's cities, each clustered around an I-94 interchange. First was Detroit, stuck to the eastern edge of the state as if trying to escape. An old pilot's trick question: If you take off from Detroit and fly due south, what's the first foreign country you pass over? The girls always loved the answer: *Canada*.

Over the years, Detroit has spread west, toward Ann Arbor, planted at the intersection of U.S. 23. After Ann Arbor, fields take over, then there's Jackson, hanging by the thread of U.S. 127. Then more fields until I-69 marks Battle Creek, where you sometimes see the flash of a fighter jet streaking toward the Air National Guard base. In another twenty miles, as regular as county lines, another freeway, U.S. 131, with Kalamazoo tumbling outward around it. Due north of Kalamazoo you can see Grand Rapids, and due west you can see the lake. Somewhere in that quadrant, too small to be seen from the air, is Ryville, the town where Will grew up, the town where he's standing now.

Whenever a plane passes overhead, Will imagines the view from above, just as when he flies over Michigan, he imagines being on the ground looking up. Flying over Michigan is both familiar and strange, like looking at a well-known face upside down. He sees the puzzle pieces of farms below and imagines himself down there, the huffing of the tractor, the smell of stirred-up earth. When he was young, he wanted to avoid that. That's why he enlisted in the Air Force, working the motor pool and taking night classes until he finally made it to flight school at Laughlin Air Force Base in Del Rio. He lived in a cardboard duplex ten miles from the Mexican border, and every morning he burned a supersonic trail over the bleak expanse of western Texas. Even if he could see the ground, he didn't look. He'd put over a thousand miles between him and any ground that could call him back.

The wind picks up with a heavy sigh, like a horse standing bored in the barn. The whiteness is darkening to gray. There's a brief splatter of tiny raindrops on the top of his head, where his hair has thinned enough to be considered no longer there. He walks to the end of the driveway and looks down the road, aware of a fearful sensation that seems out of proportion. It's only a county road, but cars travel fast on it. They lost two cats and a horse to that road, and the people down the street lost a child. He remembers being sad for them at the time, but it felt distant, someone else's sorrow. Now his heart tightens with anxiety at the thought. Every year his heart, old fool, pounds harder for the past's close calls. Danger seems closer to him now than it did then, as if every time it missed him, it took another step in his direction.

Still, he has to cross the road. Their mailbox, like all the others on the rural route, is on the other side of the road, so the mailman can pass by once. That's why he's out here, to get the mail. That and to get out of the house. He glances back over his shoulder. In the flat, fading light, the house windows look dark, as if brimming with the energy that pushed him outside. Carol is in there, eddying through each room in a last-minute surge of nervous preparation.

Today is Wednesday, a day set aside for the girls' arrivals, one with her husband and son, one with her husband-to-be. Tomorrow is slated for preparations and Friday is the wedding rehearsal. Bucking tradition, there won't be a rehearsal dinner, but a cocktail reception for family and close friends in their home. He supposes that's what's got Carol all worked up, the thought of forty people milling around, all of them needing drinks and elegant little snacks. Carol likes to do things right. He used to love that about her. When he was in flight school, he was proud to bring his fellow pilots home, pleased when she cooked Easter dinner for his family. But lately, there's been something desperate about it. She'll be sweating every last detail until the party is over, and then she'll be worrying for weeks about the little problems, going over it all in her mind. Even when everything's perfect, she seems discontent. But maybe she's always been that way. Maybe he's only noticing it now.

A truck whizzes by, a piece of farm equipment rattling in the bed, and then from the other direction, a single blue minivan. The truck driver raises his hand in a slight wave, not because he knows Will but because that's what people do in the country. The minivan driver is a woman, and she doesn't even look at Will. Her van is new and boxy, a strange, almost aqua, color. Will makes her to be someone from the new high-end suburb growing west of town, on the edge of the state forest. The houses are big, all variations on the same theme, a young architect's supposedly creative reinterpretation of the midwestern farmhouse, rife with gables and peaks and trim. Their lawns are studies in contrast: rich green expanses of unrolled sod punctuated by scrubby trees from the local nursery, some still sporting orange tags with their name and price.

Everything is changing, even here. He's seen it in nearly thirty years of flying over the country. In the seventies, at night, you would go for hours without seeing a single city, only scattered individual lights. Now every town has sprawled outward, and every part of the country, even the desert west of the Rockies, is carpeted with tiny pricks of light. Throughout the Plains states, the lights follow the dark line of the freeways, just as they must have once followed the great rivers.

"The Great Trajectory," he murmurs. It's the title of a book he's reading. The author, an anthropologist at a university out west, argues that the progress of all human civilizations mirrors the course of a single human life. The first phase is simple needs fulfillment. Then there's a steep learning curve, leading to greater self-awareness and socialization. An era of increasing achievement follows, which the author calls "the Ambition Years." Then comes the decline: first a slowdown in accomplishments, then the tailing off of ambition itself. Decadence: an era marked by physical decline. In people it's an aging body, in cultures a depletion of the natural resources that made them successful. After that it's just a matter of time until the end.

Will likes the theory. The author argues that Western civilization is solidly into its decadence, and that makes sense to him. There are accounts of all sorts of ancient civilizations—the Romans, but also the Mayans, the Taino, the Babylonians—and the story is always the same. It reminds him of the biographies he used to love reading: Andrew Jackson, FDR, Patton. There was always a fresh one under the tree at Christmas, but after a while, he couldn't read them anymore. You always knew how the story would end.

With the road finally free of traffic, Will walks across to the mailbox. It's an extralarge metal one from Farm and Fleet, big enough that it won't overflow, even when they go away for a few days. Over the years it has proved roomy enough for Christmas cards and tax forms, for Margaret's college catalogs, for the design magazines Carol ordered when she was planning to start an interior-decorating business, for the continuing-education bulletins she got when she thought she'd go back to school and become a teacher. *Carol and her projects,* his sister Janice always said, shaking her head.

The mailbox door opens with a metallic squawk, revealing a modest bundle of mail, still rubber-banded together. The girls haven't lived at home for fifteen years, and Will and Carol don't get as much mail. Today's small group of letters is protectively encircled by a shrink-wrapped magazine. Will looks at that first, because it's bound to be for Carol. *Olde Country Inns.* The cover shows a picture of the deck of a large white farmhouse. A wicker and glass table is set for brunch, everything in shades of blue. He looks back at his house. This is Carol's project now: she announced it last week at dinner. She wants to turn the farm into a bed-and-breakfast.

"You mean have strangers come and stay in our home?" Will asked.

"For a price," she said.

"But why would they want to stay here?" he continued, pressing it.

She gave him an inscrutable look. "For the wholesome country atmosphere, of course," she said, her voice level enough that he could hear her sarcasm but couldn't call her on it. "For the spiritual rejuvenation of a return to simpler times."

Two of the letters are wedding-related: something from the caterer and something from the church. Bills, no doubt. Will has shelled out hundreds of dollars in deposits already, and he knows it will tally up to thousands before it's over. He shuffles those to the bottom of the stack and looks at the rest. Another bill, this one from the phone company. A quarterly report from his pension plan, now worth one quarter of what he had expected, since TWA went bankrupt and got absorbed into American. A credit-card offer. And there, at the bottom of the stack, the letter he's been waiting for without really thinking about it, the real reason he came out to get the mail so soon after hearing the gravelly roar of the mailman pulling off the shoulder, why for over a week now he has beaten Carol to the mailbox every day. The return address is embossed with the aqua logo, a wispy bird drawn in one stroke like a Chinese character. Next to it is the name: Cathay Pacific Airways.

So it's really happening. A couple months ago he ran into Harris

Grolier, a fellow captain from TWA. The flak over American's acquisition was in the process of dying down, and while no one's worst fears were fulfilled, no one was exactly thrilled either. Even with reasonable seniority and a better salary, few TWA pilots were happy about flying for American. How do you shed thirty years of loyalty to one company and put on your competitor's uniform just like that?

"There's always the Far East trick," Harris said to Will. "I hear Cathay's hiring."

The Far East trick is what some guys do after retiring. The U.S. and Europe have mandatory retirement at sixty. Far Eastern airlines don't. Everyone knows guys who went to Japan Airlines or Cathay Pacific and flew well into their seventies, starting out in freight and then moving into passenger service. As long as you pass the physicals, you can stay in the sky.

Will sent an application to Cathay. His sixtieth birthday is coming up in July. All his life he has planned to retire when his time came, settle into the farm and do what he moved back there to do. In retirement, he can be a real farmer, full time. Now, with commercial planes being used as weapons, he should be eager to turn in his wings. But for some reason, the thought terrifies him. He tries to imagine his life without flying, but he can't. He can see himself driving to Farm and Fleet, fixing the door on the barn, walking the fence line, seeding the western field with George's John Deere. But he can't see himself doing all those things knowing he's never going to fly an airplane again.

Ever since he was twelve years old, he wanted to fly. It came to him in a moment, when he was plowing his father's field, his skinny boy arms still having to crank double time to turn the tractor's large steering wheel. He looked up and saw a plane, a Gooney Bird or a Constellation, buzzing its tinny path to Midway, and he wanted so much to be up there, cleaving a furrow through the sky, that something in him slammed shut and he knew he was gone. He knew right then that he would put tractor and field and farm behind him and learn to fly.

He opens the letter and flits his eyes over it—*Asia Pacific freight routes, standard benefits package, transfer to passenger fleet*—and it's almost like takeoff, something you know is going to happen but still sucks the stomach out of you when it actually does. He went to work right out of the Air Force, straight from Vietnam. What will it be like to go back to the Far East as a pilot, even on commercial jets? He could find himself flying into Bangkok again, or Saigon, or even Hanoi. He imagines the lush green jungle, the neat geometry of rice paddies, the long low plateau just north of Hanoi they called Thud Ridge because so many F-105s went down there. His buddy Rogoff's plane—what's left of it—is on that ridge. Rusting on the damp Hanoi ground. The great trajectory. A tight hard knot seems to be resting not in his stomach but lower down in his gut. He needs to go to the bathroom.

He turns and faces his house again, waiting for a chocolate brown SUV to pass before he ambles back across the road. He folds the Cathay Pacific letter in half and shoves it into the front pocket of his hooded sweatshirt. He hasn't made a decision yet. But Carol doesn't even know he's thinking about it.

The concrete walk up to the front door is lined with flower beds. Most farmhouses don't have a front walk, but Carol had insisted.

"We're not farmers," she said when they first moved in, "so there's no reason to pretend to be." She was using the tone that meant the subject was closed, so Will had kept silent. In fact, as the son of a farmer and the owner of a farm, he qualified for the label. But he didn't say that. *If we're not pretending to be farmers,* he thought, *what are we pretending to be?* He didn't say that either—it would have started a fight. Those were the early days, when Margaret was three and Leanne just a baby. They avoided fighting then, much as they do now. It was the middle years that were full of battles, shouting, nights spent stewing in anger, whole days without speaking.

He puts the mail down on the front porch and goes back to the flower beds, where he noticed a few weeds. If Carol sees them, she'll ask him to pull them. She's determined to have everything perfect when people come over for the dinner. Kneeling down on the sidewalk, he feels a lightening in his heart, an automatic satisfaction triggered by the action of doing something that will make Carol happy.

The weeds are reedy and green. They look healthier than the delicate pansies and nasturtiums Carol has laid out with obvious care. Somehow the sight of the flowers, bravely trying to live up to an ideal of luxuriant beauty, makes his heart ache. For all her efforts, Carol never seems to get it exactly right. And yet what she wants is simple: beauty, elegance, control. He grabs a weed by the base and yanks.

He works methodically, rolling the idea of Cathay Pacific over in his mind, thumbing the possibility like a pebble. According to Harris, freight pilots are based in the U.S., New York or Chicago. So that won't be a big change. But when you switch over to passenger service, you have to be based in Hong Kong. He could leave George in charge of the farm, as he always has when going away on trips. He and Carol can have the excitement of living somewhere exotic for four or five years while he finishes up his flying career. It won't be such a long time, really. He isn't going to do it forever, just long enough for him to wrap up his flying years with grace and a sense of completion, not the abrupt disappointment of seeing the airline he worked for all his life simply fold up and disappear like a bad restaurant. Not the ignominy of turning sixty and being officially declared unfit by the FAA.

"How would you like to live in Hong Kong for a couple of years?" he imagines himself saying. Carol should be thrilled. She has never loved the farm—in fact, she's spent much of her life regretting their move from the nice Chicago suburb where she started her career as an airline pilot's wife in 1968. She has often pointed out how much the girls would benefit from a year or two abroad. The girls are no longer an issue, but living abroad is still a glamorous prospect. They'll live in one of the world's most cosmopolitan cities, socialize with other pilots and their wives. The food's supposed to be good. And the shopping—that alone should make her want to go.

He's plucking the last few weeds from the main bed when he

notices a sparkle on the back of his hand. He stops and sits back on his heels, examining it. Veins cross his hand like highways, curving up over the hill of his bones. Around them blooms a dark mottled colony of age spots. Now there are lighter spots among them, shimmery teardrops of rain. He looks up, and another one hits him in the eye. It's only a splattering, but he can see from the gray banks of cloud that real rain is on its way. They're the clouds that look like a solid thing from above, a fuzzy wool blanket some giant has thrown over the earth. He stands up, bones aching from just five minutes of crouching. Turning to the west, he squints toward the lake. It's thirty miles away, but from the air he could see it, could determine whether or not Margaret and David will be starting out their drive in the rain, or whether they'll have clear going for fifty miles. Once they get to this side of the lake, they'll be in it.

Drive safe, he thinks, sending the thought out along this road, along the county road through the state forest and down the long gray tunnel of I-94. He thinks of his daughter and son-in-law in the front seat, his grandson on his booster in the back. He's four, but they make boosters for bigger kids, too, now. When Will was young, they just put the kids in the car and called it safe. These days it seems parents have to contemplate danger lurking whichever way they turn.

He goes toward the ditch and tosses the weeds into the brackish water that has pooled there since the thaw. Then he goes back to the porch and picks up the bundle of mail. He puts his hand against his sweatshirt pocket, and there's a slight crackle. As if in answer, a quick flash of lightning is followed by a low growl of thunder. The wind picks up quickly, then stops. The world stands still, expectant. Will is moving toward the front door, mail in one hand, the other reaching for the knob, as the clouds seem to break apart and a curtain of rain drops down.

There's a service plaza coming up, Margaret knows it. She remembers it as a childhood landmark, her father driving them home from

O'Hare after a flight from San Francisco or Phoenix or Fort Lauderdale, some trip he thought might be fun for the family. It's not an exit—she doesn't want to risk an exit, which might cause confusion about getting back on the highway, might involve her in stoplights and left turns and merges, any of which could spoil her forward momentum—but a freestanding service plaza, with gas stations on both sides of the highway and a restaurant perched on the overpass above the traffic. It's somewhere just east of the city, because when they drove to Chicago, the sight of that plaza was always a sign that they were nearing O'Hare. Once they drove by it after a tornado, and every window of the restaurant was blown out. Long blue curtains trailed out the windows, swaying like the leaves of an underwater plant. Margaret was surprised when they next passed to see it put back together, lights bright, people inside eating chicken nuggets or french fries while traffic zoomed by underneath. Quick restoration was unusual for Chicago, a city not gifted in the art of renewal. Margaret always envisions it as entropic, an explosion moving outward as the center goes from bad to worse. She used to love its urban shabbiness, because it was so far from the rural shabbiness that surrounded her childhood, in spite of her mother's vigilance. Now she can't help but see Chicago's decrepitude as something darker, a metaphor for all the winding-downs she's living through— of empire, of prosperity, of youth and expectation and love.

Love. Love is what got her here.

"Don't do this, Margaret." It didn't sound like him, her husband of seven years. It was his voice hollowed out, as if a knife had scraped it clean of something that wasn't essential to him, perhaps, but was essential to her loving him.

Margaret looks in the rearview mirror. Trevor has his head resting against the backseat, turned to the side so he can stare out the window. His eyes don't seem to be following anything; he'll probably be asleep soon, she thinks, glancing ahead to where a rickety little delivery truck is valiantly trying to overtake an eighteen-wheeler. *David and Goliath,* she thinks, and the cold stab of fear hits her stomach again with the name. *David.*

She's going to need gas. If she and David had driven to Michigan together, as planned, they would have brought what has always been considered "their" car, a reasonably new Toyota Corolla with gray upholstery and a CD player and air-conditioning. Instead she is driving "her" car, a powder blue Volkswagen Rabbit that has somehow survived, through underuse and sheer doggedness, since her grad-school days in Irvine. She hadn't considered what she was doing, but when she picked up her suitcase—packed since yesterday, before the fight began—and took Trevor's hand, the keys she lifted out of the Mexican ceramic bowl by the front door were not the Corolla's but the Rabbit's. Her car. It was what she said when she left the message for Vasant. *I'm taking my car and driving to Michigan.*

"I don't care about some stupid wedding," David had said. "This is about our life together. You'll stay until we've sorted this out." It's ludicrous, really. She bites her lip, remembering. How did they end up arguing that way, she and David, like some couple on *Jerry Springer*? How did her perfectly rational, well educated husband, the likely next chair of physics at Northwestern (and what could be more rational, more dedicated to the steady, dispassionate, judicious pursuit of solutions than physics?), how could this man have such words in his mouth? But even worse than what he said was what he did when she quietly moved toward the door. He stepped between it and her. It was deliberate and immediate, and at that moment it seemed that some completely different consciousness was ruling the father of her child. His hands were clenched at his sides. He wasn't going to *let* her leave. For the first time since she met him in college, she felt afraid of him. Not afraid that he might hurt her—that seemed likely, but not the real tragedy. The real thing to fear was what would happen after that. How much things would change. How unfixable it would all be then.

Up until now she has felt jittery and wired, as if something in her was goading her to push things to a breaking point and then make a run for it. All of a sudden, the sheer awfulness of it all sweeps over her, and her eyes fog up with tears. Sniffing hard, she wipes her eyes with the back of her hand. She can't risk crying on the Dan Ryan at sixty-five miles an hour. She glances in the rearview mirror again and is dismayed to see Trevor's eyes on her, fixed and wide.

"Go to sleep, sweetie," she tells him. "It's going to be a long drive." To her relief, her voice sounds normal, and Trevor lets out a little sigh, a habit of his that makes him seem, for an instant, more like fifty than pushing five.

They might have survived all of it—David's girlfriends, Vasant, the awkwardness, the anger—their marriage was based on rational principles, after all—but the phone call shattered it. And there's no taking it back.

The worst part of it, the thing she keeps mentally replaying with a frantic, nauseated feeling of regret, is the laugh. It was right after she hung up the phone. David was sitting on the deacon's bench in their entryway, looking at her, eyes wide, as if seeing her for the very first time. She could see he was still in the process of realizing that she was capable of what she had just done. Suddenly, seeing it from his eyes, she realized what she *had* done, realized that her act of pure and simple desperation was in fact a brilliant first move in a battle that had just commenced. And then she laughed.

It wasn't humor, it wasn't even triumph; it was a desperate hysterical impulse, because it seemed the whole world had turned upside down and the only person who might understand exactly how crazy everything had become was David, sitting there staring at her. Her laugh released him from his stillness, and for a moment she thought he might laugh with her, the two of them might crack up and forget the whole thing, might reverse course and go back to where they were before, turning the awful night and more awful morning into a funny story to tell good friends at dinner parties, after a bottle or two of wine. *The night David tried to be a tough guy. The night Margaret called the cops to arrest me.* For an instant, things hung in the balance as their eyes met and her laugh hung in the air.

"Well then," he said, and looked away. And that was it. She couldn't take back the phone call, and worse, she couldn't take back the laugh. She felt frozen, immobilized against the telephone table, as her husband stood up slowly. His moves were casual but deliberate, as if calculated to prove how far he was from requiring legal restraint. The thing that had scared her, made her pick up the phone and dial, wasn't gone but had retreated to somewhere further down inside him.

"I'm not going to wait around to be arrested," he said, and as if something in him suddenly jerked into gear, he moved, quick and agile, to the foyer. Before anything more could transpire between them, he opened the door and left.

A semi towing two containers roars by her, and Margaret realizes that she has been stuck behind a slow car, a large Galaxy that looks like a relic from the sixties. She's edging left to pass it when she sees up ahead, like a beacon, the service plaza she's been waiting for, crouching over the highway. Relief washes over her, and she slows down to move right instead. At least she won't run out of gas.

It's been so long since she drove the Rabbit that she has forgotten which side the gas tank is on. She gets it wrong the first time, pulls forward, backs into another spot, finds herself too far away, pulls forward again to back in closer to the pump. Her hands are shaking on the wheel. *Calm down,* she tells herself.

Trevor's eyes are half shut, so she leaves him in the car as she uses her Amex card in the automated gas pump. The sight of the card causes another icy lump to form in her stomach. Will he cancel all her plastic? Can he do that? She makes a mental note to call American Express tomorrow. Somehow this makes her feel better. Everything has changed now; they're playing a whole new game, with new rules, but at least there *are* rules. As soon as she has a chance, she will sit down and think through every single thing he might do, and try to formulate a plan.

And then there's Vasant. She won't allow herself to think of him, his thick eyelashes, his graceful hands. She holds that thought in reserve, a treat she's saving for herself, the way when she was writing her thesis, she used to buy a beautiful piece of fruit and save it for when she had completed a section.

The wind has picked up, and she breathes deeply. There's the smell of gasoline and something fried coming from the restaurant area, but there's still a fresh smell in the wind—perhaps the rain, or perhaps something coming off the lake. It's a warm June wind, not yet the hot, fetid current of summer in the city. She finishes filling the gas tank and starts to get back into the car, but then on second thought, gets the squeegee from its tub of gray blue water and does her windows. Something about the methodical motion calms her down: wet the window, scrape the wetness off with the rubber edge, wipe the tool with a paper towel, do it again. The front window is quite dirty, and cleaning it off is so satisfying that she does the sides, even though they're not that dirty, and then the back window, which has sticky brown marks on it from leaves falling on the car. She and David have a parking lot attached to their apartment building, but they get only one covered space. That was always reserved for the Corolla, so Margaret's car has been sitting out in the weather for months without being driven. It's a wonder she even got it started. She stops to experience a satisfying feeling of gratitude toward the Rabbit.

Perhaps this is what her life will be from now on, a series of small graces, now that she's awake to the world again. Vasant did that, she thinks with a small, shuddery thrill. She looks around the service plaza, and suddenly the living, breathing, sensory fullness of the place overwhelms her, as in movies where a video simulation gives way to reality. She breathes in the oily gas-station fumes, and the wind picks up a strand of her hair as gently as a lover would. The orange red of the neon sign, 24 HOURS, the iridescent black of oily spots on the cement, the bottle green of a beater car full of teenage boys pulling up to the next bank of pumps: all of these impressions triple, quadruple in intensity, and her capacity to receive them seems to yawn wide as well. She puts one hand on the car to steady herself. She feels disoriented, as if she were in an airplane and a trapdoor in the floor fell open, plunging her into limitless emptiness. It's a rush of terror and exhilaration: she's no longer going where she was once going, but who knew about this? Who could have imagined the boundlessness of the space that existed outside that tiny moving tube? Who could have imagined the thrill of falling from it?

There's a burst of music, a last gasp of sonic self-assertion as the teenage boys in the beater turn off their engine, and the extraordinary feeling vanishes. A couple of them glance Margaret's way as they pile out of their car, and her neck prickles with a sense of potential danger. Quickly, but with a studied attempt to look calm, she moves back to the driver's side and gets in her car. She locks the doors before starting it.

A sign directs her to the freeway entrance, with arrows pointing to westward and eastward ramps. The possibility flashes up: she could go back. She could turn around and drive straight back to Evanston, and maybe she would get back to the apartment before David returned, maybe he would never have to know that she climbed into her car and drove away from their marriage. Maybe she would even get there before the police did, and she could explain to them, *No, no, I'm so sorry, it was all a big mistake. Yes, I called, but it was just a misunderstanding, everything's fine now.*

She points her car east, toward Michigan.

Somewhere around Michigan City, she notices in the rearview mirror that Trevor has fallen asleep. She drives steadily, four miles above the speed limit, so she'll get only a warning if stopped. When she sees the large blue WELCOME TO MICHIGAN sign, she presses her lips together in a thin line. In the midst of everything, she can't help noting the irony of what she's doing, the ridiculousness of fleeing to Michigan when she has spent the last fifteen years of her life—at least fifteen—trying to put Michigan and everything it stands for behind her. What was the University of Chicago, what was Irvine— what was David, with his Westport family and his cultured upbringing and his nontraditional ideas about marriage—if not a wholehearted rebuke to the flat, rural landscapes, the solid midwestern values, the low expectations that proclaim themselves from every shabby farmhouse, every blue Harvestore silo, in this state?

A few miles inside the Michigan border, she drives smack into what feels like a wall of rain: the silence is wiped out by the tinny roar of water banging onto her car. As if in answer, her eyes fill with tears, and this time she lets them fall, silently, so she won't wake Trevor. She drives and weeps, windshield wipers on high, gas-tank needle still close to F. *The pathetic fallacy,* she thinks, the notion that the weather can represent interior states. But as her strange exhilaration drains away, she knows that it's not really sadness that makes her cry. She's crying because she's turned a corner that was not on her carefully mapped life plan. She's crying because she's on her way, alone, to celebrate her sister's wedding, an event that has been in her plans for months, but not like this. She's crying because she's Margaret and she has just passed Benton Harbor, which means she has only sixty more miles to cry before she'll stop, wipe her eyes, practice some of the deep ashtanga breathing she has learned in yoga, and pull herself together to face her family as the ambitious, confident, self-sufficient woman they all know her to be.

The doves are okay.

The vacuum cleaner growls along. Carol's back is showing the first signs of getting sore, but she keeps going, putting her full wrist, arm, and shoulder into each stroke across the living room carpet. She'll be doing this even more regularly once she has the bed-and-breakfast up and running. The vacuum hums going out, haws coming back in. Its baleens sift through the deep pile of the fawn carpet she fell in love with at Carpet World. When she's done with the living room, she'll move on to the dining room. Back and forth, thrust and parry. Not. One. Speck. Of. Dirt. Will. Remain.

The doves are okay.

She's been saying it all morning, a kind of mantra. She pictures them in their wooden cage in the garage, turning in futile circles or huddled bleakly, in the corner. Every now and then a soft trilling, like a fairy princess gargling, comes from one of them, it's never clear which.

But they're alive. At that thought, she redoubles her vacuuming efforts, throwing her lower back into it, as if nothing but an impeccable living room carpet can possibly testify to her gratitude for the lives of two small grayish birds. Sparks of pain crackle up the ladder of her spine, but she ignores them.

"Why are you so worried about it?" Will said at breakfast. "It's not like there's any shortage of poultry in these parts." He'd already proposed that Leanne's guests might appreciate it more if she bought a couple of turkeys to release and let everyone bring their rifles. That's Will's sense of humor, hiding his deep-down inability to understand. Leanne wants one still, beautiful moment at her wedding—she and Kit will release the doves after the kiss—and Will has never been one for still moments, beautiful or otherwise. Life for him is a highway: the faster you move forward, the more you'll see along the way. After thirty-six years, Carol understands that much about him, has learned to accept it and even sometimes laugh at it. Still, she can't help but chafe against his continued desire to bait her, even when the second-to-last full day for preparations is upon them. The wedding is Saturday. The girls are coming today with Kit and David, Trevor must be lapped with grandmotherly attention, Kit's mother comes on Friday, and somehow Carol must be ready to host forty people for cocktails on Friday night ("Let's skip that whole dull rehearsal-dinner thing," Leanne said on the phone) when the Harding's in Ryville has never stocked an artichoke, let alone fresh shrimp. Can't Will see that she's stressed and try to be nice? Instead, he's been mocking her practically since the moment she awoke this morning with an icy hand squeezing her heart, convinced that something was drastically wrong.

Years of experience have taught Carol that leaping out of bed and trying to check on everything is inevitably counterproductive. She has taught herself to lie still and clear her mind, not addressing the fear but not banishing it, either, just allowing it to float in like fog. She stares right into it, and eventually, as happens when you stare into fog, something will glide into view—usually the thing that generated the anxiety. Then she can get up and address it calmly.

As a mother, Carol always prided herself on her intuition. "I've got eyes in the back of my head," she would tell the girls, and for years they believed her. Fights were nipped in the bud before they began, guilty silences always led to a shout: "What's going on in there?" Even Will was impressed by how quickly Carol could burrow to the heart of a lie. But all of those things come with mothering's territory, if you just pay attention. The only thing Carol considers unusual is her talent for predicting disaster.

So this morning, when anxiety struck, she lay very still and looked at the ceiling until the image came to her: the doves. It wasn't clear what had happened to them, but something was wrong. Immediately, her brain raced through scenarios: poisoned feed, lethal stray wires, foxes burrowing into the garage. She stood up and threw on a robe, trying not to wake Will. He lifted his head as she moved toward the hall.

"What's up?"

"Nothing. I'm just checking on those doves." She slipped out before he could say more.

Her heart pounded as she pattered down the staircase and to the door. The garage was gloomy and still. She moved toward the cage and heard a rustle of distress at her approach. She could see two soft gray lumps in the dim light, but she couldn't tell if anything was wrong. She went back and turned on the light. There was a small cooing sound, as if the birds recognized the light as a sign to wake up. Returning, she stared at them. They were both hunkered down, feathers fluffed around them like quilts. They regarded her steadily with beadlike black eyes. She willed them to get up and walk around, do something to prove their well-being, but they didn't move. Finally, she unhitched the cage door and stuck a hand in, fluttering it clumsily toward them. They both rustled to their feet, eyes fixed on the hand, and scuttled back. Perfectly fine. When she pulled her hand out, they looked at her with obvious reproach.

Now, finished vacuuming the living room, she is tempted to check on them again, but she has gone into the garage four times already this morning, and if Will comes in from the mailbox and finds her there again, she'll never hear the end of it. She decides to focus on the problem of Doug.

Already she can hear her own voice, defensive but unconvincing. She can imagine the look of absolute horror Margaret will give her when she finds out what Carol did. Margaret has always been good at killer expressions.

He seemed so genuinely pleased for Leanne, Carol hears herself saying. *It just slipped out before I thought about it.* It's all true. She considers adding how nice he looked, there in Harding's, his cart full of frozen dinners and granola bars and instant vitamin shakes. Shopping for his mother, he explained. Mrs. Johannsen had a hard time getting around these days. Doug's devotion to his mother was widely accepted in town as the reason he had never married, and he had smiled such a fond smile when he spoke of her that Carol's heart melted. The fact that he was a pig farmer's son who had dated Margaret slipped her mind, and all she saw was a fine young man— nice broad shoulders, too—who remained, in his thirties, an attentive and loving son.

No, strike that. Margaret would be angry at her for singing Doug's praises in front of David. In fact, Carol has no idea whether David even knows about Doug. Presumably, a woman who teaches history at one of the nation's very best universities—*She could be teaching in the Ivy League,* Carol always tells people, *but she wanted to stay close to home*—doesn't go around bragging about the Future Farmers of America she dated in high school. Carol makes a mental note to herself to speak only of "your old friend Doug."

There's even some hope that Margaret's reticence to admit her connection to Doug might save Carol from her daughter's scorn. After all, who could possibly get upset about her mother inviting a childhood friend to her sister's pre-wedding cocktail party? In fact—and here Carol recognizes the flash of maternal insight that is the only thing preventing worldwide familial discord—Carol can simply pretend to have forgotten that Doug and Margaret were ever romantically involved. After all, they were just kids. It wasn't as if it was some big passionate love affair. (A little voice in Carol's head

pipes in that her own dislike for Doug always suggested the opposite—that he was actually a threat even then, and ever since, she has
secretly suspected him of never getting over Margaret. Decisively,
she squelches it.) As long as Carol refuses to acknowledge that there
might be a problem, Margaret can't create one without explaining
exactly why she doesn't want Doug there.

How did it come to this? Carol wonders as she winds up the
vacuum-cleaner cord. Margaret was always determined, always
focused on the next thing, while Leanne was Carol's baby, clingy
and content. But Carol always encouraged Margaret, always appreciated her drive. She nurtured ambition in both her girls, pushing
them to use first-rate manners, to succeed in school, in short, to rise
above the place where they were raised. And Leanne, her baby, was
the one who rebelled, running off to New York, while Margaret
achieved everything Carol hoped she would: college, graduate
school, an impressive career, a brilliant and cultured husband, a
lovely son. Now, with everything Carol has ever dreamed for her,
Margaret seems to have forgotten who helped her find those
dreams in the first place, who encouraged her to think big and
promised her she could do or be whatever she wanted. She comes
home and looks around with disdain, and Carol is the one who's
terrorized. "Mom, how can you stand those curtains?" Margaret
will say, or "Really, Mom, you ought to be eating better," or "What
do you mean you told Brenda Moran I'd be in town?"

It's always been easier to be close to Leanne. Even after her decision not to go to college, a decision that still makes Carol's throat
feel dry and tight, as if she's choking. Even after Leanne moved to
New York and lived God knows what kind of life for several years
after high school, working in some awful bar. By the time of
Margaret's wedding, Leanne was drinking so much she appeared to
be slightly waterlogged. Although this was something Carol never
could have imagined for either of her girls, she felt like she could
talk to Leanne. After Margaret's wedding, Carol flew to New York
and stayed there a month and talked to her. Through sheer persis-
tence—simply refusing to pack up and leave—she found a way to

help. Now Leanne lives in Cold Spring, an hour north of the city, in an adorable small house she bought with her own money once her store—specialty high-end crafts—became successful. Though Carol still thinks Leanne could have been anything—a doctor, a lawyer, an architect—she has to admit that Leanne's life suits her. It ought to— it cost Carol fifteen thousand dollars.

The front door opens, and Carol hears a strange clattering that she recognizes, after a few seconds, as heavy rain. Okay, so it's raining. The wedding is three days away. Saturday's sure to be gorgeous. June weather is reliable; that's why it's traditional to have weddings then. She glances at the clock. They need to go to the airport to meet Leanne and Kit, and she wanted to stop at Meijer in Grand Rapids on the way, to pick up some items the Ryville Harding's won't have. She also needs to grab a few sundries—shampoos, fancy soaps, hand creams—to stock the guest bedroom. Kit's mother flies in on Friday morning from Atlanta, and after many phone calls with Leanne, Carol has prevailed on the woman to stay with them.

"Tell her it will be good practice for me," Carol kept saying, "for running my bed-and-breakfast." Kit's mother had been concerned about Carol having too many people in the house, but Carol told Leanne to explain to her about rambling midwestern farmhouses. With the attic Will fixed up on a whim, the house has five bed-rooms.

In the end, Bernice Lewiston was prevailed upon to stay with her son's future in-laws. This will give a Carol a chance to try out her hostessing ideas, and it will be a lot easier, because the closest motels are in Kalamazoo, over thirty miles away. That's another reason her B&B will be a success.

Her stomach flutters happily as she thinks about the project. Will doesn't know it yet, but she's already scheduled and paid for an ad to run in one of the special advertising sections of the *Chicago Tribune*. It's not a glossy ad, just a small one-eighth page of text, but she worked long and hard on the copy, getting every word just right. It will appear in a few weeks, at the end of June, just as people in the city will be in the mood for weekend getaways. Carol is sure she can have everything ready by then. This is one project that's really going to happen.

Leanne's wedding is really going to happen, too, and Carol needs to make sure she's thought of everything. She sits down at the kitchen table and contemplates her shopping list. Shrimp. Cocktail sauce. (Margaret will disapprove—she would make her own.) Cherry tomatoes for the vegetable tray. Olives from the deli section. ("Canned olives?" Margaret yelped on a visit last summer. "You guys are still eating canned olives?") Sun-dried tomatoes and goat cheese for a recipe Carol tore out of a magazine. Some nice crackers. Everything else, she should be able to get in Ryville.

Water runs upstairs, and then she hears the thud of Will's feet coming down. She looks around for her purse. Once he's ready to go, he can't stand waiting for anyone else to get ready. When the girls were little, Carol was always scooping them up and rushing to the car, shoes untied and jackets unbuttoned, hair ribbons clutched in their hands. If she grabs everything now, she might have time to dash out to the garage and check the doves one more time.

"Okay!" Will booms, bursting into the kitchen like an event. "Time to go to the airport!"

Planes always wait to take off at Newark for at least half an hour. Leanne would have preferred to fly out of the Westchester County airport, or even La Guardia, but the only direct flight to Grand Rapids leaves from Newark. Kit didn't mind having to come down. He works in the city, as a video production editor, so the Metro-North trip from Cold Spring to Grand Central is no big deal for him. Leanne proposed taking the Carey bus from there, but Kit pointed out that with luggage it would be a huge hassle, and a cab wasn't that expensive.

"Besides, you only get married once," he said, "at least to each other." His voice was level, but he raised an eyebrow in his arch way, and Leanne, as always, had to laugh. Kit's dry wit puts people at ease, rather than making them feel left out. It's what makes his real work—documentaries—so good.

They stood on line for forty minutes before having to remove their shoes and jackets for the amped-up security screening. Kit was sent back to empty his pockets a second time, because on the first he had forgotten to remove his BlackBerry and the metal detector pinged him. Leanne was carrying the box containing her wedding dress, and the security screeners watched it glide through their machine without so much as a smile. It's all grave intensity now, the fun and excitement of travel forgotten.

Kit steered Leanne to a coffee bar for double lattes. "Don't you feel safer now?" he asked her, only half in jest. He held his hand out to her, palm up, his habit whenever he asked a question. As if waiting to take hold of the answer, cradle it like a small bird.

Now they are sitting on the tarmac, inching forward every few moments, in an excruciating waiting game that seems designed to mimic their earlier slow progress through security. Leanne twists in her seat and sighs. All of this would be fine—nothing has gone badly, really—if only she had done what she has been promising herself to do for weeks, what she swore to do last night. If only she had told Kit.

With the trip in motion, telling him will be even more complicated, because what if it changes everything? Before this moment, they could at least have canceled their trip if he freaked out, avoided the embarrassment of arriving in Michigan and then not getting married. She will have to tell him on the plane and hope for the best, breaking the news that his intended wife is a drunk—a reformed one but a drunk nonetheless. That's putting it melodramatically, of course, and she despises melodrama, which is perhaps why she has avoided speaking of it all this time.

The right moment to bring it up just never seemed to come. She couldn't tell him right off, when they met in a Cold Spring café a year and a half ago, or when they went on their first date, or even their second. It was too early then, and then suddenly it was too late. By the time he moved in with her six months later, he had asked her so many questions—he was inquisitive, after all—and they had talked about so many things, it seemed like he must know everything about her. When he proposed marriage on a hike up Storm King Mountain, Leanne looked down on Cold Spring, its steepled church and clapboard houses nestled between hills and river like a model of a town, and thought, *What is there to tell? It's not important.*

But it is important, and as they have thundered down the track toward the wedding, she has felt guilty and anxious, as if she was purposefully deceiving Kit. Because her past has an effect on their future together. On Mexico. Kit has received a grant to go to Mexico City and make a documentary about street kids, and he wants Leanne to go with him. But she can't. Somehow she knows that if she ends up in Mexico City, her carefully cultivated life of restraint and respectability will fall apart, and Kit will see her for what she really is: a lost cause.

The engines wind up and the plane bounces twice before moving forward ten feet. Once they get to Michigan, it will be impossible to talk. Leanne leans back and stares at the window across the aisle. Her heart clamps down on a cold, dull sensation: regret. What led her to say yes to this? She has never had a strong desire to be married. In truth, the thought alarms her. Kit is great, and they really enjoy being together, but a husband? She looks at his arm, taking up all of the armrest. He has a mole on his wrist, and she never noticed before that it has three or four very light hairs growing out of it. She stares at them, outlined in the glow of his reading light. There are probably a million things like that she doesn't know. She has no idea what's going on in his head, whether he has secrets, too. Suddenly, the whole idea of marriage seems ludicrous, just a way of pretending to be together when people are actually alone.

The arm moves from the armrest, and Kit's hand drops onto her leg. His fingers burrow toward her inner thigh.

"We're going to have a good time," he says. Leanne looks up at his face. It's a young, open face, but little knowing crinkles radiate out from his eyes. He has blond hair. Of the Gruens, only Trevor, Margaret's little boy, is blond, and his hair will no doubt darken to the family's signature brown.

"A good time getting married?" she says. "It seems like a big hassle to me."

"*Being* married," he says. "Although that might be a hassle sometimes, too."

Leanne puts her head back against the seat and closes her eyes. He wants to be married to her when he doesn't even know her, just as he's sure he can make his documentary when he hasn't met any of the subjects yet. His Spanish is great, and he's been to Mexico City before, but still. Part of her can't help but suspect his certainty, his ability to be so positive about things, like Margaret, or their father. It's not Leanne's nature. Maybe she and Kit are a bad match.

It's nice with her eyes closed. She doesn't have to look out the window at the New York skyline minus the Towers, a sight that, almost a year later, still makes her stomach lurch with shock. She concentrates on how good it feels to do nothing. The last few days have been a frenzy of annoying preparations, with multiple phone calls to Michigan to confirm details with her mother. The country club is booked, the caterers confirmed, last-minute changes to the luncheon menu have been approved, the photographer and church have received their deposits. It's a June wedding, but not a traditional one. She wanted something simple and short, even declining to have a wedding party: Margaret will stand up with Leanne, and her cousin Eddie will stand up for Kit, who has no male relatives of his own.

The plane inches forward. She can't talk to Kit while the plane is on the ground, she decides, because if something happens and they don't take off, it will seem as though fate has ordered them not to marry. And all of a sudden she *does* want to marry him. She wants to tell him everything and, in telling it, have it disappear, so he can understand why she can't come to Mexico, and then they can go forward from there. She'll tell him when they're in the air. She has always liked being in airplanes. They're a place where time has stopped, where you're not home nor yet away, but suspended, you and the small world around you. It's the closest thing there is to being nowhere.

"We should have gone by Greyhound," Kit murmurs next to her. "At least then we'd be in the bus lane."

Leanne wakes up when someone screams. Her head has been leaning sideways, and her neck is so sore she holds it still, avoiding any quick movement. As she reaches a hand up to massage it slowly back into place, the plane pitches violently to the left and snaps her upright.

She leans out into the aisle. Everyone else in the cabin looks frozen, some sleeping or feigning sleep, others simply holding still. The only movement is the synchronous bobbing of heads as the plane commences a strange, shuddery wobbling. There's another stomach-churning jolt, and Leanne turns to Kit. He has his hands clenched together in front of his stomach and is holding himself in an oddly tight way. His face is pale, but he smiles at her. Her heart jumps with concern, and in that moment, it's clear to her that she loves him. She reaches a hand out and touches her fingertips to his balled fists. Because of the plane's wobble, they tap up and down on the back of his hand, as if she's trying to wake him up.

"What's going on?" she whispers.

"Turbulence," he says. She notices that his knuckles are stretched thin and white with tension.

"Someone screamed."

It takes him a moment to reply. "*Bad* turbulence," he says. He takes a deep breath, and Leanne realizes that his tight posture and pale countenance are the result not of fear but of nausea. She leans forward and paws through her seat-back magazine compartment. There's an in-flight magazine, an in-flight catalog, an in-flight entertainment guide, and a couple of crumpled napkins. Don't airlines provide airsickness bags anymore? Or were they somehow a security problem, too?

"I'll be okay," Kit says, his voice slightly strained. He watches her with a worried expression, as if afraid she will produce what she's searching for and that will push him over the edge. "I almost never get motion-sick."

"I heard it helps if you use the pressure points on your wrists." Leanne holds out a forearm and encircles one wrist with her other hand, pressing her thumb down where it's supposed to help.

Kit looks as amused as a nauseated man possibly can. "My God, why didn't I think of that," he says.

The plane drops what feels like fifty feet. The falling sensation is scary, but there's a deep throb of pleasure in it, too. Leanne thinks of her father. He fell from the sky once, when his fighter jet was shot down in Vietnam and he parachuted into the ocean. Was there a thrill in the long ride down? It's funny, she has never heard him talk about it. Somehow the subject of the war was one they all left alone, even though it was always there, a shadow in the background.

The plane shakes and accelerates, and the overhead compartments creak. One of them has a rattling door that looks like it might give way at any moment. Leanne looks out the window. The sky is white, giving no clue about why the air should be so choppy. The plane seems to be descending, but there's no ground visible beneath them, just shreds of white on top of thick white soup. She tries Kit's approach, pressing her body back into her seat. When she was small, airplanes seemed so big. Of course, they really were more spacious then, before the airlines started cramming in as many bodies as they could. Things were more elegant, too. Leanne remembers dressing up to fly. When she was three, the family took their first trip abroad, to London. Carol bought Leanne and Margaret matching fur hats and muffs. They took a 747, and the upstairs was a piano bar. At dinnertime, an attendant came to their seats and carved a chateaubriand.

The plane drops again, and Leanne reflexively grips her armrests. *It would have been easier to die in those days,* she thinks. You'd have gone out in a blaze of glamour, like Princess Diana in the backseat of the speeding limo. Now it would be like falling off a cliff in a Greyhound bus. Leanne imagines the plane ripping apart, crammed overhead compartments disgorging their cargo, passengers melding with their downsized economy seats. Pretzel bags, plastic cups, and fanny packs would fuel the fireball.

This is always how it is in the air. Part of her believes with all her heart that these are her last moments on earth. What else is there to believe, thousands of feet in the air, powerless inside a small metal tube, tossed and jolted around like so much baggage? Every bump, every jerk, is like a message from the higher power of nature: *You do not matter. You are insignificant in the greater course of things.*

And yet another part of her cannot believe that anything could possibly happen to her here. Not because of the statistical safety of airline travel, not because, as her father always told them, more people die of bee stings than plane crashes, but because this is not her life. The airplane is nowhere, merely a conduit from one part of her life to another. Cold Spring, her store, her East Coast friends: all these dwindled in significance the moment the plane rumbled into the air and turned them into tiny toylike objects. At the same time, the realities of Michigan—her family, the home she grew up in— exist only as ghosts, stored in her memory.

This nowhere enfolds her, above and outside her real life, which will restart when she lands in Michigan with her fiancé, greets her parents, drives to Ryville, and, two days later, walks down an improvised aisle outdoors at the Green Lake Country Club to become a married person. That is her real life, opening before her like a brightly lit corridor. Even the dark spots are already visible: Margaret will inevitably find fault with some aspect of Leanne's dress; her cousin Eddie will find the most inopportune moment to call her by her old nickname, Pester; some simmering tension between her parents will make everyone uncomfortable. These things seem so certain that there's something exhilarating, almost glorious, in the idea that they might not occur.

And so she sits, suspended between two certainties: the certainty of her imminent annihilation and the certainty of the life mapped out for her. She shifts in her seat.

"Kit," she says, "I have to tell you something."

There's a short silence before Kit's hand finds hers. "Can it wait?" he says, his voice tight. "I'm just holding it together here."

"It's important."

Kit closes his eyes. His fingers work their way between her own.

"Yowza!" It's not the same person who screamed before but someone in front of them. The yelp follows a loud thud that sounds like some part of the aircraft being wrenched off. Immediately everything feels different. There's a noisy drag on the plane, as if the thing hanging off is disrupting its aerodynamics, and at the same time there's a strong surge coming from the left, like a crosswind. The nose points steeply down, and Leanne concentrates on how the curtain between first class and coach falls forward, marking their angle of descent. It holds steady at about 18 degrees.

At her side, Kit has gone limp, eyes closed, breath measured. Leanne lets go of his hand to grip her armrests. She's still staring at the curtain when the impact comes. There's a smack, a screeching of tires, and a roaring of engines, and everyone in the airplane seems to tense, as if pressing the brakes themselves. Then it's over. They're on the runway, slowing down. A single apple rolls down the aisle, and with it the old beliefs, the old certainties and expectations, come crowding back into place.

The plane slows to normal speed and turns a corner at the end of the runway as if nothing unusual has occurred. The low gray terminal can be seen outside the left windows. A collective sigh of relief breaks the spell. A few people in the rear clap. Outside, a dark curtain of rain drums on the wings.

"Ladies and gentlemen," comes the captain's voice. "Welcome to Grand Rapids."

two

RAIN POUNDS THE CAR ALL THE WAY TO GRAND
Rapids. Highway depressions become flat pools. Will feels the tires
beginning to skim along the surface of the water a few times, but he
responds the way he responds to snow: step on the gas. Get the car
to engage with the road. Everything else will sort itself out.

"This'll be good for the corn," he says at one point. "It was looking a little dry."

"It's all coming down now," Carol responds. "So Saturday can
be perfect." It sounds more like an order than a prognosis.

At Twenty-eighth Street, Carol reminds him that they're stopping at Meijer so she can get a few things. Reluctantly, he pulls into
the massive parking lot.

"Twenty minutes," he says in his businesslike voice. "Or else
we'll be late picking them up."

Carol doesn't answer, just climbs out of the car. He follows
behind her, registering his concern for their timing by refusing to
walk at her side. When she pulls a cart out of the corral and heads
off toward the grocery section, he drops back, thinking he'll wander
over to hardware and meet her at the checkout. There's a big display of gardening tools, and he looks at that for a minute. Then he
starts walking toward the far wall, where he thinks the hardware is.
He passes through some racks of clothing, then an aisle lined with
books.

The book section is notoriously bad at Meijer, populated mainly
by large *Family Circle* cookbooks and rows of shiny, thick paperbacks with lurid pictures on the cover. At the end of one aisle is a
large display of September 11 books. Will stops, arrested by an
image showing the second plane's impact with the Tower. He's seen
it a million times, and every time it causes the same shortness of
breath in him, a combination of anger and impotence. It could eas-

ily have been him. He flies for American now. *I wouldn't have let them do it,* he can never help but think. He knows that's absurd.

He looks over the selection, surprised at how many books there are. Not even a year later, there are commemorative books, books about firefighters, memoirs, books purporting to explain Islam's problem with the West. He picks up a profile of one of the passengers who died in Pennsylvania, trying to retake the fourth plane. The guy's picture is on the cover. He looks like Joe Average, smiling, buoyant, in charge of his life. He's young, too—younger than Will. Young enough to fly for years, if he'd been a pilot. *It could have been me.* Disgusted, Will puts the book back on the shelf and turns away.

Carol is glad Will wandered off. She can get everything done faster without him. She guides the massive cart expertly down the wide aisles, aiming for produce.

She finds cherry tomatoes quickly, good ones. Pleased, she piles three pints into the cart. She looks around for sun-dried tomatoes but doesn't see any. She goes over to the cheese section and locates a nice big log of goat cheese. Boxes of fancy crackers are stacked beneath the cheese display, and she spends some time deciding which ones to get. In the end, she decides on stoned-wheat crackers in a large box that prominently displays the British flag, and fancy biscuits that come in assorted shapes. She gets four boxes of each.

On her way back toward the fish counter, she sees a clerk and asks about sun-dried tomatoes. He directs her to the condiments aisle, where she finds them nestled among the pickles, relishes, and ketchups. She sees olives and almost grabs a couple of cans before remembering her intention to get them from the deli counter.

Margaret involved Carol very little in the plans for her wedding. She was married at the University Club in Chicago, and she and David began the festivities with a cocktail reception at the Drake Hotel. There was a rehearsal dinner at some sort of ethnic restaurant north of the city center: the food was lentil-based and very spicy. The wedding dinner was catered by the University Club, and Margaret made all the choices without even consulting Carol. The only thing she asked for help with was shopping for her dress, and even that required little input, since Margaret had already found a dress in a magazine and simply had to try it on at the bridal salon. She tried on a few others, but Carol got the impression she did so only out of a diplomatic urge to make her mother feel involved. In the end, Margaret bought the dress she had pre-chosen, and the two of them had a nice lunch at Water Tower Place.

Carol was happy for Margaret. Everything was exactly as she would have wanted it to be. Still, at the wedding she had almost wished for some last-minute disaster, some unforeseen event that would require her intervention and offer her an opportunity to prove how useful she was, remind her daughter that she was the woman who, for years, had solved all of her problems—sickness, sadness, confrontations at school. Carol could remember being all-powerful. Why was she now treated like the child? She could look at her daughter, so capable, so determinedly in control, and remember the day—not so long ago!—when she found the four-year-old Margaret sitting rigid on the floor of her bedroom, her mouth a perfect O of horror, tears sliding lasciviously from the corners of her wide eyes. Her favorite doll's head had come off. Carol fixed it and rocked Margaret—clingy for once—on her lap, her heart aching to see how gingerly her chubby hands held the doll, unwilling to be subjected again to the appalling sight of the mute, decapitated body.

But Margaret's wedding went off like clockwork. Guests arrived to find their hotel rooms stocked with a welcome basket put together by Margaret. Each wedding event unfolded exactly as planned: the waitstaff and caterers were as accommodating and gracious as one could wish, and the music for the ceremony—Margaret refused the traditional wedding march—was played beautifully by a string quartet from the University of Chicago. Even the weather was perfect, which was a waste, because the wedding wasn't outside.

The only disaster at Margaret's wedding, as far as Carol could see, was Leanne. She arrived looking dragged out and sullen, she wore awful thrift-store getups, and she was drunk from the get-go every night. The worst night was the rehearsal dinner. That was when Carol knew something had to be done.

They were in a dimly lit banquet room somewhere on Chicago's north side, and Carol was exhausted. She and Will had driven down the day before, arriving just in time for the cocktail reception. The next day they had tried to do some things from the list of recommended Chicago activities Margaret had included in the welcome baskets, and barely made it in time to the rehearsal dinner. There, they were stuck sitting with David's parents for the entire dinner, and once it was over and everyone was up and mingling, David's parents remained staunch at her side. Somehow, Will had escaped and left her to man the ship. Running out of conversational topics, she got stuck on her latest project: opening a children's clothing store.

"I've always had a thing for kids' clothes," she told David's mother. "Ever since the girls were little." David's mother was nodding and smiling in what could only be described as a matronly way. She was gray-haired and plump, and she treated Carol as if she were Margaret's sister, not her mother.

"It's so brave of you," she told Carol. "Starting up a new business like that. Your own store! I'm sure I wouldn't have the energy." She glanced at her husband, propped blandly at her side, and Carol wondered if the kindly matron was quietly disapproving.

"Oh, lots of people are doing it these days," she said. She could feel the tightness in her smile. "It's so much easier with all the new computers and software they have to help you do the accounting part."

She glanced around the room. During the endless string of small courses—what kind of cuisine had Margaret said it was, anyway, Armenian? Andalusian?—she had noticed the waiter refilling Leanne's wineglass at least five times. David's parents stood, waiting for her to carry on.

"I'm hoping to find a commercial space in Kalamazoo," Carol

continued, at a loss for anything else to talk about. "It's a good-sized town with lots of kids." Her eyes traveled to a group of smartly dressed young people, standing close together and laughing loudly. "Pre-millennial angst," she heard one of them say. Chicago friends of Margaret or David. Leanne was not with them.

"So there really is a Kalamazoo?" David's father cackled. Carol pressed her lips together in an attempt to smile at the worn-out joke.

"But Will flies out of O'Hare? Isn't that awfully far?" asked the matron.

"Not for a pilot," Carol said. She hoped that would suffice. She had been waiting for years for Will to get sick of the three-hour drive to O'Hare. But even after all the airlines shifted over to the hub-and-spoke system and he was required to fly out of St. Louis, Will stayed in Michigan. He flew down to Missouri on a competitor's airline. It added half a day to every trip, but he thought it was worth it.

"You'll have to travel, won't you?" David's mother said to Carol. "To do your buying and such."

"Oh yes," Carol answered vaguely. "I've always liked traveling." It wasn't strictly true, but it was part of her new persona as entrepreneur. She imagined herself driving to the Chicago Merchandise Mart, dressed in a smart jacket and pants.

Leanne emerged from the little hall leading to the restrooms and stood surveying the room. Carol tensed with predatory alertness. Leanne couldn't get past without walking by Carol. The minute she was within reach, Carol grabbed her arm.

"Leanne, have you met David's parents?" she said brightly. She felt Leanne stumble a bit, thrown off balance. She was wearing high, tottery heels and a formfitting black dress that showed off her trim figure. It had cutouts in sheer black netting around the waist. She had never dressed that way before moving east.

"Leanne lives in New York!" Carol told David's parents. "You guys are almost neighbors." She was aware of a slightly galled feeling as she said this. One daughter in New York, another heading for

San Francisco. She had always wanted them to get away, and once they did, she was surprised at how keenly she felt left behind.

"Oh well—," David's father began, but his wife interrupted him.

"It's true it's not so far from Westport to New York," she said, nodding benignly. "We ought to get down there more often. We do love the opera." Carol, still gripping Leanne's arm, felt her squirm subtly, in exactly the way she used to as a little girl, trying to get away from something her mother thought was important.

"I can't afford the opera," Leanne said. Belligerence edged the gaiety of her tone. She was clearly drunk.

David's mother smiled fixedly at her, unperturbed. "We've just been talking about your mother's little project," she said. "I think it's so brave of her to start her own children's clothing store." She nodded, buffing the conversation to a quiet sheen. "And creative, too."

"A children's clothing store?" A waiter passed by, and Leanne, in a surprising burst of agility, managed to slide her arm out of Carol's grasp and neatly snag a glass. "Didn't you always say that after we left, you were going to pack up and move somewhere civilized?"

Carol heard a thudding in her ears. David's parents pretended not to have heard. Leanne lifted her glass, and for the first time ever, Carol saw determination in her—determination aimed at oblivion.

David appeared then and took possession of Leanne. He told everyone she'd had enough to drink and he was going to drive her back to the hotel and see her to her room. There was something confident and commanding about David. Everyone agreed with what he decided.

Carol watched them leave. From behind, Leanne looked tiny and fragile. She had always been far more pliant than Margaret. From the beginning, Margaret had tested boundaries, complained, made demands. Leanne drifted along, apparently content with whatever life doled out. Occasionally, Carol would find herself trying to crack the veneer of complacency. *What do you want?* she would ask, trying not to sound critical. *What are you doing with yourself?* Leanne would shrug and look away. She could never be drawn into talking against her will.

Once, when Leanne was about five, Carol lost track of her on the beach at Lake Michigan. She never forgot the feeling, a chasm of fear, as her body yawned open to receive a dark terror. Her knees shook and her groin clenched. She staggered down the beach, frantic. When she found Leanne, she wanted to drop to her knees and shriek out all the fear. Leanne was just twenty or thirty yards down the beach with a group of older kids. She had let them bury her up to her neck in sand.

"Oh, Leanne," Carol whispered, watching David lead her away from Margaret's party. Embarrassed, she glanced around to see if anyone had heard. David's parents looked discreetly away. Carol looked down at her glass. She had found her unforeseen crisis.

Two weeks later, she flew to New York and showed up at Leanne's place. Leanne was shocked at first, but eventually, she did what Leanne always did and accepted the state of things. She was unhappy with her life. Carol assumed a love affair had failed, but Leanne didn't want to talk about it. Instead, they talked about what Leanne might want to do now. Two months later, financed by Carol, Leanne moved to Cold Spring and started her store.

Carol has reached the fish counter. She draws her mind back to the present, focusing her eyes on the display. The first things she sees are little jars of cocktail sauce so cute even Margaret will have to admit they're elegant. The labels look handwritten, and the lids are wrapped in a sweet gingham fabric. Carol takes two of them and then looks for the shrimp.

To her infinite delight, the fish man has a huge bowl of the most beautiful shrimp Carol has ever seen. They are large and pale, with striking gray stripes. The only problem is that they still have their heads. And they're twenty-four dollars a pound.

"What are those?" she asks, pointing.

"Tiger shrimp," the fish guy says, beaming. "Just got them in from New Zealand. Best shrimp you'll ever taste."

"Would they be good boiled?" she asks.

"Perfect," the guys answers. "You can't go wrong with these critters."

Carol admires the shrimp. She imagines arranging them around the rim of her large crystal bowl, a heap of crushed ice in the center. She can perch a small colorful bowl of the cocktail sauce in the center of the ice. It will be like a work of sculpture.

"I'll take four pounds," she says.

The man begins scooping the shrimp into a plastic bag.

"Wait," Carol says. "Can you take their heads off?"

The guy stops and looks at her. He picks up one of the shrimp and, as neatly as a child plucking a dandelion, pops its head off. "It's that simple," he says. "Besides, they'll taste better boiled heads on."

Heads on is not the kind of thing Carol likes. Margaret does, though. Once when Carol was visiting Margaret's house, Margaret baked a whole fish, its belly filled with some kind of mushroom stuffing. She brought it to the table like that—head, eyes, tail, and everything—and rolled her eyes when Carol looked away.

"All right, then," Carol says. "Leave the heads on. My daughters are coming today, and they can help me with them."

The bag of shrimp is so heavy she almost drops it. She puts it gently in the cart's child seat, where nothing else can touch it, and heads for the deli counter, her heart swelling with triumph.

"Some olives, please," she tells the deli man. "A pound of French country mix."

After wandering aimlessly through hardware for what seems like twenty minutes, Will heads back toward the checkout counters. He didn't expect to see Carol finishing up on time, but there she is, nudging her cart toward lane seven. She looks pleased as she pages through an issue of *House & Garden*. It must be the excitement of picking up Leanne. While the girls were little, Carol and Margaret were always in cahoots—planning home improvements, organizing school outings—but Leanne was always her baby, the silent shadow attached to her leg.

Will stops next to a stack of charcoal and lighter fluid so he can watch Carol, unobserved. She's fifty-five, but other men still notice her. She has continued to pay attention to her appearance, her makeup always carefully applied, her hair blown shiny. When they were first married, she wore it long. Now she has it cut short and layered. It's not unattractive. But something about her is harder than it used to be. Her angular beauty is turning into a kind of flinty coating, like the shell of an exquisite crab.

When he met her, she was in what she called her Jackie phase. She wore neat shifts and matching jackets in bright colors. Her shoes and bags always matched. He was intimidated by her. She had grown up in Dayton, where her father owned a successful furniture store. Ed Timmins, the Duke of Dining Tables. He had a series of billboard ads showing him robed and crowned, with a different title for each type of furniture. The Baron of Bedroom Suites. The King of Couches. The Regent of Recliners. Will was just a farm boy, an officer-in-training in the Air Force. He wore his dress uniform on their first date; it made him look more impressive. Within a week, he had proposed. He didn't want to risk losing her.

They married before he went to Vietnam. When he came back, there was Margaret, and if anything, they were happier together. It was when he decided to move back to Michigan that things changed. He had been with TWA only a couple of years, and the bankers had gotten control of it from Howard Hughes, so things were looking up. Carol was happy, too. She hadn't wanted him to give up his Air Force career, but the war scared them both. And the airline wasn't that different at first. They lived in a suburb of Chicago with lots of other pilots. Their wives would come over for coffee to talk about their husbands and swap airline gossip. Carol belonged to the tennis club and was looking forward to joining the nursery school board when Margaret went. It was a perfect life for her. But not for him.

After they moved, he kept thinking she would learn to love the farm. It seemed like she was trying. First she went back to school, but she dropped out before she even finished her first semester.

Then she was going to start some sort of farm-style baked-goods business, but that idea disappeared when something happened to their chickens. Later, she spent a long time taking a correspondence course in interior design and then redoing the house in anticipation of starting a decorating business. Then she switched from that to children's clothing. She had put together enough money for the initial investment when she gave that up, too. Now there's the bed-and-breakfast. He doesn't expect to see that happen any more than any of the other things happened, but he won't say so. Carol doesn't seem driven to finish things. He's always figured the charge came from having a project.

If they move to Hong Kong, perhaps she won't need one. They'll get a knockout apartment overlooking the harbor and entertain other expats. There's a tennis club; they get good shows. He's even heard there are fancy eating clubs, like private restaurants. It would be the kind of life she's always wanted.

He approaches her from behind. Casually, he swings his arm back, intending to slap her ass, but something stops him, and he puts a hand on her shoulder instead. She jumps, glancing not at him but at the hand.

"Will!" She slaps the magazine shut. "I found some really fabulous shrimp for the party!"

As soon as they step off the plane, it's as if the whole scary experience in the air never happened. Leanne takes Kit's hand as they walk down the jetway. It feels a bit damp, but she's glad to have it to hold on to. That small, soft lump of warm flesh steadies her, makes her feel more in control. Because just looking out the jetway window at the flat, tree-lined fields edging the airport gives her a sense of being enveloped by home. She can feel the family momentum tugging on her, pulling her into its trajectory.

Kit met her parents already, when the two of them came out to look at the country club. It's strange for him to be getting married in a place where he knows almost no one, but he insisted it made as much sense here as anywhere. His oldest friend lives in Cleveland and can drive up for the wedding. His mother lives in Atlanta, but he has no one else there, so she would have to travel no matter what. And he and Leanne each have a few good friends in Cold Spring and New York, but not enough that it made sense to have the wedding there and make Leanne's family travel east. That would have been a real ordeal. For their Cold Spring friends, they can have a separate party, a barbecue or something, when they get back home.

Rain beats on the jetway roof. "You're lucky we came to Grand Rapids," Leanne tells Kit. "Kalamazoo doesn't have a jetway. You climb down the stairs and make a run for it across the tarmac."

"I wouldn't mind getting wet right now," Kit says. He's still a little pale, a thin gleam of sweat delineating his hairline.

"Poor thing," Leanne says. "We should get you something to settle your stomach. Some crackers, maybe."

"Or some Scotch," Kit says, and Leanne glances at him quickly. Is he trying to tell her something? His face is blank, communicating only an effort not to look sick.

"Leanne!" Her mother and father are standing at the gate, the only people there to greet the flight. Will is grinning like a kid who expects to be punished. Carol has her arms thrown wide.

Leanne goes to her mother first. Carol pulls her tight for a real hug, and briefly, the world winds down around Leanne, the way it did when she was a child and would hide in her mother's arms. Her mother has a slightly lemony smell in addition to the familiar celery-like scent of the perfume she has worn forever.

"How did you get through security?" Leanne is jolted from childhood by Kit's voice beside her.

Carol releases Leanne and laughs. "One of the perks of being airline people." She beams at Kit, then impulsively throws her arms around him as well. "Soon you'll be my son-in-law!" she cries.

Leanne gives her father an awkward kiss on the cheek. He puts a hand on the back of her shoulder and reaches another toward Carol, steering them in the direction of baggage claim.

"Everything is all ready," Carol tells Leanne as they start walking, her eyes bright with pleasure. "It's going to be so lovely, Leanne. I've done everything just as we planned. I got the doves—" She stops short, as if momentarily confused. Leanne shifts her bag to the other shoulder, letting herself be propelled by her father, even as she's eddied about in the rapids of her mother's enthusiasm. A familiar feeling of passivity washes over her. Others will pilot the wedding from here. She glances back at Kit. He's following a few steps behind, carrying the box with her wedding dress, and watching them intently, like an anthropologist arriving in some remote village. Her documentary genius. *Kit Burns,* she started calling him after he won the grant. He'll look at Mexico with that intense, searching gaze.

"Yes," Carol is saying, "I got the doves. They're in the garage in a nice little cage. And I just went to Meijer here for the things we can't get in Ryville, you know, and I found the most fabulous shrimp. Oh, they're going to look so wonderful!"

"That's great, Mom."

"I was thinking we could use that big crystal punch bowl, only fill it with a mound of ice and perch the boiled shrimp all around the edge. With the cocktail sauce right there in the middle. It will be very impressive, right at the center of the table!"

"That sounds perfect."

"A veritable shrimp Matterhorn," Kit puts in. He wants to be accepted by the natives. That's what anthropologists do.

"Come on," her father says, exerting just enough force on Leanne's elbow to speed up her steps. "If we hurry, we can beat the rush to the escalator."

three

BY THE TIME THEY REACH THE BAGGAGE CLAIM, THE belt has already cranked into action. Will sees it with relief: there's something he can do. So far, he and Kit have been extraneous, holding themselves apart from the women's barrage of chatter by maintaining an awkward silence. Now they can make themselves useful. Will steps over and begins scanning the bags trundling by before remembering that he has no idea what Kit and Leanne's luggage looks like.

"Leanne's suitcase is gray. It matches her shoulder bag," Kit says, as if having read his mind.

"Look at that, the luggage is already here!" Carol cries, a fountain of cheer now that Leanne has arrived.

"Yeah, maybe they hired a second guy to help unload the baggage," Leanne says, and she and Kit grin at each other. Will sees it and looks away. Let them make fun of his Michigan backwater. They don't know about Hong Kong.

Kit steps forward and pulls a black bag off the belt, quickly turning it upright and pulling the handle out in one smooth motion. He sets it next to Leanne. As he turns back, Will notes that he looks a little pale and sweaty in the face.

"Rough landing?" he asks.

"How'd you guess?" Kit asks, and a small, mean feeling of triumph flickers in Will's chest. *You're a bit green around the gills,* he almost says, but Leanne's grown-up, serious self standing there stops him. He looks out the doors to the parking lot and shrugs instead. "I figured, with that weather," he says.

"There's mine," Leanne says, pointing.

Will is stepping forward when Kit steps in front of him.

"I've got it," the young man says. He sets down the first bag and reaches over to pluck Leanne's suitcase off the belt. Will steps back, trying not to feel annoyed all over again.

It's young men. Only lately, Will has been noticing how quickly they get on his nerves. The first time he remembers it happening was when he was doing his initial training on the 767. He was paired with a newbie, a young copilot named Warren Gliss. It was a few years back when things were getting strained at the airline: TWA had been through two financial reorganizations. They were employee-owned and bankrupt, and it wasn't clear if they were going to make it. Everyone was tense, but it wasn't just that: Warren Gliss was annoying in his own right.

"Can you carry this one, Dad?" Leanne asks, pushing the handle of the black bag toward Will. He nods and goes to pick it up.

"It has wheels," Kit says. "That button releases the handle."

"Got it," Will says. He heads toward the door, dragging the bag behind him like a recalcitrant dog.

"Oh, Leanne, is that your *dress?*" he hears Carol squeal. He quickens his pace, yanking the bag over the edge of the curb and humping along, separate from the others.

Warren Gliss started bugging him on their first day in the simulator, when Will got taken through his dead-stick landing. The instructor had been putting him through the wringer: hydraulic failure, loss of cabin pressure, two go-arounds, and an electrical fire that killed his right engine. He was thinking the instructor might let him land when the left went, too. He was calm. After twenty minutes without the right, this would be easier: the plane would no longer strain to the right like a stubborn horse angling for the barn. The first thing he did was drop the landing gear. He remembers Gliss making a noise to his right as he did, a little *pop!* of surprise. He thought Will had dropped the gear by mistake. Will checked the speed, did the calculation. Altitude times nine. He was under thirty miles from the simulator's virtual Dulles—he'd make it just fine. He didn't say a word to Gliss. He had no idea why they had paired him with a kid twenty-five years his junior. Will had thought of him as Kid Flyboy since the first day of training.

Fifteen minutes later, after he'd brought the simulated 767 down for a perfect landing, he felt better than he had the whole first week. That was flying, he thought. Not the poking-your-fingers-at-a-computer crap aviation had become. Kid Flyboy loved that part, zipping through computer screens like he was fragging video space aliens at the local arcade. Will liked it best when the computers failed, when the autopilot was off, when he could put his hand on the stick and fly.

"Nice" was all the instructor said as he cleared the control panel. Some Delta guys were waiting, standing in a small cluster by the door as Will and the other two clumped down the metal steps. Desperate for cash, TWA was renting simulator time to other airlines. Delta pilots were said to make double the TWA salary. They nodded, giving off a little buzz of confidence as Will's crew walked by. *I chose TWA,* he always told people, *when Delta was still dusting crops along the bayou.*

Then Kid Flyboy started his whining. "Hey," he said, jogging a bit to catch up with the instructor. "When am I gonna get my engine failure?"

"If I told you, it wouldn't be the same, would it?" the instructor said. Will couldn't help laughing. He knew how to fly a plane. He knew the feel of it, the tug of a headwind over steel shoulders, the effortless glide of a machine in perfect trim. He didn't need a computer second-guessing him, but if they wanted to install one, fine. In the end, he knew what he was doing. That was more than he could say for the Kid.

"What are you doing?" Carol demands. "Trying to run between the drops?" Will looks up from the back of the van, where he has been rearranging Carol's grocery bags to make room for the luggage. He charged across the parking lot so quickly that the others had to trot in a vain attempt to keep up.

"What?" Seeing them all hunching under their umbrellas, Will remembers the rain. Funny, he hadn't noticed it on the way to the car. It's still coming down, dull and steady.

"Just chuck that in here," he tells Kit as the young man arrives at his side with the other large bag. Leanne steps forward with her box.

"Oh yes, get that inside before it gets wet," Carol says. Will tosses it lightly on top of one of the suitcases and she raises her eyebrows. He sees her make up her mind not to speak.

"Okay, everybody in," he says, trying to sound hearty and unconcerned. For a moment, as Kit and Leanne move to opposite sides of the van, it's true. He *is* unconcerned, and hardy enough to stand out in the rain for the rest of the day, if that's what's required to move things forward. He pauses, an impulse of defiance making him reluctant to climb into the van, as if doing so will indicate weakness, a triumph of the weather over him.

"What now?" Carol says. He can see her leaning forward to look back at him around the driver's seat.

He reaches into his pocket for the keys. "It's just a little water," he says, climbing into his place at the wheel. "It's not like you'll melt."

Kid Flyboy kept after the instructor: "When am I going to get my engine failure?" He couldn't stand that Will had shown him up with a beautiful dead-stick landing. But the next day was their last day of ground school. The morning was all lectures. Will squinted at the screen for a while, finally giving in and getting out his glasses. He thought he saw Kid Flyboy smirking into his notebook. *Let him smirk,* Will thought. He needed to see the instructor's PowerPoint slides. They were going over the electrical system, an area where Will had learned to be slow and deliberate. All those circuit breakers to memorize.

Learning the new autopilot interface was even worse. After lunch, they were seated at computers for the electronic tutorial. Will could feel the sweat breaking out on his forehead. His neck itched, his chest itched underneath his shirt; he shifted forward and back in his seat like a restless high-schooler. He hated this part. In the old days, there was an actual physical connection between the pilot's controls and the rudders. Now it was fly-by-wire, electronics and software sending your signals for you, computers butting in on the instincts you'd honed over a lifetime.

At the end of it, he felt exhausted, though he'd been sitting all day. His eyes were wrecked from staring at the blue screen, and his head was beginning to ache. He drove his rental car from the training facility to the hotel and pulled into a parking place. For a moment he sat there immobile, hands on the wheel, thinking about dinner. The idea of driving to a depressing chain restaurant and sitting at a table alone was unbearable. He got some chips from the vending machine and went to his room. He undressed and turned on the TV, but the endless election coverage made his jaw tense up and his heart pound. He switched around until he found sitcom reruns: *Seinfeld* or *Frasier.* He didn't really pay attention, but he found the familiar cadences, the building crescendos of dialogue followed by canned laughter, comforting. He turned the sound down low as he started drifting off to sleep.

When the telephone rang, he jumped. People rarely called him when he was in training, even though he gave everyone his number. To his surprise, it was Margaret. She sounded like she'd been crying, though she tried to hide it. She explained that she and David were having a fight. She just needed someone to talk to.

He tried to be comforting, to say things that were blandly helpful. He couldn't help but wonder why she was confiding in him. She had never done so before. It made him nervous—it would be too easy to say the wrong thing—but deep down he felt a small glimmer of satisfaction. She wanted his help. But he worried that he was letting her down. He told her to call whenever she wanted. *Anything,* he said to her. *I'm always happy to talk.*

That Saturday he had dinner with the Kid. He'd been studying all day, sitting on his hotel bed with his back against the headboard and the little room radio playing a jazz station. He had a color-coded highlighting system: pink for crucial information, orange for places where the 767 differed from the DC-9, blue for items the instructor said the FAA guys were asking that year. He'd lost track of the time, surprising himself when he looked up to see that it was six o'clock. All he had eaten for lunch was a packet of cheese crackers from the hotel vending machine, and he was starving. Almost unwillingly, he closed his book.

In the bathroom he surveyed his face. He'd put on weight, and it showed in a paunchiness around his jawline. His beard was coming in, spilling gray like a cloud across his cheeks. It made him look old and haggard, but he decided he could get away without shaving this once. He'd go, get some dinner, and come back. Who cared if the folks at the local Pizza Hut thought he was a wizened old grandpa? He changed his shirt and headed out.

As he was walking through the lobby, he heard a jovial voice.

"Will!" It was Kid Flyboy, parked on an ugly lobby sofa with a newspaper.

"Hey." Will hesitated, not sure if he could get away with simply greeting him and walking out. The Kid was folding up his newspaper and standing up. His hair was damp, sticking to his face around the edges.

"Did Bart call you up?"

"Uh, no." Will looked over his shoulder at the door as if expecting someone. "I was just heading out for some dinner." For some reason, he thought of Margaret. Was she having dinner alone tonight, too? He'd call her later, see how things were going.

"Perfect! Come with us. Bart knows some place that's supposed to be great."

Will looked toward the elevators, and sure enough, here came Bart, an affable fellow captain, smiling as he bore down on them.

"Steaks, Colonel!" he called out. "Best steaks to be had for a hundred miles."

They took Bart's rental car. The restaurant was pole-barn-sized. Outside it was a large cement pedestal topped by a giant cow. Their waitress was a chirpy blonde, and when she leaned forward to pick up their menus, her uniform gaped open to reveal tanned breasts tucked into a shiny black bra. Bart raised his eyebrows across the table at Will and the Kid. They had all ordered rib eyes. Will was annoyed that he got dragged into this, but he didn't feel out of place. This was what it meant to be a pilot: eating dinner in some strange town, ogling the local college students, confident of receiving some measure of respect. He and Bart were used to it. Female attention as they passed through hotel lobbies in uniform was the air they breathed. It was a tribute to their position, to their responsibility for strangers' lives. The Kid was still taking it all in, delighted with his new persona. He gave off, like heat, a desire to make himself known.

"So, Will, how'd you end up at TWA?" the Kid said, breaking off a piece of bread.

Will looked at Bart, who nodded as if to give him the go-ahead. "The way all the best pilots did," Will said. "I came up through the Air Force. Trained on the Century series. I flew sixty-two missions in 'Nam."

"I met Will on the transport home," Bart put in.

"What happened?" The Kid looked seriously interested.

Will shrugged. "Got shot down over the Tonkin Gulf. Broke an arm and a leg on a rough ejection. I came back and joined TWA. Thirty-one years ago."

"Will and I have been around," Bart said. "We've flown every one of the airline's routes."

"That used to be something, too," Will said. "We used to fly to Cairo and Bombay and Tel Aviv. I flew into Rome two days after the terrorists bombed it."

"Those were the days of constant hijackings," Bart added. "You youngsters probably don't even remember that."

Will nodded. "I flew every piece of jet equipment TWA ever bought," he couldn't help saying, "from the Convair 880 on up."

The Kid grinned. "I knew I was working with a pro," he said. "Even before the end of ground school, Will here is flying the thing like an angel. Got his total engine failure yesterday and brought her in like there wasn't a thing wrong."

Will didn't know what to say. It was a pretty landing, but he couldn't tell what the Kid was playing at.

"Will's up there with the best," Bart agreed. "You watch and learn, young man."

Kid Flyboy nodded and started buttering his bread with great care. "So the first thing he does when the second engine goes is drop his gear." The Kid was acting casual, but suddenly, Will got it. Kid wanted to know if dropping gear was the right thing to do, so he could show off in his own engine failure. His heart sank. He busied himself with his own piece of bread and tried to act as if the conversation didn't interest him at all.

"You don't say," Bart answered, and he looked at Will, a slight furrow of concern bisecting his brow. "Every guy has his own way of flying," he said, looking around the room in a way that ended the conversation.

A flash of anger sparked through Will. Surely Bart knew he did the right thing, knew the only way to judge whether you'll make it dead-stick or not is to dirty up the plane right away. Drop your gear at the last minute, and you're in for a nasty surprise. He didn't want to say it, though, because that would educate the undeserving Kid. He picked up his water glass and looked at Bart over the top of it.

Bart surveyed the restaurant far too casually before turning back to the Kid and grinning. "How do you like those new computers?" he asked, and then Will saw it. Bart was on his side. Bart didn't want to tell the Kid, either, so he was letting the Kid think Will was wrong. Will wanted to laugh out loud. He concentrated on buttering his slice of bread. Good old Bart. *We old guys stick together,* Will thought. *They can't get ahead of us yet.*

"It's really coming down, isn't it?" Leanne says.

Will starts at her voice. No one has spoken for at least fifteen minutes. The thud of the wet highway against the van's tires, the regular thump of the wipers, the flat gray light—everything has combined to hypnotize them into drowsy silence. Even Carol looks up in surprise, as if she has forgotten the presence of the young people.

"It's only passing through," she tells them, although they haven't asked for reassurance. "Everything will be fine by Saturday."

"I'm surprised at how flat it is here," Kit says. "I didn't notice that last time." Will looks at him in the rearview mirror. Kit's gazing out at the fields with a small squint. When he moved in with Leanne, she told them he was a filmmaker of some sort. Perhaps he's seeing it all as a film, visualizing a landscape shot.

"You should see the Great Plains states," Will says. "Now that's flat. Michigan is actually hilly." He waves a hand toward the landscape. "Glacial terrain. That makes us lucky in water, too. We have the Great Lakes. The Plains states don't have lakes. There's not one natural lake in the state of Missouri." He's surprised by the strength of his desire to defend his little corner of the world.

"That's right," Kit says, seeming to like the topic. "I read something about that. There's an aquifer underground in the Plains, right? That's where the water goes."

"The Ogallala Aquifer." Will tightens his hands on the steering wheel. "But it's drying up." He feels himself warming to the task of explaining how things are.

"Oh yeah?"

"Out there," Will tells him, "they irrigate on a center-point system. They drill wells down into the aquifer and bring the water up into a pipe that rotates around the well like the hand of a clock. You can see it from the air. Each one makes a green circle." He pauses, visualizing it. "Twenty years ago, there were hundreds of them. You'd fly over and see green polka dots for miles across the yellow plains. Now one in three is brown. The wells are dry." His voice cracks as he says it; he's overwhelmed by his own words. That's what his book is trying to explain. The great trajectory. A tremor rises in his throat, almost as if he might cry. He looks in the mirror again, to see if Kit has understood.

The young man is looking out the window. "No shortage of water here," he says.

"But that's just it," Will tells him. "Now that they've pumped the aquifer half dry, they want to start pumping water down from the

Great Lakes. But it'll be the same problem all over again. It just delays the inevitable."

"The inevitable?" Kit is flagging. Carol is glancing at Will as if wishing he would be quiet. He looks away, back to the road, where water sluices toward them from the wheels of the car ahead.

"The depletion of our natural resources," he says. "The end of our culture. It's all wrapped up together."

Leanne moves in the backseat, and Will glances at her in the mirror, thinking she might say something. But she, too, is gazing out the window.

"Yeah, well, you may be right about that," Kit says. He speaks lightly, drawing the conversation closed like a neat little sack. Placating the old guy to get him to shut up. Will glances at Carol, casting about for a way to keep asserting his point until the young man gets it. His impulse is a tiny flame persisting in a doused fire.

As if sensing this, Carol moves to stamp it out for good. "That's farmers for you," she says. "Always full of dire predictions." She turns to them with a conspiratorial smile. It's meant as a joke, but Will can hear the edge in it.

"Well, you laugh now," he says. He tries to think of a better rejoinder, an eye-opening way to finish, but nothing comes. Like birds, the words flit away.

Will had his FAA oral the Monday after the steak-house dinner.

"How does the fuel-dump system work, and what is the jettison rate?" All FAA inspectors looked like retired G-men. This one read the questions off his clipboard, and Will answered slowly and carefully, not getting anything wrong. When he was young, he used to try to answer quickly, to show that he didn't have to think about it. Now he knew it was more important to get it exactly right, even if that took a few seconds more.

"What's the maximum starting exhaust gas temperature?"

Will joined TWA in 1968. It was the end of a big hiring spree at the major airlines: United, Pan Am, TWA. He had agonized for weeks over which airline to join, ultimately choosing TWA over United. It was the wrong decision, he knew now, but how could he have foreseen it? "I want us to be able to travel to Europe," he had told Carol. TWA and Pan Am were the flagship carriers, worldwide symbols of American prosperity and glamour. United was the poor relation in those days, the country cousin back home. Now Pan Am was dead and TWA was in perpetual trouble. Its refusal to die was an industry joke. By the year 2010, the joke went, there would be only three U.S. airlines left: American, Delta, and "the financially struggling TWA."

They did get to travel. When the girls were little, Will gave Carol tickets to London in her Christmas stocking. He wasn't there to see her surprise. He was away on a trip, as he always was on Christmas through the long years he spent at the bottom of a huge seniority list. Being hired at the end of a big wave meant he flew flight engineer for fifteen years before even getting promoted to copilot. Now they didn't even have flight engineers anymore. Only the last few 727s required three guys in the cockpit, and those planes were being phased out.

"Name all the electrical circuits on the same bus as the cabin lights."

The weekend's cramming paid off, and Will answered every question correctly. He felt like his brain was melting slightly at the end, an overloaded circuit board. Still, he got through it. The FAA inspector shook his hand absently, already looking at the next name on the list.

The Kid was waiting in the hall as Will headed outside.

"How was it?" the Kid asked, his face upturned and eager.

"Piece of cake," Will replied, pleased with the way it came out. Careless, unsurprised, cool. *Piece of cake.*

When he went back to his room, there was a message from Margaret. *Just calling to say hi,* her voice said, sounding vaguely distant in the hotel's crackly voice-mail system. *No need to call back. Maybe I'll try you later.*

He lay down on the bed and closed his eyes. Leaving the training center, he had felt mentally exhausted. But now he couldn't stop his brain from cycling through the questions and answers of the oral. *Jettison rate, twenty-six hundred pounds a minute,* he thought. *Circuits on the right forward bus.*

The Kid seemed cocky for his second simulator test flight, eager to show what he could do. He and Will traded places for it, Kid Flyboy settling into the captain's seat, Will sliding into the copilot's.

"Where shall we go today?" the Kid joked as he pulled out the simulated flight-ops pages churned out by a training facility computer. The instructor had a huge cup of Starbucks coffee. Smelling it, Will made a mental note to ask the guy where he got it as soon as they left the simulator. On the other guy's day, he always tried to say as little as possible. That was only good manners.

Kid Flyboy moved quickly, entering the performance data into the inertial reference system. Will had a sinking feeling, watching him go. It was clear that the software stuff made an intuitive kind of sense to him.

"Do you have the final weight from the load control agent?" Kid Flyboy asked, and Will had to snap back to the present and turn to his own monitor. He loaded the information, then mistakenly went to hit execute before activating it. The Kid looked across at him quickly.

"Sorry," he told the Kid. "Guess I needed one of those gallon coffees this morning, too." The instructor chuckled a little and settled into his seat.

Why am I doing this? The question rose up, gassy and disruptive, at least once a day. Will had fewer than five years before mandatory retirement. He didn't need the 767. He could keep flying captain on the DC-9, where he was senior enough to get his first-choice bids every month, never flying on holidays or getting stuck with undesirable layovers. But the DC-9 made short hops around the U.S. all day long: Chicago to Kansas City to Cedar Rapids to Omaha. If he wanted the plum trips now, the transatlantic flights or the twenty-four-hour layover in Hawaii, he had to fly the 767. He didn't want to spend his last two years checking in and out of Omaha. He wanted to do what he had joined TWA to do.

"Okay," the instructor said as Kid Flyboy got the plane launched into the digitized sky over Dallas–Fort Worth. Will suspected the Kid would get his full engine failure. But the instructor took him through a pretty standard routine: interrupted climb, 45-degree turns, stall maneuvers, a nonprecision approach. On his second takeoff, the instructor failed one engine, and the Kid handled it with surprising ease. He looked pleased when they climbed out of the simulator, and the instructor looked satisfied as well. As they left, Will's heart sank at the thought of the lousy cafeteria lunch and then a long afternoon of the same routine for him. He saw the Delta guys and looked over to see if the instructor had remembered his coffee cup. He hadn't. Will felt a secret satisfaction as the door slammed behind him. Let the Delta pukes clean up after them.

"You got kids?" They were parked in the noisy cafeteria. Kid Flyboy had a shred of lettuce stuck to his lower lip, and Will couldn't help but watch it as the Kid talked. It made him look absurd, undercut his tightly held posture of cool.

"Yeah, two," Will said. "Two girls. They're grown up now." He looked down at the chef salad he had selected with his health in mind and wished he had gone for the grilled cheese. It was hard to ruin grilled cheese. The Kid was demolishing a BLT. A side order of fries spilled over onto his orange tray.

"Either of them ever consider flying?"

Will was jolted out of his food funk by the question. *How stupid can you be?* he wondered. Or maybe it wasn't so absurd. When Margaret was about ten, she got obsessed with space. They had planned their family vacation so they could make a stop at Kennedy Space Center. They toured the site, watching a film about astronaut training and taking photographs of the girls in front of Apollo-era rockets. Will had never thought much of her obsession, and sure enough, the next summer it was replaced by horses.

"Well, when my older one went to college, I thought she might join ROTC," he told the Kid. "She objected on anti-militaristic grounds." He tried to make it sound jokey, and the Kid grinned. Will had in fact once suggested ROTC to Margaret, but she had slapped the idea down with the fervor that marked her entire college era. He had never suggested anything to Leanne.

"She's a historian now," he told the Kid, wanting him to know that she turned out okay, that she wasn't some flake chaining herself to fences at missile sites. "Teaches at Northwestern."

The Kid nodded, just sufficiently impressed. "Mine's four," he offered. "A boy. What a demon." He shook his head in awed pride. "He's so cocky, he's sure to be a fighter pilot. But he's a lot of work for his mother."

Will nodded. "They are work," he said. It sounded stupid. He longed, foolishly, to demonstrate his superior knowledge. "Of course, it only gets worse," he told the Kid. "I think the girls gave my wife the most grief in their teen years."

"She must be relieved now, to have them all grown up and settled," Kid said, and Will felt a surge of anger. What was up with the third degree? He wasn't about to go into Margaret's rocky marriage with a guy who didn't know how to land an engineless plane. With great control, he made his voice calm. *Relax your jaw,* his doctor always told him.

"It's good to have your kids settled," he said. "Shall we get going now?" He picked up his tray, and the Kid, after one more slurp of his soda, followed Will's lead.

That night Margaret called before he was asleep.

"He left us, Daddy. He didn't come home last night." Her voice was twisted and strange, as if the wires had gnarled, keeping it from getting through clearly. "I don't . . . I can't . . ." She didn't finish, and for a moment it seemed as if she had disappeared.

"Honey?"

"He hasn't even called!"

"Okay, let's think about this." Will's eyes took in the hotel room. Blue patterned bedspread. Fake brass lamp. Dark wood cabinet with television inside, minibar underneath. The thick blue drapes were pulled shut over the window, and a notebook and pen were laid out on the table, as if someone had expected him to sit there taking perfect little notes. His actual notes were piled on the dresser, neatly stacked by the maid. He scratched his head, aware of how thin his hair had become.

"Okay, let's think about what to do. Where has he . . . Where is he likely to go?"

"I don't know." The way the words tapered off to a wail suggested she had said this too many times. "I've called his mom's place and his sister and all the friends I can think of. I even called his girlfriend."

Will pinched the bridge of his nose, where his glasses had left an indentation. He didn't want to think about Margaret calling her husband's girlfriend. When it came down to it, he felt lost in his daughters' world. Drugs, the Web, alternative lifestyles. Things had changed too much.

"Any information?" he asked.

"Everyone denies seeing him. But now I don't know . . . I don't even know who to trust." He heard something in her voice, a mournful edge he'd never heard before. It was a hollow echo, the sound of someone who had seen her own mistakes. Margaret had never been one to make mistakes. Every step in her life had been carefully planned and carried out with absolute conviction. Now she radiated uncertainty.

"Your counselor," he said. "What does your counselor say?"

"My counselor . . ." She sighed heavily. "My counselor says to sit tight. She says he's probably just trying to get my attention so we can address things more directly."

"Well, I guess that's what you'd better do."

"I don't know how I can!" she cried. "How can I?" She broke then, and he could hear a single sob on the other end of the line.

"Oh, honey," he said. "Look. I don't know what to say. Like I said . . . people get crazy. He's frustrated. He's done the only thing he can think of. He'll come to his senses, and you guys will sort this out. He will." He was silent, listening to her weep.

"You and Mom never got like this," she said, controlling her tears but talking in a small voice, like a child. "You and Mom would fight without getting so out of control."

"We were just different people," he answered, as if he had expected this reply. "We got crazy in different ways." It was true but not true at the same time. Some part of him suspected that the craziness could still come. "Get some sleep," he told his daughter. "Do what your counselor tells you. There's nothing else you can do."

"I know," she said, her voice now under control. "I know it; I just hate not being able to do something."

After he hung up, he continued to sit on the edge of the bed, unable to move. He felt an enormous sadness dragging him toward the earth. Finally, he stood up and went to his pile of manuals. He saw his face in the mirror as he walked by. An ineffectual old man. There wasn't a damn thing he could do. He might as well study.

But when he picked up the flight manual, he found his arm hurtling through the air, launching the book across the room. It smashed into the wall on the other side of the bed with a tremendous smack, dropping to the floor open. He looked down at his hand. It was shaking. *How did that happen?* he wondered. Something had taken him over. He couldn't do anything, not even control his movements. *Old man,* he thought, and a phrase came into his head. *Tattered coat upon a stick.* He could remember someone reading it to him once. Margaret, maybe. Something she was studying in school.

It was Kid Flyboy's third and last period when he finally got his engine failure.

"I bet I'll get my engine failure today," he had announced that morning as he caught up with Will in the parking lot. "Here, I brought you a coffee." He held out a Starbucks bag. "Creamer and sugar in there. I didn't know what you took."

"Thanks," Will said, surprised. He couldn't even bring himself to wonder what sly motivation the Kid might have had, because he was too tired. At eleven Margaret had called to say David had been located: he had gone to the home of a mutual friend. Margaret had talked to David on the phone, and Will had reassured her that David was just getting away to think clearly for a while. At seven that morning she had called again to say that maybe he was right, because David had agreed to go to couples therapy. Margaret sounded exhausted but slightly hopeful. Will had tried to encourage the feeling. He had tried to sound confident and consoling, sure that everything would work out fine. The effort left him feeling blank and empty. He looked at the Kid and didn't even have the energy left to resent him. He just wanted to get it over with.

They did a normal instrument departure, and the Kid launched into his airwork. He did some steep turns and then a go-around into a holding pattern. The Kid's face was relaxed beneath his headset, his hand loosely on the stick. He was in control of the plane.

Will looked at the sky and earth playing on the windows of the cockpit and wished it were a real plane and he could walk right out. Just open the door and free-fall to the earth. *This isn't what I signed up for,* he thought. He was getting old, and what had become of his life? When he was twenty or thirty or forty, this wasn't how he imagined himself approaching sixty: unable to fix anything or make anything work out right. *I want to do it over,* he thought. What would he change, though? He couldn't see how he could make things end up any different. If only there were a single moment where things went wrong, then he could go back and fix that, or at least know the right thing to fix.

When the engine failure came, it was both engines at once. The Kid was confident, jumping to attention, easily beginning the standard procedure. He measured his ground speed, checked his altitude, did the calculation. The computer agreed he could make it, just. He didn't drop his gear.

"We'll make it," he told Will. Will nodded his okay, careful not to look at the instructor. A phrase from his Air Force years popped into his head. *Ain't no way.*

At first everything went smoothly. The Kid decreased altitude at the right rate, the plane gliding sleekly through the air. It kept its speed so well that the Kid had to introduce drag with the flaps as they neared the airport. The runway was in sight, and they were moving at the right speed when the Kid dropped his gear.

It happened as Will knew it would. The gear dragged the plane down, not much, but just enough, and there was a sickening lurch as the simulator's hydraulic nose dipped toward the ground. There wasn't much the Kid could do with no power. He tried to bring the nose up, but the plane was low and out of trim; even a pilot with decades of experience would have fought to regain control. The last thing they saw was an approach light rising in their path. Fifty yards from the runway, the screen went blank.

The three of them sat there in silence. "Well," the instructor said at last. "Hit the approach lights."

"Yeah," said the Kid, deflated.

"Dead-stick landing is not on the rating ride," the instructor said. "Still, you could use a few more hours." He rifled through his schedule pages. "I need to get Thursday's schedule," he said, rising in a rustle of paper. "Wait here." He clunked down the stairs.

Will and the Kid sat in the silent cockpit. With the windows black and the computers off, it didn't feel like an airplane at all.

"All I've ever wanted to do is fly," the Kid said, surprising Will. His voice was flat in the cockpit's dull gloom.

"It'll go in your record," Will said, "but it probably won't matter." Guys had crashed the simulator before. "At least it wasn't your rating ride." Surprisingly, he felt bad for the Kid. Maybe he should have helped him out. It was an easy mistake, after all.

"I built model planes when I was three," the Kid went on. "As soon as I knew about the navy, I planned to join. I went to the Gulf War."

Will was surprised by that, too. He hadn't taken the Kid for someone with any real action in his past. Maybe that explained his confidence.

"Everything went like I wanted. I got back from the Gulf and joined up with TWA. Lately, I've been wondering if I chose the right airline."

Will laughed. He felt a sense of relief. His hatred for the Kid seemed small and faraway, a town seen from miles above.

"I grew up on a farm," Will said. "I drove a tractor every single day in the spring. I'd be plowing my dad's field, looking up at the planes going by overhead, and all I wanted was to be up there, flying." He paused, and the Kid half turned in his seat, encouraging him to go on.

"Now I'm in the opposite place, you see? Now I'm flying, and I look down and see the fields. Corn, apples—whatever. Combines and harvesters. And I think, *Man, I wish I was down there.* Now I'm up in the air, I wish I was back on the ground."

He stopped and met the Kid's eyes. The Kid didn't understand the story. Will wasn't sure he understood it himself. It was the story he'd always told to explain why he left the farm and why he went back. But it meant more than that. The Kid still thought all motion was forward. He didn't understand how much would drag him back. Maybe Will couldn't tell him that. He doubted if anyone could have told him at the Kid's age.

"Thursday night," the instructor said, filling the doorway. "Eight o'clock."

"Yeah, okay," said the Kid. He looked downcast again.

The instructor turned. "How about you, Will? You okay with coming in at night? If not, I can fly it with him."

"Yeah, all right," Will said. He didn't want to, but he felt a sudden desire to do something nice for the Kid.

"Flying all night," the Kid said. "And getting nowhere. Sorry, Will."

Will shrugged. He thought of Margaret's voice on the phone that morning, cautiously hopeful. He wanted her to keep the hope, and the caution, too. "That's the name of the game," he said. For the first time, he really looked at the Kid. He was young, but that wasn't all. Sitting there in the half-light, he had a slight sheen to him, the glow of a person at the beginning of everything.

The rain is quieter by the time they get off the freeway and head down the road toward home. No one has spoken for thirty miles. Will looks in the rearview mirror at Kit. Sitting there, one arm draped lightly behind Leanne, he has that same glow, that newly made look. According to Carol, he just won some grant to make a film. But it's more than that. He has the eager energy of someone who still believes, in some corner of his heart, that he has all the time in the world.

"What's that?" Carol cries, and for the second time on the trip, everyone starts at the sound of a voice. She's looking ahead, toward their house. The rain has slowed; it's still steady, but lighter, like a fuzzy curtain. Will makes out a car in their driveway, but not the one he expected, not Margaret and David's black Corolla.

"Whose car is that?" Leanne says, her voice betraying the first sign of nervousness about the impending three days of preparations and festivities.

"It's not George or Janice," Will says. "Maybe it's the caterers."

"It's Margaret," Carol says, so softly she might be speaking to herself.

"Margaret's driving a Rabbit?" Leanne says.

"It's her old car—the one she had in graduate school." As soon as Carol says it, Will realizes something must have happened. He glances at Carol, who's frowning slightly.

"Maybe the Corolla's having trouble," he says. "I told them to buy American." His tone is less than convincing, but she turns to him with an almost grateful look. She smiles, the tight smile of forced optimism.

"Yes," she says. "Those Chicago winters are really tough on cars. All that salt." She turns and looks back at Kit and Leanne, as if to reassure herself they really are there.

"Well," she says cheerily. "We're all here now!"

four

I'M CALLING BECAUSE MY HUSBAND IS, UM, KEEPING me prisoner in our apartment, and I was wondering if someone might, um, might come and convince him to let me leave.

Margaret is lying on her old bed, the one she slept in as a little girl.

Have the two of you been fighting?

Yes.

Her mother had to redecorate Leanne's room to make it feel more like a guest room, but Margaret's room always had a formal air. It features a wooden four-poster bed and a dark walnut dresser topped by a curving, ornate mirror. They were a Christmas gift when she was in seventh grade. It was what she had asked for: a real grown-up bedroom suite. In the corner, there's a matching armoire.

Yes.

Has he harmed you?

No. Not yet.

The comforter on the bed is a graceful blue chinoiserie with trees and people walking over arched bridges. It looks like the pattern on a china tea set.

Not yet.

Margaret rolls over and tries to clear the voices from her head by focusing on a tree outside the window. In the carpeted basement, Trevor is bouncing something against the wall again and again. Carol keeps a box of toys for him down there.

Thud-slap, thud-slap, thud-slap, goes the ball.

Not yet, not yet, not yet.

Margaret stares at one of her bedposts. It's a long, grooved taper, topped with a small carved knob. Pinecones, the American acanthus leaf. She left the bedroom suite when she went to college and grad school. Students slept on futons. Fancy meant having a frame for your futon, so you weren't on the floor. When she and

David moved back to Chicago, Margaret proposed collecting the bedroom suite from Michigan, but David said he preferred the firmness of the futon. He didn't have to say what Margaret had already learned to see: that the bedroom suite was tacky, a striver's idea of gracious living. She didn't want it, either. Still, she couldn't help but feel vaguely insulted by David's rejection of it.

We'll send a squad car out.

Okay. Thank you.

Margaret's call did the police's work for them. It got David to leave, so she could. She's lucky they live in Evanston. In Chicago she wouldn't have had the nerve to call 911. How much did she really require help? Enough to take an officer away from a woman whose husband was already hitting her, not just acting like he might? From an old man hearing gunshots outside his apartment? A little girl whose crack-addicted mother had passed out on the living room floor? Chicago had bigger problems than hers. It couldn't be bothered with her, and she wouldn't have asked it to.

And yet some part of her recognizes that when she dialed the phone, it was blind instinct acting, with no reference to her ideals or beliefs, her understanding of the larger forces—social, political, historical—that gave her situation a context and a relative meaning. Lying on her childhood bed, clutching her pillow to her, she can't stand thinking about what she did, but she can't imagine having done anything else. He had crossed a line. If he was willing to threaten her physically to hold her prisoner in her own house, what else might he be willing to do?

Now the skein of anxiety tangled around her heart is half for the past and half for the future. What has she done? And what will happen next? She imagines David coming home, walking through the apartment, finding them gone. Will he see the note she left? Will he look out the window and see the absence of her car?

The thudding from the basement has stopped, and a suspicious silence ensues. Margaret listens for a moment.

"Trevor!" she yells. "What's going on down there?"

The silence changes character slightly before Trevor yells,

"Nothing." Margaret can tell from his voice that he has moved closer to the basement stairs.

Just envisioning him standing there makes her shaky with love and fear for her son. She wants to go check on him, to calm herself by putting her arms around him. She's beginning to sit up when she hears the unmistakable thud of a car door outside. Immediately, she feels exhausted at the prospect of talking, and at the same time relieved that something has arrived to distract her from her endlessly cycling thoughts. She gets up and goes to the doorway of her room. The house seems frozen with anticipation of some imminent epiphany. There's a knot of poised tension in her stomach. She stands, waiting. Voices outside are approaching, but they sound muffled, like harbingers from another world.

"Where's my grandson?" Carol is the first one into the house, and her shout cracks the stillness. It's as if light, as well as noise, has flooded the rooms. There's a brief pause and then the sound of Trevor running up the basement stairs.

"Grandma!" he cries. Margaret finds herself able to step forward, and she moves toward the family room. Everyone has trooped in through the garage. She sees Leanne first and is struck by how good her sister looks, tall and lean, her hair long and gleaming, her eyes bright. Behind her is a blond man—Kit, presumably—whose hair is slightly longer than the Midwest considers appropriate, and whose thin nose and lips edge him from the category of "handsome" and into "interesting-looking."

Then her father comes in, awkwardly and unnecessarily lugging a rolling suitcase under one arm, and a quick breath catches in Margaret's throat. His hair is thinner than it was the last time she saw him, but more surprising is how haggard he looks, how his cheeks and shoulders and neck seem to have dropped, like a tired man falling into a chair. He looks up at her, and worry flickers in his eyes. She wonders if he has told Carol about the phone calls they exchanged a while ago, when he was in training on the 767 and she and David were fighting. Somehow she always felt he wouldn't.

"Oh, you're getting to be such a little man!" Carol is on the floor embracing Trevor.

"Hey, there," Will says, coming to embrace her, and the image of him as an old man vanishes. He's tall enough that her face disappears in his chest, and as she inhales the musty dampness of his coat, Margaret feels a rush of gratitude for the fact that regardless of the cost, she left Chicago and came here, to be part of a family event. She's safe here, she tells herself, and for the moment, she feels that way. She lets go and turns to Trevor.

"You won't believe what I've got for you," Carol is telling him. She puts one hand on the ground to help herself get back onto her feet. Margaret sees Leanne move forward and quietly put a hand under their mother's elbow. Her sister, too, has grown older and more mature.

"Oh, Margaret!" Carol tears herself away from Trevor to throw her arms around her daughter. Margaret returns the embrace with her usual slight discomfort. Her mother's angularity has become something more fragile than beauty. Margaret draws back to greet the others.

"How was your drive?" Leanne asks, leaning in to give her sister an awkward one-armed shoulder hug.

"Fine. It wasn't raining until Michigan."

Carol has turned her attention back to Trevor. "I've been saving a surprise for you. Come see." Leaving the groceries and the others behind, she takes his hand and heads for the kitchen. Margaret and Leanne exchange a look that says *She's still the same.* Then Margaret leans over and grabs one of the bags of groceries, and they all move toward the kitchen.

"Oh, Margaret, this is Kit," Leanne says, offhand as ever, as if it's no big deal to introduce the man she's bringing into the family.

Margaret turns to him. "Good to meet you," she says. "Is Kit your real name?"

"It's Kitto, actually," he says. "Kind of embarrassing. My father was English, and it's a perfectly reasonable name over there."

"I don't think it's unreasonable."

"Well, that's a relief." He smiles in an open way, making a joke but including her in it, and Margaret decides she likes his soft, unhandsome looks. Leanne puts a hand on his shoulder blade, as if wanting to assure herself that he's really there, and he acknowledges her touch by leaning in ever so slightly. There's a current between them. Margaret glances away.

In the kitchen, Carol has opened a high cupboard and dragged out a large plastic canister. "I've been saving them," she says, handing the canister to Trevor. Trevor's eyes go round with amazement at his good fortune. Inside the canister are at least thirty different cereal-box prizes.

"Oh, look at that." Margaret nudges him. "What do you say?"

"Thank you," the boy breathes, unable to take his eyes off the cornucopia of molded plastic joy awaiting his excavation.

"I got Janice to save them up as well. And I added a few things from bubblegum machines." Carol looks slightly sheepish at this admission of fraudulence, and Margaret surprises herself by laughing. She disapproves of both sugary breakfast cereals and cheap plastic toys, and has instituted strict rules about what Trevor is allowed to bring home from his grandmother's, but today she finds herself relieved to be engaged in normal conversation, an exchange of family pleasantries in a bright, cozy kitchen.

"How about some coffee?" Carol asks, and Margaret puts an arm around her mother and squeezes.

"That'd be great, Mom," she says.

Leanne starts unloading things from the grocery bags, and Kit goes off to help with the luggage. Margaret can hear Will lecturing Kit on how to assess the corn crop, which is looking frail and tentative in the field west of the house.

"Where's David?" Carol asks. "Resting up after the ride?"

Margaret experiences a slight hiccup in her steadiness, like a car going over a speed bump too fast. She concentrates on watching her mother scoop Maxwell House from a can into her drip coffeemaker. With any luck, it won't be the disgusting flavored kind. Margaret always makes espresso at home.

"He couldn't come," she says, her eyes on her mother's hands. "Departmental stuff. One of the adjuncts quit, and he had to fill a summer-school teaching position at the last minute." She hadn't intended to lie, but somehow the lie manifested itself more easily than any version of the truth she had contemplated telling. How can she ruin her sister's wedding by dragging her own unhappiness across it? Lying is only fair to Leanne, so she can have a perfectly happy day, as Margaret did when she got married. Or appeared to.

Not yet. Not yet. She pulls her mind away forcibly and looks at her sister. "David says to tell you he's really sorry, Leanne."

Leanne looks down at the counter and shrugs lightly. Her hair slides forward over her shoulder, shining in the kitchen's overhead light, and Margaret wonders if she's been doing something special or just using a good conditioner.

"It's okay," Leanne says. "These things happen."

Carol has added water to the coffee machine—too much water, given how little coffee she used—and now she turns a skeptical face to the girls.

"But I don't understand," she objects. "Why can't someone else take care of hiring a summer-school teacher? That's not such a big deal, is it?"

"Oh, Mom, you don't understand what goes on in a high-powered department like David's," Margaret says. It's true: Carol has never understood the amount of pressure academia imposes on its denizens. Still, in order to avoid her mother's eyes, Margaret begins rifling through the last grocery bag.

"But it's his sister-in-law's *wedding,*" Carol says.

Margaret has found a large damp package at the bottom of the paper sack. "What's this?" she says, dredging it up. The bottom of the paper bag is wet and threatening to give way.

"Oh, Margaret, those are the shrimp. I found the most *wonderful* shrimp." Carol's mood improves immediately.

"Shrimp?" Margaret studies the package. "Good shrimp out here? Where'd they come from?" Exasperation darts through her, overwhelming the tenuous feelings of goodwill and affection. It's so like Carol to convince herself that something is wonderful when it can't possibly be.

Carol looks surprised. "From South America," she says. "They were flown in this morning."

Margaret shrugs and goes to the drawer that holds plastic wrap and tinfoil.

"Well, it's dripping," she says. "I'll have to rewrap it." She finds the plastic wrap and begins rolling the package of shrimp in a long piece. "There must be almost six pounds here," she says, trying to regain her generous spirit.

Trevor weighed six pounds at birth. He was three weeks early. She was home alone the night she went into labor, David still at the office. Later, she found out he'd been having take-out food with one of his grad students, an attractive Asian woman named Mei. Margaret had gotten angry about it, and David had laughed.

You're just flooded with hormones, he had said. *You can't help but start spouting the dogma of mandatory monogamy. Don't worry, it'll pass.* Why didn't she remember that line when David was getting so furious about Vasant? Spouting the dogma of monogamy.

"This might be more shrimp than we need," Margaret says as she rewraps the bundle. "How many of us are there, only six, right?"

Carol looks uncomprehending for a moment. "Oh no," she says, getting it. "Those aren't for us to eat. Those are for the party Friday night. For shrimp cocktail."

"Shrimp cocktail Friday night?" Margaret pauses, the package in midair. "Mom, you can't be serious. We can't eat these Friday night."

"Why not?" Carol's eyes take on the hardness they get when she's gearing up to be stubborn in her own defense.

"Because, Mom, it's Wednesday. You can't freeze them if you want to use them for shrimp cocktail, and you can't keep fresh shrimp in your fridge for two whole days. They'll go bad." Margaret glances at her sister for support, but Leanne looks away, out to the dining room where Trevor is unpacking his goodies. She hates conflict.

"South America to Michigan," Margaret adds, annoyed to have to explain something so obvious. "They're at least a day old already."

Carol looks confused, and Margaret feels bad. She saw the price tag on the paper package. Immediately, however, her sense of rightness overrides her sympathy. It's so typical of Carol to rush into buying something without even understanding all the exigencies, to grasp at an ideal of luxury without securing the means to achieve it. She wants Leanne's party to be elegant and sophisticated, but she hasn't thought through every step of it with the care a real sophisticate would know was required.

"I'm sorry, Mom," Margaret says, softening her voice a bit, "but you don't want to feed your guests rancid shellfish." She glances again at Leanne, who has disengaged completely. "They'll all get food poisoning and be too sick to come to the wedding."

Carol's face falls. It's clear she was preparing to fight back, to insist that Margaret was being ridiculous, but the vision of the wedding emptied of guests, Leanne herself hunched over a toilet in her wedding gown, trumps every argument in her head. She surrenders completely.

"Oh no," she says, visibly shrinking. "What do we do now?"

Margaret squelches a feeling of guilt. Maybe she's being overscrupulous, but it's for the best, just as lying was for the best. Somehow, disaster is going to have to be averted for three days, so her little sister can get married and fly back to New York, and Margaret can go home and sort out the wreckage of her imploded life. Neither Carol nor Leanne seems up to the task, and her father will be charging ahead on his own track, so the anticipation and prevention of disasters is clearly falling to her. Now, one crisis headed off, the next is already brewing in Carol's downcast face. Her mother's dismay at the shrimp debacle is going to leach into the fabric of the next two days and color all their preparations unless a way can be found to stop it.

"Don't worry, Mom," Margaret says. "We can cook this tonight. We can make a really nice dinner. I can make gumbo from it. I just need a chicken and a few other things."

"Gumbo?"

"A celebratory dinner, just for the family."

"Five pounds of shrimp? Isn't that going to be a giant gumbo?"

"We can freeze the leftovers. Gumbo freezes well."

Carol shrugs. Now that her vision of a gorgeous platter of shrimp has been dashed, she'll refuse to care what happens to them. "They still have their heads on," she says glumly, but Margaret just smiles.

"All the better," she declares. Encouraged by her mother's lack of objections, she begins digging around in the fridge to make space for the shrimp.

"Oh, Margaret," Carol says. She has turned to the sink now and is busy scrubbing the label off a jelly jar. "I ran into your old boyfriend Doug in the grocery store last week. You should see what a nice man he turned out to be."

Margaret rummages in the fridge, only half listening. Carol presses on. "He was talking about his mother, and then I mentioned Leanne's wedding to him, and he seemed truly excited and happy to hear about it, so . . ." She pauses and leans over the sink, attacking a particularly tenacious piece of label.

"And so . . . what?" Margaret demands, her attention captured at last. She turns from the fridge and uses the dish towel to wipe her hands dry while fixing Carol with a no-more-nonsense stare.

"Oh, well . . ." Carol stops scrubbing and sets the jelly jar on the counter before turning around to reply. "I invited him to the cocktail party. I hope you don't mind."

Margaret knows what this declaration is: immediate revenge for the shrimp but also, at a deeper level, a belated revenge for the very *fact* of Doug, for the way Margaret tortured her mother with the possibility that she might just run off with a farmer, abandoning every hope Carol held so dearly for her future.

"No, I don't mind," she says coolly. "It will be good to see him again."

She meets her mother's gaze, her calm footing reestablished, but if Carol is disappointed in Margaret's failure to be upset, she gives no sign. Instead, she turns to the sink and gives her jelly jar a pat, then whirls back around to confront Leanne.

"Sweetie, your dress!" she cries. "I haven't seen it in person yet! Let's go try it on!"

In a cotton tank top and underwear, stepping into a pooled circle of wedding dress, Leanne nurses a secret happiness. David isn't coming. From Margaret's expression, the way she cast her eyes down when she answered their mother's question, it was clear there were parts of the story she wasn't telling. But it's not just that. Leanne has never really liked David. As she thrusts her arms through the dress's tulle armholes, she asks herself whether she disliked him from the first time Margaret brought him home, or whether it started with Margaret's wedding.

"Oh, Leanne," her mother breathes. "It's stunning."

"You *are* planning on wearing a bra with it, aren't you?" Margaret asks. "Because that bodice isn't doing a whole lot for you."

"Yes, I'm wearing a bra. Here, zip me up."

Everyone else seemed to like David. He was smart and sophisticated, and ambitious, like Margaret. He had grown up in a wealthy Connecticut family, spending summers on Martha's Vineyard and getting his bachelor's degree from Princeton, but he didn't act like a snob. When he came to Michigan, he complimented the food and acted interested in Will's farming tales. He seemed to fit into the family better than Margaret. He was clearly the motivation behind his and Margaret's push to get jobs in Chicago, and he even talked about buying a summer cottage on the lake in Michigan, the way a lot of Chicago people did. He gave Will and Carol every reason to approve of him.

And yet Leanne can't help but suspect that they never warmed to him. Perhaps it was a lingering discomfort with his upper-crust background, or maybe he seemed too good to be true. Their coolness was never apparent in things they said or did, but in what they didn't do. Carol made elaborate formal dinners when he visited, but never the cozy grilled-cheese-and-tomato-soup dinner the family traditionally had on Sunday nights. Will answered questions about the farm, but he never dragged David out to the barn to inspect his new backhoe or offered to let him drive the combine.

For Leanne, David was a more familiar problem. He was the kind of man who raised eyebrows, dropped hints, let his eyes linger, and held goodbye hugs for a second too long. It never extended into anything that could be considered a breach of manners, and she never thought anything of it—until Margaret's wedding.

"What shoes are you going to wear?" Carol asks, and Leanne points to her suitcase. On the top rests a small flannel shoe bag. She didn't want standard bridal shoes, something she'd never use again, so she went to Bergdorf Goodman in the city and picked out the most beautiful pair of white shoes she could find. They are so exquisite she can hardly stand the thought of wearing them.

"These are really nice," Margaret says as she takes the shoes out of their soft bag, and Leanne can't help but feel a stab of pleasure. It's rare for Margaret to compliment Leanne's choices.

"Are they high enough?" Carol asks. "Put them on." Leanne does as she's told, bunching up her dress to slip them on. The three of them contemplate the image in the mirror. Leanne scrutinizes the hem, but her eyes keep being drawn back up to take in the full effect. The dress is simple and barely ornamented, but it hugs her body tightly before dropping to the ground in a dramatic sweep of satin. She looks like someone else in it.

"It's too long," Margaret says at last.

"Oh, I don't know," Carol says hopefully. "As long as she can walk, it will be fine."

Leanne kicks one foot in front of her and watches the dress drift slowly back into place. The bottom edge just touches the carpet. "Margaret's right," she announces. "It's too long. I didn't have the shoes when they hemmed it, and I guess they thought I'd go higher. They left half an inch too much." She leans over. The white satin rests lightly on her mother's carpet. "I look like somebody cut off my feet."

"Oh no, you're right." Carol's face seems to wilt. "And if the ground is still a little bit wet from all this rain . . ."

"I don't suppose there's anyone around here who can do anything for us." Margaret's lips are a thin line in anticipation of Ryville's usual shortcomings.

"It's okay," Leanne says. "I can do it."

"What do you mean you can do it?" Margaret raises her brows, and Leanne fights the familiar feeling of intimidation. "Hemming a wedding dress is complicated. Even a professional seamstress won't do it unless she's really good."

Leanne turns back to the mirror, where the reflection of an unfamiliarly beautiful woman looks back at her. "I can do it," she says simply.

"Leanne is as good as a professional seamstress," her mother says, jumping to her defense. "You should see how people in Cold Spring come to her store for advice."

Margaret, obviously calculating this particular argument's importance, raises a hand to stop it. "Okay," she says. "Mom, why don't you get us some pins?"

Pins in hand, Margaret and Carol drop to the floor to debate the merits of various lengths. Leanne tries to join in, but whenever she leans over, they both sit back in annoyance and cry, "Stand up straight!"

"This skirt is fuller than mine was," Margaret says, on her hands and knees. "You're going to be hemming for a while."

"Your dress was beautiful, Margaret," Carol says, conciliatory now that Margaret has acquiesced on the hem issue. "Your whole wedding was picture-perfect."

"Well," Margaret is scooting around to the back, concentrating hard on the evenness of the hem, "I had a lot of good people to work with. People who understood the idea of standards."

Leanne thinks of the people who worked at the Drake Hotel. They were certainly accommodating. Margaret had a cocktail reception there the night before her rehearsal dinner. Leanne wore a mint green dress that she bought at a secondhand shop on St.

Mark's Place for two dollars. Drunk, she fell into bed wearing it. The next morning, when the housekeeping staff made up her room, they picked the dress up off the bathroom floor and hung it carefully in the closet, as if it were an Armani suit.

Mostly, she remembers the bathtub. After the rehearsal dinner, she floated there for hours. The water cooled down, but she didn't want to get out. She had a stack of empty bottles from the minibar by the side of tub. She just lay there, watching the bubbles on the surface pop and vanish. She had used the entire bottle of hotel bath and shower gel, and that still wasn't enough to make her feel clean.

Even then she couldn't quite remember how David had ended up in her room. She recalled him telling her mother he'd get her home safe. In the hallway, he had cupped her elbow in his hand, like a nineteenth-century gentleman. *Oh, I'm so glad you're here,* she had joked. *I couldn't have made it without you.* She meant it to sound sarcastic and wry, but it came out sounding stupidly true. She could have taken a cab home; that's what she would have done in New York.

When they arrived, David took Leanne's key and opened the door. She had her shoes off and her dress unzipped before she realized he had followed her into the room. He was leaning against the closed door, watching. They exchanged some more banter, and then somehow David had her up against the wall and was slipping one hand into the back of her dress while hiking up the hem with the other. She felt his finger slide up her thigh and under the elastic of her underpants, and she wondered disinterestedly if his touch felt good because he was used to Margaret, if sisters liked the same thing. But she and Margaret never had. Like David, for instance. Leanne certainly wouldn't be marrying him in under twenty-four hours. That was enough to make her put her hands on his chest and gently push him back.

"I think you should go," she managed to get out.

"I know you do," he said, and then he moved his hands onto her hips and his mouth to her collarbone. Leanne felt oddly reluctant to push him away. She didn't want to be rude. She leaned her head against the wall, hoping he would get bored with her lack of response. After a few moments, when his enthusiasm wasn't appearing to slacken, she shimmied down the wall and slipped sideways away from him.

"I think I need to sleep," she said. Like that, he gave up. They exchanged a few words—niceties, as if agreeing to put themselves back on an even keel—and then he grinned at her and left.

Once he was gone, Leanne went straight to the minibar. She filled the ice bucket with everything that looked good, filled the bathtub with the hottest water she could get, and climbed in. The heat scalded her skin so that it turned pink and didn't even feel wet. She twisted the tops off the tiny bottles and stretched her toes to the end of the tub and thought of her sister. Margaret would never get drunk alone in the bathtub. Even if she knew that her soon-to-be-husband had made a pass at her sister the night before their wedding, she wouldn't respond by sedating herself. She would proceed calmly along some sensible and efficient path for fixing the problem. That was how Margaret was.

The next day, Leanne knew, Margaret would marry David, for better or worse. Later on, if she discovered one of David's infidelities—because Leanne knew she couldn't be the only one—she would move on to the next thing. Margaret never stood still. She moved forward all the time, just like their father, who couldn't wait to leave home and then couldn't wait to return. Thinking about it made Leanne exhausted. She wanted to stay in one place, hovering, floating, indefinitely. She closed her eyes and floated so that only her heels were touching the tub.

Now, standing in her own wedding dress like an oversize doll, she experiences a wave of the same feeling. She doesn't want to hem the dress, because then it will be done, and that will be one more step toward the wedding actually happening, toward Kit and Leanne being married, which means she will have told him about her past and they will have stepped through the ceremony into their future as a married couple. And then what? The trip to Mexico, kids maybe, a bigger house, middle age, the empty nest, retirement.

It's all laid out, a perfect path forward, with no regard for the idea that she might want something else instead.

"There," Margaret says. She leans back and scrutinizes her work in the mirror, squinting. "That's as even as I can possibly make it under these circumstances."

"It looks good," Leanne says. "At least I won't trip over it this way."

"That satin won't be fun to deal with." Margaret is gathering up the remaining pins and putting them back in Carol's sewing box.

"It's okay," Leanne says. "I find sewing relaxing." Margaret frowns at the dress, trying to find a mistake in her work, and watching her in the mirror, Leanne feels sorry for her sister. Margaret is like one of those characters from Greek mythology, perpetually longing for something just out of reach. That's how her standards work: her expectations are always increasing, so that as soon as her abilities catch up with them, the bar moves a little bit higher, and she is disappointed again.

"It looks good," Leanne says softly, and Margaret looks up and meets her eyes in the mirror. Over the years, the two of them have grown to look more alike than they did as little girls. *Look at the picture upside down,* their mother used to say. *That's when you see the resemblance.*

"It'll do," Margaret says.

Will and Kit are sitting in the living room. They have hauled the luggage in, the girls and Carol have unpacked the groceries, and now the women are all upstairs seeing Leanne's wedding dress. Will knows Carol well enough to know that not only should Kit avoid going upstairs, he should stay away himself. He's not the groom, but he's a man, which allies him with the groom. He can't be trusted not to report back some detail—a beaded bodice, a sweeping train, a plunging neckline—the anticipation of which would spoil Kit's delighted surprise when his bride comes rustling down the aisle.

Now, not quite sure what to do, the two of them have retreated

to the living room, awaiting further orders. Will eyes the remote.
There's probably a game on, or news. That means more endless terror coverage. Yellow alert, orange alert, red—who wants to hear it?
No TV, then. He wonders if he should offer Kit a beer. He's not sure
if there will be any in the fridge, what with all the party stuff Carol
has been stockpiling. It occurs to him that no one has had lunch. In
the old days, Kit and Leanne would have eaten on the flight, but
now even the occasional in-flight meal is usually a little box of cold
sandwiches that passengers pick up on the jetway. Will doesn't even
bother to eat them. He brings his own food now, like a passenger on
Greyhound.

"How about something to eat?" he says. Kit looks up, almost as
if he'd forgotten Will was in the room.

"Yeah, okay," he says. "Actually, that would be great. I'm a bit hun-
gry." He nods, confirming this new understanding of his physical state.

Will gets up and leads the way to the kitchen. "I don't know
what Carol's got in here," he says, opening the fridge to check it
out. He spies a small jar of red sauce with a fancy label and red-
checked cloth covering the lid. Must be salsa. Carol had a Tex-Mex
phase last year, bringing home black beans and fancy blue-corn tor-
tilla chips and expensive jars of salsa that, as far as Will could tell,
didn't taste any better than Old El Paso. But at least there's something he can serve to Kit without embarrassment.

"Here's some salsa," he says, grabbing the jar and heading for
the pantry. "I'll find some chips." There's a bag of chips on the top
shelf, not the fancy blue-corn kind but something called "restaurant-
style." Will puts them on the table and then, in deference to Carol's
complaints about his lack of civility, he finds a ceramic bowl and
dumps the whole jar of salsa into it. It's thick and red, and he's
relieved that it doesn't seem to have any chunks of peppers or
onions in it. During the Tex-Mex phase, he was constantly dredging
things out of his salsa that shouldn't be there: corn, beans, raisins.

Kit has the bag of chips open by the time Will gets to the table. "I
needed this," he says. "I was feeling a little queasy on the plane."

Will's mistrust of the kid eases up a bit. He helps himself to a chip, loads it up with a heaping pile of salsa, and leans back in his chair. "So you make videos, right?"

"I work as a video editor right now. But I make documentary films."

"And those aren't shot on video?"

Kit breaks a chip in two. "Yeah, they are these days. Digital video— it's a lot cheaper than celluloid." Will is about to point out there's little difference, then, between videos and films, but Kit speaks up first.

"So Leanne tells me you'll be retiring from flying soon."

The chip and salsa, which had been tasting perfectly salty and sweet and tangy in Will's mouth, go as dry as cardboard. He grinds his jaw up and down, but it seems as if he'll never get the mouthful down. Kit watches him patiently, waiting for an answer. Finally, Will swallows the whole dry lump. It sticks in his throat.

"How about a beer?" he rasps, heading for the fridge.

"No, thanks," Kit says. Will locates a Bud Light and cracks it open, getting a few swallows down before returning to the table. The beer is cold and malty and slowly removes the lump from his craw.

"It's damn stupid," he says, sitting back down. "The FAA plays God, but they don't have the good sense to do it on an individual basis."

Kit has taken a bite of a chip heavily loaded with salsa. He frowns, looking confused. Gently, he sets the chip down on the table. "So it's mandatory retirement?"

"At sixty. No matter what." Will gulps another swallow of beer and feels it fizzle down his throat. He gestures with his can out the kitchen's sliding glass doors. "The world is full of second-rate pilots. Not because they're old. Because they don't know what they're doing. Most of the new guys haven't even come up through the military. They learned to fly on a computer." He snorts.

"Maybe I *will* have that beer," Kit says.

Will nearly tells him to help himself, but a vision of Carol's face stops him. He gets up and goes to the fridge. "Here you go."

"Thanks. So what will you do with yourself?" Kit opens his can and seems to be sniffing at the top before taking a drink.

Will lifts his own beer in a gesture of uncertainty. Suddenly, he's tired of talking. "Oh, I don't know," he says evasively. He's not about to play his Far East hand now. "Farm. Raise chickens."

"You like chickens?" Kit has begun taking neat, slightly prissy sips of beer.

"Aaannnh." Will shrugs. "We had some once." He's reverting to midwestern farmer-speak: short sentences, few words.

Kit looks out the window. "What's up with Margaret?" he says out of the blue.

Will gazes down into his beer can. There's a small bit of liquid left in the bottom, giving off a slightly gold shimmer. He's not surprised by the question. Something is definitely up with Margaret, something he hopes she might tell him about, but he suspects that's not what Kit means. Kit must mean *What is Margaret really like?* That's not an easy thing to summarize.

"If Leanne makes sense to you," he tells Kit, "Margaret won't."

Kit makes a funny gesture with one hand. "Leanne doesn't make sense to you?" It's a real question, and Will ponders it.

"No," he says after a few moments. "I guess she doesn't." It's odd to hear himself say it, but as he does, he knows it's true. He has never really understood Leanne the way he has understood Margaret, even at her most dogmatic or defiant. Perhaps he shouldn't admit that to Leanne's future husband, but something about Kit makes him speak honestly.

Kit takes a drink, a real drink this time, and gazes out across the farm. From the sliding doors, the deck extends out toward the barn. Behind the barn, the cornfield stretches in both directions, wrapping back around the house in a giant U.

"I don't think she makes sense to me, either," he says. "At least not all the time. But I don't really need her to make sense. I need her to fit in. With me. With my not making sense." He looks back at Will. "You know?"

Will nods. "Yeah," he says, although for as much as he's following, the guy might as well be speaking ancient Greek. "Sure."

"Besides," Kit continues, "you reach a certain age . . ." He pauses.

"And they ground you," Will finishes. Kit laughs softly, an almost sad little laugh, staring down at his beer can. He picks it up again and drinks.

"Grandpa, I found a frog in the basement!" Trevor comes into the room, sheer delight illuming his face. Kit raises his eyebrows at Will.

"What'd you do with it?" Will asks his grandson.

"I chased it!" Trevor cries with glee.

"Did you catch it?"

Trevor pauses, looking serious. "I chased it," he asserts.

Will nods. "Once your mom caught a skunk in the barn. With her bare hands. It was only a baby." He looks at Kit. "That was when she really loved the farm." He stands up, crumpling his empty beer can in one hand. "I'm the only one who loves it now," he says.

There's a clatter of feet on the stairs, and he hears Carol talking to the girls.

"Your rooms are so close together, with that bathroom in between," she is saying. "So if we put a door in the hall just past the linen closet, we can make that into a whole separate suite. People could rent one or both rooms."

"But those rooms are so small," Margaret says.

"It's a bed-and-breakfast," Carol answers. "People don't expect four stars. They want atmosphere and country charm."

"And breakfast," Leanne says. "That's what they'll come back for." Will recognizes her conciliatory voice, her quiet, unobtrusive way of defusing conflicts.

"Oh yes." Carol laughs. It's her real laugh, an authentic welling up of happiness, because no matter how much Margaret picks on her, or Leanne evades her questions, she loves nothing more than having her daughters home again. The three of them burst into the kitchen.

"Will!" Carol cries. "We need you to go to the store!"

"I'll go with you," Margaret adds. "I've been making a list."

five

THE RAIN, NO LONGER A MONSOONLIKE DELUGE THUD-
ding on the roof of the car, has throttled back to a dull, steady
downpour. As he backs out, starting the grocery run, Will imagines
how intensely Carol will watch the eleven PM weather report. Not
that the pudgy, cheerful meteorologist on the Grand Rapids channel
ever gets it right. Still, Carol will believe him if he says what she
wants to hear. If not, tomorrow she'll be ordering Will to turn on
the computer and dredge up a better prognosis from some weather
website. Fussing with the computer always makes him tense.

"What's the almanac say?" Margaret asks, and it takes him a second to realize that she's talking about the weather, too. She's always
had a way of doing that, registering what people are thinking and
stepping right into their thoughts. The question isn't serious. *The
Farmer's Almanac* is a sort of joke to her, an amusing piece of
regionalia. He's expected to answer like a farmer.

"Whatever it says, it's lying," he answers. Margaret smiles,
expectations fulfilled, and he lets himself believe that she's happy to
be here in the car with him, speeding toward the next task.

She's quiet as they start down the road to Ryville. He glances
over. She's looking down at her list, frowning slightly, determined to
ferret out whatever has been overlooked. She looks old; not just
grown up but aging. Her face has grown thinner, losing the glowing
roundness of youth. A few gray hairs mix with the brown at her tem-
ples. How did he get so old that his children are no longer young?

"All right," she murmurs to herself, looking out a window and
considering something. She feels very faraway. He wonders if she'll
tell him what's up. He noticed her looking at her Rabbit as they left
the driveway, but she didn't say anything. Now that they're here,
alone in the car like this, she might confide in him the way she did
when they talked on the phone a few years back.

"How's Trevor doing in preschool?" he asks. It's a safe topic, he figures, but one that might open up a door for her to tell him what's going on at home.

"Oh, great. He loves it." She leans forward to fiddle with the radio, then changes her mind and sits back. "His teacher is really great."

"What was her name again?"

There's a pause, and he wonders if she's forgotten. But when she speaks, it's in a soft, dreamy voice, as if she's only half paying attention to the conversation. "Jana Keplin," she says. "They all call her Jana."

"They call her by her first name?"

"Yeah. That's the way they all are now." It's not clear if she means the teachers or the kids. She goes back to gazing out the window. "Lots of American flags," she says.

"The Peddet farm sold," Will says. He feels annoyed—awkward and then frustrated to know that he's awkward. Here he is, making small talk with his daughter. And yet he doesn't want to engage her, doesn't want to get dragged into a conversation about Afghanistan or terrorism or the crimes of America, because he knows how that will go. She'll start in with her liberal dogma, and he'll stumble around trying to explain himself, and they'll both end up mad and sullen. He doesn't always disagree with her views; what he hates is the fierce conviction. He wants to talk to her, but about things that really matter—how she's doing and why she came alone and what's going on with David. He considers telling her about his Cathay Pacific plan, bringing her in on his secret. That might spur an exchange of confidences.

"The Peddet farm sold? To whom?" Interest sharpens her face, pulling her into focus. The Peddet farm, adjacent to theirs, is a beautiful piece of land. It's classic Michigan: neat farmhouse and outbuildings, rolling fields, a pretty piece of woods once used for maple sugaring. When he was little, Will was sometimes taken to the sugar cabin in late winter, during the sugaring off. It was a tiny log cabin, and to a kid, it seemed deep in the woods. Inside, it was warm and noisy, filled with men and the heat of the fire. A vat of maple syrup was always boiling on a brick hearth in the center of the cabin. He would step inside and think, *I never want to leave.*

"The Lanskys bought it."

"The Lanskys? That farming conglomerate?"

"Yeah." He looks out over the wheel. "They're buying up a lot of the farms around this part of the state."

Margaret presses one hand to her face, considering. It slackens her cheek, making her look even more like a middle-aged woman. Will resists the urge to tell her so.

"That's kind of sad," she says after a moment. "Old Mrs. Peddet always looked forward to getting her sign."

"Yeah." He slows down to pass a combine that's crawling down the shoulder of the road. "I don't know if the state is even giving those out anymore." In the past, when your farm was in the family for a hundred years, the state historical commission gave you a sign for your property: MICHIGAN CENTENNIAL FARM. Will hasn't seen a new one in a long time. They may have given up doing it, since so many people are selling their family farms. *The great trajectory,* he thinks. One of the first signs of decadence is a lost connection with the food supply.

"You can't make a living on eighty acres anymore," he says. "The Peddet boys all went into construction, and the girl went to cosmetology school, I think. She lives in Kalamazoo now." He can't keep a trace of bitterness out of his voice. Margaret is part of the problem, after all. She couldn't have been in more of a hurry to abandon the country for city life. *You don't like the Lanskys?* a small voice inside him says. *You're helping make sure they succeed.*

"What's Mrs. Peddet going to do?" Mrs. Peddet was a widow, at least eighty years old. Will used to take her a chicken sometimes, or some nice pork chops when they had them. Old Peddet had been a friend of his father.

"I think she's going into a home—one of those assisted-living places in Kalamazoo," he says. "She sort of lost it after September eleventh. She was stockpiling stuff. Food. But not stuff that would keep. She had this old dead freezer full of rotting eggs, carrots, hamburger. One of her kids finally went in there and found it. I guess the place was a real mess."

Margaret is silent, and right away he regrets his bitterness, regrets that he's even allowed himself to think of his brilliant, successful daughter as part of any problem. She only did what he did—set off to find her own dreams. The difference is that he came back and she hasn't. He wants to compensate for his bitterness by making the Peddet story less dark. "At least this way she'll see her daughter more," he says lamely.

Margaret nods and looks out the window again, leaning her head against the taut shoulder strap of her seat belt, and Will senses a kind of exhaustion coming off her. He wants to tell her she shouldn't worry about making dinner. She should go to her room and rest and let someone else handle things. Carol and Leanne can cover the party preparations for now, and he and Kit could put a frozen pizza or something in the oven.

But he knows that wouldn't work. Margaret hates halfhearted measures like frozen pizzas. If there's something to be done, she'll be there doing it, because that's how she is. Without realizing it, he sighs heavily and loudly. Margaret doesn't seem to notice, and they're silent for the rest of the run to Ryville.

In the grocery store, she is quietly efficient, piloting the cart up the aisles and making decisions quickly. She wears a determinedly patient expression, as if willing herself not to waste time complaining about the poorly stocked store. Will follows behind, amazed all over again at the adult his daughter has become. She's been grown up for years now, but when she's away, he still thinks of her as a child, so that when he sees her, he has to accustom himself all over again to her maturity. For her part, she acts like he's the child, asking him occasional questions as if trying to include him, to make him feel useful.

"Mom wants some new sponges," she says. "Which kind does she usually get?"

Will looks at the packages she's holding up, one blue, one green, and has to shrug. He has no idea.

"Well, these are the better ones," Margaret says, tossing the blue into the cart.

He gets involved only when asked until they reach the meat department and he sees her frowning at the chickens. They're the usual grocery-store Tyson chickens, wrapped in partly opaque plastic. They have huge breasts and short stubby legs. Will doesn't like the look of them, either. They look abnormal, their breasts so oversize it's hard to believe they could walk when they were alive.

"Peterson has some chickens this year," he tells her. "He brought one over not long ago. We could stop by his place and see if he'll sell us one."

Her eyes are bright as she looks up at him. "That'd be great, Dad!" she says. "A fresh free-range chicken would be perfect!"

They finish up at the store and drive out to Peterson's place, a smallish gray house with a long, low barn in the back. Margaret hovers behind as Will knocks on the door. Ted Peterson himself answers.

"I got none in the fridge right now," he tells them. "I took a whole lot over to the farmer's market, down to Kalamazoo. People was paying two-forty a pound." He chuckles, and Will joins in, shaking his head at the promiscuous spending of city folk. Even Margaret puts on a smile, but Will can sense her shifting her weight, wanting to move things along.

"I'd go kill one for you, if you didn't mind waiting," Ted says.

Will glances at Margaret, but her face is serene. "Sure," she says.

Ted heads for the barn, leaving Will and Margaret standing in silence under the small roof of his back-door steps. Margaret crosses her arms and looks out over Peterson's cornfield. One foot taps lightly. She's not going to tell him anything here.

"Somewhere in that barn, a chicken is meeting its maker," Will says, and Margaret laughs once, shortly.

"Do you know what a freshly killed free-range chicken would cost in Chicago?" she says. Her voice is too cheerful, as if she's forcing herself to think about the chicken instead of something else. "It's almost a shame to put it in gumbo."

"Remember our chickens?" Will asks her.

She puts her hands down on the railing and leans back, looking up at the rusting metal of Ted Peterson's porch roof. "Oh yes," she says. "How could I forget?"

Will grins, remembering. The idea of getting a flock had hit him when the family returned from a trip to Mexico. Leanne and Margaret must have been about six and eight. "It will be good for them," he remembers telling Carol. "They can learn how to take care of something. Did you notice how the chickens in Mexico were always taken care of by the little kids?" They had been living on the farm for years without any animals. He figured chickens were the perfect starter livestock—easy to take care of, not a huge investment, with a good rate of return. "We can have fresh eggs," he told Carol. "Think how nice that will be!"

He looks at his grown daughter standing opposite him on the tiny porch. Sometimes he sees an expression out of the corner of his eye, or catches a gesture she's making, and there she is, the little girl he knew before, hiding inside this grown woman's body. But most of the time that girl is missing in action.

It was a Saturday when they went to get the chickens. Will made breakfast for the girls first. Carol was sleeping in.

"You've got to have a rooster," he remembers telling them. "Even if you don't want chicks, it's better to have a rooster."

"Why?" Margaret had reached that age: whenever she asked him a question, she waited for the answer as if her entire opinion of him hung on it. Leanne wasn't even paying attention. She was just happy they were having toast and jam and instant hot chocolate for breakfast, something Carol would never allow.

"Having a rooster around makes the hens happier," Will said, and before Margaret could say "Why?" again, he continued. "It makes them feel like someone is looking out for them."

"Is he?"

"Is he what?"

"Looking out for them."

"Oh yes." Will took the kettle off the stove and filled their cups with hot water. "He sure is." The brown powder dissolved into liquid, with tiny white specks on top.

"Why?"

"Because that's what roosters do." He grinned. "Now, hurry up and drink your hot chocolate. We want to get to the feed and grain before the farmers fill it up."

"But we're going to be farmers now," Margaret told him. "We're going to be farmers of chickens." She got a satisfied tone whenever she could correct her parents.

"Even without the chickens," Will corrected her back, "we're farmers. We live on a farm. We grow corn and hay. That's farming."

"But Uncle George always drives the tractor."

Will set down the kettle. It clanged down too loudly on the burner. The girls blinked with surprise. "Uncle George drives the tractor," he said. "But it's my farm."

They went to the feed and grain, which was busy, as always on weekends. Still, old Dan Curran made everyone wait while he talked to Will about flying. Like most people in Ryville, Dan Curran had never been up in a plane, so he loved hearing about them. Will always went along with it, but he didn't enjoy the attention. He wanted them to see him as a farmer, like everyone else. He'd rather talk about the weather or wheat prices. Unconsciously, he'd find himself reverting to rural pronunciations when he talked to someone like Dan. Carol always accused him of putting on an act. "Playing farmer," she would say. She rolled her eyes when Will said "them cows" or "crik" instead of "creek."

Dan Curran told them to go see Ted Peterson. Peterson must have been younger then, but Will remembers him looking just the same. He and Will crated up the chickens and loaded them into the back of the truck. The girls were wide-eyed on the drive home, riding backward in the cab to see that the chickens didn't fall out.

"I don't think they like this very much, Daddy," Leanne said.

"Do chickens talk to each other?" Margaret asked.

"They cluck and squawk. They go, 'Bawk! Bawk! Bawk!'" Will made a chicken face as he squawked, and Leanne giggled between them. Leanne's giggle was deep and luscious, water welling up from a spring.

"That's talking," Margaret said. "For chickens." She pressed her lips together, disapproving of the others' silliness.

"You girls will go and gather the eggs," Will told them, becoming more serious.

"Do the chickens want us to take their eggs?"

"They really don't know any better," Will said. "They're just chickens." He felt her skeptical gaze. "Chickens are not very smart," he told them. "Did you know that when it rains, you have to put them inside? Otherwise they look up and drown."

Even Leanne looked skeptical at that. They watched him to see if he was joking. He felt the need to reassure them somehow.

"I think they'll be real happy with us," he told them.

"*Very* happy, Daddy," Margaret said.

"Well, here you go then." Ted Peterson ambles toward them from the barn, upright and unhurried, as if he doesn't notice the rain. Under his left arm he carries a brown paper parcel. When he reaches the steps, he holds it out to Will, but Margaret steps forward and takes it, gently, as if not wanting to hurt what's inside.

"I plucked and gutted it for you," Ted says, "but I left it whole."

"That's great," Margaret says. "Thank you so much."

"'Preciate it," Will says, handing Ted a five-spot. Ted crumples it into his pocket, and Will waits. He knows Margaret is eager to get going, but he doesn't want to be rude.

Ted looks out over his cornfield. "Lotta rain for June," he says. "Corn could use some sun now."

"I guess the rain's gonna quit by Saturday," Will says. "My other daughter's getting married then, and the wife won't permit it." He feels a tremor in Margaret, a slight move of impatience, when he says "the wife."

Ted chuckles. "Aaaah," he says. "Guess not, then." He works his mouth, locating an old wad of tobacco or just moving to do so out of habit. After a moment, he looks at their car. It's the sign that they're dismissed, that they've made enough small talk for their visit to count as friendly and not purely commercial.

"All right, then," Will says. "Be seeing you, Ted."

"That's right," Ted says. "Bye now."

Margaret holds the chicken on her lap as they leave. "Thanks for that, Dad," she says.

"Hey," he says, trying to be jovial. "What's the country good for if not a nice dead chicken."

Margaret glances at him quickly, then looks at the parcel on her lap. "I hate those factory-farmed chickens," she says. "Did you know they cut off their beaks so they won't peck each other to death?"

Will can't tell if she's making conversation or if a lecture is in the offing. He doesn't want the friendly mood spoiled with a tirade about the evils of commercial food production. No one hates factory farms more than he does.

"So whatever happened to those chickens of ours?" he says. "I can't remember."

Margaret stares. "You don't remember what happened to the chickens?"

Will doesn't, but her surprise stirs a vague memory of something bad.

"We lost them, right?" he says. "But I don't remember how it came about."

Margaret looks back at her lap. "We had them for one summer," she says. "Mom was planning to start a baked-goods business with the eggs. But those dogs from the Wagners' came down the street and killed them all. All at once."

"The Wagner dogs?" Will frowns.

"Yeah, the Wagner dogs. A hound and a little mutt. The chickens were out, and the dogs came into the yard and caught them all. They didn't eat them, they just grabbed each chicken and sort of shredded it. For the fun of it. Then they ran on to catch the next one."

"I don't have any memory of this," Will says.

"No," Margaret agrees. "I don't think you were home."

"Was Leanne there?"

"Leanne was there. She and I stood on the porch and watched, and Mom chased the dogs all around the yard with a rake, yelling, 'Bad dogs, bad dogs!' like they were trampling her roses or something. But they just kept going until every bird was dead."

Will knows he must have heard this story before, but it seems new to him. Perhaps he's heard it only from Carol's perspective, filled with acrimony and claims about how *this* was exactly the reason they didn't belong in the country. He might not have listened carefully.

"What happened then?" he asks.

"Mom sent me to the garage for a rope, and she and I caught the dogs."

"Were you scared?"

Margaret shrugs. "They weren't actually vicious or anything. They came up to us, friendly as anything, once the chickens were all dead." She looks out the window. "I remember the little mutt was a pale color, and he had blood staining the fur around his mouth. But he just sat there and wagged his tail like he was Benji or something."

"What then?"

She glances over. "You must remember this. We killed them."

"You killed the dogs?"

"Well, we had them killed. We took them to animal control and told them they were chicken-killing strays, and they put them to sleep."

"Weren't the Wagners mad at us?" This he would have remembered, surely.

Margaret laughs once, a short, bitter exhalation. "The Wagners?" she says. "They weren't exactly intellectuals. We went over there and told them their dogs had killed our chickens, and she—Mrs. Wagner, I guess—stood behind the screen door and said, 'You folks'd better shoot the motherfuckers, then. Them dogs got the taste of blood now.'" Margaret affects a rural midwestern accent for this, and Will is surprised at how convincingly it comes out.

Will shakes his head. "Where was I?" he says, more to himself than to her.

"At work, I'm sure," Margaret says. She puts her hand to her face again, and Will thinks the story is over. He wonders if she's expecting him to apologize for not being there, or for forgetting.

"The really weird thing," she says, "is that afterward, when the chickens were dead, we were walking around the yard to collect their bodies, what was left of them, and they had laid all their eggs." He can feel her looking at him, and he keeps his eyes on the road. "They must have done it out of fear or something, because there were eggs everywhere in the grass. Big ones, and then the ones that weren't quite ready to be laid—almost full size but a little soft. And then smaller, softer ones. And then even smaller, little white eyeballs, and then teeny-tiny ones. Like caviar, just scattered in the grass."

Will frowns. Margaret's story has reminded him of a game he once played. *Ad misericordia.* It means "for sympathy": you tell a story in order to try to gain sympathy. He played it in Vietnam. He shakes his head, expelling the memory. "People and their damn dogs," he says.

Margaret laughs that short bitter laugh again. "Didn't you ever wonder," she says, "why Leanne and I never asked to get a dog? We both hated them after that."

No one is around when they get home. Margaret goes into the kitchen with the chicken clutched to her. The package is warm. Behind her, Will deposits the rest of the groceries on the counter.

"Thanks," she says. Her voice wavers slightly, but she doesn't think he notices. Where's Trevor? Why didn't he come running when he heard them drive up?

"Okay," Will says. He goes out to the living room, and she can hear him turning on the news.

There are soft voices coming from the basement. Margaret goes to the head of the stairs and listens. Her heart expands with relief when she hears Trevor's voice. He's explaining something in exhaustive four-year-old detail.

"Hey, down there," she calls. "How are things?"

"Just fine," Carol's voice comes back.

The knot of anxiety that burned Margaret's stomach all the way to the store and back lessens. She vows not to leave the house again without Trevor. She just feels funny when she's separated from him. What if David should show up after all?

"Do you need some help up there?" Carol's voice is slightly sleepy.

"No, I'm fine. You guys stay down there and have fun." Margaret goes back to grocery bags. She prefers to have the kitchen to herself when she cooks.

She unpacks the groceries and puts the ingredients she needs for gumbo out on the counter. The first and hardest part is making the roux. She feels almost cheerful at the prospect. There's something satisfying about cooking: following the instructions, chopping and measuring and blending. It's a neat, controlled process, each step creating something new out of raw ingredients, until you end with something entirely other, a whole greater than the sum of its parts.

She opens up Peterson's brown paper package. The chicken lies there in a pose of limp abandon. It was alive half an hour ago, walking around the barn. Ted has taken off the head but left the feet on. Margaret goes to her mother's knife drawer in hopes of finding a cleaver.

Something about the chicken story is still nagging at her. She remembers it exactly as she told her father, but there's more. After the chickens, she never quite saw herself or her father in quite the same way again.

The first time she and Leanne gathered the eggs, Margaret got to the chicken coop first. The rooster and a few hens were clucking around on the floor, scratching back and forth. The other five hens were tucked into their boxes, like eggs in a carton themselves.

"How do we know they've laid their eggs?" Leanne asked. Margaret lifted her shoulder carelessly, reaching for the basket their mother had given them.

"They just have." She was a little scared of the chickens, but she didn't want Leanne to know it. They had glittery eyes like tiny black beetles, and pointy hard beaks. They didn't blink. Their feathers were beautiful: brown and white and burgundy and a deep greenish black color, but up close, the birds were alarming. The way they looked at her made her think they were plotting against her.

Holding the basket in one hand, she walked up to one of the hens, a brown and white one that seemed less intense than the others. Margaret clucked softly, trying to act like she knew what she was doing.

Leanne went over to another hen, slipping her hand under it without hesitation. "Hey!" she cried, surprised and joyful. "There's two eggs under here!" She held one up in triumph.

Not to be outdone, Margaret slid a hand under her hen. Its feathers were soft and its body squishy underneath, unlike chicken on your plate. It felt good beneath the hen; it would be nice to be a little chick there. Her hand moved through the slippery straw until she came upon a hard, warm egg. She pulled it out. The hen regarded her without seeming to notice that anything had changed.

After that, it was like Easter Sunday. They went from hen to hen, pulling out the eggs and putting them carefully in the basket.

"Wow," breathed Leanne. "Our own eggs."

They made the chickens go outside, as they had been told to do, and took the eggs inside to their mother.

"Look at these eggs!" Carol exclaimed. "They really are excellent, aren't they?" She held one up to the light and admired it. "We could really do something with these."

Margaret finds a cleaver in her mother's drawer. She lines the chicken up on the cutting board and brings the cleaver down as hard as she can. There's a satisfyingly loud thud, and she's holding a foot in her hand. It's golden, the color of chicken stock, and lined with tiny scales. In a dim-sum place in San Francisco, she and David once ate chicken feet. They were visiting a Chinese friend who joked that chicken feet separated real foodies from amateurs, so they had to try them. Both Margaret and David claimed to like the feet, but Margaret remembers being unimpressed. It was like the last joint of a wing: bony, with little threads of meat. She sets the foot on the counter.

Not long after they brought the chickens home, Margaret went out to the coop alone. She watched the chickens and thought about the roast chicken their mother made, how she and Leanne liked to eat crispy, burned pieces of skin off the bottom of the pan. There was one chicken she liked especially, a brick red hen she and Leanne had named Rose. She watched Rose peck along the floor. Underneath her feathers there was skin.

"Are you delicious?" she asked the hen. She wondered if they would eat her one day. When she had asked their father, he just laughed and said the chickens were young and would lay good eggs for years, so there was no need to think of eating them now.

Looking back, she knows she didn't want to eat Rose. But part of her did, wanted to grab Rose and squeeze her thigh, find the part she would bite into. But when she thought of her father catching Rose, she felt different. Growing up on a real working farm, their father had killed chickens. Sometimes he joked about how a chicken would run around the yard with no head, and Margaret would feel a hard white anger against him, something akin to hate.

She remembers nursing that feeling. Sometimes she would get a strange desire to hate him, and she would bring to mind things he had done, like killing chickens. Surely he had killed people, too—he had fought in Vietnam. In high school she got interested and read several books about Vietnam: that was when she started loving history. But she didn't talk to him about it. He had never spoken of the war, so no one brought it up. It was hard even to imagine. Instead, when she wanted to hate him, she would recall something that happened on a family trip to Mexico. Her mother was lying down because she didn't feel well, and her father wanted to go and get sodas at the village store to calm her stomach. He asked Margaret if she wanted to go with him.

They walked down the middle of the street to the tiny store. The heat beat down on them from above and rose up again from the road. Inside the store, it was dark and cooler. Margaret stayed close to her father's side. As he was paying for the Cokes, Margaret saw a young boy in the store. He was about Margaret's age but skinny in his baggy shorts. He was coming toward them, saying something in Spanish and holding out his hands, begging. Margaret remembers freezing as she looked at him, because one of his hands wasn't a hand at all but a twisted thing, like a bird claw. It had two tiny deformed fingers that curved toward each other like pincers. It wasn't even where a hand should be, but higher up, right after his elbow.

Now she can imagine the possibilities: thalidomide, industrial waste, poor pre-natal care. The boy is a symbol for her now, of corporate greed, injustice, the appalling callousness of the first world for the third. Thinking of him makes her angry in an abstract, distant way. Then her horror was more direct. She stared at the boy, appalled, until her father pulled her out the door. He kept a hand on her shoulder as they silently walked back to the hotel, and as she stumbled along beside him, Margaret began to feel angry, not at the things she knows to be angry at now but at her father. She hated him so much she almost wept with disgust. She wanted to tell him to go back and give the boy some change, but something in the way he walked made it clear that he would never do that. Margaret hated him for his certainty, hated him more completely than she had ever hated anyone, even Leanne when they fought. She hated him like the chickens must have hated him, a grubby farm boy, when he grappled them onto the block.

That day in the chicken coop, she watched Rose, and she thought of how her father had lifted the chicken out of the crate and tossed her lightly to the ground. All of them, even Margaret, even Leanne, had the power of life and death over the chickens. They fed them, let them live in their coop. Someday they might decide to kill them.

"I think you are delicious," Margaret whispered to Rose. She said it with a mean tone in her voice. She said it like something the chicken didn't want to know but had to.

Once she has the feet off and the few remaining feathers plucked, Margaret cuts up the chicken. She takes off the legs, then the wings, then separates the breast from the back. She drops the back and wings into a bowl to make stock later, then cuts the rest into smaller pieces, dividing the breast in half lengthwise and crosswise, splitting the thighs apart from the drumsticks at the knuckly joint. She sets the chicken pieces aside and gets the shrimp out of the fridge. She heats up oil and adds flour to make her roux. She has even found okra in Ryville, which surprised her. It's going to be a good gumbo. They'll all sit down together for dinner: her parents, Leanne and Kit, soon to be her brother-in-law, and herself with Trevor. They'll have a wonderful meal, and David won't feel like an absence, or a presence, either. This is their family now.

Leanne and Kit are in their room. Kit is on the bed with one of Will's *Airways* magazines. Leanne is hemming her dress. Her mother would be shocked to know she's doing this with Kit in the room, but he promised, laughing, not to look. There's something comforting about the regular sweeps of the needle, in and out, over and under. Leanne has always liked sewing. It's steady and pre-dictable, and if you make a mistake or end up with something you didn't intend, you can always go back and change it. It's nice that nothing is ever permanent. Sometimes she takes whole dresses apart and puts them back together another way, just for the fun of it.

From downstairs they can hear the ongoing monotone of the news. Her father seems to listen to the television at higher volume than he used to.

. . . reports that bin Laden may have been hiding there turned out to be false . . .

Leanne had been hoping this might be the moment, her chance

to have her talk with Kit. But he kissed her when he came upstairs, and she tasted beer on his mouth. She can't say anything now, because it would sound like an accusation of some sort, a remonstrance for having had a drink. She doesn't want to do that. She has never joined AA, never subscribed to the twelve steps, the higher power, the one day at a time. Alcohol was just something she did too much of and had to stop. She found it easier to stop cold turkey than to cut back, so that's what she did. She's not convinced that one drink will undo her efforts. She's not even sure she qualifies as an alcoholic—she always considered herself a drunk. A person who was throwing her life away and didn't care. A person who aimed for numbness. "Alcoholic" seems too clinical to describe a failure she had willingly embraced.

In a way, that's what she fears about Mexico. It's not that she doesn't want to go—it's that she does. The trip is too appealing. She's got the store set up and her senior assistant trained well enough to run things smoothly without her for a long time, months even. And she has always been fascinated by Mexico. Her family went there when she was little, but she can't remember. There are hazy seventies photos of her and Margaret standing in scenic spots—in front of a baffled burro, or perched on a cliff overlooking the ocean. But that's not Mexico City, which she imagines as a sprawling metropolis full of low adobe buildings and twisty streets beckoning to be explored. There, she could lose herself. That's a seductive idea, and she's scared to be seduced.

"Ow, damn," she says. A red bead appears where the needle jabbed her. She puts her finger quickly to her mouth, to avoid getting blood on the dress's pure white expanse.

As if on cue, Kit, closes his magazine. "We should probably talk."

Leanne presses her finger against the inside of her teeth. It feels good somehow. "What do you mean?"

"Leanne, don't be evasive." He sets his magazine aside and sits up. That's one nice thing about Kit, he always gives his full attention to conversations. "I know you. I can tell something is bothering you."

Leanne leans over and peers closely at her stitches, checking their evenness. "Why would you say that?" she asks.

"Leanne."

A dull resistance overtakes Leanne. It's like the conversations she used to have with her mother about what she was doing with her life. Even letting the subject come up was a kind of defeat. "I don't know what you're talking about," she says.

"Okay." Kit lies back down on the bed and takes up *Airways* again. "If you don't want to talk, that's fine." There's a hurt edge in his voice.

"Kit." Leanne wants to stop sewing and say something, but she can't think of what. She leans over even farther, sewing furiously. Downstairs, the news drones on.

. . . *CEO resigned after an indictment for failure to pay sales taxes . . .*

"I don't know," Leanne says. "I'm sorry. I have been feeling odd."

Kit stops reading but doesn't sit up, just raises his head to look at her.

"I mean, doesn't it all seem a bit strange to you? With what's going on in the world?"

"Doesn't all what seem a bit strange?"

Leanne stops sewing to raise an arm and gesture around her. "All this." She waves a hand over her dress. "Satin. Tulle."

"You'd prefer a nice cotton-lycra blend?"

"You know what I mean."

"Actually, I'm not sure I do."

Leanne drops her hands into the satiny pile in her lap. The fabric is smooth and shiny, untouched by the world's rough edges. It feels like hope, like promise. "It's just so . . . absurd," she says.

Kit pinches the top of his nose. "Well," he says, "if you mean the ceremony and all the hoopla—for lack of a better word—I guess I agree with you. White dresses and rice-throwing and big fancy cakes that are always too dry—all those things are absurd. If you mean that, yes." He looks at her, and there's a hollow feeling in her stomach. "Is that what you mean?" Kit sits up and moves to the edge of the bed. "The wedding itself? Or do you mean the marriage?"

Leanne feels empty, drained of all emotion. She puts her hands on the heap of white froth in her lap. "Of course that's what I mean," she says. "I mean the wedding."

Kit watches her closely, some debate playing itself out in his mind. After a moment he blinks and looks away. "The world *is* falling apart," he says. "For me, that makes something like marriage seem even more important. It gives you something to hold on to."

Leanne looks down at the dress again. Froth. How can you hold on to that? "You're right," she says. "We'll just have to live through the hoopla, won't we?" She makes her voice sound light.

"Mott the Hoopla," Kit says, going back to his magazine. "Weren't they a band in the seventies?" It sounds forced. His real sense of humor is dryer.

Leanne puts in a few more stitches. "This is killing my eyes," she says. "I think I'll finish it later."

"Why don't you have a little rest?" Kit pats the bed beside him.

Leanne stands and drapes the dress over the back of the chair she's been sitting in. "Don't look," she says jokingly, and she notices that he does, in fact, glance away. Perhaps he really does want to be surprised. She moves to the bed and crawls onto it, stretching herself out beside him.

"Isn't that better?" he says. He keeps reading but puts one hand on her calf. It rests there heavily. Her thoughts scrabble about, but she blocks them by focusing on the feel of his hand on her leg, warm and solid as a small animal.

Only that, she tells herself. *That's all any of this is about.*

"Whatever you're doing, it smells great." Carol comes up the basement stairs in an expansive mood. She has been lying on the couch, half dozing while her clever grandson played with his cereal prizes and the plastic farm animals Will bought him last year. Trevor's steady stream of chatter has soothed her, like those machines that make the sound of ocean waves or rain on an old tin roof. Now she feels refreshed and generous, ready to make peace with everyone, ensuring their help and support for the arduous two days ahead.

Margaret has a giant pot simmering on the stove. Two of Carol's cutting boards are on the counter with scraps on them, and a bowl of something disgusting—chicken parts, it looks like—is sweating on the counter. Averting her eyes, Carol picks up a wooden spoon and turns to the stove.

"Don't touch that," Margaret says.

"I was just looking at it. Is that the gumbo?" Carol sets the spoon down casually, pretending not to have noticed the bossiness in Margaret's voice. *Family togetherness,* she reminds herself.

"Yeah, that's it." Margaret wipes her hands on Carol's apron and takes a more conciliatory tone. "It's going well. We can eat in twenty minutes or so."

"Can I do anything?"

Margaret starts to shake her head but stops herself. "You could set the table," she says. "I think you've moved things around since I was here last."

Carol nods and goes to the linen cupboard. She finds six of her favorite place mats—yellow plastic ones with large red poppies—and carries them out to the dining room, arranging them neatly on the table. When she returns to the kitchen, Margaret is hovering by the stove, hesitant. She starts to say something, then balks.

"What?" Carol looks up on her way to the silverware drawer.

"Um, why don't we just eat in the kitchen? It'll be homier."

Carol looks at the kitchen table. It is homey, but it's not her idea of sophisticated.

"I thought we could keep the dining room nice for Friday," Margaret adds.

It could be about Trevor, Carol tells herself. Margaret probably doesn't want him making a mess. There's no reason to think she's insulting Carol's nice dining room. "All right," she says. She goes out to retrieve the place mats.

"You know," she says, coming back in and rearranging the mats on the kitchen table, "I wasn't sure whether, when I have the B&B up and running, I should serve breakfast in the dining room or the kitchen. We always eat in the kitchen. But if there are more than six people, it will be tight." She gets out the napkins that match the place mats and distributes them, stopping to admire the effect. The napkins are the same pattern in reverse colors: yellow flowers on a red background.

"Do you expect you'll ever have that many guests at once?" There's a funny strained tone in Margaret's voice, as if she's making herself join the conversation.

"We could have six guests at once with the three bedrooms fixed up, which makes eight, counting the two of us." Carol turns to putting out silverware. "Should we have forks and knives or just spoons?"

"Both, I think."

"I'm going to redo the dining room, too," Carol goes on. "I think it should be a little more country. Maybe blue-flowered curtains and tablecloth and white dishes. And I thought I'd bring in some of those pieces from when Will's mother died: the old butter churn and the milk can and that big washing tub and washboard." She pauses, imagining the room finished. She had planned on putting potted plants in the big washbasin, something with tendrils like ivy that would droop down over the edge. And then she'll fill the hutch with appealing rustic pieces of stoneware. She already has a lot of classic country pieces from flea markets and antique fairs: milk jugs with flowers on them, creamers shaped like cows, teacups sporting tiny rural scenes.

Margaret has stopped fussing over the stove and is contemplating her mother. "But Mom," she says, "you've always hated that country style."

Carol laughs and waves a hand. "I hate ducks in bonnets. All country isn't bad."

"You've spent the whole time you lived here doing everything possible to make this house look less like a farmhouse!" Margaret's voice is light, but there's something almost like anger behind it.

"Oh, well, you know," Carol says. "People will come here expecting that kind of thing. Gotta give the customers what they want!"

Margaret watches her, then turns back to the stove. "So," she says casually, "when do you expect to have this endeavor up and running?"

Carol goes to get water glasses from the cupboard. "Oh," she says, "it's hard to say. What with all the preparations for Leanne's wedding . . ." She stops to fix a crooked fork and, unable to resist, blurts out the secret she's been keeping like a talisman. "I've already placed an ad," she says. "In the *Chicago Tribune* special section. The one on Midwest getaways."

"You've placed an ad?" Margaret sounds incredulous.

"Not a big one." Carol leans over to remove the centerpiece from the kitchen table. "Just one of those small-print ads in the back. It wasn't very expensive." She doesn't mention the copy and how she agonized over it.

"When is it scheduled to run?"

Carol tries not to notice how Margaret couches everything in hypothetical terms: *when is it scheduled, when do you expect.* "It's running at the end of June," she says.

"Just before Dad's birthday?"

"Oh, that." Carol waves a hand. "He's insisting we don't make a big fuss."

Margaret stiffens as if about to say something else, but then she moves to the fridge instead. "Shall we have wine with dinner?" she asks.

"I don't care. Your father and I probably wouldn't."

Margaret nods and pulls a bowl out of the fridge. She's made a large green salad. "We should probably get everyone together," she says. "I'm just going to taste the gumbo and see if it needs more salt."

"Well," Carol says, succumbing to an irresistible urge to have the last word, "remember your father's blood pressure."

Leaving Margaret in the kitchen, she goes to the bottom of the stairs.

"Kit, Leanne!" she shouts. "Dinner's ready!" She calls downstairs for Trevor, then goes into the living room, where Will is watching the news. A tank is slowly rotating its way into a small street, while crowds of young men shake their fists and shout. It's somewhere in the Middle East, Israel probably. Something catches in her throat.

"Do you have to have that on all the time?" she asks. "Dinner is ready."

"I don't have it on all the time," Will says. "I watch the news for one hour every night. That's not all the time." He takes the remote from the coffee table.

"It's not exactly what we all want to be hearing when we're planning a wedding," Carol says. She doesn't like the way her voice sounds, but it's too hard to explain the feeling the news story gives her, the sense of being lost, of not mattering.

"It's the news. It's about what's going on in the world, not about planning weddings."

"That's what I mean," Carol says, unable to back down. "It's not helpful." She stands there, fighting the sinking feeling, as he draws himself up from the couch, pressing his thumb against the remote several times.

"You're doing it wrong," she says, exasperated. "You have to aim it at the thing."

The TV shuts off with a staticky pop. Will tosses the remote onto the couch and ambles over to Carol. "I guess I know where to aim it after all these years," he says. He reaches out as if to grab her, then pokes the side of her hip with a finger, like a kid.

"Cut it out," she says. "Margaret made dinner." She turns away from him, but she feels a slight, unbidden smile tugging at her lips. Half the time, he's like an unruly dog. You don't want to laugh at its tricks, but occasionally, you can't help it.

In the kitchen, Margaret is ladling out bowls of gumbo. Carol notes with disappointment that she has chosen some heavy ceramic bowls from the kitchen cabinet, not the fancy china from the dining room hutch. It's almost as if she's refusing to make things nice for Kit. But it's too late to change without a fuss.

Carol goes to the sink. "Trevor, did you wash your hands?" she asks. "Come here so Grandma can help you get them clean." Reluctant but not willing to disobey, he pads over. She takes hold of his hand and he pulls back slightly but doesn't dare yank it away.

"Smells like fresh chicken!" Will says.

"It's gumbo," Carol corrects him, handing Trevor a towel.

At the table, Kit and Leanne are sitting in silence. Leanne looks tired. *Wedding nerves,* Carol thinks. Or maybe the hemming is turning out to be harder than she thought. Kit nods politely and murmurs his thanks as Margaret serves him first.

Carol sits down between Trevor and Leanne. "I can't tell you all how happy I am!" she says. She beams at Margaret, who's handing out the bowls of gumbo, and even when she looks down and sees, floating on top, a whole shrimp, unpeeled, head and feelers still attached, the flame of her enthusiasm flickers a bit but doesn't go out.

"I'm so happy," she says again. "I've been looking forward to this for months: sitting down to dinner with my whole family!" She beams around the table. Leanne and Margaret glance at each other before returning the smile.

"Of course, it's sad that David can't be here," Carol adds quickly. "But I have all the rest of you!"

"We're happy to be here, Mom," Margaret says, and Leanne nods.

"Thank you so much for all your help with this, too," Kit says. "With all this wedding stuff. We couldn't have done it without you."

"Oh," Carol says happily, pushing the shrimp to one side with her spoon and digging into the gumbo beneath. "It's only just begun."

six

A DROPPING SENSATION WAKES LEANNE. IT HAS something to do with a dream, but she can't remember how. She stares at the ceiling. The silence is so complete it's startling. From the character of the light—gray and flat, the way it is before the sun clears the horizon—she guesses it's between four and five AM. But Michigan light can fool her after living out east. Here, at the western edge of the time zone, everything is shifted back. The sun rises later and sets later; twilight drags on until ten PM at this time of year. Now, even in this half-light, it could be as late as six.

She can sense Kit next to her. His body is solid and turned away from her, a ridge on the horizon, inscrutable pathways in the darkness of its near side. Is there an approach on that sheer wall? She could reach a hand out and touch him. Even in his sleep, he responds to her touch, gravitating gently toward it, the way a magnet moves. If he stayed turned away from her that would make it easier to talk. But where should she start? *I can't go to Mexico with you.*

Kit is the talker in their relationship, the one who tries not to let things go unsaid. Leanne is willing to let pain go untended or sorrows unvoiced in order to avoid scenes. Her mother was always a big scene-maker. Leanne still cringes when she hears her mother's voice take the tone that means she's spoiling for a fight, looking for an action or statement on which to hang her sense of injustice. When she gets like that, nothing Will says can appease her. Even though Leanne always automatically took her mother's side, she would end up feeling bad for her father. For all his energy, he could make no headway with Carol.

That's the danger of talking. Too often it descends into pointless recrimination or complaint. That was the beauty of Hoyt. When Leanne and Hoyt were together, they hardly ever talked, and when they did, it was never like that.

Of course, she and Hoyt weren't actually together; they couldn't even be said to be seeing each other, really. Looking back, Leanne knows she didn't love Hoyt, not the way she loves Kit. Eating breakfast, she sometimes watches Kit dip his toast into the yolks of his fried eggs and she loves the gesture, simple as it is, because it's his. She never loved Hoyt like that. She loved his blankness. He wasn't a love object so much as an escape, a place to lose herself.

She met Hoyt while she was tending bar at the Dingo, a grubbily hip bar on the Lower East Side. She'd been in New York a year, most of which she had spent waitressing. Bartending seemed cooler and more grown up, especially at a place like the Dingo. Leanne had been there about a month when Hoyt came in, settled himself on the bar stool, and parked his arms in a neat circle, marking off territory.

"So," Hoyt said to Leanne. "What are you doing with your life?"

"Who are you, my mother?" At the time, Carol was telling everyone that Leanne was taking some time off, as if life were a nice job with benefits and Leanne was on vacation from it.

Hoyt regarded her intently. His eyes were large and slightly droopy; in fact, his entire face looked like it was migrating downward. Leanne made him to be in his midforties, not bad-looking but not as well preserved as he might be. *Probably a painter,* she thought. Only three kinds of people strayed east of Avenue A: artists, drug addicts, and tough Latino kids. Occasionally, those categories overlapped.

"Jim Beam, neat," Hoyt said, raising two fingers like a blessing. "I'm Hoyt."

Leanne was nineteen. When she applied for the job at the Dingo, she had said she was twenty-one, with experience tending bar.

She handed Hoyt his Jim Beam, and he stared morosely into the glass as if it disappointed him.

"Are you a painter?" she asked. Being friendly, they'd said, was part of her job.

"I don't like the word 'painter,'" he said. " 'Painter' implies will and intent. One who paints takes action. I do not. Art is made through me, but I am only a passive medium for its creation."

Leanne nodded. After three months of life in New York, she was used to people talking that way.

"Sometimes," she said, "I think people are just fooling themselves. They think they do a lot of things when really things just get done to them."

Hoyt raised his head. "How old are you?" he asked.

Leanne looked at his sad-sack eyes. He was taking her in the way a large man might eye a chair, wondering if it would hold him.

"Twenty-two," she said. "I look young for my age."

That was how it started.

Even then, after a year, Leanne wasn't sure what she would eventually do in New York. Most people seemed to arrive in the city with big plans: go to school, act, get rich on Wall Street. Leanne thought she might do any of those things; she just had to figure out what she wanted. She thought that would be easier in New York, a world of strangers and new ideas, not driven by the desires of her family. At home, she sometimes felt caught in a slipstream, pulled forward in the wake of others. Her father's dreams of farm life, her mother's projects, Margaret's ambition—each of them hauled Leanne along, heedless of her own desires.

And for the most part, she had none. Content to be pulled along, she drifted through life until high school graduation. The most self-directed, assertive thing she had ever done was move to New York. Even that was someone else's suggestion: her high school friend Julie was going to NYU and driving out with a truckful of stuff. Leanne could go with her, she had said, take turns with the driving and help pay for the gas.

"What you should do," Julie had told her as they pounded the highway, talking about the millions of possibilities awaiting them, "is open up a shop for arts and crafts. You are so *good* at all those things."

Leanne had smiled. She might do that one day. She might do anything. For the first time in her life, the paths she could take seemed endless. She didn't want to make any decisions. She wanted to enjoy the feeling of potential, the sense that as she went to work or drank with friends or wandered down the crowded, grubby streets of the East Village, her real life was still out there somewhere, waiting for her.

Hoyt came back the next night. Leanne's heart skipped a beat when she saw his face coming toward her. But he barely seemed to recognize her when he sat down at the bar.

"Hey," he said flatly. "Jim Beam, please."

"How are you tonight, Hoyt?" Leanne asked. He looked up, vaguely surprised, before settling back into a slump.

"I'm here," he said glumly. As if to underscore the point, he pulled a book out of his backpack. The title spilled across the cover: *Be Here Now.*

Leanne handed Hoyt his drink and noticed for the first time that his hair was bright red, or at least used to be. It was now the color of a dried-out scab.

"Have you ever read this?" he asked her. She shook her head. "You should." He closed the book and examined it, nodding.

Leanne looked at the book. "I think my mother had that book on her shelves," she told him. "But I doubt if she ever read it."

"Why not?" Hoyt's face looked younger when his attention was roused.

"I don't know. My parents weren't very good at being anywhere now. They were always chasing after the next thing."

Hoyt shook his head. "That's the problem," he said. "The future—it's just as oppressive as the past. You can't get sucked in by either of them."

Leanne studied Hoyt's face. His presence felt light, indeterminate, as if he might fade away on his bar stool. She was drawn to him the way one is drawn to a perfectly flat green lake. The smoothness of the water is both what you want to be part of and what you disrupt if you try.

Hoyt drank steadily from ten PM to two AM. As Leanne was wiping down the counters and loading the last glasses into dishwasher trays, he looked at her with that summing-up expression again. She spoke quickly. "How about a nightcap?"

Hoyt laughed, slow and world-weary. "Where?"

"I was thinking your place," she said.

He shook his head. "Bad idea."

"No pressure," Leanne said, concentrating on the last stretch of counter. "I just thought we might, you know, be there now."

He leaned back and looked at her, and it was as if he were studying her through glass. He narrowed his eyes. "I hope you have cash. 'Cause we'll have to get a bottle."

Liquor stores were closed, so they went to a bodega where Hoyt nodded to the counter guy and waved Leanne's twenty. They were ushered to a curtained doorway, and a small Indian man looked Leanne up and down with a dark stare. Then he disappeared behind the curtain and returned with a fifth of Beam.

Hoyt lived in a largish building on Ludlow Street. The staircases sagged in upon themselves, and the hallways were painted a lurid purple. His apartment, however, was surprisingly clean. In the kitchen, black-and-white linoleum squares gleamed as if no one ever walked on them, and the porcelain sink in the bathroom had been scoured to a suedelike nap. They sat on the living room floor, Leanne cross-legged, Hoyt leaning back against a pine green couch, his knees up, his head resting on the cushions. He smoked Winstons, ashing them into an incongruously delicate china teacup.

They drank Jim Beam and listened to music. Hoyt had hundreds of cassette tapes lined up in perfect rows across a set of built-in shelves. The tapes all appeared to be bootlegs, labeled in the same precise handwriting. Leanne didn't recognize the music, but she liked its slow trancelike beat. Sometimes there were words, sometimes not. Hoyt closed his eyes, his jaw pulsing slightly. Leanne sat still and watched him for a long time. She had never done anything like this before. She'd had sex only a few times, each time with someone who seemed so bent on getting her into bed that giving in was the easiest path. This was entirely different. She watched Hoyt until he seemed to be asleep. Then she crawled over to where he sat, and placed her palm, fingers spread, on his stomach. He opened his eyes but didn't move. She slid her hand down his stomach to his belt buckle. Still he didn't move or speak, just watched her. One hand on his buckle, she used the other to unbutton her own blouse.

"You'll have to do everything," he said. She nodded and kept going.

After that, Leanne and Hoyt saw each other regularly, but there was never a plan or an agreement. Hoyt came in two or three nights a week. On one of those nights, sometimes two, he would stay until closing time, and when he did, Leanne went home with him. He didn't speak or acknowledge her in any way; he would just stand up, and Leanne would get her jacket and follow. At his place they drank, listened to music, talked, went to bed. Sometimes they had sex, and sometimes Hoyt would roll over and fall right asleep, his back to her. She would trace his tattoos with a finger. He had two, an American flag and a dead dove. When she saw them, Leanne wondered if he had fought in Vietnam. He seemed about the right age.

Leanne always left first thing in the morning. Sometimes Hoyt would go with her. They would meander in silence, roaming the streets of the East Village, where artists had adorned vacant lots with sculptures made from scrap metal or stuffed animals. Farther east, between Avenues C and D, there was a shantytown where chickens roamed among cardplaying groups of men. Occasionally, they walked through the East River Park, a grubby, forgotten strip of land between FDR Drive and the river. Autumn had set in, and they scuffed over leaves, lost socks, chicken bones, menus. On the park staircases, their shoes crunched the glass of empty crack vials, scattered there like tiny jewels.

Hoyt dealt drugs. There was no particular moment when Leanne realized it, just a series of small things that added up: cryptic late-night phone conversations, vagueness about his activities, the precise way he lived. When they left his apartment together, he would open the door slightly, surveying the hall before stepping outside. Keys in hand, he'd turn and fasten the locks—two Medeco cylinders and a police bolt. Then he'd take Leanne's hand and wordlessly lead the way to the building's rear stairs.

She knew it should bother her, but it didn't. Dealing didn't seem like a vocation to Hoyt so much as a habit he had slipped into, casually and with no intent, the way he seemed to have fallen into the rest of his life. There was something admirable in that ability to move through the world rudderless, living entirely in the moment and taking things as they came. Leanne had never known anyone who could do that, but she recognized it immediately as a quality she had always harbored herself.

It was what made her enjoy the fact that she never knew what was coming next with Hoyt. Sometimes he came into the Dingo and reached over the bar, fingers tucked into the waistband of her pants, to pull Leanne toward him. Other times he would come in and barely speak to her, or look at her darkly, as if she had done him some wrong. On those nights he would leave before closing, and Leanne would walk home alone, dropping the change from her tips into the cups of Avenue A's panhandlers, by that time asleep or staring straight ahead, lost in memory or blankness.

One night Hoyt took her to a party. It was the launch of a magazine called *Playground,* a fat, densely printed review of alternative culture edited by one of his customers. It was in a warehouse on Clinton, a street so far east and edgy that even Leanne avoided it. At the door, a large man with dreadlocks slid his eyes down her before stepping aside to let them in.

Inside the cavernous warehouse, the magazine people had set up an X-rated playground. There was a sandbox filled with sex toys and a jungle gym to which a man was being tied with nylon cord. At the center of the room, a long swing was suspended from one of the building's rafters. A man in leather pants was swinging.

Leanne had seen a lot of interesting and strange characters at the Dingo, but she had never seen so many in one place. There were men in dresses and a woman with a real beard. There was a bald man with a tattoo of a large hawk covering the back of his head. When he turned, Leanne saw that he was wearing a beak, melded so realistically with his face that it gave her a small shock. Other women were gotten up in gorgeous excess: corsets, leather dresses, sparkly evening gowns, plastic, space-age minis. One woman was completely naked except for a pair of silver boots. Blindfolded, she was following a man in black jeans who was ringing a tiny bell. He never touched the woman or spoke to her, just rang the tinkly bell every time he moved. She would lift her chin slightly and follow the sound.

Hoyt got them beers from the bar. They wandered around the party together, not speaking. Near one wall, a large, upended wooden box was punctured with round fist-sized holes. Attached to each hole was a long black cotton glove. People outside the box were putting their hands into the gloves. Leanne and Hoyt approached. He held out a hand, welcoming her to try it. Leanne reached her hand into a glove and extended it into the box. There was a person standing inside. Her hand landed on his or her hip. Feeling strange, she ran it up the person's side. Other people were groping more freely. She could feel their hands, too, reaching in, slipping over her own hands in their excitement to explore the stranger.

Hoyt turned to her. "Let's go on the swing."

They got to the swing just as a woman in a black evening gown was finishing. She smiled at Leanne as she handed over the seat. It had a been a long time since Leanne was on a swing, and she had forgotten what a rush it was, the slow, smooth glide forward and up, the loosening at the top and then the swift drop back to earth. The swing was long, and she swung higher and higher, skimming through the crowd and up above it, into the rafters, then back down through all those bodies. She pumped her feet to go faster, higher. It was exhilarating. She found herself laughing out loud. Her heart had never felt so light.

It was a strangely happy time. Leanne went to work, walked home, went out at night with work friends or with Hoyt. She never made plans, and she never worried about the future. The future was there, ahead, like a bubble or a sealed room, waiting patiently for the time when she would break the seal and enter it. Until then she could do as she pleased, be who she wanted. She dyed her hair blond, then red, then cut it all off and put a blue streak down the side. Each time she did it on impulse, looking in the mirror and walking right out to the drugstore to buy the dye. She wore a gorgeous flapper dress to work one day, frayed jeans and a Metallica T-shirt the next.

Slowly, almost unnoticeably, Hoyt's visits to the Dingo grew less frequent.

"You should stop hanging around me," he said one day as they sat having their coffee at noon. "You're young, you're pretty. You're wasting your time."

"Maybe I want to waste my time," Leanne said.

He never mentioned the war, although once, looking through his kitchen drawer for a knife, she found a pair of dog tags with his name. She closed the drawer silently, never mentioning it. She liked their arrangement, wasn't willing to risk it by trying to talk about things he wanted left alone.

Even so, he stopped coming to the Dingo. It was January. A week went by, then two, then three. Leanne told herself that this, too, was part of Hoyt's attraction, that the uncertainty she loved had always included the possibility of his not coming at all. But she missed him. She didn't have his phone number, and he'd never given her a key to his apartment. There was little she could do.

One night, walking home, she went by his building. She couldn't say exactly what she wanted. To see him or touch him, yes, but there was something more. When she lay in bed at night, it seemed to her that she wanted to hear him say her name. *Leanne.* She stood on the street looking up at his window. His light was on. A couple came out of the building, and Leanne grabbed the door as they left. Once inside, she decided to go up to Hoyt's apartment and say hello.

But when she got to the door, she stood outside, unable to knock. Who was she to Hoyt, after all? Just some girl he had picked up a few times, hung out with a few more. She didn't know any-thing about him. She had no right.

She was turning to leave when the door opened. A woman stopped, startled, when she saw Leanne. She didn't look like anyone Hoyt would know. She was older than Leanne, probably in her late thirties, with high, heavily sprayed hair. She was wearing acid-washed jeans and a T-shirt with a sequined flag.

"Who are you?" she said, unfriendliness in her face and voice.

"Oh, just . . ." Leanne stumbled, unsure how to answer, taken aback by the woman's hostility. "I'm a friend of Hoyt's. I was look-ing for him."

The woman glared at her. "Hoyt's dead," she said, cold and slightly wild at the same time. "You druggies keep coming around asking for him. Don't you have a phone network or something?" Leanne knew she must have looked shocked, because the woman modulated her tone slightly, looking back over her shoulder and lowering her voice as though someone in the room might hear. "He overdosed, okay? Why don't you take that as a sign from God and get yourself to the methadone clinic."

Leanne was speechless. The woman stood there, waiting for Leanne to leave.

"I'm sorry," Leanne squeezed out. The woman shifted on her feet, and Leanne saw that she was holding a garbage bag. She must be cleaning out Hoyt's apartment. Her face had a family resem-blance. A sister, maybe. She didn't look old enough to be his mother. Suddenly, it was too hot in the hallway. Leanne stared at the half-open door. Hoyt would never walk through it again. She turned and fled.

All the way home, she searched her heart. Had she known? She had seen marks on his arms and legs. But she'd never known a junkie before—she didn't know what tracks would look like. Hoyt was skinny and ate badly. He smoked and drank. Bad skin just seemed like part of his general unwholesomeness.

Then again, she hadn't wanted to see it. It was hardly a surprise. He sold drugs, and he was a vet: lots of guys got hooked on heroin in Vietnam. But if so, he had been addicted for years. If he had over-dosed, it must have been on purpose. She clutched her arms around herself. The worst of it was, she'd had no idea Hoyt was that much on the edge. She just hadn't known him that well.

She went home and drank a whiskey, then another. The numb-ness that began to spread through her felt almost like peace. She sat on her floor, the way she and Hoyt had always done, and worked her way through half the bottle before crawling into bed and falling into a heavy, overheated sleep.

Her life wasn't much different with Hoyt dead. She went to work at the Dingo, came home, drank herself to sleep. She didn't answer phone calls from Julie or her mother. Occasionally, she had drinks with the bar manager, Mike. They would end up in bed back at his place, but Leanne felt none of the excitement she had felt with Hoyt. Once Mike asked her what had happened to Hoyt, and she shrugged and said she didn't know, he had just disappeared.

Spring came, then summer. As the days got longer, Leanne found she was unable to fall asleep without enough to drink. That August she went to Margaret's wedding, and her mother decided to visit her in New York.

Carol didn't lecture Leanne. She set about helping her figure out what to do next. She didn't mention the possibility of Leanne going back to school, even though that was surely her own secret wish. When Leanne proposed opening a crafts store, Carol immediately started looking into locations. They stumbled upon Cold Spring on a friend's recommendation, and Leanne found the town oddly appealing in its old-fashioned simplicity. She wasn't worried about whether she would live the rest of her life there. Like her trip to New York, the move to Cold Spring was a reaction, not a plan. It was a place to get away for a while, somewhere she could sort things out and figure out what she really wanted to do with herself.

Leanne never told her mother about Hoyt. Once she mentioned a friend who had died, but she didn't go into the details. It would be too hard to explain her attraction to him. Sometimes she thought about the naked woman at the *Playground* party, following the bell. She imagined herself, blind and exposed, following that tiny but clear sound through a room crowded with things to see.

Kit rolls over next to her. For a second Leanne thinks he's awake and about to speak. His heavy breathing resumes. She listens to it rise and fall. Kit is the opposite of Hoyt. He offers her not surprise but certainty. If Leanne wanted that from anyone, it would be him. But she's not sure she wants it at all.

There's a crisp, wheaty smell drifting into the room. Quietly, Leanne gets up and finds her thin robe. Kit is still fast asleep when she slips out.

Her mother is at the kitchen table with coffee and toast. The dishwasher is running. They did last night's dishes after dinner, so it must be the party glassware. As Leanne comes in, she is sitting still, staring out at a deck dark with rain.

"It's still raining," Leanne says, and Carol turns her head. Seeing her mother's face in profile, Leanne is struck by how it has changed. Carol looks thinner and sharper, her cheeks more defined, her nose the blade of a knife. On the handle of the coffee cup, her knuckles are like bony marbles.

"Shhh," she says. "Your father's still sleeping."

seven

WILL IS FLOATING ON HIS BACK, LOOKING AT THE SKY.
The water feels warm. He worried all the way down about getting
tangled under his chute, about the heavy anti-G suit dragging him
down and drowning him. But everything worked as it was supposed
to. His chute released, his life raft actually inflated, and now here he
is, arms thrown over it like a kid with a pool toy, gathering the
strength to climb in. He rests his face on its side and stares up at the
blue Asian sky. It's funny about sky. No matter where you are on
earth, it's the one thing that looks the same.

There's an ache in his right leg. He knows it's broken. He knows
he'll discover before the end of the day that his right arm is also broken, that within two weeks he'll be on a C-130 transport out:
Saigon to Yokota in Japan, Yokota to Hawaii, where Carol is sitting
out the war. "Say goodbye to Vietnam, Captain," the young doctor
will tell him. He already knows that, too; his whole path is already
mapped out—it fell into place the instant he heard the metallic
chink, brief and purposeful, that meant he'd been hit. Immediately,
he punched the button to turn off his air-conditioning. If there was
going to be fire outside, he didn't want it coming in.

Within minutes there was fire, plenty of it. His wingman told
him to jump.

"Cobra One, you're burning bad," he cried. "You better ditch
now."

"Negative" was Will's reply. He didn't have time to talk. He
shouldn't have to explain why he didn't want to touch down in the
middle of a jungle full of guys who wanted him dead. Better to get
his feet wet. He was heading for the coast, thirty miles away.

The Thud lurched and coughed. It was a tough plane, known for
its ability to limp home. He knew he had it made when he saw blue
shimmering ahead like a mirage. There was a thick trail of smoke

behind him, and it got worse when he used his afterburner. He avoided the afterburner until he could see the water, then he laid on it with all he had. The plane shot forward, and as soon as he figured he was a safe distance from shore, he blew his canopy. Noise rushed in like water. Papers, screws, sand, and dust, even a few loose cigarette butts blasted into his face. A map of Route Pack Six covered his mask for two seconds before vanishing with the rest. Things caught fire. He'd made a mistake. He was going too fast for a safe ejection, but it was too late. The next thing he knew, he was hurtling backward through the air, and he could see his plane shooting off ahead of him like a horse that had thrown its rider. He hadn't even had time to get his feet in the stirrups; he felt his right leg whack the side rail as he went. Then his neck snapped back when the chute opened, and he thought, *Shit, my neck's broken,* but before that thought could stick, he was heading for the water and his neck was forgotten and it was time to worry about touching down. Knees together, feet together, eyes on the horizon. Lose the chute at the last moment so it wouldn't drag him down.

Now he's floating and rerunning the whole thing in his head, and it feels as if several key parts are missing. Where did the plane go down, for instance? He can't remember seeing it after that initial look, because he was focused on how to hit the water. Somewhere, it's sinking to the bottom of the Tonkin Gulf, all forty thousand pounds of it, surprising the fish with its flashy silver gleam. He imagines it settling into the mud, becoming part of this foreign place. Sea turtles will glide through it like one of those little plastic wrecks at the bottom of a fish tank. Octopuses will grope its slippery sides; eels will hide in the cockpit.

Those are the pearls that were his eyes.

He remembers the lines from high school, when he had to memorize the whole poem. *Full fathom five thy father lies, of his bones are coral made.* He stops thinking about that right away. He doesn't want to think about sinking down, and he especially doesn't want to think about what might be living in the water around him, because he keeps feeling little pricks on his legs, as if something is nibbling on him. It's probably pain from the break, he tells himself. Lots of guys have been picked up in the gulf. No one has been eaten yet.

The thought of getting picked up makes him grope instinctively for his radio. He must have ejected even farther from shore than he intended to, because he can't see land anywhere. But that's to be expected. Everything looks closer together from the air. You get a false sense of distance and scale.

He looks at the sky. He has to pee. After a few minutes he thinks, *What the hell,* and lets it go. A warm spot spreads around his crotch, and his eyes fill with tears of relief and joy. It's over. It's really over. He won't be expecting to die every day, won't have to look out the window of his plane and see the smoking remains of someone else's world. He'll return to his own life. He'll see his daughter for the first time. They'll fly him home, and Carol will hand him a tiny package, and there she'll be.

Again the feeling comes, pinpricks like hundreds of miniature mouths. It's things like this that can drive a guy crazy. He's seen it happen. He breathes deeply and hauls himself farther out of the water and onto his raft. Hold the position and wait for the *chop-chop* of a Spad. Those are the instructions. He can't go anywhere now. When the pinpricks come, he stares harder into the blue expanse above. It doesn't look like the place he came from. It doesn't look like somewhere he ever could have been.

"Hello there, Margaret," he says to the sky. "It's your dad."

There's a strange *thunk*.

"Sorry, Dad," she says.

"Margaret?" He opens his eyes. The sky is white outside. Carol is standing in the room. No, it's Margaret. Margaret, fully grown.

"I didn't mean to wake you." Her voice remains soft, as if she still wants to avoid waking him. She has a ball of white in her hand. "I needed to borrow some of Mom's socks. I'm going for a run."

"What time is it?" He feels disoriented. Things are flying around in his head, and he tries to nail them down. Socks. Gumbo. Cathay Pacific. Chickens killed by dogs.

"It's about seven thirty." Margaret moves closer to the bed. "You should get some more sleep."

"Is everyone up?" It's all slotting into place now: Leanne's wedding, Carol's preparations, Margaret here without David. Something has happened between them, but she isn't saying what.

"Trevor's still asleep, and I think Kit is, too. Leanne and Mom are having coffee in the kitchen and planning their attack." She picks his book up off the bedside table. "Are you reading this?"

Will squints at it. *The Great Trajectory.* Society in decline. He lifts his head. "Yeah, You know it?"

She sets it back down carefully, as if afraid of breaking it. "The guy came to Northwestern and talked. Most people think he's kind of a lightweight."

Will looks at the book on his bedside table, confused. It's too early to deal with Margaret. Should he defend the book or apologize for reading it? Is he meant to come up with an excuse—*It was the only thing I could find in the airport bookstore?*

"I guess I should get up," he says, letting his head drop back on the pillow with a soft *whumph.*

"No, sleep some more," she says. "I'm sorry I woke you." She glides to the door clutching the ball of socks to her chest. He sees now that she's dressed in running gear: shorts, T-shirt, a pull-on windbreaker. Her hair is tied up in a ponytail.

"I'll see you in a little while," she says, her voice still low. She slips out the partially open door.

He rolls over and tries to go back to sleep. But now he can smell the warm yeastiness of toast, hear the low murmur of voices in the kitchen. From Trevor's room, across the hall, comes the sound of motion on sheets, that twitchy restlessness kids get just before they wake up. From anywhere, anytime now, all hell could break loose.

Just as he thinks it, he hears shouts from downstairs. The door to the garage slams, and then Carol yells up from the bottom of the stairs.

"Will, wake up! We need you! One of the doves is hurt!"

The door shuts behind Margaret with a satisfying thud. She stops on the porch to kneel and tighten one of her laces. She doesn't have her running radio with her; she wasn't that organized, but this morning she will be happy to enjoy the silence. The house is always so full of her mother's activity. Buzzing—that's the only word she can think of for it. Her mother is always buzzing.

Margaret straightens her legs and keeps her hands on the ground for a minute, stretching her hamstrings. Then she stands up and surveys the sky. A light mist is falling. It won't be bad to run in.

No one else in her family ever works out. Margaret works out four days a week, alternating between running and going to the gym to lift weights, but at her parents', she runs every day. It's partly because it makes her less tense, helps her maintain a sense of calm in the midst of her family's chaotic inefficacy, but also she feels she should set a good example. Her mother and father, for instance, should be taking brisk walks every day. At their age, they're risking heart trouble by being inactive. And Leanne could probably use some strength training. She's always been thin and willowy, but she doesn't look as if she could pick up a sack of potatoes with those arms, let alone a baby if she should have one. *Strike that thought,* Margaret tells herself. That's her mother's job, planning Leanne's future for her.

She heads down the road, scanning it for cars. There's one in the distance, and she squints at it, trying to make out its shape. As it draws nearer, she makes out a small pickup. She veers left to stay well out of its way.

She will run down to the first east crossroad, then turn around and go back to the first western one. Michigan's back roads were laid out by surveyors before anyone really lived there. They're set down in a grid, with half a mile between them. Ten laps back and forth between the two roads will be five miles, as accurately as on a treadmill, and she'll never leave sight of the house. She'll be back before Trevor even wakes up.

She assesses the visit as she runs. So far, so good. There has been no word from David, which could mean that he's still angry, or that he's taking this time to calm down. She hopes it's the latter, and that he'll interpret her not calling as giving him some space to cool off. When she goes back, they can sit down and talk things over in a reasonable way. That's what they've always been good at, being reasonable.

As for the family visit, that's going okay. The whole shrimp thing could have been a disaster, but Carol seemed happy with the gumbo. Who cares if she didn't eat her shrimp, leaving it lying at the bottom of the bowl like an affront? Will is crashing around, preoccupied with God knows what, and Leanne is acting vague, but they're always like that. Leanne probably has pre-wedding nerves. Margaret remembers crying a lot in the weeks before her wedding. Two weeks before the scheduled date, she had to fly to Irvine and find them an apartment. She had chosen Irvine for grad school over Princeton because David had a two-year visiting appointment there. When she got home, David confessed that in her absence, he had picked up the hostess at the Denny's out by the expressway.

"It wasn't a big deal," he said, wearing an expression of pleased contrition that would become all too familiar. "We just went to my car for a blow job."

"The *hostess*?" Margaret remembers saying, as if that were the hard part to believe. Not the manager, not even one of the ugly-uniformed waitresses, but the hostess, the girl who sits at the cash register cracking her gum and checking her nails, her jaw pausing with the difficulty of calculating change for a twenty.

Why did I marry him? she asks herself. The question thuds along with the beat of her sneakers on the roadside: *why, why, why, why, why.* She has reached the first cross street and turns around to head back in the other direction.

She always kept a mental list of things that were right about David. He was smart—that was first. People called him brilliant. He was attractive. He had a good sense of humor, and he got along well with her friends. His was one of those East Coast Waspy families in which everyone seemed to be a lawyer or a judge, but they liked her.

And David was ambitious. He wanted what she wanted: a successful academic career, a nice home, kids. He had an idea of the kind of wife he wanted that fit Margaret, just as he fit her ideas about what a husband should be.

His inability to be faithful she saw as a glitch, though he assured her it was actually a strength.

"People have ridiculous expectations," he told her. "I'm not saying I'm going to spend our marriage sleeping around. I'm just saying that as soon as you tell me I can't do something, it's all but guaranteed I'll want to do it."

That had a certain logic that Margaret couldn't help but acknowledge. That was one thing you could say about David—he was logical. She had always liked that in men. She was logical herself. David was not the kind of man who would pack up his family and move to the country on a whim, when it would clearly make his wife miserable and hobble his children's education. He saw marriage as she did—as a partnership, one conducted in a sane and rational manner by two intelligent people. They would approach the institution as adults, he told her, not like lovesick kids. She agreed. How could she not? David was brilliant and worldly. He was a man who was going places.

Besides, the wedding date was approaching. She had seventy-five people arriving in Chicago to see her get married. She had made up a basket to be delivered to each of their hotel rooms with a bottle of wine and a typed list of attractions they might want to visit. She had handed over eleven thousand dollars in checks from her father for the wedding and banquet at the University Club, and she and David had paid a thousand for a cocktail reception at the Drake. She had reservations for a family breakfast and a rehearsal dinner for twenty. She had appointments for a manicure, a pedicure, a facial, and for a stylist to sew pearls into her hair.

Her father was going to walk her down the aisle, and then this impressive, ambitious man was going to stand in front of all those people and agree to be her husband. What was a blow job here and there, she reasoned, compared to that?

It had gone fine for a couple of years, while they were still delighted with each other, and then for a few more while they were each too busy worrying about their work—Margaret's dissertation, David's first book—to have time for other concerns. When they both landed interviews at Northwestern and managed to get their departments to urge each other's appointments, everything seemed to be going even better than they could have expected. Getting two academic jobs in the same place was an almost unheard-of coup. They laughed and toasted their good fortune, though secretly they both knew it wasn't luck but hard work and determination paying off.

It was in Evanston that things started going wrong. After they had achieved exactly what they both set out to do, a strange dissatisfaction set in. When David started an affair with a woman who taught in the art department, Margaret couldn't turn her head anymore. They fought, and the result was that they decided it was time to have a baby.

Margaret reaches the other road and turns around again. She finds it so hard to think about Trevor in the context of her own unhappiness. She hates to admit that not only was the child she adores conceived in a desperate attempt to save her marriage, but he contributed to its decline. Once Trevor was born, everything changed, and the change seemed to be to David's advantage and her disadvantage. He spent more time at his office, citing the difficulty of concentrating with Trevor around. He suggested they hire a nanny so she could do the same, but Margaret couldn't bring herself to do that. Even as she resented the baby's demands on her, she couldn't find it in her to hand him off to someone else.

Physically she was exhausted, and mentally she felt drained. The baby required so much attention, so much love and care, that it seemed there was nothing left after giving it. And yet the worst of it—Margaret finds it difficult admitting this even to herself—was the strange transformation in desirability they both underwent. David, as a father, became more attractive. Margaret saw it in women's eyes as they walked across campus, David carrying Trevor in the backpack. Even the undergraduate girls oohed and aahed, and their admiration moved easily from the baby to the father. It was as if, in some cold calculus of sexual partnering, David's stock had gone up.

Margaret's, meanwhile, had fallen. Even after she began working out again and lost the pregnancy weight, even when she cleaned the milk stains and strained carrots off her blouse and put on a nice outfit and heels, walking down the street with a stroller, she had become another sort of creature. No longer a desirable female, she was absorbed into the sentimental landscape of maternity. It felt like a black hole.

This is what you have always wanted, she told herself. She had ticked off everything on her list: degrees, job, husband, child. Why, in the flush of such fulfillment, should she regret losing something that had never been important to her? She found herself feeling angry when construction workers saw her with Trevor and only nodded politely. How could she miss attention that had been unwelcome?

It was all too predictable that she would turn to someone else to make her feel attractive again. That it was one of David's colleagues causes her to cringe in embarrassment and self-recrimination. But the ground rules of their marriage had been clear: no strings attached when it came to sex. And even as she acknowledges that what she feels for Vasant Devaraj is qualitatively different from what David seemed to have felt in his many dalliances, she can't help but feel that he applied an unfair double standard when he became so furious about it.

Vasant. She lets herself dwell on the memory of his graceful hand running down her leg. *I want to kiss you, I hope that's okay,* he had said. Margaret had lowered herself onto his couch, straddling him, and taken his face in her hands. She had never done anything like that. Even now, a thrill blooms in her stomach as she thinks of it. How it can ever work out is unclear, but Margaret knows one thing: she can't give that up. She wants to feel his hands on her again.

A tractor passes her, pulling a flatbed wagon. The farmer lifts his hand at her, and Margaret waves back. She's relieved that she doesn't recognize him. It could have been her uncle George, or worse still, some member of Doug's family. She hasn't thought of Doug in years. Now she'll have to make small talk with him. And yet, after what's happened to her, the thought isn't unpleasant. She watches the tractor moving down the road, the orange triangle wobbling with its jerky back.

After six laps—three miles—her hair is sticking to her head. The rain is only mist, but instead of cooling her off, it seems to make her sweat more. She's burning off nervous energy, but she longs for some organizational task to put her mind to. Something she can concentrate on and solve. She turns her steps toward the door.

Weep! Weep! The car passes quickly, so that by the time Margaret turns around, she can't identify it. It's local habit to honk when driving by the home of friends or family. It could have been George, or Aunt Janice, or Eddie, Janice's son. It's hardly likely, she tells the little voice inside her, that it was Doug. Doug has his own life now. Besides, honking is what friends and family do, and it's been a long time since Doug considered himself either. Still, she watches the car fade away in the distance before turning back to the door.

"I think his wing is hurt." Carol hovers over the cage, on tiptoes with the effort of supervising Will's movements. Will, looking half asleep in pajama bottoms and a T-shirt, is reaching a hand slowly into the cage to prod at the larger dove. The other dove flaps around, doing a hat dance of anxiety as her mate—Carol has assumed that they are mates, and that the larger is the male and the smaller the female—huddles forlornly in the corner, one wing oddly flattened and sticking out from his body.

"Maybe we should just leave them and check back later." Leanne is standing, still in her bathrobe, at the doorway to the garage. She has a coffee cup in her hand.

"Don't poke him!" Carol cries out. "You'll make it worse, whatever it is."

"It could be that he's holding his wing funny," Will says. "I want to see if he'll pull it back in."

"Well, don't hurt him!"

Will lifts his shoulder and makes a funny twitching motion with his head, shaking her off like an insect. She knows he's going to do something rash. He turns his finger over and prods gently at the dove's stiff wing.

"Ouch, damn!" he yells.

"You were hurting him!" Carol says. But she moves to inspect the hand. "Let me see." The bird's head moved so fast she couldn't see how hard he pecked Will.

"It's just a little peck. He didn't even break the skin." She pats the back of his hand absentmindedly.

"I should wring his stupid neck," Will mutters, pulling his hand away from Carol, refusing her sympathy.

Carol lifts her hands and steps back, in turn refusing blame. "Don't say things like that," she tells Will. "It's your daughter's wedding."

In the doorway, Leanne makes an impatient move. "It's not worth fighting about," she says. "Maybe he's just cold. It's kind of chilly and damp in this garage." She pulls her robe tighter around her body and holds the coffee cup to her cheek.

"Oh no!" Fear grips Carol's heart. "Do you think I should have had them in the basement?"

Leanne looks remorseful. "No, no, I didn't mean that. You've been taking great care of them, Mom. I just meant maybe nothing unusual is wrong." She puts one hand on the doorknob, as if that will move them all toward the door.

"I don't know enough about birds to say if anything's wrong or not," Will pronounces. He looks at his hand again and then wipes it on his pajama pants. "I could call Tammy down at the vet's, see if she has any ideas."

"Oh, Will, would you?" Carol is filled with sudden gratitude. "Would you do it right now?"

"Yeah, all right." Will climbs the stairs and pauses near Leanne, who smiles at him apologetically. He puts a hand on her head. "All right, then," he says, before clumping inside.

"You know, I knew something was wrong with these guys since yesterday," Carol says. "I felt it in that way, you know. I could feel it coming." Leanne takes a step into the garage and then, unexpectedly, plunks down on the cement step.

"Oh, Leanne, it's probably filthy there." Carol paddles her hands as if to shoo her daughter away. "And that's such a pretty robe, too."

Leanne makes no sign of moving. "The doormat is clean enough." She has her elbows on her knees and the coffee cup in both hands.

"Oh, what will we do?" Carol moans quietly, as if to herself. "What if he dies or won't fly away when it's time?"

"It's not that important," Leanne says.

"But you wanted it!" Carol looks at her watch. It's still early on Thursday, two days away from the ceremony. "I could go to the pet store in Kalamazoo and get more, but last time they had to order them, and it took two weeks."

"I wouldn't go to that much effort," Leanne says. She hugs her arms to herself and ducks her head to bite the edge of her coffee cup. Huddled there like that, she looks like the injured bird, her robe pooling around her on the cement step.

"You know, I almost didn't marry your father," Carol says. Leanne looks up, interested. It's not the usual story. The family wedding story has always been Will and Carol's whirlwind courtship. They met in San Antonio, Texas, where Will was in officer candidacy school. Carol had driven down for graduation with a friend who was engaged to another student. Will was presented to her as a fellow midwesterner; she was from Dayton. When Will told her he was from Michigan, her first thought was *country boy*. Still, when he asked her to dinner at the officers' club, she agreed. Kelly Air Force Base was known to have a posh O-club. She bought herself an exquisite shift made of peach silk and used a borrowed sewing machine to make a matching jacket. Will and his friend wore their dress uniforms. He told her that his application to flight school had just been accepted.

For the next week, they saw each other every day. At the end of it, Will presented her with a shiny red suitcase, the kind a serious traveler would carry. "It's a gift," he said. When she opened it, she found the ring.

"I'm the kind of man," he told her, "who knows what he wants and goes after it."

She always wondered how he managed to get a diamond ring like that out in the middle of nowhere. Years later, he admitted he had bought it with an IOU from a fellow student whose fiancée had returned it after meeting someone else. Carol would have considered that bad luck. But at the time, she was impressed with his ability to manifest the thing he needed. A man like that was surely going places.

"How did you almost not marry Dad?" Leanne asks, leaning forward.

"Well, you know my ex-boyfriend Rick," Carol tells her. Leanne nods. Rick also looms large in the family mythology. As teenagers, the girls loved hearing about his James Dean haircut, his '57 Chevy. He and Carol dated all through high school, and everyone assumed they'd get married. But they broke up right after graduation.

"Rick called me the week before the wedding. I hadn't heard from him in almost a year. He'd heard about the wedding, and he said he was calling to tell me I was making a big mistake. I should never marry a military man, he said."

"Why would he say that?"

Carol shrugs. "I guess he thought we'd move around a lot, stuff like that. Or maybe he thought I'd be lonely when Will went off on postings."

Leanne nods. "That was reasonable."

"But there was more to it, you know?" Carol gazes off into the dimly lit garage, envisioning herself in her father's study, the phone clutched to her ear. She'd had curlers in her hair, and tissues stuffed between her toes because she had painted them, and she worried that those things might somehow telegraph themselves through her voice. She didn't want Rick to envision her like that.

"I think he wanted another chance. But he couldn't bring himself to say so. He was too cool."

"And if he had said so?"

Carol shakes her head, dispelling the vision. "Oh, who knows," she says, suddenly cranky. "You never know what you would have done, do you? You become a different person, and it's hard to imagine how you made the decisions you did."

Leanne laughs, a short bark with no mirth in it. Carol is about to ask her if she's having doubts of her own when Will appears in the door behind her.

"Tammy says let him sit there for a while. She says birds act weird all the time. Just make sure he's drinking and eating." He steps around Leanne, who leans against the doorjamb to let him by. "Can you tell from the food and water if he's had any?"

"Will, how would we know?" Carol says. "The other bird might have eaten it all." She stares forlornly at the unmoving dove. "Didn't Tammy say anything else?"

"She said if he bit me, he's probably not croaking," Will says. "They go all passive when they're on the way out."

"Oh, *that's* encouraging."

"Let's not worry about it," Leanne says. There's something strained in her voice. "It's really not a big deal."

"What's going on here?" Margaret, red from exertion, has appeared in the doorway behind Leanne.

"One of the doves is sick," Carol says. "And we don't know what to do."

"Do nothing," Leanne says. "Let's just have some more coffee."

"Kit's hogging the shower," Margaret says. "He's been in there since I left to go run."

"Margaret . . ." Carol starts to tell Margaret that someone phoned for her, but then she can't remember the person's name. Some impossible Arab-sounding name, what was it? Vitor? Vikram? He had asked for her so formally, in that strange accent, wanting to know if he had "reached the residence of the parents of Margaret Gruen." He sounded polite and cultured, but something about him makes Carol hesitate to pass on the message. It's not that the man sounded foreign, she assures herself, it's that she has never heard of him before. Who would be calling Margaret at her parents'? When David isn't with her? Some instinct makes her not trust this man, and Carol always pays attention to her instincts.

"What?" Margaret is looking at her, waiting.

"I need your help bringing some things up from the basement," Carol tells her. "Let's do it before you clean up."

eight

"WHERE ARE WE GOING AGAIN AND WHY?" KIT ASKS.
He's dressed in jeans and a polo shirt, and it occurs to Leanne that
he might be cold. She should ask him if he'd like to borrow a
sweater from her father, but something is stopping her from being
too solicitous. She is suspicious of the impulse. It's obviously some
sort of overcompensation.

"We need to go tell the people at the country club exactly how
we want things arranged," Leanne says. "The caterer is meeting us
there with some things she wants us to taste. And then we have to
stop by the florist and give them their check."

"It's only lunch," Kit says. "Besides, I thought your mother
already picked out all the food."

"She did, but they want us to make some decision about sauces
or something, I don't know." Leanne runs a hand through her hair.
Another thing she was supposed to do was call a salon and make an
appointment to have her hair properly put up for the wedding. She
hadn't thought it necessary, but at dinner last night Margaret
assured her it was. Most brides, Margaret pointed out, would have
had at least one practice session at the salon already.

"What are we driving?" Kit asks.

"Margaret's car," Leanne says.

Kit rolls his eyes. "Perfect," he says dryly. Leanne giggles but
immediately feels guilty. Laughing about Margaret's stupid car and
making sly jokes about the caterers and country-club people and
florists is all well and good, but it implies that they're in this
together. And Leanne has not let Kit in on all of it.

"I need another cup of coffee first," he says.

"I'm sorry about my mom's Maxwell House," Leanne tells him.
"There's not a Starbucks for miles."

Kit holds his hands up, stopping her. "I adore Maxwell House," he says. "You have no idea."

"I'll get you a to-go cup," she says.

They drive in silence. The rain is still coming down lightly but steadily, enough to require the windshield wipers occasionally. Margaret's car doesn't have an intermittent setting, and the slowest speed is too fast, so Leanne pushes the wiper lever every twenty seconds or so. Kit looks at her sidelong but doesn't say anything. The little Rabbit feels thin and metallic, an insufficient barrier between them and the elements. The engine is noisy, the dashboard flat and no-frills. Leanne wonders why Margaret would have agreed to drive it all the way up to Michigan.

You know, Kit, I'm a drunk, she could say.

"It's not a very impressive landscape, is it?" Kit says. He's looking out the window at the flat fields, mushy with rain and dotted with run-down barns and outbuildings. They have just passed the old Vandenburg farm. The house, a flat brown structure with peeling, scraped siding, has an orange couch on the front porch. There's an old Gremlin and a truck in the driveway, along with two mangy dogs. A blue snowmobile in the corner of the front yard wears a handwritten sign: FOR SALE.

"It gets prettier north of here," Leanne says. "The U.P. is really gorgeous."

"But why?" he asks.

"Why is the U.P. gorgeous?"

"No, why did your father come back here? It's not exactly my old Kentucky home."

Leanne can't tell if he's being facetious or if he truly wants to know.

"Our dad always said that when he was a boy, he used to look up while he was plowing and see airplanes overhead and all he wanted was to be up there, in the sky," she says. "So he went off and became a pilot. And he found himself flying over Michigan and looking down and seeing tractors in fields, and all he wanted was to be down there, on a farm." She pauses. She's heard the story countless times, but now it seems to explain something, something she'd love Kit to understand.

"He was malcontent," she says. "And he dragged my mother along with him."

Kit gazes out at the miserable homesteads, the rain-battered corn drooping in saggy rows. "I guess it looks better from above," he says.

The country club is on the outskirts of Kalamazoo. As they near it, the fields drop away, and the landscape begins to look more suburban. There are neighborhoods with curving streets and boxy new homes on large lots.

"All of this used to be farmland," Leanne tells Kit, "but farmers have been selling their land in small parcels. It's worth more as residential real estate than it is as agricultural land."

Kit nods. "Tough luck on your dad," he says. "I guess you really can't go home again."

Surprised, Leanne nods. She'd never thought about it that way.

A long driveway through a sloping lawn heralds the entrance to the club. The building itself is old, probably built in the sixties, in the faux-colonial style that was current then. Behind it there's a small lake. The golf courses are to the left. They pass a small bank of tennis courts and park as near the door as they can.

They are given a cheerful midwestern welcome. The events coordinator introduces herself as Lori, an energetic blonde a bit younger than Leanne. They follow her around, nodding in acquiescence to all of her plans: the tables laid out in a circular pattern, the bridal table here, the cake table in the corner. Her energy is so enormous, her manner so confident, that to suggest any changes—a little less frippery for the cake, a smaller bridal table—would be trying to derail a speeding locomotive.

They go outside to see her layout for the ceremony itself, Lori grabbing one of the club's golf umbrellas from behind the main desk.

"Here," she says, "one of these is plenty big for newlyweds-to-be!"

Kit holds the umbrella. Leanne takes his arm awkwardly. It's like they're becoming the bride and groom on top of the cake. It makes her feel all the more uncomfortable for the false pretenses under which she's here.

Lori shows them the strings in the grass where she has measured out the space for the chairs. "Now, don't you worry about that," she says. "They're all safe and dry in the basement, and our boys will set them up just before the ceremony so they don't get wet. Not that it's going to rain! I'm sure you're going to have a *perfect* day!"

She leads them to the trellis arch where the minister will perform the ceremony.

"We're ready for anything here," she says cheerily. "Big Catholic weddings, little private ceremonies with a justice of the peace. Yours is easy. Our last couple was Latvian. Russian Orthodox! Boy, did they have a complicated ceremony! But we had everything they needed. We even have a chuppah for Jewish weddings!" She beams at them, pleased to have such a tangible expression of the club's open-mindedness.

How about an imam? Leanne wants to say. *We're Muslim, you know.* It would amuse Kit. In fact, she realizes, it's something he would say, not she. She glances at him sidelong. He's looking at Lori in a genial way, absent all his usual archness.

The grass is sodden, and Leanne's feet sink into it as they walk back toward the building. Its squishiness mirrors how she feels. *What are we doing?* she thinks. Kit is clearly playing the good bride-groom to make Leanne feel better, but it's only making her feel worse, as if the dry, witty man she loves has had his brain rewired by earnest midwesterners. Maybe he doesn't even want to go to Mexico anymore. Maybe he just wants to go back to Cold Spring and be a video editor. She glances at him again. No, this is Kit, the real Kit. He really does want to be married.

But that's only because he doesn't know her. He thinks she's good wife material, a sweet, crafty girl who has had the ambition and energy to go out and start her own business, when she's a self-destructive, lazy girl whose mother bailed her out and set her up in a store to keep her from being a total loss. He thinks she's going to walk cheerily down the aisle and become a nice wife who will run her little store and keep him company while he zips around making prizewinning documentary features. And why shouldn't he expect that? He has been completely clear from day one about his hopes and dreams. He's like everyone else in her family.

How can I be sure I want to do this? she wants to scream at Kit as he climbs the wooden stairs to the country club's porch, looking solid and confident and calm. *How can I be sure of anything?*

"Now," Lori says, relieving them of their umbrella when they get inside, "the caterers are here with some samples, and boy, I can tell you one thing! You're in for a treat!"

Wheel disk, post-hole digger, sickle mower. A neat row, like birds on a telephone wire. The three pieces of equipment have been sitting in front of the barn for the last three months. Carol has asked Will to put them in the barn several times, and every time he has said okay, then promptly forgotten. He knows this drives Carol crazy, but he doesn't do it, as she seems to think, on purpose. He just forgets, because in the end, it's not clear to him why moving them should be so important.

But that's not entirely true, he tells himself as he heads out the back door toward the barn, pulling up his sweatshirt hood against the light rain. He understands all too well. Carol doesn't want anyone looking out back and being reminded that this is a farm.

He stops and contemplates the three hunks of metal, figuring out where to start. They are unsightly, he has to give her that. The post-hole digger looks like an oversize corkscrew, and the wheel disk squats on the grass like a discarded set of false teeth. The sickle mower is downright frightening, with its sawlike blade sticking up in the air as if waiting to drop down on some toddler's unsuspecting head. Carol is right, they should all be in the barn. It's better for them, anyway. The wheel disk is going to start rusting if it sits out in the rain much longer.

He starts with the post-hole digger, because it's the smallest piece. He gets himself under the tall end and drags it toward the barn.

"Damn it," he says as he gets to the barn and realizes he hasn't opened the door. He sets the digger down and gets his foot in between the doors, shoving the right door aside. It roars on its track. His father's barn door made the same sound. It's almost a surprise to see the interior of his own, larger barn instead of the small one he grew up with. He looks inside, letting his eyes adjust to the light. He should probably move some things around, make enough room for the three pieces of equipment. They're awkward and oddly shaped. He shoves the flatbed wagon backward a few feet, then moves some large spelts barrels to the side.

He goes back out and gets under the post-hole digger again, giving it a friendly pat as he does. He's always appreciated equipment. His father taught him how to fix a tractor when he was barely seven. Will liked knowing how one part led to another part, how the fuel worked its way through and caused the small explosions that moved the machine forward. It made his first Air Force job in the motor pool easy. He felt even stronger about airplanes. Up until the 767, he got excited every time the airline ordered new planes. Just three years before ceasing to exist, TWA put in its largest aircraft order ever, 717s and Airbuses. It was an optimistic moment. They had finally gotten rid of Carl Icahn, who had been milking TWA dry to line his own wallet. The airline was employee-owned, and a pilot had been named CEO. Customer service and on-time performance had improved, because the employees were giving it their all. Will thought then they were finally going to make it work. Shows how much he ever knew.

"Hah," he says, shoving the post-hole digger into the spot he's made for it.

He goes back outside and starts at the sight of Margaret, standing in the rain, her hands in her pockets and her shoulders shrugged up close to her ears.

"I thought I'd give you a hand," she says.

"Well, okay." He wonders if Carol sent her out. *Go make sure your father gets those things inside.*

"Let's get this disk in the barn. I can pull it around by the hitch and get it through if you can open the door a little wider." He expects her to object, to insist on helping drag the thing, but she only nods and goes to the door. There's something stiff and anxious about her bearing. Maybe it's just the rain.

Luckily, the disk rolls easily when Will pulls it. He goes in a large circle to get it lined up straight on with the door, then ducks his head and pulls it quickly inside.

"Look out!" Margaret grabs on to the frame from behind to help slow it down and keep it from crashing into the flatbed wagon. It pulls her a short distance, the soles of her shoes scuffing as they slide across the cement floor. She laughs, looking for that instant like a child again. Will's heart lightens. He brushes raindrops off his sleeve.

"I'm getting wet," he says. "I've got a jacket in the tack room. I'm going to go put that on."

The tack room hasn't been used for tack since Leanne sold her horse and moved to New York. Will used to love the way it smelled, the saddles all soaped and shiny on their sawhorses, bridles and leads hanging on the walls. It was like the girls' clubhouse in those years when their world centered on horses; they hung ribbons from horse shows and pictures torn out of horse magazines on the white walls.

Now there are only a few leads left, hanging forlornly on the wall. The saddles and bridles have all been sold. At some point Margaret pulled down all the ribbons and stored them away some- where, but the magazine pictures are still there, brittle and yellow with age. Will has been using the room to store random items. He wrestles his sweatshirt off, tosses it over one of the sawhorses. He takes his work coat from one of the pegs and shrugs into it.

Margaret is outside surveying the sickle mower when he comes back. "This thing looks lethal," she says. "But I think if you pull on that side and I guide it around, there's a small chance we can avoid decapitating ourselves." Will nods and leans over to grab his side of the frame. Slowly, they rotate the mower without moving the blade.

"So what do you think of Kit?" Margaret says as they begin shoving the mower toward the barn door. Will is surprised. Is she just making small talk, or does she really care what he thinks? Maybe she's trying to open a conversation about something else, something that relates to her.

"I don't know," he says, grasping for the right answer. What does he think of Kit? The kid seems sure of himself, but that's just youth. If there's anything about Kit that bothers Will, it's that he seems to watch and listen more than other men his age. It strikes Will as somehow cautious, and that makes him suspicious. Then again, it could be a good quality, couldn't it?

"I don't know," he says again. "Seems nice enough, I guess." It's what his own father would have said, he realizes upon hearing it. Margaret glances up at him, and he wonders if she heard that echo, too. She stands up and brushes her hands together. The mower is lined up with its buddies.

"Okay, then," she says. "It's all inside now. That should give Mom about ten minutes of satisfaction." She smiles at him and he grins back, accepting the brief moment of complicity. Then it's over, and she puts her hands on her hips. "I'd forgotten about this barn," she says, surveying the place like a real estate agent. "It's funny to think how much time Leanne and I spent out here. Those long summer days. Where'd all that time go?"

"It comes back to you," Will says. "As you get older. You start getting it all back."

Margaret's gaze comes back to him, and she stands there taking him in. Her eyes narrow with thought. After a moment, her face softens, as if she remembers she's seeing her father, someone she need not figure out.

"You think so?" she says, and a light smile touches the corners of her mouth. "Well, I need to get into the shower, or I'll never be ready to help with the cooking. See you inside!" She lifts a hand toward her face, a funny half salute, then turns and heads back out-side, but pauses at the open doors. "Don't forget your sweatshirt," she says.

Will stands alone in the barn, next to his mower. The only illu-mination comes from the open doors; the day's gray light is too weak to penetrate the dusty haymow windows a level above. He feels oddly abandoned. Here he stands at the center of his domain, yet no longer at the center of anything. He's a king, Lear in a brown Carhartt coat. *Who loves me best?* He opens a hand and examines it. *Here I am, a living, breathing creature. Taking up space in the pres-ent.*

The barn smells dank and metallic, more like oil than animals. Will closes his eyes and summons his father's barn, the way it smelled when, as a boy, he slid the door open on a summer day. There was first the cool, muddy smell of the concrete floor, then the sweet pungency of the hay, and then the musky, manure-like smell of two pigs and two cows. Behind that was the sweeter, sweaty smell of their solid old horse and the acrid smell of chickens in the attached coop. He can smell all of it, right here, standing in his own barn, a barn that hasn't seen an animal in fifteen years, except for mice and swallows. Those old smells are as real to him as anything he can smell today. And what, he asks himself, does that say about the present, about its bossy assertion that it, and only it, can be here now?

Margaret is in the shower when the phone rings. She's already exhausted. After her mother had her bring a ton of things up from the basement, she asked Margaret to go out and take the padding off all the deck furniture and hang it in the garage in hopes that it might dry out. With Kit and Leanne off at the country club, Carol had become obsessed with the yard.

"Mom, it's going to be dark," Margaret said. "No one will be able to see it."

"They will at the beginning," Carol said. "They'll all be wandering around looking out the back windows at the beginning, and it will still be light outside. I know. You act like I've never had cocktail parties here before."

Margaret sighed and went out to weed the flower beds, as her mother wanted, but that didn't take long, because there were hardly any weeds. When she walked around the house to check the back-yard beds, she saw her father lugging the old, unsightly pieces of farm equipment into the barn. Something squeezed her heart at the sight of him, hunched over in the rain like an old man. She went to help. By the time she came back into the house, it was time to eat lunch. Will was fed a sandwich and sent to Kalamazoo to pick up his tuxedo and more groceries. Margaret collected Trevor from the playroom, and the two of them sat down with Carol for some canned tomato soup.

"This is great!" Trevor said happily. Margaret's heart always sank when she saw how happily her son, who got homemade bread and organic vegetables at home, ate awful, prepackaged junk. High-fructose corn syrup, she told herself. It's irresistible.

But the tomato soup tasted good even to her, sweet and warm-ing. She split a cookie with Trevor after the soup, and let him sit on her lap to eat it. Against her sweaty skin, he seemed impossibly clean and soft. She rested her chin on the top of his head and breathed in the smell of his hair.

When she came up to shower, it was with a sense of having made progress toward the ultimate goal: getting Leanne married without having Carol melt down.

She is under the water, rinsing her hair, almost content, when she hears her mother's shout. "Margie! Telephone!"

She turns off the shower and stands there, not wanting to have heard it.

"It's your husband!"

Acid fills her stomach. Can she tell him to call back? No, that will just prolong the agony. Better to get it over with. Besides, maybe he's calmed down. Maybe they can have a reasonable con-versation that will move them toward some sort of rapprochement.

There's even still time for him to get here, to act as though nothing has happened. Clinging to that flicker of hope, she wraps a towel around herself and, dripping heavily, goes to the upstairs extension in her parents' room. Vasant, she reminds herself. His hands. His eyes.

"I've got it," she shouts before easing the door shut.

"So." David's voice is cold, and the minute she hears it, Margaret's heart begins to thud loudly. He's still angry. He's still that other person, the one who threatened her. Her hands begin to sweat, making the receiver slippery. She wipes her free hand on the towel she's wearing and switches ears.

"So," she says, striving to make her voice sound normal. "How are things?"

He laughs. It isn't a pleasant sound. "Do you have any idea what you've done?" he asks.

Margaret feels dizzy. "Yes, I do," she manages to say. "I've come to my parents' home to attend my sister's wedding." She can hear him breathing on the other end. "As we planned," she adds, but it sounds lame and defensive. Her breath catches, and she swallows hard. She can't let herself be intimidated.

"The police were still here when I got back," he says. "They were knocking on the door."

"David . . ." Margaret doesn't know what she wants to say, but she has to say something. It's going to be her only chance.

"They were knocking on the door," he says, determined not to be sidetracked. "They asked me who I was, and I said I was your husband."

"Okay." She won't be able to do anything besides let him get through the story, she can see that.

"They asked me to unlock the apartment so they could have a look around. They stood right next to me with their hands on their guns. I could tell what they thought."

"David, it doesn't matter what they thought. They have to think that way, they're police officers."

He isn't listening to her. "I could tell that they thought I had done something to you. They were just waiting to have to arrest me."

Margaret can feel tears filling her eyes, not for David but for the awfulness of the whole situation. She regulates her breathing carefully so he won't hear her crying.

"So we got inside, and I saw that you had left a note on the table by the door. I picked it up and put it in my pocket so the police wouldn't see it."

This confuses Margaret. She dashed the note off quickly—*I've taken Trevor to my parents for Leanne's wedding. We can talk when I get back on Sunday. I don't want to fight. M.*—but she doesn't understand why he would hide it from the police.

David continues. "So they looked around the whole apartment, and they saw there was no one else there, and then they asked me what had happened. I said that we had argued about you sleeping with my colleague, and I had left to get some air. When I got back, you were gone. And then I said, 'Oh my God, our son!'"

"What are you talking about, David? You knew Trevor was with me."

"I ran upstairs and looked for him. I told them he was gone. The police asked if I had any idea where you had gone, and I said no, none. And then I started crying."

It's a confession, but it's bragging, too. David is describing his next move in the game she started unintentionally when she called 911.

"You know what, Margaret? They started to feel bad for me then. They said I should contact a lawyer. They said if you had taken Trevor out of state to hide him from me, it could be kidnapping. They said I had rights."

The full horror of the call is dawning on Margaret. "But David, you knew exactly where I had gone. I left that note for you. I wasn't trying to take Trevor away from you, I was going to my sister's wedding!" She despises the rising tone of desperation in her voice.

"What note?" David says, and even in his cold, flat tone, there's a glimmer of triumph.

Words crowd into her head, but she stops herself from speaking. *You were threatening me! I was scared of you!* She breathes deeply and tries to make her voice calm, reasonable. "David, what are you trying to do?"

There's a pause as David seems to consider this question. Margaret's mind races, trying to come up with something she can do or say that might jolt him out of this, might make him see the absurdity and awfulness of turning their unhappiness into all-out war.

"I'm doing the only thing I can do," he says. "I'm fighting to get my son back."

"But you haven't lost him! Why are you saying this?" It doesn't escape Margaret's notice that he says nothing about getting his wife back, and she doesn't bring it up, either.

"Goodbye, Margaret," David says. She waits, tensed, for him to say something that would be in keeping with the melodramatic tone of the conversation: *I'll see you in court* or *Have a nice life.* But there's just silence, and then a click as he hangs up. The phone sounds empty. Margaret clings to the receiver, unwilling to accept that the conversation is over, with no chance of bringing it to a better end. After a few moments, the off-the-hook tone starts warbling.

Margaret returns the phone to its cradle and sits down on the edge of her parents' bed. She feels completely drained. She can't get the energy to walk to the bathroom and finish drying off. Numb, she slumps over to her side. She closes her eyes, but she's too drained even to cry.

After knocking several times, Carol comes in and finds her there.

"Margaret, honey, what's wrong?" she says. She sits down by Margaret's side. Margaret feels herself sliding toward the hollow her mother makes.

"I don't know what to do," she says.

"Why don't you start by telling me what's going on," Carol says.

Margaret opens her eyes. "You can't tell anyone else," she says.

"Of course not."

Margaret doesn't know where to begin. She's afraid that if she opens her mouth, a pathetic, childlike wail will find its way out.

"It's okay," Carol says. "Whatever it is, we'll try to sort it out."

"It can't be sorted out," Margaret says. "There's no *sorting it out*."

"Then we'll just deal with it."

Margaret puts her hand over her eyes. She shivers, freezing from lying there damp and barely covered up. She wiggles her toes to try and work them under the blanket. Her whole body is shaking with cold. She can't bear another second of not being under the covers.

"Whatever it is, Margaret, I'm on your side." Carol sits there, emanating an unusual patience. *I'm on your side.* Margaret repeats the words in her head, trying to squeeze some comfort from them. Her mother is on her side. She always has been. Although why should she be? Every choice Margaret has made has been a direct rejection of the life her mother has lived.

She gets her feet under her parents' blanket. Shakily, she reaches a hand down and pulls it toward her chin. She gets herself covered and huddles there, trying to focus as much of her consciousness as possible on the awareness of the blanket's softness against her skin, the small warmth beginning to grow underneath it.

"I've been asleep," she says. "I've been like a person asleep at the wheel."

"That's okay," Carol says softly, in a lullaby voice. "You're awake now."

The country club is all set, tables, chairs, trellis all ready to go. The florist has been paid. The caterers know what sauce to use with the salmon and which wine to serve with the soup. Everything has been arranged, and Kit and Leanne are almost home, driving in the rain without speaking. Leanne has never felt more uncertain about the wedding happening.

"Well," Kit says, as she pulls into the driveway and stops the car, "I guess the wheels are in motion, aren't they?"

Leanne turns off the car. Rain runs in tearlike trails down the windshield. "I think I'll take a walk," she says.

"An excellent plan." Kit's voice is light. "Stop and smell the wet roses for me, would you?" He pulls the handle and shoves his shoulder against Margaret's sticky passenger door. "I'm going to go in there," he says as he gets the door open, "and ransack the cupboards, because I'm sure that somewhere, hiding, leftover from a holiday basket or an office party or the visit of some previous gourmand, there's a bag of whole coffee beans. And I'm going to find it and make some coffee. So don't be too long." He climbs out of the car. "Tallyho!" he cries as he slams the door.

Leanne sits at the wheel, watching Kit walk to the front door and enter the house. He seems to be becoming a part of the family even as Leanne feels she's drifting away from him. She rests her forehead on the steering wheel and closes her eyes.

After a few moments, she picks her head up and is surprised to see eyes regarding her from the porch.

"Trevor, what are you doing there?" she asks as she gets out of the car.

"Is it raining now?" he asks, and Leanne notices that the rain has stopped. The sky is still a grayish white and the day still gloomy, but for the first time since she arrived, there's nothing falling. Still, the air feels so damp it might as well be raining.

Leanne runs her fingers through her hair. "No, it's not raining anymore," she says, walking over to her nephew.

Trevor looks up at the sky. His brow furrows with concentration, making him look like Margaret. The blond hair at the crown of his head swirls around in a perfect miniature spiral. He stands there, head tilted back, studying the sky. His face moves up and back, as if he's trying to take in every inch of it. She watches as he looks up, up, up, until he goes too far and tips over backward, falling onto his behind. Trying not to laugh, Leanne squats down to make sure he's okay. He doesn't seem to mind.

"The clouds are really the rain," he says. "They're the rain waiting to fall from inside the air."

"That's right." She smiles at him. She's always felt comfortable around kids, more so than Margaret. It's funny that Margaret was the one to have the first grandchild. Whenever they used to go to restaurants or other places where there were rowdy kids, Margaret always fixed them with an icy stare. "Don't people even *try* to control their kids anymore?" she would mutter.

"You want to come outside and play?" Leanne asks Trevor. He smiles at her as if he has been waiting for exactly this.

"Yes," he says calmly. "I want to."

"Do you want to play ball?" Leanne is trying to remember whether there are some toys in the garage.

"I want to see the barn," he says.

Leanne looks at the front door. "Maybe we should ask your mother first," she says. "The barn is kind of dirty."

"No," the boy says, grave. "You shouldn't ask my mother."

"Why not?"

"Grandma says she's sleeping and not to bother her."

"Oh." Leanne stands there, unsure what to do. *Oh heck,* she thinks, *the barn's not so dirty with all the animals gone.*

"All right," she says, holding out a hand. "I'll take you to see the barn."

They stop in the garage to check on the doves. The larger one is no longer holding his wing in a funny way, though he still seems subdued. The other one scrabbles around, rustling in the seed shells at the bottom of the cage.

"Those are Grandma's birds," Trevor says, watching them.

They walk outside again and go around to the back of the house, where the large deck extends out toward the barn.

"My dad built that deck," Leanne tells Trevor, "when I was really little. Your mom was about your age."

"Grandpa Will is my mom's dad," he says, serious with the knowledge, but his attention is focused on the large barn as they draw near it.

"Those big doors are for tractors," Leanne says. "And this small one is for people."

"Which one do horses use?"

Leanne laughs. "Either one," she says. "We used to take them in the small door and straight back to their stalls."

"What's a stall?"

"I'll show you."

The door creaks as Leanne pushes it open. A thousand memories crowd into her head. Taking her horse out, cleaned and groomed, to put her on a trailer for the horse show. Riding out for an afternoon jaunt, ducking her head down to go under the lintel. Rubbing saddle soap into bridles in the little tack room. The smell of it fills her nostrils. Strange, how physical sensation can reside in a place and just reappear.

"That's where the saddles and bridles were always kept," she tells Trevor, pushing open the tack-room door. He looks in hopefully.

"They're gone now," she says. "We sold them when we sold the animals."

"What's that?" He's pointing to a large round bin.

"That's where we kept the spelts. That's sort of a treat for horses—like cookies for you."

"It's a big cookie jar!" He laughs, pleased with himself, then follows her to the row of stalls at the back.

"My horse lived there," she says, pointing, "and your mom's lived over there. But they spent most of the summer out in the pasture." She shows him the door to the pasture, how the stalls could be opened to let the horses go freely in and out. She leans on the stall gate, staring at the open door to the pasture. The smell of the pasture grass on a hot summer day, the buzzing of flies around her, the roughness of a lead rope wrapped around her hand. In the summer sometimes, they rode in shorts and sneakers, the damp warmth of the horses' bodies pressed against their bare legs.

"I love horses!" Trevor cries, a spontaneous burst of enthusiasm. His shriek is immediately lost in the barn's emptiness.

"This room is where we brought the hay in for them to eat," she says, leading him into the large tractor room. Above them, the hayloft windows let in a fraction of the day's white light. The air seems to be filled, even now, with tiny motes, particles of hay perhaps, so that everything looks slightly out of focus.

"We can go up in the hayloft!" Trevor breathes.

"I don't know if we should do that," Leanne says. "It's dirty up there, and it's dangerous for little kids. You might fall down."

"I won't fall down. I'll be very *very* careful." He is almost whispering, as if telling her a secret. Leanne eyes the hayloft ladder. It's not a ladder, really, just thick planks nailed to the wall, entering the loft through a small square cut in the floor. Going up it was always scary—you emerged into the hayloft and reached your foot over from the plank ladder to the hayloft floor—but going down was worse. Then you had to reach one foot out over the square hole in the floor and let it fall onto the plank. For one dizzying moment, you were stepping onto nothing.

The first time Leanne went up to the hayloft, she refused to come down. She remembers seeing the hole in the floor and knowing there was no way she was going to take that step. The ground was so far down she couldn't even see it. Her cousin Eddie was there, and he and Margaret made fun of her, but she wouldn't budge. She was going to stay in that hayloft forever. Eventually, Eddie's stepfather, Uncle Rem, came up and got her, hefting her over his shoulder like a sack of wheat.

"That ladder is difficult," she says. "It's really only for grownups." Trevor looks up at her and his face is filled with disappointment.

"There's nothing up there to see," she tells him.

"I really, *really* want to see the hayloft," he says, pressing his lips together and squinting at her as if he's sorry to have to break it to her. Leanne almost laughs.

"Oh, all right," she says. "But you'll see, it's scary." It will serve him right if he gets just as terrified as she did.

She follows him over to the ladder and gets him started on the first rung, which is high off the ground. His stubby arms and legs begin climbing so quickly that she has to hurry and get on herself so she can stay right behind him. *This is really stupid,* she tells herself. What if Trevor falls and breaks his arm? Margaret would be furious.

"Be careful, Trevor," she says.

He slows down when he reaches hayloft level. The ladder keeps on going; there's another level above this one, stretching toward the other end of the barn, but Leanne doesn't tell him that.

"Stop there," she says, and then she climbs up so she's right behind him, her feet on either side of his on the same rung. "Take my hand," she says, and he does. He holds her hand and reaches a leg for the hayloft floor. It's just barely long enough to reach. With one leg on the floor and one leg on the ladder rung, he starts to feel scared—she can feel his body tighten and his motions grow jerky.

"Wait, wait," he starts to say, but she lets go of his hand and pushes his butt to shove him into the hayloft. She pushes a little too hard, and he stumbles forward onto his hands and knees. Quickly, she steps over to the hayloft floor herself.

"There, look at you!" she says, before he can get upset. "You're in the hayloft now!"

Trevor stands up and looks around, satisfied. "Wow," he breathes. He heads for the edge.

"Don't go anywhere near that edge," Leanne says, surprised at the command in her tone.

Trevor freezes and looks back at her. "Please take me over there so I can see over the edge?" he asks.

That's Margaret's training, Leanne thinks, and for once she's grateful for her sister's bossiness. "Sure," she says, catching up to him. "Here, hold my hand."

They walk to about two feet from the edge and look over. A few farm implements are parked below; she recognizes a disk tiller. Farther over, there's a red canoe hanging between two of the barn's rough-hewn posts and a small sailboat under a tarp. There was a short period when Carol decided the girls should learn to sail, but all the lakes in the area are small and don't get much wind, so they quickly lost interest.

"We're up high," Trevor says.

"Pretty high," Leanne answers.

"But buildings are higher."

"Yes."

"Chicago has the Sears Tower," Trevor says. "That's one of the tallest buildings in the world."

"That's right," Leanne tells him. "They built that when I was a baby."

"New York had the Twin Towers," Trevor says. "But some airplanes came and knocked them down."

Leanne looks down at him. "That's right," she says. "That was very sad." It feels insufficient. Suddenly, she wants to cry. How would it be for a four-year-old to know such awful things about the world? Leanne has never before considered what an exercise in uncertainty being a mother must be. It must be hard for Margaret.

"I have to go to the bathroom," Trevor says.

Leanne laughs. "Okay," she tells him. "Come on. I'll put you on the ladder."

Trevor is surprisingly calm about going back down. Leanne gets on the ladder first, then reaches out to take his hand, and he steps easily over and starts right down. He must really have to go.

On their way out, she notices that the tack-room door has swung open again. She's about to shut it when she sees a sweatshirt lying on the floor inside. It's the one her father was wearing earlier; he must have taken it off out here and forgotten it. When she picks it up, an envelope falls out of the pocket. Leaning over to retrieve it, she sees the return address: Cathay Pacific Airways.

He must have bought some tickets. A surprise for her mother perhaps, to celebrate his retirement. The thrill of being in on a happy secret flickers through her. She turns the envelope over. It's open.

She's surprised to see that the contents are pages and not tickets. Before it occurs to her that she shouldn't be reading it, her eyes have flicked over the first paragraph.

We are pleased to offer you the position of first officer at Cathay Pacific Airways. Please call Jim Chan in our New York office to discuss the details of your assignment . . .

No one expects her father even to consider flying past retirement. They all expect him to retire and settle in on the farm, as he has always said he couldn't wait to do. And Cathay Pacific. Is he planning to move to Asia? Obviously, her mother doesn't know anything about it.

Leanne's heart pounds. She never should have looked. Quickly, she stuffs the letter back in the envelope and the envelope back in the sweatshirt. Her hands shake slightly. She rolls the sweatshirt up in a ball and puts it under her arm.

"Okay, let's go," she says to Trevor, who is pacing back and forth like a tiny basketball coach. He follows her eagerly. When she opens the barn door, she sees that the hard rain has started again. She holds the crumpled-up sweatshirt over her head for protection, then reaches for Trevor's hand.

"Come on, run!"

nine

THE FRIDGE IS TOO FULL. CAROL REARRANGES A FEW jars, but there's really no hope. She won't be able to squeeze in any of the things Will is bringing home. She's going to need the bottom shelf, which is currently being taken up by leftover gumbo. She'll have to freeze it. Shutting the fridge door, she goes to collect a stack of plastic containers.

A low television hum emanates from the family room. Kit is in there, watching CNN. He said hello to Carol when he came in, seeming slightly distracted. She asked him where Leanne was, and he said, "Outside, with Trevor." That's a good sign, Leanne getting to know her brilliant nephew. Leanne has always been good with kids.

Carol takes a deep breath. Margaret is upstairs on the phone. At least Carol was able to talk her into making some calls—right now—to find herself a lawyer.

Carol stops and steadies herself against the counter, one hand on her forehead. It's too much. Leanne's wedding, all these people coming over, the bed-and-breakfast, and now this. And of course, she's the only one who knows about it. Margaret was quite insistent about that, and Carol can see why. Leanne would be upset if she knew what Margaret was going through at her wedding, and Will—who knows how Will would react. These things are easier for a mother to understand.

And yet what things, exactly, is she being asked to understand? The first and most important thing is that David is being a jerk. That much Carol gets, and in that she is entirely on Margaret's side. That he would even think of threatening to take custody of Trevor from Margaret—the thought is too terrible. She looks at the phone on the kitchen wall and considers picking it up. It would be for Margaret's own good, so Carol could understand what was going on and be in a better position to help her. But she knows it would make Margaret furious. And since Carol is her daughter's only ally right now, it's best if they stay on good terms.

She begins to unload glassware from the dishwasher. She started running them through this morning, but they'll all need polishing with a clean dish towel. She can't be putting out glassware with soap spots at a cocktail party. She goes to the linen closet for a clean rag. Returning, she takes up the first wineglass and begins polishing. Her daughter doesn't need oversight, she tells herself. She needs understanding. Even if she's not exactly admitting what needs to be understood.

Carol knows now that the phone call from the man with the accent probably has something to do with all of this. Margaret didn't say so. She just insisted, categorically and unhesitatingly, that it was all over between her and her husband.

Carol picks up another glass. What if Margaret *has* had an affair? Somewhat to her own surprise, the idea doesn't shock her. She hates that word—"affair"—as if it were something involving tuxedos and engraved invitations. But if Margaret was involved with someone, it would hardly be surprising. Carol never really let herself think it, but somehow she always knew David wasn't faithful to Margaret. Why shouldn't she have retaliated? Even if David was a loyal husband, Margaret might have had a weak moment. Everyone has those.

What's upsetting is that Margaret clearly feels she can't talk to her mother. Perhaps she fears disapproval. And, Carol realizes with a pang of sadness, that makes a certain kind of sense. After all, Carol has always tried to set an example for her girls. She has never talked to them about her own weak moments. How does one talk to one's children about things like that? She finds it hard even to think clearly about them herself.

There was, for instance, the spring early in the seventies when Will was laid off. He was part of a group of two hundred pilots that TWA put on furlough. Being Will, he didn't do what anyone would expect him to do—sort out his finances, figure out a plan for economizing. Instead, the very day he was notified, he stopped at K-1

Auto on his way home, traded in their old Ford Fairlane, and bought a brand-new '73 Buick Riviera, brown with a white leather interior. He drove the Riviera right off the floor and home, where he honked until Carol opened the front door. She wasn't sure who it was. The car was shining like waxy new chocolate in a white haze of exhaust. After a moment, she saw Will.

"Get the girls!" he called to her from the window. "Let's go for a ride!"

Margaret was six then, old enough to be interested. Leanne had just turned four. Carol herded them into the car. It was beautiful. The dashboard was leathery, the insides of the doors shiny imitation wood grain. Everything was as polished and sumptuous as the interior of a limousine.

"You got laid off, didn't you?" she said, and Will grinned.

"This may be the last time in my life I could walk up to a car dealer with an airline pilot's credit."

Even thinking about it now, Carol experiences a stab of frustration, deep down and indistinct, like a mitten frozen in ice. It wasn't that she didn't like the Buick. It was seductive, a sable coat of a car. She had always wanted a car like that. But buying it in those circumstances—that was Will all over the place. Impulsive wasn't even the word for it. Impulsive was buying an outfit on a whim, or deciding to go to a movie as you drove by the theater. Will had big thoughts and acted on them, with no regard for what anyone else might think. It was like that when he joined the Air Force, infuriating his father. Or when he bought the farm in Michigan, uprooting them from their nice Chicago suburb and signing himself up for a two-and-a-half-hour commute to O'Hare. Will wasn't impulsive. He was driven to remake the world, for no better reason than that he could.

Carol picks up another glass and holds it to the light. She wraps the towel around her hand for a firmer grip. It's a soothing task, watching the smudges disappear, the glass grow shiny and bright.

She always went along with Will's latest impulse. When he signed on for fighter pilot training, she went along like a good Air Force wife, even though it landed him in Vietnam. They were lucky.

He was back in under a year, recuperating and planning to join TWA. She objected at first: why throw away a career he'd worked so hard for? But Will was determined. After his airline training, he decided they'd live in Chicago—she thought for good.

It might be easier for her girls if things were still that way. It's not that she wishes women didn't have careers and lives of their own. But just look at the mess Margaret has to deal with. There was something simpler about it when one person called the shots. Sometimes Carol wonders if she did her girls a favor by raising them to be independent. She told them all along to go and make their own lives, to be ambitious and focused, but how much could she really equip them to do so? She was like a ground squirrel raising baby birds, telling them they could fly without having the means to show them how.

But that's not fair, she tells herself. She did her best. When Will got laid off, Margaret was in first grade and Leanne was starting nursery school early, so Carol decided to go back to college and get her degree. She signed up for two morning classes, two days a week at Plaingrove Community College. Will hadn't liked it when she suggested it. "Colleges have turned into zoos these days," he said. "Look at the mess at Kent State." But Carol convinced him that Plaingrove was different, a community college mostly filled with housewives like herself. It had no dorms, no student newspapers, no teach-ins or SDS meetings. The few young kids there were biding their time until they could transfer to Western or MSU. Still, looking back, she supposes Will was right. Plaingrove was where she met Bryan.

Bryan taught her favorite class. Cross-listed in sociology and literature, it was called "The Utopian Impulse." They were assigned a variety of books about utopian communities, starting with the Book of Genesis. They read Thomas More's *Utopia* and works by other people Carol had never heard of: Benjamin Disraeli and Charles Fourier and Edward Bellamy. She found it fascinating, far better than the European-film class she had to sit through before it.

Bryan was young and didn't act like Carol expected professors to act. He was always late, hurrying into the classroom at five past nine, a disorganized sheaf of papers under one arm. He was tall and lanky in his blue jeans, with brown eyes and curly brown hair that just touched his shoulders. He had a habit of pushing his hair behind one ear, revealing full brown sideburns. Will would have called him a hippie. Bryan never sat at his desk or lectured. Instead, he made them pull their chairs into a circle and "rap." He listened patiently to everyone's ideas about what they'd read. If anyone interrupted another student, he'd hold up his hand gently. "Everyone is owed equal time to express his or her opinion fully," he would say.

It was near the end of the semester when Will came home with the Riviera. That night he went to his study after dinner. Carol put the girls to bed and went to his door. He was at his desk, drawing.

"What are you going to do?" she asked.

"I'll tell you what I'm going to do first," he said. "I thought I'd build us a deck." He held up a drawing of a small deck extending from the kitchen's sliding glass doors. That wasn't what she'd meant. In the window behind him, she could see his hand, holding up the notebook, an offering.

They had always known furlough was a possibility. When the first round of layoffs came, they talked about what Will might do. The farm didn't make enough money for them to live on. But neither of them could imagine Will doing anything other than flying. It was all he had ever wanted. Carol suspected Will was happiest in the air. It was the only time he was moving forward as fast as he wanted to go.

"Are you sure we need a deck?" she asked. "Won't it cost a lot of money?"

Will waved a hand, dismissing what he didn't want to consider. "Wood is cheaper than laying concrete. Besides, won't it be nice in the summer?"

The word "utopia" had always given Carol a particular feeling. She imagined a world in the clouds, or a gleaming city like Oz in the movie. She imagined girls in frilled dresses drinking root-beer floats, children singing in the streets. Utopia was an imagined place, an ideal existing only in books. She was amazed to learn how many people had actually tried to create one.

In class, Bryan would point out the flaws in the utopian schemes they read about: the repression of individuality, the assumption of physical perfection, the failure to allow dissent. With him as their guide, they dissected one beautiful dream after another, until Carol began to suspect that his point might be that the very notion of utopia was dangerous and wrongheaded.

The Tuesday after Will was laid off was when it all started. Bryan gave them their final paper assignment. They were supposed to analyze a contemporary instance of utopian thinking.

"I'm not necessarily talking about a cult or a special school," he told them. "The utopian impulse is everywhere. We talked about how advertisers try to sell you a utopia. Look around you. Find the same urge somewhere else in your world and take a good hard look at it."

Carol was agitated as she packed her things. Something about the assignment appealed to her. She wanted to do it well. She imagined writing a brilliant paper, Bryan handing it back to her slowly, reluctant to give it up.

Bryan leaned against his desk as the class clattered toward the door, joking and chatting with them as he always did. When Carol passed, he put his hand on her arm.

"Do you have any idea what you'll write about, Carol?" he asked. Flustered, she shook her head. "Bring in some ideas on Thursday," he said. "We can look them over after class."

Will started on the deck. He went to the lumberyard and came back with what seemed like more wood than he could possibly need for the little deck in his drawing. He started hammering things outside. Carol would come home from class, and there he'd be, at work in back. On Thursday she told him she had a research project to do, and she needed him to watch the girls.

"Okay, fine," he said. "They can help me block out the flooring."

After class, Bryan was waiting for her. "Do you like falafel?" He had a way of looking at her that made her feel self-conscious.

"Do I like what?"

"Falafel. It's a Middle Eastern sandwich. I think you'd like it. I know a place in Kalamazoo."

"Oh." Carol hesitated.

"I mean, wouldn't it be nicer to discuss your ideas over lunch? I'm starving."

"Well, yes." Carol knew she didn't sound like she meant it.

"Not if you're in a hurry, of course."

"No, no, that's okay." She watched the buttons on his coat as he did them up. The coat looked at least two sizes too big for him. "I'd like to try that," she said. "Something new."

He smiled. "Which of us should drive?"

They decided to take Carol's car, hurrying across the parking lot to avoid the cold wind that had started to blow.

"Nice vehicle," Bryan said as they settled into the Riviera's white seats.

"Thank you," she answered.

"I'll bet your husband is a doctor." His tone was overly casual, as if he were making her into a sociological specimen.

"He's an airline pilot," she said. She had always liked saying that. But with Bryan, it fell flat somehow. They were silent as Carol drove.

"Do you have a tape deck?" Bryan asked. "Ah, you do."

"What?" Carol looked to where he was pointing. "No, that's just the radio."

"It's a tape deck, too." With an index finger, he pressed the station-selector panel, and it gave way, swinging back to reveal a tiny rectangular cavern. "You see? For eight tracks. It's hidden so the thieves can't see it." He said "thieves" with an ironic tone, as if he disapproved of hiding things, or of keeping them for yourself at all.

"What do you know!" she said with false enthusiasm. "A tape deck!"

"Now all you need are some tapes," Bryan said. Carol looked at the sneaky radio and suddenly hated their car. She hated its flashy white upholstery and its funny humped-up rear. She wished Will had never bought it. Looking through Bryan's eyes, she saw it for what it was: a striver's car. A car for the man who was going somewhere. Never mind that you couldn't see much out the rear window. This was a car for someone who never looked back.

It was late afternoon when Carol got home. The girls were outside with Will, wearing hooded coats and mittens over their school clothes. It was like that when he watched them—he let them play in their school clothes, gave them peanut-butter crackers and fruit cocktail straight from the can for lunch. Whenever she came home after leaving them, Carol would find herself wishing she hadn't gone. She missed their rituals, felt the loss of an afternoon with them as if it were a year.

The deck was beginning to take shape. A skeletal foundation was extending out from the wall. It reached into the yard twice as far as the drawing had. Will was inside it when she got there, pounding a nail into a corner. Carol collected the girls and thanked him for watching them.

"I have to do some more research on Tuesday," she told him. "If you can watch them again, that would be great."

"Yeah, all right," he said, pounding. When he looked up, she got the feeling that he wasn't really seeing her; he was seeing his future deck, gleaming and perfect.

After that, Will just assumed that on Tuesdays and Thursdays, he would pick up the girls with his truck. Between Carol and Bryan, there was an unspoken agreement that they'd go for lunch after class. They'd talk about all kinds of things—politics, movies, ecology, Bryan's career as a professor.

"Sociology isn't an easy discipline," he told her once. They were at the falafel place, where they always went. Carol had decided she liked falafel a lot.

"You have to let go of the old narratives," he said. "The old teleologies. Question common sense. That means taking ego out of the equation entirely. Buddhism gets that right. You have to let go of the self and everything it has learned."

Carol was never sure she understood what Bryan was saying, but she liked the sound of it. She liked the focused way he sat there, caught up in his words, having forgotten the food in his hand. He wasn't always thinking about the next thing. He wasn't driving at anything.

Sometimes she would watch him surreptitiously while he ate. When he focused on his lunch, he became as caught up in that as he had been in what he was saying. He was a man who lived in the moment, she told herself. That was why he was against utopias.

Watch out for the future, he told them in class. *It can hang you up just like the past.*

Once he looked up and caught her staring. He pushed the sandwich basket aside and leaned forward. "You have an astonishingly open face," he said.

Carol looked down at her hands, resting on the table. Bryan's hand came across and rested on one of them. She looked at the two hands sitting there, one nearly covering the other, as if they belonged to total strangers.

"I'm embarrassing you," he said. He took his hand away. "Why don't we get our check and go?"

"Yes, okay." Disappointment thudded in Carol's heartbeat. Bryan got up and began shrugging into his coat, and for a minute she saw him not as a whole person but as a nearly overwhelming collection of parts. A torso, pulling his shirt taut. A belt buckle. Thighs wrapped in denim. A hand, emerging from the coat. An elbow. Knees.

Another time he gave her a book. "Have you read Ram Dass?" he asked, and Carol thought that must be the book's title until he handed it to her. *Be Here Now.* Ram Dass was the author. "It will change your life," he said in a tone of warning she was clearly meant to ignore.

She took the book home and read it. It was disorienting and strange. Ram Dass, it seemed, used to be a professor named Richard Alpert. Then he took LSD and it opened his eyes. Carol disapproved of that. But it was exciting somehow that Bryan had given her such a wild book. And some of the things Ram Dass said were interesting. People shouldn't be so attached to the future, he said. The idea of progress was harmful. Something about that bothered Carol. After all, the girls were her future. How could she not be attached to them?

Meanwhile, the deck just seemed to keep on growing. Will began to build what looked like a trellis on it. He showed her a sketch on a napkin, something he had copied from a hotel in Kansas City.

"They had a grape arbor that made a sunroof," he told her excitedly. "You could sit on the patio underneath it, and it was shady, with grapes hanging down." His eyes glowed. "You wouldn't believe how many grapes there were on that one small plant! We could make our own wine."

Carol looks down at the dishwasher. She has finished polishing the glasses. They're lined up on the counter, a shiny battalion, eager to do their duty. She could put them on trays for the party. She goes toward the cupboard, where the large platters and trays are kept, but finds herself drifting to the sliding glass door instead. Outside, the deck is a deep, wet brown. Over the years it has cracked and split in places. The grape arbor is still there, but the plant is spindly and yellowing. For a while they tried to foster it, but it never yielded anything other than tiny, bitter clumps of grapes that would drop to the deck before they got ripe, leaving oily purple stains that Carol could never get off.

Beyond the deck the barn hulks, the cornfield sodden and dull behind it. A spindly tree line marks the field's edge. On the other side is Will's parents' farm. His ancestral home, except his ancestors never lived there. His father, a German immigrant, bought it from a pig farmer who went bankrupt in the Depression. Like their own eighty acres, it's flat, hard clay skirted by a nameless, muddy creek.

Why did Will want to come back to this place? When people asked, Carol gave out various answers: he missed working the land. He couldn't imagine the girls growing up in a city. You can take the boy out of the country . . . Privately, she thinks it has to do with his father. Will's father didn't want him to enlist in the Air Force, and he was even angrier when Will went to Vietnam. He refused to write to Will while he was on his tour. All he would say was that Will had left him with too much work, even though his farm was barely functional by then. Will's brother, George, tended the fields, and the animals were long gone, except a small flock of chickens watched over by Will's mother.

Will was sad about his father's anger, but he wasn't haunted by it until he came back from the war. Then it was as if he had acquired a sense of his own betrayal, and he felt compelled to make up for it.

The last book they read in Bryan's class was H. G. Wells's *The Time Machine*. Their class discussion about it was heated.

"I didn't like this book at all," one student began.

"Why not?" Bryan always looked eager to hear what they thought.

"I guess it just seemed ridiculous," the woman said, hesitating. "I just didn't find this world believable."

"I agree," put in another student. "It was described in such a hokey way. Silver trees. Huge flowers."

Carol raised a hand, although that wasn't required. "I think I took it more symbolically," she said. "I took the beauty of the world to be the way the narrator saw it at first. Before he realizes it's all a lie."

"It's all a critique of capitalism," the other woman insisted. "The Morlocks do all the work, and those little people live like gods."

"Before we address that," Bryan said, "let's see if Carol can expand on her point. What exactly is a lie?"

"The future world," Carol said. "The way the Time Traveler sees it."

"And how does he see it?" Bryan was watching her intently.

Carol paused. "He thinks the future must be better. He believes in progress. He thinks the world is becoming a utopia, but it really isn't changing at all."

Bryan smiled at her. "Excellent point, Carol," he said.

By then the deck was nearly finished. From the sliding glass door, Carol surveyed its vast expanse. Will was on his hands and knees, nailing down planks. Boards were jutting up at intervals. Staring at them, Carol realized they were the frames for built-in furniture. There was a long base for a bench, four legs for a table, tall posts to support a grape arbor. Their skeletal forms were silhouetted against the dull landscape's fading light.

One night after putting the girls to bed, Carol sat down at her typewriter and began.

Some utopias are big and others are small. My husband Will's is the size of a large backyard deck. He built it from the ground up, from plans he drew himself.

When Will purchased the farm, he did it without her. He drove up to visit his parents. His brother, George, had called him and told him the farm next door was for sale, but Will never mentioned that. He said he was taking Margaret for a weekend with his folks. Leanne was a baby, so Carol didn't mind. Her mother came to visit from Dayton, and they worked on little projects, a new slipcover for the couch, bright new curtains for the kitchen. Carol had friends over for coffee, took her mother to the tennis club to show her where their league played.

When Will came back, Margaret tumbled from the car and raced to the house.

"Dad bought us a barn!" she shrieked. Carol's mother laughed, because she thought Margaret was being cute. But Carol had seen

Will's face. He looked half guilty, half triumphant, the expression of a man who had just changed the course of their lives.

Like most utopias, Carol wrote in her essay, *my husband's is an entirely personal one. It is based on the particular dreams and beliefs of one individual. Because of that, it cannot help but fail to create a better world.*

Eventually, something had to happen. In their second-to-last class, Bryan seemed slightly distracted, not his usual jocular self. When the students left, he didn't stand near the door chatting, as usual. Carol stayed seated at her desk, unsure of what to do. A few moments of silence passed before he looked up.

"I'll drive" was all he said.

They went out to the parking lot together. In the new spring sun, he seemed to loosen up. He looked at Carol with warm eyes. When he unlocked the passenger door and held it open for her, the sun shone through his shirt, showing the dark form of his body within. Carol could see the silhouette of his upper arm through the blue fabric, and she shuddered with what she thought must be desire. Quickly, she looked away.

She had never made love to anyone but Will. Her high school boyfriend used to try to talk her into it, but it was the early sixties: having sex was not something good girls did. Even his asking for it wasn't entirely in earnest. It was the accepted game: he asked and she said no. Neither of them would have wanted it any other way.

But in the seventies, sex was everywhere. Carol was shocked by the wispy girls she saw strolling around town, their sandals and bra-lessness and torn jeans all proclaiming their availability. She was a young woman, too, and this was supposed to be the sexual revolution, but she had gotten married and it had passed her by.

It wasn't that she didn't have a good sex life. Will was passionate and eager, which had put her off at first. But eventually, she grew used to his energy, and he learned that a little gentleness would go a long way with her.

How would it be to make love to Bryan? She imagined he knew things she didn't. He was thinner than Will, only a few years younger, perhaps, but a completely different type. His hands on the steering wheel were brushed with a fringe of dark hair. She didn't know if she liked that or not.

When they got near town, Bryan didn't take the usual route to the falafel place, turning down a residential street instead. The car stopped in front of a large pink Victorian house.

"Where are we?" she asked.

"These are my digs," he said, putting his hand on the door. "I thought I'd make you lunch for a change."

She followed him inside. The house was spacious and barely furnished. In the front room, a sofa slouched behind a cluttered makeshift table. Hundreds of records lined the floor along one side of the room. She saw a poster for Godard's *Weekend*.

"We saw that in my European-film class!" she said, happy to recognize something, even though she had found the film confusing and strange. Bryan led the way into a large kitchen at the back. There, too, clutter ruled. The counters were lined with tea, coffee, nuts, a row of jars containing oils, honey, vinegars. Every surface was coated with crumbs. A small flame of understanding flickered to life in Carol's head.

"Do you live here alone?" she asked.

Bryan turned to her. "No, there are seven of us: four in bedrooms on the second floor and a trio who share the attic. We're a cooperative household."

"Like a commune?"

He smiled. "Yeah, sort of like a commune."

"Oh." Carol didn't know what to say. She looked around again. *A utopia,* she thought. Bryan's utopia. "Where did you all meet?" she asked.

"Most of them are graduate students at Western," he told her. "We all met there. When I finished my degree, I stayed on."

Carol was oddly disappointed. She hadn't thought of Bryan as a Western Michigan grad. She had thought he must come from some other, more exotic place. Princeton, maybe. Or the University of Chicago.

"Our house is vegetarian," Bryan said. "So I have some nice veggie soup for us." He was scooping soup out of a Crock-Pot.

"Oh, that's fine," Carol said quickly. "It's quite interesting, really. Vegetarianism, I mean."

"Yes, well, it's a house rule." Bryan turned toward her with a bowl in each hand. "Of course, I cheat sometimes when I'm not here. I can't resist a nice piece of ham."

"Of course." She couldn't stop being flustered.

"And rules are made to be broken, aren't they?" Bryan smiled at her, and for the first time, Carol thought, *I really don't know this man at all.*

"Have a seat," he said, pulling out a chair at a large country-style table. "I'll just grab us some bread."

The bread was dark and grainy, the soup thick and warming. Carol began to feel better as they ate. Bryan finished quickly and then sat back in his chair, regarding her steadily as she sipped soup. She shifted uncomfortably. The desire she had felt in the car had vanished; in its place, she felt an oddly fervent longing for her family. What were the girls doing just then?

Bryan stood up and retrieved a packet of cigarettes from the sidebar. "Smoke?" he asked her.

Carol shook her head. She looked up at Bryan and made the mistake of meeting his eyes.

He walked behind her chair and rested a hand on her shoulder, kneading gently. "Let's go upstairs," he said.

Carol didn't know what to say. How did one turn down such an invitation? She didn't want to insult him. But she didn't want to go upstairs. "I think I have to be getting home," she said miserably.

There was a pause. "You think you do?" he asked.

"I do."

"I see." Bryan didn't move his hand right away, but it stopped kneading and became a thing, a deadweight on her shoulder. He stood there for what seemed like minutes, as if waiting for her to say more.

"Maybe you could take me back to my car now," she said, her voice almost a whisper. It worked; it broke the spell.

Bryan took his hand back and moved away. "Yes, okay," he said. There was a new brusque tone in his voice. "Let's get you back to your vehicle."

Carol drove away on autopilot, following an instinct that led her home. She expected Will and the girls to be outside, but as soon as she opened the front door, the girls launched themselves at her, propelled by pure need.

"Mommy!" Leanne cried, in one of her rare moments of protest. "I want to be a dog and not a cat. Margaret always is the dog."

"Oh, sweetie." Carol picked her up. Will was on his back on the floor, asleep.

"Mom," Margaret said, "does a carrot know when it gets picked?"

Carol stood at the threshold, looking at Will. He took up over six feet of carpet. There were small toys on his stomach, as if the girls had been using him as a table.

This is only temporary, Carol thought. *He'll get his job back soon. He has to. It's what he does best.*

Margaret made a small sigh, a *humph* of displeasure. She hated being ignored. "A carrot doesn't have a brain; it can't think," Carol told her. For an instant, she wished she were back at the house with Bryan, his hand resting on her shoulder. But that made no sense: when she'd been there, she only wanted to be home.

"I want to be a dog!" Leanne yelled, even though Margaret seemed to have forgotten the game.

With a jerk, Will started awake. He took a deep breath and looked around, lost. "You're home," he said. "I was just having a little nap while the girls played." His voice trailed off, and his head dropped back down onto the carpet.

"Come on," Carol said to the girls. "You want to help Mommy start dinner?"

Will's head popped up again, and now he seemed awake. "No, let's go out for dinner!" he said. "Let's get spaghetti and celebrate! I finished the deck!"

That weekend, spring arrived. The sun turned from white to golden, and the trees unclenched into buds. The girls wanted to play on the new deck, and Carol let them. They ran up and down it, clomping as hard as they could, so that Carol could hear them from inside, where she was finishing her paper. *Thud thud thud thud thud thud thud.* Then a pause as they turned around, giggling. Then all the way back the other way.

Carol wrote about her husband. She wrote about his desire to build something most people realized was impossible. She wrote about how a man who moved forward for a living tried to find his own bliss in going back. When she was done, she reread her paper. It was a beautiful essay, she thought with surprise. She didn't know if it was what Bryan had in mind, but the satisfaction of having written it filled her body like a warm drink.

What she didn't write about was herself. She didn't write about how, two weeks before they moved to Michigan, she had called an attorney to ask about divorce. She didn't write about the ugliness of the man's voice, or the awful things he had said. How uncertain he told her the future would be. She didn't write about how she had decided to forget the phone call, how she had packed up their household with care. How she had unpacked here and tried to see beauty in Will's farm. How, when she watched the girls run giddy circles in the field or sat down to read them a story, always saying one word wrong to give Margaret a chance to correct her, she was filled with the feeling that it could be her utopia, too.

The last day of class was a gray Tuesday. Will drove her so he could use the car. They dropped the girls off first.

"I can't be late," Carol said. In European film, they had an exam.

Bryan didn't believe in exams. They were going to turn in their final papers and write self-evaluations.

"I'll get you there," Will said. He sped up, glancing at her, and for an instant, Carol could see that for all his complaining, he was secretly proud of her.

They pulled into the Plaingrove parking lot with five minutes to spare. Carol had watched the school as they neared it. It was low and dull, not welcoming at all.

"Okay, then," Will said. "Give 'em hell."

"Yeah." Carol hesitated. She thought about giving her paper to Bryan, Bryan reading those things about her husband in his grubby living room. Maybe he would read amusing bits out loud to his commune buddies. Maybe they would all laugh. *Bored housewife,* they would say. *Frigid, too,* Bryan might add.

She climbed out of the car. Will pulled away, and she watched the Riviera gliding off, smooth as a shark in water. She turned to look at the college. She had five minutes before the start of her film exam. It would cover everything they watched: a long, dim Czech film. A Spanish film with no plot. An Italian film about a wife going mad. "This is a beautiful film," the professor had said, but to Carol it looked industrial and depressing. She and Will had seen *Doctor Zhivago* together. That was a beautiful film.

TWA had been the first airline to show films on board. Now all of them did it. It was only the beginning. Will had said. The airlines were on the way back up. People were going to travel more and more. The layoffs were only temporary.

For days Carol had been trying to think of what to write in her self-evaluation for Bryan. *The past is illusion,* she could say, *and the future, too. So anything I have done in this class is an illusion. What matters is that right here, right now, I deserve an A.* The sad thing was, Bryan would give her an A for that.

Something caught her eye. It was the Riviera. Instead of leaving, Will had circled the parking lot and was coming back toward her. She turned to face the car as it passed her and kept on going. She could see Will grinning behind the wheel.

He circled the lot three times, driving too fast. Each time he drove by, he raised his eyebrows at her, as if his not stopping surprised him, too. She was laughing by the time he stopped in front of her. The passenger window glided down, and Will leaned toward it.

"Don't you want to go?" he asked. Carol shook her head. She imagined folding her paper into smaller and smaller squares, until it was tiny enough to swallow.

"I don't want to go," she told her husband.

"Well, get in, then," he said. If there was one thing Will understood, it was this. He opened her door. She looked back. Then she stepped forward, ducked her head, and got in.

ten

"TELL ME AGAIN WHERE YOU ARE NOW."

"I'm at home. My parents' home. It's my sister's wedding."

"And you have your son with you?"

"Yes."

Margaret is on her second lawyer. The first, someone recommended by a friend of Carol's, dismissed Margaret out of hand when he heard she lived in Illinois. No jurisdiction, he'd explained. She'd have to get an Illinois lawyer.

She called Caitlin, her closest friend in Evanston. She told Caitlin she couldn't talk about it right now—yes, she'd call her the minute she was back in Evanston—but she needed a divorce lawyer right away. Caitlin's voice became soft and low in response to the urgency of the situation. Thankfully, she avoiding asking questions or expressing dismay and did as Margaret asked, hauling out her copy of the Chicago Yellow Pages to read Margaret some of the larger display ads. Together they selected a few, and Margaret wrote down the numbers. The first one was a single-lawyer firm, and Margaret was surprised when the receptionist put her through to the man himself. Richard Guattari. The text in his ad read: *Custody cases my specialty.*

"Who is divorcing whom?"

Margaret is surprised by the question. "I don't really know," she says. "We're divorcing each other, I guess."

"But you've been living together until now?"

"Yes."

Richard Guattari coughs, a short sound, like he's squelching an impatient snort. "Illinois has no-fault divorce only for couples who have been living separate and apart for six months. And that's if both parties agree in writing. If one party brings the case against the other, it requires two years. And custody changes everything. There really isn't no-fault divorce if custody is going to be disputed."

"So what does that mean?"

"One of you needs to file against the other, with grounds. Your best bet would be to beat him to the punch there."

"You mean I need to accuse him of something?"

Richard rattles off the list. "Impotence, adultery, abandonment, drunkenness, gross habits, cruelty—look, lady, do you think he's going to file against you?"

"Maybe. I don't know." Margaret tries to imagine David having this conversation.

"If he does file against you, does he have substantiated grounds?"

"You mean can he accuse me of any of those things?"

"More important, can he make it stick."

Margaret cringes. Talking about this with a stranger is even more awful than she expected. There's something so cold and factual about the man's voice. *He's just doing his job,* she tells herself.

"I guess only adultery," she says.

"Right." His voice gets marginally less friendly. "And if you were to file, it sounds as if you've got cruelty, based on the 911 call. That's good. Anything else?"

"Um, adultery, too, I guess," she says. Her voice, frustratingly, comes out small and hesitant.

Richard Guattari sighs in earnest. "Open marriage?" he asks.

Margaret stifles a sudden, nervous urge to laugh. *Open marriage.* It sounds so old-fashioned, so seventies. Flower children and free love. She can just see the scorn on David's face if he heard the phrase. *Rational marriage*—that's what he always called it.

"I guess so."

"His idea?"

"Yes." She clears her throat, trying to moderate her voice's tendency to sound like a little girl in trouble with her father.

"Okay, look." He talks fast, and she thinks she hears the sound of papers shuffling on his desk. "It doesn't look great. He's got adultery, you've got adultery. But in court, women always look worse for agreeing to these—situations than men do for proposing them. I'm not saying it's right, that's just how judges are. On the other hand, you've got the kid. That's good. Hang on to the kid. If your husband comes around, hide. Don't let your parents tell him where you are. Or go away. Take a little vacation. Call him up every night, let him talk to the kid. Use a private line so he can't trace the call. There's a chance he'll bring in the cops, since you went out of state. If you see cops coming, go out the back door. Have your parents say you're gone. Otherwise, they could take the kid. It depends on Michigan law, but there's a good chance. Meanwhile, your best bet is to file quickly, use the cruelty thing, draw attention away from the adultery. I can do that today. Serve him with papers tomorrow. That's what I'd recommend."

"Oh God." Margaret's head is spinning; her feet and hands feel icy. "Isn't there any way I can, it can . . ."

"What?"

"Can't it be some other way? Not so . . . hostile?"

There's a short silence on the other end. Richard's voice sounds more strained and, if possible, colder when he speaks again. "Look, Mrs., uh . . . It sounds like it's hostile already. I'm just telling you how to protect yourself. You do what you want. This was your free consultation. If you want to talk to me again, I'll need a retainer of one thousand dollars. Call my secretary, give her your fax number, and she'll get you the paperwork. You can wire the money or FedEx it. Certified check."

"Okay." Margaret is relieved the conversation is drawing to an end. She wants to be off the phone with this guy.

"In the meantime, you've got to consider how you'd feel being a mother without custody of her child."

"Okay." Quickly, instinctively, Margaret hangs up the phone. For a moment it seems as if Richard Guattari is still there, a presence infecting the room. She crosses her arms and hugs them to her, trying to get warm. *Rewind,* she thinks. *I need to rewind.* But where to? Three days ago? Three weeks ago? Three years ago? Would it be enough to go back to the night Vasant invited her up to his place for a cup of tea, or would she need to go back further?

She closes her eyes and imagines Vasant. She longs more than anything for him to be here now, to put his hands on her shoulders and pull her toward him. She could melt into him and everything else would disappear.

The thought gives her a new resolve. She can't go backward. She can't give him up. But the idea of ever speaking to Richard Guattari again, let alone meeting him in person, is unbearable. And the vision of a court case, the two of them fighting over Trevor, trying to prove each other unworthy, is even worse. It's false. David's a good father. In spite of everything, she knows his connection with his son is strong. Why would she want to ruin that?

Of course there have been moments when he was impatient with Trevor, even annoyed by his presence. Margaret has had those moments, too. There was one night when Trevor was a baby and the two of them were arguing over the graduate student. Trevor began crying, and Margaret felt a hard rage settle in. She sat on the couch, immobile. *Let him go pick up his son,* she thought. *It shouldn't always be me.* She glared at David and he glared back, aware of her protest and settling into his own refusal. Trevor cried harder. Margaret heard every wail as an accusation of David, as if he himself were inflicting the pain. It went on that way for what seemed like hours, though it was probably only ten minutes. Trevor's wails turned to howls, then shrieks. When they became gasping, rattling screams, as if he would scream his breath away, Margaret got up and ran to him. He was deep red with effort, his tiny body shaking with exhaustion and fury, his belly contracting and expanding as though it would pop. She picked him up and held him. But as she paced and quieted him, feeling his fragile, shaking chest, she didn't feel moral satisfaction. She felt only a huge and immutable rage against the fact that David could hold out longer than she could. Her sympathy, her love—they were weaknesses, and he was not above using them against her.

And he will do so now. She doesn't want this war. But she can't go back. She started on this path, and there's nothing to do but to keep going. If she's going to do it, she has to do it right, and although he's awful, Richard Guattari sounds like someone who can do it right for her. Awfulness might be exactly the quality she needs.

Instinctively, she looks around for a piece of paper. She'll make a list of all the things she needs to do. First she has to figure out how to receive a fax. There isn't a Kinko's or anything nearby, but downstairs in the study, her father has a relatively new computer that must have a fax modem in it. She'll just have to load up the software.

The next problem, and it's a substantial one, is how to get the thousand dollars. She and David, being academics, never have very much money in the bank, but even if they did, she can't exactly demand money from David in order to divorce him. The most likely avenue would be to ask her father for it. But then she'll have to tell him why she needs it. Perhaps she can get a cash advance on her credit card.

She should take some money from their joint checking account while she's at it—exactly half, and open her own account, redirecting her direct deposit from Northwestern to it. Then she should call the credit cards to establish a separate line of credit. And she should tell Carol what the lawyer said about the police. It seems unlikely, but the thought of anyone coming and taking Trevor away makes her heart quicken all over again. Carol should know, just to be sure there are no tragic mistakes.

Margaret feels slightly ill. When she stands up from the bed, she feels dizzy. She steps to her parents' dresser and leans on it, avoiding looking in the mirror. David always said she was aging nicely, but Margaret took it as a backhanded compliment. To her eyes, she looked exactly the same. That's how it happens—the changes are so small you can't notice them yourself. Sometimes when she sees herself in pictures, she realizes she used to look different. Nothing specific, just younger. Her grandmother's skin slackened until two long jowls hung down at the sides of her face. Margaret puts a hand to her own cheek, wondering if that will happen to her.

At least now there's something she can do. Her mother was right to make her call a lawyer. As awful as the conversation was, Richard

Guattari has laid out her path. There is action she can take to move forward. Margaret takes a deep breath. She'll go down to the study. The first thing she'll do is find a piece of paper to make her list. Then she'll start with the first item and work her way down.

When Will gets home, Carol is acting strange. He brings the groceries in from the garage—it's raining again—and she doesn't paw through them right away, finding fault with the produce he chose or looking for the one thing he has forgotten. Instead, she just nods from the sink, where she's scrubbing a large punch bowl, jerking her head toward the kitchen table to indicate that he should leave the bags there. He clumps over and sets them down, then turns to watch what she's doing. She has a toothbrush and is going at the cut crystal.

"I don't know how this punch bowl got so dirty," she says, her back to him. "It was sitting on those shelves in the basement. I don't know what you do down there to get everything so filthy."

This line of conversation is a little more normal, but still, she's hunched over the sink as if protecting something from him, not wanting to give anything away.

"Where is everybody?" he asks.

"Margaret's upstairs. Kit and Leanne are watching CNN in the living room. Trevor's in there with them." She stops and half turns toward him. "I think he's getting a little bored. Maybe you could take him downstairs and amuse him for a little while."

There it is. A blatant attempt to get rid of him. Put out to pasture with the kiddies, just like the FAA is going to put him out to pasture on his sixtieth birthday. Something is going on, but he's never going to get it out of Carol. Or anyone else, for that matter. Nobody tells him anything.

Ex-pilot, he thinks. *Ex-patriarch.*

"Yeah, all right," he says.

Carol goes back to her punch bowl. Will wanders out of the kitchen into the living room. Kit and Leanne are on the couch.

Leanne is curled up on her side, clutching her knees to her chest just like she did when she was little. Carol used to hate seeing her lying there in her last years of high school. *Don't you have anything better to do,* she would ask, *than turning your brain to jelly?* Leanne would shrug. Carol's disapproval had been a new thing. When Leanne was younger, she and Carol would watch television together. Will would find the two of them together, curled up on opposite ends of the couch, mirror images of each other. Margaret didn't watch much TV. She always had homework or somewhere to go.

Now it's Kit slouched on the couch with Leanne, one arm draped behind her. The news is on, but they have the sound down so low Will can hardly hear it, especially with the water running in the kitchen.

"Hey," Kit greets Will. Leanne looks up and doesn't speak, but she smiles at him. A small, rather sad smile, he thinks. He looks around for Trevor.

"I hear there's a bored five-year-old around here," he says.

"I think he went down to the basement," Kit says. Leanne has turned back to the news. Will stops and watches. They're showing a satellite feed of military action. Small, dim lights are bobbing forward into darkness. The reporter, blurry and digitized, is leaning toward the camera, speaking urgently about their position. His description of the terrain—hills, rocks, roads, gullies—could be coming from anywhere, though it must be Afghanistan. The war has dropped from the headlines, but Will keeps up with it. It's all happening on the ground now, U.S. troops sealing off caves along the Pakistan border. Earlier it was all about air power. With the GPSs and the laser-guided bombs, air superiority is finally the advantage the joint chiefs of staff insisted it would turn out to be in Vietnam. They were wrong then. Now they're right. They looked smug when he saw them being interviewed on TV, showing satellite maps of targets or computer simulations of pilots dropping bombs. They were even using unmanned airplanes to deliver ordnance. That would have saved a few guys in 1967.

The segment ends and a report about hurricanes takes over. The National Weather Service is predicting six to eight this year. Will watches the computer simulations. Lately, whenever he watches the news, he has an odd sensation that he's waiting for something. There's a story in all that noise that belongs to him. The thing that will finally get him.

"All right," he says, "I'll guess I'll go see how Trevor's doing."

"Okay," Kit says, his eyes flicking up briefly from the television. Leanne's head drops onto the back of the sofa, and her eyes close. For an instant Will thinks she going to speak, but she doesn't move. He makes his exit unwatched.

In the finished part of the basement, Carol has set up a small toy area for her grandson. With the kid-sized furniture that used to belong to the girls and the box of toys Carol has collected, it's usually the first place Trevor heads when he arrives. But he's not there now. He's standing at the other end of the carpeted rec room, in front of Will's glass cabinet. His airplane models.

"I like these," Trevor breathes as Will approaches. "Look at that one."

"That's a Lockheed 1011," Will tells him. "That airplane was way ahead of its time when it came out. We were all excited to fly it."

"My mom's daddy used to fly airplanes," the boy says.

"That's me," Will says. "And I still fly airplanes."

Trevor looks at him, his brow furrowing just like Margaret's did at his age. "Do these ones fly?" he asks.

"No," Will says. "They're model airplanes. I built them all."

"Do you play with them?"

"No." Will laughs. "Not really."

"What do you do with them?"

Will pauses. "I look at them," he says. "They make me remember flying the real ones." He points to a 707 mounted on a gray curved stand, the old TWA logo on its tail. "See that plane? That was the first commercial jet they ever built in this country." He loves the shape of it, the solid fuselage, the wings swept back 35 degrees, as became the jet standard, the tail with its snazzy forward-pointing spike. They weren't thinking about cramming people into narrow seats back then, or reducing fuel consumption, but about the speed and excitement of air travel. Even the old red and gold TWA logo suggested elegance and glamour. Not like today—the MD-80, a cheap filter cigarette, the generic 767, stripped of any detail that might give it personality. The new TWA paint jobs weren't bad, but now they're being methodically blasted off, replaced with American's boring red, white, and blue stripes.

"Before there were jets, people rode horses everywhere." Trevor's eyes are wide, and he nods, encouraging Will to agree with him.

"Well, not exactly," Will says. "There were a few steps in between horse carriages and jets. First there were little airplanes. Then there were propeller planes." He points to a Constellation, also mounted on a small stand. "See how that plane has four propellers?"

"I like that one," Trevor says.

"So do I." Will admires the airplane. "In those days, TWA was the most glamorous airline. Everybody dreamed of flying it—movie stars, politicians."

"T double A," Trevor repeats quietly.

"That was my airline, you know. Until a man named Carl Icahn came along and destroyed it. Now it's gone." He can't help the bitterness in his voice. Right up until American's acquisition, Carl Icahn was undercutting TWA's sales, using the Internet to sell the cheap tickets he got in his buyout deal. TWA agreed to give him the tickets because they were so eager to get rid of him. They didn't realize they were shooting themselves in the foot.

Trevor looks at Will, confused. "What did they do with the airplanes?" he asks.

"They sold them to another airline."

"What did they do with the airlines?"

Will laughs. "You said it, Trevor," he tells him. "That's the question I've been asking myself. What did they do with the airlines?"

He says it in a joking tone, but his voice cracks slightly, and a wave of sadness washes over him. What did they do with the airlines? What did they do with the world? Icahn was a businessman for today's era, when making a good product or offering a good service is no longer a sufficient corporate goal. It's all about shareholders now, and shareholders are interested in only one thing: selling their stock for more than they paid.

He and Carol were so excited when he got the letter offering him a job at TWA. They were in Hawaii. Will had been transported out of Bien Hoi in Saigon in December 1967. A month later, it was overrun in the Tet Offensive. He watched the reports on television, from his hospital room. A metal pin had been inserted to hold his leg together. He would be fine, but he wouldn't be a fighter pilot anymore.

Four months later, they moved to Kansas City for his TWA training. They flew to San Francisco, then took a train to Kansas City, sitting up all the way to save money. Will was still in uniform, waiting for his discharge papers. Martin Luther King Jr., had been shot two days before. Cities were rioting, college girls were weeping in public. Lyndon Johnson had announced he wouldn't run for reelection. The war was an increasing disaster. The tide of public opinion had swung for real.

As they got on the train and took their seats, a woman across the aisle stood up. "I'm moving," she announced loudly, grappling her bag from the overhead rack. She looked stiff with fury as she glanced his way. "I don't want to sit near a baby-killer."

Did you ever kill a baby, Will? Carol never asked him that question. But Will heard it hovering, shimmering in the air between them.

"I want to play with them," Trevor says. He's still standing in front of the display case. Will looks around for something else to distract the boy. No one ever touches his planes. But then he thinks, *What the hell.* He opens the case.

"Just one," he tells Trevor. The boy waits, rigid with eagerness. Will reaches for the Connie, then changes his mind. The propellers could break off. He takes the 707 instead, lifting it gently off its stand.

"Be careful with it," he says.

Trevor beams at the airplane in his hand. Then he shoots his arm out, lifting the plane as high as he can. "To the moon!" he cries.

Will slumps onto the cast-off couch they keep in the rec room. He rests his palms on his thighs, giving in to tiredness. Thirty-three years—that's how long he flew for TWA. He can't get used to being an American pilot. Last month, when air traffic control hailed him as "AA 77," he failed to answer. He was used to blocking out other flights being hailed. Finally, after two or three times, the guy on the ground guessed what was happening. "TW 77," he said loudly, and Will heard him. It became a big joke in the cockpit.

Now he'll have to adjust to flying for Cathay Pacific. At least that will be his own decision, not something imposed on him—like pay cuts and pension reductions—by a corporate merger. Or retirement forced on him by the FAA. He clasps his hands behind his head. Trevor is loping from one end of the room to the other, the 707 held high.

"Grandpa's going to tell you a secret, Trevor," Will says. "You want to hear it?"

Trevor stops and looks at Will. "Okay," he says. He takes the 707 down to a lower altitude but keeps it airborne.

"TWA is gone. But Grandpa's going to fly for a new airline now. One in Asia. Do you know where Asia is?" The boy shakes his head. "Well, it's where China and Japan are. Would you like to come visit China some day?"

"I don't know." Trevor looks back at the 707, starting a holding pattern at shoulder height. "I might have a playdate."

Leanne and Kit are watching CNN when Margaret comes downstairs. Leanne looks up as her sister half enters the room. "What's up?"

Margaret doesn't answer. She looks strange. Her hair is messy, but her clothes are perfect: blue linen pants and a perfectly ironed white blouse. Her face is set in a blank hardness. The effect is grim and vulnerable at the same time.

"I need to use Dad's computer," she says. "Is he in there?" Her voice has a tone that forestalls any speech but a direct answer.

"He's in the basement with Trevor."

"Good." Margaret opens the door of their father's study and sighs before stepping inside.

Margaret's presence infects Leanne with a restless feeling. She ought to be doing something. She sits up. Kit's attention is gripped by a story about the resurgence of mountain lions in California. His hand drags lightly along her leg as she leaves.

Her mother is in the kitchen. "Do you need some help?" Leanne asks.

Carol looks up from an array of small candleholders on the kitchen counter. "I'm just putting tea lights in these votives," she says. "But you could help by starting dinner, if you like."

"What are we having? Leftover gumbo?"

"I guess so," Carol says. "There's so much of it."

"Where is it?"

"In the freezer. There just wasn't any more room in the fridge."

Leanne goes to the freezer. "Okay. I'll just pop it on the stove."

She waits for her mother to say the microwave would be faster. That's what she would do with Margaret. Margaret hates microwaves, and Carol always feels obliged to defend them. But with Leanne, she doesn't seem to need to assert herself that way. Leanne doesn't like the microwave any more than Margaret does. But if her mother had suggested she use it, she'd have done so.

Leanne finds the gumbo containers in the freezer and empties three of them into a large pot. The gumbo has just started to freeze, and it slides out of the plastic in a slushy stream. Leanne pours it slowly, watching the little crystals flow downward.

"I think everything we need tomorrow is clean," Carol tells her. "I washed the table linens today. Tomorrow morning, after the rehearsal, we'll get started setting up."

"What time are people arriving?"

"Six."

Tomorrow night it will be over. There really will be no turning back after forty people come over and toast her and Kit. After that, there's only the ceremony. Leanne pushes the gumbo around with a wooden spoon and looks at the trays of glasses, the platters and serving bowls her mother has assembled on the counter. All these solid objects somehow make it seem possible. It's not such a big event, really, just a formalization of something that's already true: she and Kit are together. All the fuss is a way to make her mother happy, to offer family friends and relatives a chance to see that she has grown up, that she has a life of her own now. Afterward, she and Kit will go back to their lives in Cold Spring. Very little will have changed. They can sort out the Mexico thing then. She thinks of Mexico City, sprawling across a dried-up lake bed, ringed by blue mountains. There are volcanoes on three sides of it.

"If you want any of these things after the wedding," her mother says, gesturing to the countertop array of serving ware, "you should pack them up and mail them to yourself."

"But why?" Leanne asks. "Aren't you going to need them for the bed-and-breakfast?"

"I'm getting new stuff," Carol says. "Country-style things."

"You're replacing all the china and glassware in the house?"

"Not everything, but the things I'll need for serving guests. Actually, I have a lot already. There are those big boxes we got from Will's father when your grandmother died."

Leanne contemplates her mother. When Will's mother died, his father had assumed Carol would want a lot of her stuff. "What am I going to do with all this junk?" Carol had said when the box arrived. She had the girls help her repack everything neatly and put it away in the basement. "We can't sell it," she told them, "but it's not exactly our style."

"So this bed-and-breakfast idea," Leanne says, swirling the spoon aimlessly through the softening gumbo. "You're sure you want the hassle of it?"

"What hassle?" Carol says. She's setting the table. "It will give me something to do out here, with you guys so faraway."

"Yeah, but you could find something else to do. You and Dad could travel."

Carol snorts. "Your father's not going to want to travel once he's retired," she says. "He's sick of flying. He hates American. He's going to want to sit here and play farmer boy, like he's always dreamed."

Leanne thinks of the letter she found in the barn. So her mother knows nothing about it. Cathay Pacific is based in Hong Kong. He's probably expecting Carol to pack up and go there with him. When did he plan on telling her?

"When's dinner?" Her father has clumped up the stairs from the basement. Trevor hovers behind him, a small airplane in his hand—one of her father's models. Leanne glances up, surprised.

"Dinner's in about five minutes," she tells him.

It would make sense for him to be sick of the airlines. It must be even more stressful to be a pilot today. But flying is what he has always loved. He claimed to love the farm more, claimed to miss it on his trips, but when he was home, she could see him getting restless, itching to be airborne. She looks at Trevor, by the kitchen table, taxiing the plane along a plate.

"Hey, Trevor," she says, going over and gently removing the model from his hand. "Time to go wash your hands for dinner." She admires the 707 before setting it at the back of the counter, out of Trevor's reach.

Once, when she had just turned thirteen, she asked her father why he moved back to Michigan. It was late at night, and they were driving home from O'Hare. For her birthday he had taken her with him on an L.A. trip.

He stared straight ahead for a long time. His face glowed yellow every time a car passed from the opposite direction.

"In the war once, I was on a mission," he said after a long time. "And I saw a village. It looked just like Ryville." He stopped, still staring forward. Leanne wondered if that was all. He glanced over and saw her watching him.

"Only it had been destroyed," he said. "It didn't exist anymore."

"I see." But Leanne wasn't sure she did. She was uncomfortable, still young enough to be unused to her parents talking to her like a grown-up. "It was like a sign," she said, wanting to finish the tale, to mark its end so they could go back to riding in silence.

"That's right," he said gently. "A sign." He was letting it go.

Can you make a place exist by being there? Leanne wondered. But then that didn't make sense. She looked at her father, his eyes on the road ahead. The car dove forward into the night. Leanne leaned her head against the window, listened to it swim.

eleven

WILL IS COMING IN LOW, CLOSE TO THE DECK, THERE'S a staticky wailing in his ears. It's the radar-seeking Shrike, sensing a SAM site. His wing leader banks left. Will follows suit.

Ahead is a tiny cluster of what look like buildings. He can see them only when he jinks right or left. Now that they're diving in head-on, he can't see them at all.

"I'm on target," the wing leader says. "Hit my smoke." The Shrike is squealing like a stuck pig. In fact, it sounds exactly like a stuck pig. He looks out his window to the left, and it *is* a pig, attached to his wing in a small harness.

"What the hell?" he cries.

"I'm going in," the wing leader says, and then Will is diving, too, his plane following of its own accord. He keeps glancing at the pig, hearing its frantic noise, and then he sees the target. A farm. It's not Vietnam at all; it's Michigan. He sees the familiar white house, the stubby red barn, the blue Harvestore silo. Cornfield to the east, wheat field to the south, perfect rectangles of green.

"Wait!" he yells. He pulls as hard as he can on the yoke, but his plane keeps on diving. The pig has stopped squealing. Will looks out the window, and it meets his eyes serenely.

It's okay, he tells himself. *I'm only hitting them with a pig.*

He dives left. The ground tilts on its side and reaches for him. He eases the plane through the barrel roll, the ground slipping over his head, then wrapping around to his right. Slowly, with great effort, he reaches out and launches the pig. It sails away from his plane, gliding quickly on a shiny pair of wings. But as it heads for the ground, it begins to pull up and back in a big arching circle, curving around and heading back toward Will. It comes on fast, its expression no longer serene but malevolent.

He wakes up. He doesn't yell anymore, he barely even jerks. His eyes fly open and he's there, in his bed at home, almost sixty years old. The light is coming up outside. From the look of it, the rain may have stopped. It's Friday, one day before his younger daughter's wedding. He looks at the clock: 6:06. In twelve hours there will be forty guests drinking champagne in his home. He sighs and rolls over. Maybe he can get another hour of sleep.

It's funny, he never dreams about flying commercially, though there have been plenty of scares there, too. He's landed planes with engines that died, or worse, flamed out and slung compressor blades every which way, banging holes in the fuselage. He's had a rear tire blow out at V1 on takeoff, leaving him the bad option of a go-around or the worse option of aborting and risking a lethal slide off the end of the runway. Once a Cessna appeared out of nowhere on his final approach, and he had to take evasive action to avoid ramming into it. Luckily, he was flying the 707 at the time, one of the most maneuverable jets there was, and one of the fastest, until the airlines got rid of them because with four engines, they were too expensive to fly.

The clock blinks ahead a minute: 6:10. Commercial flying is safer now than when he started. The month after he joined TWA, one of their Convair 880s crashed into trees on a nighttime visual approach in Cincinnati. It was snowing, the glide slope wasn't working, and they just miscalculated. It was an easy mistake. Will knew one of the guys on the crew, and when he heard about the crash, his heart sank. Losing buddies was something he figured he had left behind in Vietnam. Sixty-five of the seventy-five passengers died in the crash. *Do I really want this responsibility?* he had asked himself. He was flying the 880 himself. What if he screwed up? Later, when the NTSB report came out, Will pored over the blow-by-blow account, determined not to repeat that mistake. It couldn't even happen now: visual flight is a thing of the past.

He closes his eyes, trying not to look at the clock. A green after-image of the red numbers glows on his eyelids: 6:13.

There aren't as many hijackings now, either, in spite of all the terror fears and heightened airport security. In his first four years, sixteen planes were hijacked, and that was just TWA. As America's lead airline, they bore the brunt of it, but others were getting slammed, too. Of course, in those days, even hijacking was more civilized. If the hijackers got nailed, they gave up quickly. If not, they got taken to Cuba or Italy or Beirut, and it ended there. Sometimes they torched the plane to make a statement, but they let the passengers and crew go first. Still, TWA got sick of it. After a few years, they stormed a hijacked plane at JFK, and that put the lid on hijackings for a few years.

Blink: 6:16. It's no use. Will sits up and rubs both hands on his face. He might as well get up. He slides his feet out of bed and stands up, feeling especially stiff in his pinned leg. It's the humidity. All this rain in the past few days, and—if his stiffness can be believed—more to come. Sometimes when it rains he gets a dull, distant ache, so deep it's almost more the idea of an ache than real pain. Collateral damage.

The house is bright as he pads down the stairs. It's funny, when the girls come home, the house doesn't feel overtaken, the way it does when there are guests staying over. It just goes back to feeling the way it always did, full of the electricity the family generates as a unit. His stomach yawns and gurgles. Margaret's gumbo was delicious, but it wasn't that filling. He could use some breakfast.

As he heads into the kitchen, he's surprised to see Leanne. She's standing at the kitchen window, gazing outside. Something about her demeanor looks closed off, as if she has withdrawn into her own skin. She often has that look, that feeling of distance. When she was little and something she'd done caused a response from people around her, she always acted surprised. It was as if she expected to make no impression on the world, but to glide through it silent as a deer.

"Hey you, what's up?" he says. His voice comes out more jovial than he means it to be.

She lifts her head toward him without turning around. "I remember you building that deck," she says. It sounds like a line intended to throw him off the scent of her real thoughts.

"Yeah." He looks at the back of her. She's taller than Carol, and her hair comes from his side of the family. His mother. "That was when I was laid off."

She's silent, and he thinks that might be the end of it. "I always thought it was weird," she says. "Having the furniture built in like that."

Surprised, he looks past her out the window to the deck, gray in the morning light. "Why weird?" he asks.

"I don't know," she says. "Just weird to put it all in there, fixed, like that. How do you know that's where you're going to want to use it? Or even that it's the right furniture to have?"

Will shrugs. "What other furniture could you possibly want?"

Leanne turns toward him. "I don't know," she says. It's a statement, clear and final, a declaration. Will is struck by how definitive it sounds. *I don't know.* That, he thinks, is all the conviction she has.

The sun is shining on the bed when Carol's eyes pop open. She looks at the clock: 6:30. Today's the day. They have the run-through this morning. Kit's mother, Bernice, will be picked up in the afternoon, and the cocktail-party guests arrive at six. Last night at dinner, Carol laid out the plan. After the rehearsal, Will and Kit will go to Grand Rapids to pick up Bernice, while Leanne makes sure the best guest room is ready: towels, toiletries, sheets, flowers. Then Margaret is going to give Leanne a manicure, since she refused to make an appointment at a nail salon in Kalamazoo. Carol will start the cooking in the morning, and the girls will help her in the afternoon. Once Will is back from the airport, he'll be on call, for any last-minute trips to the store. They will start setting up at four and make sure all the food is laid out by five thirty. That will give them half an hour to set up the bar.

"Will." Carol rolls over, but he's not there. She rises and quickly puts on the capri pants and matching T-shirt she laid out the night before. Thank goodness the rain stopped, so she doesn't have to find something else to wear. She'll shower and dress for real closer to the time of the party. She likes to do it that way, so she's fresh when the guests arrive.

Slipping downstairs, she can hear the coffeemaker's long, gurgling sigh. That's one thing she won't have to do. They won't have eaten, though, so she'll cook something quick, oatmeal perhaps, to get them going. But first she wants to check on the doves.

The flapping starts as soon as the door to the garage smacks shut behind her. Carol flicks on the garage light and goes over to their cage, leaning to see inside. They're both alive. The smaller one is still bright-eyed and active. The larger one seems better than yesterday. He's not holding his wing strangely, and he has moved from one side of the cage to the other. She hopes that means he's eaten something.

"One more day," she whispers to them. "Just one more day, and then you'll be free to fly off and do whatever you want." She wonders if the doves will live the same life they had before, or if they'll be transformed by their experience. Perhaps they'll resettle in Michigan and make a better life. Maybe they'd been living somewhere awful—Delaware or New Jersey—somewhere with polluted air and huge freeways. Now they can live a nice life amid woods and lakes and fields. Will other birds accept them? She's heard that if a person touches a baby bird, its mother won't take it back. But that's probably not true of grown doves. Besides, they'll both have the same smell. At least they'll have each other.

Carol adds a few more seeds to their paper plate and goes back in the house. Now for breakfast. It's a little warm for oatmeal, but it's always good to have a nice, solid breakfast when you have a big day ahead.

Leanne and Will are sitting at the kitchen table. Each has a cup of coffee. Leanne is staring out the window.

"We forgot something," Carol tells Will.

"What?" He looks only half awake. He should have slept longer. He must have been having his insomnia again.

"We forgot to chill the champagne. There are three cases of it down in the basement. You've got to go load it into the basement fridge."

"Okay, no problem." He says it easily, without really taking it in or moving from his position in his chair. His bare feet are planted heavily on the kitchen floor.

"Will, *now*. Please." She hates to nag, but she needs to make sure he does it. If she leaves it, it will never get done. "When you come back up, I'll have some breakfast ready."

"All right, all right." He drains his coffee mug and pushes himself to his feet, slowly, like an old man. He gives her a sarcastic salute as he ambles by her to the sink and plunks his mug down inside it.

On the way out the kitchen door, he passes Margaret. She's wearing her running clothes and carrying an empty yogurt container.

"I was just about to make breakfast," Carol tells her.

"Don't bother for me," Margaret says, stepping on the garbage-can pedal. "I just had a yogurt. I'm going for a quick run, and then I'll be back to help you. Trevor's still sleeping." She gives her mother a softer look than usual. Last night she told Carol what the lawyer had said. The idea of police coming to take Trevor away is so awful that Carol can't even let herself think about it. She's a little surprised Margaret is leaving the house to run. But she looks better this morning, calmer. Maybe knowing things are in the hands of a professional has helped. Surely David will stop acting this way when he hears from the lawyer. He'll see that he'd better shape up if he wants to see his son at all.

"Let Trevor sleep as long as possible," Margaret says. "I'll be back in half an hour."

"I'll have more coffee made," Carol tells her, meaning *I'll make sure Trevor's okay.*

"Thanks, Mom," Margaret says. She leans forward and looks as if she's going to say more, but then turns around and, taking Will's mug out of the sink, fills it with water and drains it quickly. She rises up onto her toes and bounces a couple of times, taking a deep breath, then half turns to give a small wave before moving lightly out of the kitchen.

The front door opens and shuts quietly. It occurs to Carol that this would be a good time to start making the crab dip. She has bought canned crab for it, and she knows Margaret would say something about fresh crab being better. Carol didn't even dare put the crab on Margaret's shopping list; she had Will get it yesterday in Kalamazoo. She can have the dip made by the time Margaret gets back, and she'll never know. People love Carol's crab dip, can or no can.

"So, Mom."

Carol gives a tiny jump, startled. She'd forgotten Leanne was there, still sitting at the table in her pajamas. "What's on the agenda for this morning?" She stands up, offering her lanky physical self.

Carol sets the can aside. "I was just getting started on the cooking," she says, "but I planned to make oatmeal for everyone."

Leanne looks out the sliding doors at the sun shining on the deck. Her face is a little pale. "Kit is happy with coffee and toast," she says. "And I don't think I could eat anything."

"Aren't you feeling well?" Carol's mind races to the shrimp. Maybe Margaret didn't cook them well enough. Or maybe that chicken she bought from Peterson had worms. Carol has never liked eating chickens fresh from the farm. You never know what diseases they could have.

"No, not sick," Leanne says. "I just feel a little . . . tense."

"Oh, honey." Carol moves to her daughter. "You've got wedding nerves, that's all. Something to eat will do you good."

"Whatever." Leanne sits back down, and the way she flops into the chair suggests a forlorn adolescent rather than a grown, soon-to-be-married woman with her own home and a lovely, successful business. A brief flash of anger causes Carol's jaw to flex, but she squelches it quickly. Here is her baby, nervous on the day before her wedding. She halts behind Leanne's chair.

"Later, I'll need your help washing and trimming vegetables," she says. "That's always the biggest chore." A job to do—that will perk Leanne up.

"Okay." Leanne has her arms wrapped around her own middle, and she speaks so faintly Carol can hardly hear her. Carol hovers, her hands on the back of the chair, unsure what to do. A familiar, tight feeling of annoyance with her younger daughter is rising in her chest.

"I wish we could just sit here in our pajamas all day and drink coffee," Leanne says. She leans her head back so that it rests against Carol's stomach, and with that touch, Carol's anger evaporates. She puts her hands on Leanne's shoulders and kneads them gently. The head grows heavier against her.

"That would be nice," Carol says. "We could have a yazy day." When Leanne was little, she liked nothing better than to crawl into bed with her mother in the morning, lugging a book. Carol would read, too, and sometimes the two of them would spend hours under the covers, reading and drinking hot chocolate. Carol called it having a "lazy day," and Leanne, whose l's were a long time in coming, rechristened them "yazy." It's funny how moments like that, when nothing actually happened, sometimes strike Carol as her fondest memories. As if stillness and empty time could be the high points of a mother's life.

"I wish we could do it," Carol says. She stops kneading and gives Leanne's shoulders a pat. "But we have a lot to do today if we're going to be ready for the big event."

The sun is warm, and the weather is still humid. After all that rain, it feels as if there's warm steam rising up from the ground. Margaret puts a hand up to shade her eyes and looks down the road. By nine it's going to be uncomfortably hot. It's good she got going early.

She heads west first, intending the same back-and-forth route as yesterday. She checks her watch as she starts out, determined to keep track of her pace. As she settles into her stride, breathing the slightly asphalty morning air, her mind cycles through her to-do list. Yesterday she set up the fax modem on her father's computer, and with his help after dinner, she got it hooked into the house's second phone line, the one he uses for the Web. She told him Carol wanted it for the bed-and-breakfast, which was in fact true. Carol had been delighted to hear she was setting it up.

By the time they were fax-ready, Richard Guattari's office was closed, but Margaret called anyway and left a message with his secretary, giving her the number. She's expecting the paperwork this morning. She called Visa and established her own line of credit, with the new card to be sent to her departmental address. Once the bank opens in Illinois, she'll call and move half the money from their joint account into her own. She's hoping there will be enough to cover the retainer. In case there's not, she has left her American Express card activated, so she can draw on its line of credit.

Once she has sent the money to Guattari, it will just be a matter of waiting. Divorce on the grounds of cruelty. Yes, David was cruel to her—at least briefly—but it's strange to think of herself as someone who was suffering cruelty. It's wrong, somehow. But it's the only way.

Has he harmed you?

She reaches the first road and turns around, bouncing lightly on her feet, ridding her mind of the thought. Better to concentrate on the wedding, on the day's specific tasks. Today is just a matter of following her mother's instructions. There will be cooking and setup, Leanne to help get ready, Margaret's own dress to be checked on and ironed if necessary. Other than that, there's not a whole lot to do. Leanne has gone for a low-maintenance wedding: small, outdoors, casual. She seems unconcerned with the details that drive brides crazy—perfecting her hairdo, checking on the food, giving the photographer a list of shots. She's drifting through the wedding the way she drifts through life: vaguely confident that things will work out in the end. Leanne has always seemed reluctant to make decisions about anything, as if she believes trying too hard will guarantee disappointment.

Still, it's Leanne's wedding, and if she's letting things slide, it's not Margaret's place to set her straight. She wasted a lot of time when they were young, trying to convince Leanne to be different. If

Leanne is happy with things as they are, there's no reason to intervene. Margaret's only concern is to get herself through tonight's party and tomorrow's ceremony. It won't be so bad. She can chat with her relatives, trot out her lame excuse for David's absence, let them fawn over Trevor. It will be nice to see them, to engage in normal family niceties.

But nothing in her life is normal. Richard Guattari, David, all her arrangements—behind all of it hovers the figure of Vasant. Vasant with the hands, with the eyes that made her feel like a different kind of person, the kind of person who might do anything. She takes a deep breath and stops herself. She won't think about Vasant. That's her treat, the indulgence she'll allow herself later, when everything is settled or at least under way. Now there are other things she should think about. For instance, Doug.

A fleeting anger makes her speed up her step, but she quickly slows back down, checking her watch. Slightly ahead of pace. She slows down more. She doesn't want to exhaust herself. There's really no reason to be angry. Her mother was acting like she always does, wanting everyone to partake in her triumph. And it is a triumph, getting Leanne married. For a while it had looked like Leanne was going to let her life go down the drain. Margaret doesn't know the details, but she does know that it was Carol who helped Leanne get back on track. Carol once admitted to Margaret that the seed money she gave Leanne for her store was everything she had saved to open her own children's clothing store. It might be why she's so interested in getting the bed-and-breakfast going now. She's always wanted a business of her own.

As for Doug, there's no reason Margaret shouldn't enjoy seeing him. When she dumped him just before graduation, after a year together, he never threw in her face what he must have known—that she got rid of him like a bad haircut, in preparation for going off to college and becoming a different kind of person.

As for her mother inviting him to the cocktail party, there's no reason to think she was being hostile. She always hated the fact that Margaret was seeing a farmer's son, but as soon as it became clear that Margaret was headed for the University of Chicago—with Doug playing no part in the plan—Carol's relief, in spite of her efforts to hide it, was palpable.

Carol never knew about the time Doug visited Margaret at Chicago. It was during her first semester, and Margaret had been shocked when he called and proposed the trip. She suspected his motive was to have it out with her for dumping him the year before. Still, she couldn't think of how to say no. The prospect of Doug's anger was remote to her, strangely unaffecting. She had just taken three midterms, her history professor had mentioned a summer archaeological dig Margaret might want to join, and she was in the midst of a flirtation with a guy in her "Greek Thought" class. Doug and his broken heart—in fact, everything about Michigan—seemed very faraway to her.

Now it's that trip, more than anything else, that haunts Margaret. She remembers seeing Doug arrive, watching him amble toward her and thinking with dismay what a stereotype he was. He even made his entrance like a country boy in the movies: by Greyhound. He came down the narrow bus stairs with a blue canvas satchel and a scowl that announced his intention of despising city life. *Bulldog*, Margaret thought as he moved through the crowd. Her roommate, Alexis, loved dogs, and she saw a breed in everyone. She had declared Margaret a Border collie. Doug was a bulldog: squat and solid and ready for a fight. "Look at you," he growled when he saw Margaret.

But it wasn't animosity, at least not toward her. As they rode the city bus to Hyde Park, she could sense his disapproval, but it was for the dilapidated neighborhood gliding past. It was one of the university's conundrums: reconciling its ivory-tower appeal with the urban wasteland encircling it. Margaret liked the contrast. Both worlds—the ornate neo-Gothic buildings of the college and the dilapidated row houses of Hyde Park—summoned in her a rush of gratitude. Both were as far from rural Michigan as they could be. Walking across the quad to the library or watching a homeless man pushing a shopping cart along the street, Margaret often stopped, elbows tight to her side, to hold in the thrill at having finally laid hands on her life.

So if he wasn't going to chastise her, why had Doug come? Even now his reasons are murky to Margaret. At the time, she was less inclined to concern herself with the question of his motives. She took him to the dorm room she shared with Alexis, who was on the swim team and active in intramural soccer. She had a desk planner spidery with color-coded entries to keep track of her highly sched- uled life. Early on, she had started calling Margaret "the Brain," and Margaret responded by nicknaming Alexis "the Brawn."

"Where is she?" Doug asked after inspecting Alexis's desk—the planner, the corkboard jammed with notes, the postcards and pho- tos of her Corgi back home.

"Away at a swim meet. They're in St. Louis or somewhere." When Doug had called to propose the visit, Margaret had checked Alexis's desk calendar and chosen a weekend when she'd be away. The thought of introducing Doug to any of her Chicago friends had made her cringe.

Doug looked her up and down. His gaze fell on her feet, and his brow furrowed, puzzled. She had on her new shoes, clunky men's- style oxfords. They were part of her freshman-year uniform: a long knit skirt, a white shirt, and a men's jacket from a used-clothing store. She liked to think it was an appealing intellectual look, half *Breakfast Club,* half *Annie Hall.*

Doug's eyes traveled back up the length of her to her face, and Margaret remembered, in a shivery rush, what had attracted her to Doug in high school. It was the way he projected a feeling of baffled desire. He made her feel like an exotic creature, a bird he followed because he couldn't name it.

"Come here," he said, sitting down on the bed, and Margaret almost laughed. The country boy—a man of few words and simple desires. When they were dating, she had always stopped just short of having sex. Several months into college, she had slept with more than one fellow student. "The Brain's a slut," Alexis would say when Margaret came in late on a weekend morning, rumpled in the previous night's clothes. They called each other "slut" and "tart" all the time. It was a badge of their newfound freedom.

Thinking of who she used to be and of who she had become, Margaret had a giddy sensation of power. She had always liked Doug, the way he felt and smelled. She had dumped him not out of revulsion but because she was moving on, from him, from the life he stood for. He was completely incongruous, standing in her dorm room, but he was the one out of place. This was her world, and she was comfortable in it.

"No," she said.

A tiny spark of electricity ran through her as Doug stood up and walked over to her. Without even looking at her face, he began undoing her shirt buttons, moving quickly, like a man who doesn't want to lose his momentum. He slid her shirt and jacket backward down her arms with straightforward, almost clinical intent.

It wasn't like sleeping with other guys. There, the excitement had always been the unfamiliarity, the sense of moving into uncharted territory. Doug felt familiar. They knew each other well, like childhood friends. He didn't seem awkward, or even eager, so much as focused. There was something flat and almost childlike in the way he proceeded along her. Margaret felt, for the first time, the thrilling sensation of letting someone else's desires—whatever they were—take over.

She reaches the next road and turns around, raising her eyes from the asphalt. The sky is clear and sunny. The ground is giving off an earthy smell as it warms up. She wants to get in five miles before it gets too hot. She can see a car, a tiny black speck, wavering slightly in the distance.

Has he harmed you?

Not yet.

She shakes her head. The earthy smell is tinged with the familiar, syrupy scent of something rotting. She glances around, but there's no obvious culprit. It's strange that decay should smell sweet.

There's a thin buzzing sound, a nearby swarm of flies. She picks up her pace, moving past it, and the scent is gone.

That first evening she showed Doug around the campus, the dorms, the neo-Gothic library, the large open space called the Midway. On their way back to the dorm, Margaret noticed some people she knew walking toward them. Quickly, smoothly, she turned onto another path, averting her head.

"I thought the dorm was that way," Doug said, his sense of direction infallible as a draft horse's.

"Yeah," Margaret replied, "but I wanted to show you the library. Where I spend all my time."

Back in her room, they ordered a pizza, sitting on the floor to eat it. Margaret found herself telling Doug about her classes: the tight mathematical precision of a Latin sentence, the astonishing events of the Athenian war against Persia.

"This tiny colony of democrats," she told him, shaking her head in awe. "And they just attacked the most powerful empire on earth!"

She told him how her plans had shifted from doing pre-law to majoring in history, how her adviser had suggested a museum internship, how she was thinking of grad school. Once or twice she stopped, convinced he must find it boring, but he shook his head.

"It's not boring," he said. "It sounds exciting."

Margaret was surprised by his interest, and by how comfortable she felt talking to him. "It is exciting," she told him. "It's a whole new world. I feel like I can finally be who I am."

She was surprised when they didn't have sex again, even though they slept in her narrow single bed. She lay on her side to make more room, and Doug's body curled around hers, warm but distant, as if he were thinking of other things. His arm was draped over her body, and Margaret moved her head toward his hand, which rested near her chin on the pillow. He smelled loamy, like newly turned earth.

On Saturday, Margaret wanted to go into the city. But Doug insisted on seeing more of her university world. It was early, so she took him to her favorite of the coffeehouses that skirted the edge of campus. At night they morphed into bars and filled up, but she figured no one would be there at this hour.

She was wrong. When they walked into the Daily Bean, someone called her name. It was Mare, one of Alexis's friends, a captain on the crew team. She was sitting in back, saying goodbye to a cluster of teammates, who waved to Margaret as they threaded their way out through an obstacle course of chairs. Each of them glanced at Doug.

"Margaret, hi!" Mare's voice was raspy, like an actress's. She came from Boston. Margaret had worked very hard upon meeting her to squelch the thought that no one who'd ever mucked out a horse stall would name a daughter Mare. No doubt that was exactly what Doug would think.

Mare's greeting was so vigorous that there was nothing for it but to leave Doug waiting for the coffees while Margaret went to say hi.

Mare's eyes flashed back and forth between Margaret and Doug. "Who's the hunky guy?" she demanded.

It never would have occurred to Margaret that any of her Chicago friends would find Doug attractive. It wasn't that he didn't look good standing there, his work-muscled body accentuated by jeans and a Pennzoil T-shirt. He loved that T-shirt. Looking at him again, Margaret realized that Mare liked it, too, but for different reasons.

"A friend of mine from Michigan," Margaret said, unable to think up a good lie. "He's visiting for the weekend."

"What kind of a friend?" Mare's gaze was piercing. Her long, straight brown hair was pulled back in a perfectly smooth ponytail.

"A family friend," Margaret lied. "Sort of an obligation. Nothing interesting." She tried to smile conspiratorially, but it felt forced.

"Oh yeah?" Mare said. "Maybe you're just trying to keep him from us." She laughed a tight-sounding, short laugh, and Margaret was overcome with the fear that she was coming across as snotty or evasive. They'd always been friendly, but she felt as if Mare was a shark, circling her, and the only way to escape was to throw something in her jaws.

She gave in, of course. She introduced Doug to Mare, watched with surprise as Mare tossed her hair and crossed her legs and giggled at the things he said. She didn't seem offended by his reticence. They drank their coffees, and before Margaret could engineer an escape, Mare had invited them back to the coffeehouse that evening, for some sort of art event. Margaret was horrified when Doug accepted.

After that, Margaret convinced him to go downtown. She took him to Shedd Aquarium, and then on a stroll up Michigan Avenue. They ambled through the streets, exploring Rush Street, wandering north onto more interesting side streets, stopping at bookstores and record shops. They ate sushi for lunch, which Doug had never had, and he surprised Margaret by liking it. It was a perfectly pleasant afternoon, but all day she was tortured by the thought that they would soon be going out, socializing with Margaret's new group of friends.

Why did it bother her so much? Doug was okay; at times she was even overwhelmed by the desire to tell him everything, to make him see the struggle she had undertaken, and the precarious nature of her success. She wanted to tell him how Mare and others like her had gone to prep schools—not some middling private school in Michigan but real prep schools, with recognizable names and traditions having to do with pranks and songs and dressing as Shakespearean characters. She wanted to tell him about their expensive shoes and their ski holidays and their fathers in the State Department or the office of the attorney general. She wanted him to understand how her mother had pointed her to this world, how she herself had desired it for as long as she could remember, and how she spent almost every second in it worrying she'd be revealed as the imposter she was, the girl whose father had earned some social credit being an airline pilot, and then squandered it trying to be a farmer. But then she looked at Doug, his solid shoulders, his unembellished gait, and she doubted he could understand any of it.

She checks her watch. Five miles; forty-four minutes. Not bad, but she could do better. Her heart is thudding in her chest, her face slick. She starts on another lap, walking to slow her heart rate. She rests her gaze on the field, then on the tree line at its far edge. There's a secondary horizon, an uneven, notched one, where the tops of the trees meet the sky. It looks like a graph line, the record of a stock price or the fluctuating value of gold.

Occasionally, the farm's beauty strikes her. She used to love it. She can remember summer days lying in the field when she was little, watching Queen Anne's lace swaying above her, breathing in the baked smell of the grass and hearing the occasional dragonfly fizzling by. *This is perfect,* she would think. It seemed infinite to her then, the fields and roads full of possibility, not the dead ends they came to be later. She can understand what drew her father back. But she can also see what drove him to leave in the first place, and that's what she has acted on: a desire for more. It was what caused her to push Doug away, the first time and then again, when he came to Chicago. Somehow it felt as if he was holding her back, even though, in retrospect, it isn't clear he wanted anything from her at all.

Their last real conversation was the night of the coffeehouse event. It turned out to be an impromptu poetry contest. They ate burgers at a campus diner, then walked to the Daily Bean. Margaret had been secretly hoping the place would be empty, but in nighttime hot-spot mode, it was packed. Everywhere she looked, there was someone she knew.

Mare was in the middle of a group of friends. She caught sight of Margaret and waved them over. They had to push through the crowd to get up front. Mare held out an arm when they finally made it, welcoming them into the fold.

"Did you know?" she cried in a voice so buoyant that Margaret began hoping she was blind drunk, not just trying to be heard. "Leah's going to enter the contest. She's over there signing up now."

"Leah's really good," Mare yelled to Doug. "She's a real poet. She had a poem published in *The Iowa Review.*"

"Iowa has a review?" Doug said in Margaret's ear. "Michigan better have one, too." She couldn't help but laugh. They were standing right up against each other in the crowded café, and when she looked up, she caught Mare noting their proximity.

"I'm going to get something to drink," she told Doug. "You want anything?"

"I'll go," he said, but Margaret quickly shook her head.

"I want to go," she said. "I want to say hi to someone."

She threaded through the crowd, relieved to be alone. At the counter, she lingered, making no effort to get the bartender's attention. She was thinking of gambits that would get them out of there quickly when someone appeared at her side. His arrival had a purposeful quality. She turned, expecting Doug, but it was a man she didn't know. He was tall and thin, with straight dark hair swept abruptly to one side over heavy, horn-rimmed glasses, the kind that are purposely so nerdy the end result is cool. He looked vaguely familiar.

"I don't care where you've been all my life," he said, smiling, "but where do you plan to be for the rest of it?" His tone was slightly elevated, just goofy enough to let her know he was joking without denuding the line of flattery.

"At this bar, apparently," she answered. "Waiting for a beer."

He struck a noble pose and made eye contact with the bartender, who came right over.

"Two Heinekens," Margaret said.

"Why, thank you," her companion said, grinning. "It's always nice to be rewarded for rescuing a damsel in distress."

"Excuse me, but do I know you?" Margaret asked.

"David Branford. I'm a TA in your Latin class." She remembered seeing him then, sitting in the back of the room with the other TAs. They always seemed so confident, so in the know, smiling at one another as if the whole Latin language were a private joke engineered by them.

"You're a grad student?" she asked, and he bowed his head, placing a hand over his heart.

"Guilty as charged."

"In classics?"

"In physics."

"You're a grad student in physics, and you're teaching introductory Latin?"

He grinned and leaned toward her. "I'm multitalented," he said. "I also teach courses in horsemanship, ceramics, and lock-picking on the side."

Margaret raised an eyebrow.

"Okay, I lied," he said. "About the horsemanship. I've never been on a horse in my life. But my cousin once played polo with Prince Charles. Does that count?"

The bartender arrived with Margaret's beers, and she handed him a five.

"I'm sorry, David, but I have to go," she said. "The second beer is not really for you."

David grinned, and she liked how his eyes sparkled. "Next time it will be," he said.

She could feel him watching her as she shimmied back into the crowd, and she liked the feeling it gave her.

David's appearance struck her as a portent. He had arrived to remind her that her future was full of choices. Watching Doug drink his beer, his thick arm visible through the clean T-shirt he had put on for dinner, she cringed at the thought of having slept with him. What had she been thinking? Doug had nothing for her. Her only objective, she realized, was to get through this night and get Doug back on the bus for Michigan, stripped of any illusions he might have about a future that included her.

She positioned herself as far from Doug as possible while the contestants did their thing. Leah was third. Each poet was given a first line from which they had to compose a poem, between eight and forty lines long, on the spot. Leah's first line was "The swallows are gone again."

"The swallows are gone again," she chanted. "They left with the rain. The days are quiet now, inviolate, the empty sky burnished to a sheen." Her voice was slow and almost hypnotized, as if she were channeling the poem from another world. Margaret was struck with admiration. To be able to take a first line and move forward into the unknown like that, so quickly, with confidence to spare. She was suffused with envy.

"They just say whatever comes to mind?" Doug spoke into her ear. Margaret nodded neutrally. She couldn't help but wonder if David was nearby, watching.

"That doesn't seem so hard," he said. Margaret gave him an incredulous look. The man of few words thinking poetry came so easily? She was annoyed. It was so typical of country people to undervalue whatever they didn't understand.

One more poet took a turn, and then the MC took the mike. Margaret had seen him around campus. He was the editor of the college's alternative poetry magazine, and a regular presence at all literary events.

"Folks," he said in an admonishing tone, "those four poets are the only people who signed up for tonight's contest. Four people!" The crowd "aaaaawed" in mock dismay. "Surely there are some other budding poets out there who can help make this evening worth our while!"

"How about you, Mare?" one of the girls nearby said, leaning over and jostling Mare's elbow.

"Oh, I couldn't." Mare laughed. "Have Margaret do it. She's the Brain."

"What about it, Margaret?" Several pairs of eyes turned to her.

Margaret shook her head. "On the spot like that? I'd get stage fright."

"Come on people," the MC said. "Remember the prize: one hundred dollars and publication in *Threnody.*" He held a copy of the poetry magazine aloft.

"A hundred bucks?" Doug said. "I'd do it for a hundred bucks."

"Yes!" Mare squealed. "There you go, Doug! Go for it!" She waved an arm vigorously at the stage. "We have a taker over here!"

Horrified, Margaret put a hand on Doug's arm. "It's okay," she said. "You don't have to."

Doug grinned. "How bad can it be?"

For you or for me? Margaret thought. But things had gotten out of control: the MC was giving Doug a warm look as the audience cheered. Mare was elbowing some of her crowd aside to clear Doug's path to the stage. She and her friends were riding a swell of importance at having provided another contestant.

"All hail, hearty fellow!" the MC said as Doug stepped onto the makeshift stage. He reached out and put a hand on Doug's shoulder, turning him to face the audience. Doug pinkened slightly at the contact. "Tell the nice folks your name."

"Doug," Doug said, leaning in to the mike. He blinked, almost fearful, when his amplified voice reverberated through the room. Margaret felt a surge of pity that only compounded her anger.

"Are you a student at Chicago?" the MC asked, and Doug looked at him as if he didn't understand the question.

"No," he said after a moment. "Just visiting one." He glanced out into the crowd, and Margaret shrank down, hoping not to be seen.

"Well, Doug, the contest judges are going to give you your first line. You have five minutes to speak your poem. Remember—no fewer than eight lines, no more than forty. Are you ready?"

Doug nodded. Margaret noticed that he avoided the MC's eyes. He looked at the stage floor while the other man exited the stage, then shuffled his feet and stepped toward the mike. The judges were at a table near the front of the stage, to Margaret's right. She couldn't see which of them spoke.

"Your first line is: 'I came over the hill and saw it.'"

The crowd "oooohed" dramatically, their involvement now boosted. Doug squinted toward the person who'd said the line. He seemed too wide behind the thin mike. His broad shoulders and his full chest only accentuated his awkwardness. Margaret wanted to look away.

"I came over the hill and saw it," Doug repeated. There was a pause, and Margaret was gripped with fear. As bad as Doug improvising poetry was, it would be even worse for him to stand up there and fail in front of a roomful of people who had seen her come in with him. *Say something,* she pleaded silently. *Say anything at all.*

"I came over the hill and saw it," Doug said again, but this time his voice was perfectly normal, as if he was simply telling them about something that had happened.

> *"Down in the little hollow.*
> *We call it Paulson's hollow*
> *'Cause his tractor got stuck there once.*
> *It's a little dip in the field,*
> *Hard to plow."*

He paused and cleared his throat. His eyes flickered toward Margaret, but then quickly away, as if reading her desire.

> *"That day there was something in it.*
> *A little brown lump.*
> *When I got closer I saw it was the calf,*
> *The orphan one. Her mother, an older cow,*
> *Died in the birth.*
> *We were raising her on the bottle.*
> *It isn't hard."*

Margaret glanced around the room. There was total silence, everyone listening, eager. Some people were smiling. She wondered if they were making fun of him.

> *"Until then she didn't move much.*
> *But that day she got away,*
> *And ran all the way through the field*
> *And found that sweet spot*
> *Where you're safe from the wind*
> *And the sun makes the grass warm.*
> *I didn't want to wake her.*
> *I wanted to leave her there, happy.*
> *But I had to. I had to catch her. That's my job.*
> *I keep cows."*

He stopped. Margaret wondered if he was finished or if he had just run out of inspiration. He nodded, a short, stiff nod that seemed to say he was done. The silence that followed was like the edge of a precipice. Margaret was beginning to feel sick, from anger or pity, when the applause began. The noise of it startled her. It seemed to startle Doug more. There were whoops and shouts and the stomping of feet.

They're not making fun, Margaret thought. *They really liked it.* She watched Mare clapping and thought of how she had admired Doug in his Pennzoil T-shirt.

"That was so great!" Mare cried as Doug waded toward them, grinning. "We had no idea you were so lyrical!" The others squawked their agreement, and Margaret stood back, watching Doug's pleased discomfort as the little crowd enfolded him.

For the rest of the evening, Doug was the hero. One of Mare's friends went to buy him a beer, and others grouped around him, talking and laughing.

"Was that a true story?" Margaret heard one of them ask.

Doug glanced at Margaret before answering. "Naaaaah," came his slow reply.

Doug's success emboldened a few more poets, and there were further entrants. All were well received, but no one generated as much enthusiasm as Doug. After each poem, Mare's crowd assured him that his was better. Doug seemed baffled by the attention. His head turned toward Margaret regularly.

Finally, everyone who wanted to had spoken, and the judges retired to decide the winner. Margaret stood with the others, trying to look pleased. At one point she looked across the room to see David standing at the bar. He winked and raised his beer to her.

When the MC stepped up to announce the winner, Margaret was standing next to Doug. He was on his fourth beer and starting to seem a bit dazed. Mare, at his other side, put an arm around him and squeezed. "Good luck!" She beamed.

Doug looked at Margaret. She attempted an encouraging smile. He leaned toward her, as if to say something, but then hesitated, seemingly lost in consideration. He didn't seem to hear the MC announcing that Leah had won.

"Yay, Leah!" Mare shouted. She glanced over at Doug, still clapping. "Yours was great, too," she said apologetically.

"Oh well," Doug said, tilting his head. "I could've used that hundred."

Mare tried convincing them to come to an afterparty in her suite, but Margaret demurred. Doug stood quietly behind her as she lied and said his bus left too early. They made their way to the door in a crush of people, many of whom stopped to shake Doug's hand. By the door, Margaret felt a hand squeeze her arm.

"Next week it's improv lock-picking," David's voice murmured in her ear. "We'll see who takes you home then." He winked and turned around, rejoining a circle of people who looked like faculty.

Outside, it was colder than it had been since school began.

"Smells like snow," Doug said as they walked toward her dorm. Margaret didn't reply. They walked in silence the rest of the way back.

"Margaret," Doug said when they reached the door. "Stop a minute. Are you mad at me?"

Margaret turned from the door, key in hand. "Why would I be mad?"

"I don't know, but it feels like you are." He had his hands in the pockets of his coat, a brown Carhartt jacket that ended at the waist. It made him look even bulkier than usual. Margaret had seen those coats a thousand times. They were sold at the hardware store in Ryville.

"I'm not mad," she said, but as she said it, she knew it wasn't true. There was a glowing ember of anger inside her that refused to die.

He shoved his hands deeper into the pockets, gazing up at the sky. "The stars look different here," he said. "I always wondered about that." He breathed in, turning away from her, and Margaret could sense him struggling, longing to grasp at something. "There are so many things I . . ." He stopped, the incomplete sentence breathing between them like an invisible animal. Margaret could have helped him. She could sense him waiting for a hand, for the encouragement to find his own thoughts. She turned toward the door.

"Did you like my poem?" he asked. Margaret turned halfway back and leaned over to look down at her feet. Her clunky oxfords gleamed in the light from the dorm windows. *Say something,* she told herself. *Say anything.* She felt herself shaking her head, as if to deny that the question was answerable.

"It was fine," she said at last. "It was . . . funny."

"Funny?" Doug said. "It was funny?" His brow darkened, and abruptly, all Margaret wanted was for him to be gone, back in Michigan where he belonged.

"Not funny, exactly," she said. "Amusing. It was amusing."

"Amusing?" The darkness in his face turned to confusion. Margaret felt bad. She shouldn't have said it. It wasn't even true. But something wouldn't let her retract it. She shuffled her feet.

"It seemed easy at first," Doug said. "Until I got up there. I wasn't sure I could do it. I wanted to, but I wasn't sure I could." His face was open; he was offering her something. "But then the words just sort of came. I wasn't even sure I was done until I heard the clapping and cheering."

"Yeah, well." Margaret shrugged. "They shouldn't have done that."

"They shouldn't have?" Emotion moved through Doug's face. For a second he looked insulted, but then he saw Margaret's meaning. He looked away from her, and the hurt in his face made Margaret hate herself. Why was she making him think they'd laughed at him? As far as she could tell, they hadn't. But how would she know, really? They could have been laughing at her, too. Margaret, the country girl, out of her league. She looked at Doug in his bulky jacket and wished he had never come.

"Come on," she said. "Let's go inside. It's cold out."

They slept side by side, not touching. The next day Doug took the noon bus home. In silence they rode to the station, and when they got there, they found his gate without exchanging words. There they stopped, and it seemed as if they might not even say goodbye. Finally Doug spoke.

"I really liked the aquarium," he said. "I liked the whole city." He stopped, unsure whether to go on.

Margaret stepped in quickly. "Chicago's great," she said. "You'd like the Museum of Science and Industry, too. There's a lot to see there. You should go sometime." She said it with finality.

"Maybe I will," Doug said, understanding. "Goodbye, Margaret."

"Goodbye, Doug." She looked at his elbow, a neutral place.

After a moment, Doug hitched his duffel bag onto his shoulder and turned toward the bus. Seeing the back of him, Margaret felt an urge to stop him, to grab his arm and at least hug him goodbye. In the second it took him to climb onto the bus, a wave of homesickness rushed over her. She longed to run and join him, to watch the city slide away and see flat, dull Michigan roll into view.

The bus engine turned over with an asthmatic cough. A woman ran past Margaret, and the driver opened the door. She was carrying a tennis racket. Margaret was reminded of her mother, who had always talked about the tennis club she belonged to in Chicago, before they moved to the farm. Every summer, she worked on the girls' tennis strokes. They would throw balls up in the air and serve them against the barn, racing back and forth to hit them. They would keep going until the ball hit a clump of grass or a stone from the gravel drive and bounced crazily off.

"It's a grass court," their mother would say, her eyes squinted against the sun, determination edging her jaw. "Even Wimbledon has grass courts."

Margaret swung an arm back now, as if holding a racket. Her tennis stroke was smooth and firm, perfectly respectable. *Not bad, Brain,* Alexis had said when they went to hit some balls once. *You could be a jock if you weren't such a bookworm.*

The feel of the stroke pulled Margaret backward. Following her arm's momentum, she turned around. Behind her she heard the hissing of unclenched brakes, then a long, slow grinding of gears. The bus was backing out, but she didn't stay to see it leave.

twelve

THE RUN-THROUGH IS AT TEN. ALL THE WAY TO THE country club, Leanne is thinking the same thing. *There's no way out. You have to go through with this now.* She sits with her mother in the backseat. Her cousin Eddie is meeting them there. Whatever she felt for Kit when she agreed to do this seems far off. He's wearing an ugly short-sleeved plaid shirt that she's never seen before, and his elbows are sharp and too pointed. He's riding in the front seat with her father—Carol insisted—and when he turns to Will to make a comment, he has never looked more like a stranger.

She's a stranger to him, too. She has become her former self: the quiet girl, the follower, the girl brooding in the backseat while her father drives and her sister does all the talking. Except it's Carol next to her, breathing in quickly and slapping her own thigh lightly whenever Will goes too fast or slides through a stop sign without really stopping. It's a relief when the sign for the country club appears around a curve.

"Here we are," Will says. He roars across the parking lot and pulls the car into a spot near the clubhouse door.

"Did Margaret see you make that last turn?" Carol frets. Margaret insisted on taking her own car, because in the family car, she'd have had to hold Trevor on her lap instead of having him in the car seat. "It's not even legal for him to be out of it," she had declared.

"It's just a few miles," Will had said, and Leanne had sensed the hardening around the edges that meant her sister was gearing up to get her way. Will had shrugged but then driven fast, as if wanting to punish Margaret by losing her. But every time Carol twisted around to check, she made the little *humph* that meant the Rabbit was there.

"If she didn't see me turn, she wasn't paying attention," Will mutters. But Leanne can see his face in the mirror, and his eyes are bright with amusement. Sure enough, the Rabbit appears and zooms toward them, cutting across the white parking-space lines.

"Well," Kit says in a light tone, "let's get this over with, shall we?"

"The list of things we need to do after this is on the fridge," Carol says to Leanne as they walk toward the clubhouse. "You'll be checking on Kit's mother's room when we get home, then Margaret's going to do your nails. We have to make sure you only do light work if you help us set up, so you don't wreck them."

"There are worse things than getting married with your nails unpolished," Leanne says, but Carol shoots her such a wounded look that she immediately regrets it. "Don't worry," she says, back-tracking. "I'll be fine." Carol keeps on looking at her, as if assessing her mental condition, so Leanne looks up at the sky. It's a classic Michigan sky, deep blue, dotted with a few drifting, fluffy clouds, throw pillows on a magnificent blue sofa. The sky in New York never quite looks like that—it's flatter, without as much depth. She imagines Mexico City's sky as an even darker blue, a wide azure bowl arching over the endless tangle of life below.

"Yoo-hoo! Bride and groom!" It's the determined voice of events coordinator Lori. She's standing on the lawn where the trellis has been set up. A few chairs have been put in place to mark off the wedding area. Standing with her is their cousin Eddie and another man Leanne doesn't recognize.

"Eddie!" she says, genuinely happy to see him. He grins, still awkward at thirty-five, and gives her a clumsy, tentative hug.

"Hey there, slugger!" he says to Trevor as Margaret walks up. His awkward grin warms to a real smile. He and Margaret were always close; Leanne was the third wheel. They used to lock her out of rooms, pick on her until she ran away, angry. When they went somewhere fun, they would sneak out of the house so she couldn't sulk until Carol made them take her along. Now Eddie always acts vaguely nervous around Leanne, as if she's going to reprove him for all those years of teasing.

"Hey, Eddie," Margaret says. In spite of Eddie's warmth, she seems on edge, nervously twisting her hair with one hand and holding Trevor tightly with the other, ignoring his struggle to get free. She keeps glancing around as if expecting someone else to arrive.

"Don't go over there," she says when Trevor gets loose and makes for the lake. "You stay here, near us."

"Bride and groom, this is Kevin, the justice of the peace," Lori says. She must call everyone that to avoid having to learn their names. "He'll lead you through the walk-through today."

"Okay," Kit says when Leanne doesn't respond. Some part of her has decided never to answer to the generic "bride."

"It's a pretty simple ceremony we're looking at, isn't it?" Kevin says. He's a tall, rangy man who looks too young for his job. There's a gap between his two front teeth. "Leanne, is it? You have no wedding party, right? Will your father be walking you down the aisle?"

Leanne shifts her weight. "I guess, yeah." She glances quickly at her father, then looks away. Everything seems too real, too intimate, somehow.

"Okay, then, uh . . ." Kevin glances at his piece of paper. "Kitto, is it? You'll be up here with me, and your best man, too." Kit and Eddie move easily to Kevin's left side, both grinning like kids in on a stupid joke.

"Will there be music?" Kevin asks. Leanne shakes her head.

"We've been trying to keep it as simple as possible," Kit puts in.

"Okay." Kevin smiles. "In that case, I think we should all process in." He says the word "pro-*cess*," the verb form of "processional." "Kitto, you and your best man move to the back here, and I will, too. We'll all walk in together—just casually, like this. That gives your guests the cue to be quiet. Let's do it now."

The three of them stroll down the aisle. Will appears at Leanne's side.

"Okay, sister, you're next," Kevin says. Margaret points at Carol, and Trevor obeys her signal, going to his grandmother's side. She walks quickly down the aisle. Leanne notices Carol's hand dropping to Trevor's shoulder, as if she's taking over Margaret's nervousness.

"No need to scamper," Kevin says. "I know you don't want to make it too formal, but give people time to take a look at you."

"I'm just trying to move things along," Margaret says, a little sharply. Eddie chortles.

"All right then, bride," Kevin says. "Dad brings you down next."

Leanne stiffens. She doesn't want to make a scene, but her feet feel as if they've been buried in cement. She glances down to see if they have sunk into the wet lawn.

"Bride," Kevin urges.

"Okay, Leanne," Will says. He takes her hand and puts it on his arm. But his touch is gentle, and when Leanne doesn't move, he doesn't pull her forward.

"Come on, Pester!" Eddie calls out. "Get it in gear!"

Leanne finds herself stepping forward. The lawn is not smooth and velvety, as it looks from afar, but lumpy and tamped down with rain. A hot, muddy smell rises up from it, and the grass clings in clumps that threaten to trip her at every step. She holds on to her father's arm for support and looks at Kit waiting for her. *This is it.*

Will stops by Kit and moves aside, taking his seat next to Carol, who has perched in the front row with Trevor. Leanne steps over to Kit.

"Okay," Kevin says. "The rest is pretty simple. I'll say the standard things, you'll do the vows and exchange rings. Everyone stays in place the whole time, right?"

"Don't forget the doves!" Carol cries from the front row. Leanne's heart sinks. Whatever notion she had at the time seems childish and absurd now. She's embarrassed even to mention it.

"Doves?" Kevin asks.

"I don't know," Leanne says. "One of them isn't looking so good."

"They're fine!" Carol says. "I just looked at them this morning!"

Leanne feels a surge of rage toward her mother. "It's sort of silly," she says. She waves a hand, erasing the idea.

"The plan," Kit says, "is for Leanne and me to release a pair of doves at the end of the ceremony. Sort of a symbolic moment."

"I see," Kevin says. "And who will be in charge of the doves?"

"I will," Carol says. "I can have them here, under my seat, and at the right moment I can hand the cage over."

"I don't know," Margaret puts in. "Leanne, do you really want a cage up here as part of the ceremony? It's not even a very attractive cage."

"Not the one they're in," Carol says. "I have another one, a small one that's old-fashioned and pretty. It just needs to be spray-painted white." She turns to Will. "Will, you need to do that this afternoon."

Will grimaces. "Yeah, after the twelve other things you have me doing." Margaret looks at Leanne and shrugs. *It's your disaster.*

"Whatever. That will be fine," Leanne says. She just wants this whole ordeal to be over.

"I'll paint the cage," Kit says. "I haven't got much to do once we've picked up my mother."

"Then I guess that's it," Kevin says. "I just need a check for the fee, and we'll see you tomorrow afternoon!"

"Let me," Kit says as Will ambles toward Kevin. "I know it's not traditional, but I really want to." He steps between Will and the justice.

Will stops and shrugs. Kit says something low to Kevin, so Leanne can't hear, and then the two of them laugh. Kevin turns around, and Kit opens his checkbook and begins to write, using Kevin's back as a desk.

What does this have to do with me? Leanne thinks. It feels like a conspiracy. She was in New York, independent, living her own life, even if that meant throwing her life away. It was hers to throw. But they couldn't stand that. Carol came out and got her to Cold Spring, and then Kit convinced her to get married and settle down and lock her life into an approved pattern. What they don't understand is that she was happy like she was. Out of all of them, Carol at least ought to see that. She ought to see that Leanne will be as miserable as she was, being forced to tag along with someone else's dreams.

"Somebody's starting a new life," her father says next to her, and from her tangle of anxious thoughts, she speaks without thinking.

"You, I guess, Dad," she says. "A new life flying for Cathay Pacific, huh?"

There's a slight delay before a rustle goes through the family. Margaret gapes. Her father's expression is baffled. Trevor's lower lip makes a U, as if he might cry. Carol is the first to speak.

"Oh, no, Will, you haven't!"

Will drives fast. The rehearsal was short, but the flurry afterward dragged it out so they ended up leaving for Grand Rapids later than he intended. He wants to get there and get the car parked in time to meet Kit's mother in the baggage claim. He could just drop Kit off and wait in the car, but that seems unfriendly. So he speeds up U.S. 131, slowing down only at overpasses where he knows state troopers lurk. After about fifteen minutes of speed and silence, Kit speaks up.

"Is it all right if we make a quick stop so I can buy some spray paint for the cage?"

Will glances at his watch and mumbles something vague. He wants to say no, but he can't think of a good reason.

Kit watches him. "So," he says, turning to look out the window. "Cathay Pacific, huh?"

Will smiles. You have to give it to this kid. He doesn't beat around the bush, and he doesn't try to be diplomatic. Will can't help but admire him for it.

"You start out flying freight," he says. "I'd probably be based in Chicago."

"But you'd want to switch out of freight?"

Will shrugs. "Who knows?" It's not entirely honest. He has always assumed he'd apply for passenger service the moment he was allowed. That's what guys do. But why should he, really? What's the difference between flying a load of tourists and a load of cheap Chinese electronics? Cargo's easier to get off and on, that's one thing. And it doesn't come racing up to the cockpit and try to fly the plane into buildings.

"I guess your wife was surprised." Kit leaves the sentence hanging in the air, waiting for an explanation.

Will puffs out his cheeks. All his life he has been asked to explain Carol, and after forty years he's no better at it. "I figured it would be a nice surprise," he says. "I was waiting for the right time to tell her, because I thought she'd be happy." As he says it, he knows it's false. He had thought she *should* be happy. That's a slightly different thing.

"The thing is, she doesn't like me to make big decisions without asking her first," Will says. "I've done that in the past, and it upsets her."

"You mean moving to the farm," Kit says. He's surprisingly willing to broach family topics.

"Yeah, that," Will answers. "She was never really very happy there." He runs his hand over his face. Just talking about it makes him feel tired.

"It was where you grew up." Kit keeps making open statements, waiting for Will to explain or deny them.

"Yeah." Will doesn't know what else to say about that. He grew up, he went away, he came back. Is it such an unusual story?

Kit scrutinizes the landscape as if the answer might be there. Maybe he's interested in their family story because he's marrying into it. He might want to understand Leanne better, or get a grip on what kind of extended family their possible children will have.

"What I wonder," Kit says, "is why you came back here."

Will has answered this one lots of times. "When I was little," he says, "I used to drive the tractor all the time, and I'd look up and see the planes going overhead and think, That's where I want to be." He's stopped by an impatient move from Kit.

"I know the story," Kit says. "Then once you started flying, you flew over the fields and looked down and thought, That's where I want to be."

Will nods. "That's right."

"Leanne told it to me," Kit replies. "But it isn't the whole story, really. Why did you look down and want to be in the fields?" His voice is gentle but searching. He really wants to know.

Why did he come back? Will knows it was a mistake. Carol was never happy on the farm, and the girls drank in that unhappiness every day. They learned his yearning to leave; he was never able to teach them, or even to formulate for himself, his desire to go back.

How does a man atone for his mistakes? Will has dreamed his dream at least once every week since 1967. Sometimes he dreams the bombing run exactly as it was. Sometimes he dreams it different. They abort the mission because the weather is awful. They roll in and there's nothing there. They pull out at the last minute, when they see someone on the ground. An old man doddering off to pee. A young girl in a coolie hat, baby in her arms. A farmer wading into his rice.

Other times he dreams he's the man on the ground. He dreams he's standing at the door of his hut, only it's not a hut, it's his father's house in Michigan. Four planes are rolling out of nowhere, tiny specks in the sky that he watches with only vague interest until he realizes they're heading for him. Then, as in a movie, he gets a close-up of the first pilot's face, his hand on the throttle, missiles armed and ready under his wings. He runs inside and tells his parents. They are sitting in the living room, his father in his recliner, his mother on the davenport. "Run!" he yells. They look at him as if he's crazy. "Get out of here!" Nothing. He stands, impotent, until he hears the familiar whistle.

He's never told anyone any of this. Maybe that was a mistake, too. Maybe he should have shared his stories with his family, so they could understand what was driving him, making him want what he wanted. Would it have helped? He looks at the young man sitting next to him.

"In Vietnam, we played this game," he says.

The game was Rogoff's idea. "Gordon Rogoff," Will tells Kit. "He was my best friend at Korat—that's where I was stationed. Korat Air Base in Thailand. Sometimes we called him Rog. Like 'rogue.'"

Will was never sure why he liked Rogoff. The guy couldn't have been more different from Will. Rogoff was a city boy—mainline Philadelphia—and a Harvard man. Not only that but he'd majored in classics, slogging through two years of graduate Latin before chucking it to join the Air Force. "Best decision I ever made," he said, swigging from a beer at the O-club. Will, whose hootch was across from Rog's, knew the guy had a stack of Latin and Greek books on the table by his bed. They were paperbacks, but still. Not many guys dragged books halfway around the world just to see them bloom with mildew in the Thai jungle. Rogoff was probably the only guy at Korat who could recite dirty Latin poetry and recount Hannibal's attempt on Rome.

"Hannibal's problem was not unlike ours," he told them. "He took stock of the enemy just fine. But he failed to factor in the goddamn *weather*."

Will arrived at Korat in July 1967. In August, Washington declared Hanoi no longer off limits for bombing. After that, they flew almost daily into Route Pack Six, the most heavily defended airspace in the world. Weather stopped their runs more often than antiaircraft fire. But weather they were used to. What was new was flying through a sky so full of flak there wasn't time to think. You dove in, dropped your load, and headed for the hills.

"You only get one pass," Will tells Kit. "My wing commander told me that my first time into Hanoi. One pass, haul ass. That's the name of the game."

On average they lost about one guy a week. When you stepped out over Hanoi, you took a deep breath and hoped for the best. Nobody was coming in after you. There was a saying around the base for rescue operations in Pack Six. *Ain't no way.*

It's thirty-four years ago. Will is in the officers' club at Korat.

"Okay," Johnson is saying. "I've got a good one." He's a tall, loosely jointed guy who seems like he should be shy but isn't. Others shift nervously when he speaks, embarrassed in his stead.

"I'm fifteen years old. I've got this horse." Johnson's eyes gleam in spite of the collective groan.

"Shit, not another dead pet," someone says.

Johnson is unfazed. "So it's summer in Oklahoma, and I'm riding my horse out to check on a fence. And I see up ahead something lying on the ground. When I get closer, I see it's one of the heifers."

The game, Will explains, was Rogoff's idea. Whenever they lost a guy, they gathered and drank bourbon together, sort of an informal wake. But it made them fidgety and morose to sit around staring into their glasses, so they began to invent distractions, games. At first it was just cards. Then one night Rogoff had a new idea. The challenge would be to tell a story *ad misericordia*. It meant "for sympathy," he explained. The best story would win an extra round. Anyone who failed to win sympathy could be made to keep trying until he succeeded or was declared a loser. Losers would pick up the tab.

They started that night. The wing commander, Baz, won with a story about watching his cousin slip off a dock, cracking his skull on the way down. The kid was never the same again, and Baz always felt guilty for standing there, for not being able to prevent the tragedy from happening.

Ad misericordia became part of their routine wake. The one Will's thinking of was for a guy called Reggie McPhee, a tall skinny guy with a wife and twin boys back home. "See you after the war" were the last words he said. They heard his beeper wailing desolately all the way down, but when they tried to contact him on the ground, they got nothing. "McPhee," Will said several times, violating protocol by using his name. "If you can hear me, come up voice or radio." Nothing. After a few passes, the flak got thick, and they had to get the hell out.

Now they were telling stories. Will remembers the end of Johnson's. The guy wound up shooting his own horse's leg by mistake and being forced to finish it off. No one could resist this ending, even though they were all sick of dead animal stories. Johnson's story was declared a success.

Will went next. He had yet to win, or even to succeed at getting sympathy, and his share of the bar tabs was adding up. Somehow he couldn't bring himself to play the game in earnest. It was an odd feeling, sifting through one's past looking for shreds of pathos. It made him feel sullied, slightly obscene. For some reason, whenever he tried to think of a story, an image of his father would take shape in his head; his father standing alone in the west cornfield.

Who's gonna hold things together here? he had demanded as Will packed for his first base assignment in Texas.

Will cleared his throat. "I've just arrived at Nellis for fighter training," he began, reluctant to the last. "And the first guy I see is this instructor from my old base who hates me."

There's so much to tell Kit. For instance, there's the wild beauty of Vietnam. How, after refueling over Laos, they flew in high over jungle that draped the mountains like a rumpled bedspread. How, east of Hanoi, the ocean was jewel blue, punctuated with strange, barren islands that looked like giant boulders floating in the sea. How, farther south, it flattened into patchwork farmland, miles of green rectangles edged by tree lines, just like in Michigan. Will describes how clouds and fog rolled in quickly, as if manufactured by a machine, one more thing launched against them, along with the MiGs, the SAMs, the flak from antiaircraft guns. Avoiding that mess, Will sometimes flew upside down, looking up to see the ground. Its beauty was a strange backdrop to terror.

One thing's for sure, he tells Kit: pilots had it better than grunts. The guys on the ground spent their days slogging through undergrowth thick with heat and snakes, in constant fear of an ambush. For pilots, the terror was concentrated in the two hours flying in and the one crazy, adrenaline-skewed hour jinking and dodging in a sky full of shrapnel and smoke. If you survived that, you were bright and shiny for another day, heading home to Thailand for dinner and Jim Beam and a bed that wasn't the Hilton but was better than the hard ground.

Will's hootch, like most guys', had photos from home taped on the wall over his bed. One photo was framed and sat on his bedside table. It was a picture of Carol holding a small brown creature with a frowning face and a tiny fist raised as if in defiance—Margaret, born that August. He had never seen her. Every night he picked up the picture and looked at it for a long time. No matter how long he stared at it, she remained a mysterious creature, part of another world, no more than an idea to him there.

Another wake.

"So my mother turns to me and says, 'You've got the letter from your brother, right?'"

Julep Schneider is on the spot. He's already won once, with a story about his sister's death from cancer, and now he's trying to bring an edge of misery to a story that might otherwise be funny. The others listen, fascinated to see if he'll pull it off.

"Of course I don't. But I nod. 'Let's see it,' she says. So I reach into my jacket pocket and pull out the first thing handy. I hold it up, and it looks like that's gonna satisfy her."

A couple of guys chuckle, anticipating the screwup. Julep is a southerner with a heavy drawl. He's good at telling stories. He doesn't pause and grope for words the way Will does when he speaks. Will has already told his story, a quick recounting of how his father refused to come to his high school graduation after hearing that Will had enlisted in the Air Force.

"What was it, Julie-boy?" someone shouts, and Julep tries to keep a smirk from his own face.

"It was a letter from my girlfriend," he says. "She was freaking out because she thought she might be pregnant." He pauses to let the laughter roll over. "My mom goes ballistic, of course. She starts shouting and whacking me with the letter." More laughter as everyone envisions the scene. Will raises his hand to the Thai serving girl. He puts his thumb and first finger two inches apart, the sign for a double shot.

"Here's the killer thing, guys," Julep is saying. "Here's the real sad part: I was still a virgin!"

There's more laughter and groaning, and then somebody shouts, "I don't know about that one."

The girl hands Will his bourbon, and he raises it to Julep. "I say it's okay," he says. "I'm feeling bad for you, Jule."

"Why did it help?" Kit asks. Will pauses, stumped. It was never clear why the game made them feel better. The stories they told were all ten times less awful than the stuff they saw every day: guys parachuting into nests of ground gunners, planes blowing apart, pilots breaking their necks on a rough ejection and floating to the ground like dead baby birds. In the game, no one mentioned the war; it was an unspoken rule. Somehow there was something comforting in the thought of all the shitty stuff that happened back home as well. The war might be a tragedy. But it wasn't the only one.

"It was partly about respect," Will says at last. Incomplete but true. There was nothing more important than paying respect to a downed pilot. The game became part of that. What else could they do? Whether the guy was KIA or MIA, he was gone. There was no body to recover, no cigarettes to finish, no personal talismans to pull from the guy's pocket. There was paperwork to file, and then somebody threw the guy's stuff in his locker and taped it shut.

The game was their ritual, played every time someone went down. They played even if there was entertainment that night, or journalists visiting the base, or desk jockeys from Saigon having dinner with the commander to rack up combat pay. The only time they lost a guy without playing was when some visitors came from Takhli. Takhli was a newer base than Korat, and an informal competition had grown up between them. Everyone kept track of the stats: target hits, MiG kills, rescues. It made the war more like a football game, something you could win or lose, then walk away from.

A small delegation had been sent from Takhli to see how Korat's repair setup worked. The Wild Weasels lost a guy that day. Weasels were always the first in and last out. They were Thuds—F-105 fighter-bombers—with two seats. Built as trainers, they'd been altered during the war to carry a radar operator and Shrike missiles. Shrikes were filled with shrapnel and equipped with a guidance system that honed in on the SAM site's radar. When they exploded, they took the whole site with them. The day's flight had nailed the site, but not before it got off a couple of SAMs. One of them hit its mark.

When the Takhli guys heard a pilot had been downed, they bought a round of drinks. Then the wing commander, Baz, bought a round, and then Julep Schneider did, because he was squadron leader of the Weasels. After that they all sat around until, one by one, they started to drift back to their hootches. Lying in bed that night, Will felt worse than he had since he arrived at Korat.

Goddamn Takhli pukes, he thought. *They don't know how to survive a war.*

Across from him, he could see a light burning in Rogoff's hootch. The crazy guy was probably reading Latin poetry. He had walked home with Will that night. When they got near their hootches, he didn't say good night. Instead, he stood there for a second, shoving one foot back and forth on the dirt path, scraping a little trench.

"*Vita humana est supplicium,*" he said. "Human life is punishment."

Kit is silent, listening. Will charges ahead. He tells the young man how, after each mission, a pilot penciled an X on his helmet. How he considered it a crossing-out. One more done and gone, buried behind the black mark. Will tells him how one mission wouldn't stay that way. How it regularly dragged him back, replayed itself in his head when he turned off the lights. It's the story he needs to tell.

"The time I went on a Wild Weasel run," he says.

The Weasels were looking for a one-seater to complete their flight. For a week, SAMs had been coming from a new neck of the woods, and they had downed the Weasels' fourth plane.

"Yesterday the strike force pickled a load on what they thought was the site," Julep told Will. "But they're still coming hot and heavy. It's a Weasel job." Will just nodded. It would be a counter. One more mission toward his hundred.

They told Will to hold his position and follow their lead. They flew in on the deck, fast and low. Will flew fourth, disoriented by being so close to the ground. Weasels flew low on purpose, they wanted to be seen. Shrikes couldn't zero in on the SAM site until it was zeroed in on them.

As they roared along at six hundred miles an hour, Will started to enjoy seeing what the place really looked like. The ground was covered with a lush green blanket of trees, heavy from the constant rain. Winding dirt roads cut through the woods occasionally, but for the most part, it looked almost uninhabited.

When they got closer to the target site, the land flattened out and became farmland. Occasionally, Will thought he could see someone working the land, wading in a flat green field. They always zipped by too fast for him to see what they were doing. But suddenly he had a strange feeling of vertigo, as if he were watching someone else fly a two-million-dollar piece of equipment loaded with ordnance. He saw it from the point of view of the guy on the ground, thinking about his crop, looking up in surprise as four impossibly fast, loud killing machines zoomed ninety feet over his head. *Ain't no way.*

When they neared the previous day's target area, the red launch light lit up on Will's control panel. They rolled right and dove in, following the missile's guidance. In the last few seconds of the dive, he saw it. As his right wing dipped, it appeared, no more than a thousand feet off target: a village, a circle of huts in the middle of a large field, still smoking. Every hut was flattened.

He heard Julep on the radio screaming at him to fire his missile, and somehow he pushed the button. The whole thing flashed by so quickly he could hardly remember pulling out again and following the others up to a safer altitude. He jinked right and left, as much because he wanted to see that village again as to avoid enemy fire. But it was too far back. They headed forward, because Julep had two more sites he wanted to take out that day. Will didn't know this part of the country well enough to know exactly where he'd been.

"Don't get me wrong," he tells Kit. "We all made mistakes. We bombed the wrong bridge, missed the target, came in too fast or too slow and had to abort. There's always collateral damage." There were even stories about guys who bombed civilians on purpose. They'd get to their coordinates and couldn't find the intended target, or got locked out by the weather, so they'd find a village and pickle the bombs there instead. *Fraggin' villes,* they called it. Will had tried to believe it was a myth, a story made up by pilots looking to sound vicious instead of merely incompetent.

Even if no one ever fragged villes, accidents were bound to happen. In the rush of battle, everybody had the same feeling: get the thing done and get out. *Hit my smoke* was the motto. There was no time to think about whether the first guy had dropped his bombs with total accuracy, whether the wing commander had calculated the coordinates right, whether intel had chosen a valid target in the first place. The nature of the game was imprecise.

Still, the vision of the bombed-out village haunted Will. At night he lay on his bed and stared at the ceiling. The roof was a slab of corrugated plastic, and there was a swirling pattern in it. In one place the swirls were irregular, as if they had once melted, and he had come to see the flaw as the village. He still had no idea what he was seeing. For all he knew, it could be his handiwork haunting him, the results of his bombing run the day before. He wasn't sure where they'd been that day, in Hanoi or blasting the staging area just north of the seventeenth parallel. He couldn't remember even the day of the Weasel run, and he found that suspicious, as if he were hiding something from himself.

What really happened? It was ambiguous. He needs Kit to see

that. It could have been a civilian village; it could have been a military supply camp. It could be no village at all but a SAM site disguised as a village. That wasn't unknown. Maybe they stopped it from downing even more guys. Maybe they killed old men and babies. Will would stare at the ceiling and rearrange the village huts; now it was a group of farms; now it was a Vietcong outpost, deadly and still. He imagined himself on the ground, a farmer, looking up at the sky and seeing planes coming to flatten his fields, his family. He imagined running into the hut. There was a missile launcher hidden beneath the brush roof. He saw himself listening for the planes as they came, firing the missiles to take them down. He saw himself falling from the sky.

Rogoff's wake. It's the only time Will ever wins the game. He'd been flying as Rogoff's wingman. They'd just pickled a load when Rogoff's voice came on in Will's headset, sounding cool as ever.

"Shit, my hydraulics are fluctuating. Come in and look me over, will you, see if there's anything leaking out."

Without hydraulics, the Thud was a brick. Will got as close as he could. He was twenty feet to Rogoff's right, scanning the other plane for fluid, when the SAM hit it from behind. There was no time for Rogoff to eject. The whole plane burst into flame as if it had been waiting to do so. Will saw Rogoff inside. His helmeted head was shaking back and forth. It didn't look like terror, but like surprise. Then the black smoke rolled over them, and Will had to dive to avoid the fireball.

"I'm in second grade," Will tells the guys. "I went to a one-room schoolhouse. All the kids went for lunch and recess at the same time." He doesn't feel his usual reluctance. For once he hasn't racked his brains for a story. The memory flooded into his head, complete, while he was flying back from the mission. It filled him with outrage and sadness and loss. Strangely, he wants to tell it.

"I was on the swings when the teacher rang the bell for recess to end. I jumped off my swing at the top of the arc."

"Had you qualified for ejection seat yet?" someone asks, and there's a rustle of laughter. Will grins but continues. The story is pressing against him like a river, sweeping him along with its current.

"I fell straight down like a stone. The ground was hard, because it wasn't raining that summer. It was one of the worst droughts I ever saw. All the crops were dying. Hitting that ground was like hitting a rock. I put my arms out to break my fall, and I broke them. Both arms." He pauses while the others absorb this. He picks up his drink and feels a rush of pity for himself, for his little-boy self, lying curled like a question mark on the ground. He couldn't move his fingers.

"The bell was ringing, and everybody else—all the other kids—they just ran inside." He's tumbling toward the end of the story. The last sentence is like a waterfall, and he slips over it. "I lay there on the ground," he says, "for fifteen minutes, until the teacher finally noticed I was gone."

There's silence. Will takes a deep breath. He clenches his teeth together, just as he did when he was eight, sure that if he opened them, something unbidden would come bursting forth. An animal howl or a girlish yelp of pain. His fellow pilots look at him. A burst of applause breaks the spell.

"You got it, Will!" Baz shouts.

"Call the barkeep," Julep says. "You win that one for sure."

Kit needs to understand that the war's secret was randomness. That nothing but chance decreed whose plane was in front of the SAM, who got it in the belly with flak, who on the ground got pounded while tending his rice, who survived to man his guns for another day. Training, talent, discipline—they all mattered, but in the end it was about being in the wrong place at the wrong time. And yet the pilots still watched every film intently, analyzed the details of each loss, hoping to see what went wrong. *He jinked left when he should have jinked right, sped up when he should have slowed down. I can avoid that mistake. I can stay alive.*

The night he won *ad misericordia*, Will walked home to his

hootch. The air was hot and humid, as always. He kicked off his boots and shrugged out of his flight suit. He lay down on his bed in his skivvies and stared at the village on the ceiling.

"Human life is punishment," he said out loud. The words hung in the heavy air. They weren't quite right. He turned his head and looked at the picture of his daughter. From his prone position, he could see the picture and the clock but not the door. It was eleven PM. In six hours he'd be up for the morning briefing, to find out where he'd be going that day. He remembers lying still, so as not to disturb the moment. There was one more X on his helmet. He'd made it through one more day.

There's silence when Will finishes talking. He wonders if Kit is taken aback or if he just doesn't know what to say.

"How did it end?" the younger man finally asks.

Will shrugs. "The expected," he says. "I got shot down. Ditched in the Tonkin Gulf and floated there for an hour before a navy boat picked me up. I was lucky. I broke an arm and a leg, that's all. I always say the war cost me an arm and a leg."

"And then you wanted to go home."

Will nods. "And then I wanted to go home." There's silence in the car. It fills the air with its presence, as if it were noise or water. Kit looks out the window. Has Will answered the kid's question? *What drew you back?* That's what he wants to know. Will can answer, but only with another question. *What drew me forward? That.*

"I'm getting off here," Will says, pulling to the right. "We'll swing by Meijer so you can pick up that can of paint."

thirteen

Crudité platter (vegetables—dip—olives)
Cheese ball (cheeses, horseradish, nuts—crackers)
Crab dip (crackers)
Deviled eggs (garnish with extras—parsley, red peppers, olives?)
Sun-dried tomatoes and goat cheese on toast (recipe from Bon Appétit*)*
Cucumber rounds with smoked-trout salad
Mixed nuts (use Mexican bowls)

THE LIST IS WRITTEN IN THE ORDER THINGS ARE TO be made. Carol is working her way through a sink full of washed vegetables, cutting them up for the crudité platter. For now she is putting them in plastic bags. When the buffet is set up at five, she'll arrange everything on plates. Two dozen eggs are heating up in a large pan of water, the cheeses have been taken out of the fridge so they can soften up for the cheese ball, and all the serving bowls, platters, and crackers are piled on the kitchen table.

The rhythmic but slightly varied nature of her task is soothing. Each vegetable begins in its natural state, then gets transformed to something more regular. Carrots, celery, and red peppers become neat multicolored planks. Zucchinis, cucumbers, and radishes turn into rounds. She bought yellow summer squash instead of green, even though it doesn't taste as good, because yellow looks better with the other colors, especially the red of the radishes. She focuses on the visual effect as she cuts and stacks the pieces, ignoring the endless question throbbing in her head.

How could he do this to me—again?

The eggs begin to boil, and she steps quickly to the stove to turn the heat down, taking them to a lively simmer. She flips the egg timer stuck to the fridge, then goes back to her cutting board, checking the clock. It's just after one. Will and Kit should be back from the airport any minute now. Trevor is safe in the basement, watching a video. Upstairs, Margaret is doing Leanne's nails. There's a lot to finish, but for now Carol is content to have the kitchen to herself. She doesn't feel like chatting or listening to Margaret explain how to cut a carrot more evenly or describe a fancier way to garnish a cucumber round. She has her own routine.

How could he do it again?

She could throw parties in Hong Kong. She grapples a red pepper under her knife, slicing it across the equator, and allows a vision of life in Hong Kong to form in her head. She's heard about it from other pilots' wives. It's crowded and busy. The harbor is lined with expensive hotels, shops, restaurants. Westerners live in apartment complexes in the hills above the harbor. Down in the city, there are shanties, street people, urchins eating soup from illegal pushcarts and making a living by snatching purses and jewelry from tourists. But pilots and their families live well. They have elegant apartments and hand-tailored clothes. They have drivers and cooks and nannies if they need them—servants come cheap.

"It's only freight," Will said, "and I haven't even made up my mind yet." But she could see from his face that he had made up his mind, that he would be taking the job and plotting the move to Hong Kong. And he would expect her, once again, to go along.

She has finished all the easy vegetables. Now she takes up her vegetable brush and starts scrubbing radishes. They seem especially dirty. She holds each one under the water and scrubs around the top, near the stem. The brush is made of brittle plastic, and it abrades her fingertips when she accidentally scrubs her own hand. Probably she should cut off the tops before scrubbing them, but she hates to do that. She can't stand to open a vegetable until all the dirt has been removed from its exterior.

Twenty years ago, ten years ago, maybe even five years ago, she would have been overjoyed. She would have asked when she could pack. That's what's so frustrating. Why couldn't he have planned something like this when it would have done them some good? Now it can only come as an interruption of her own plans. She suspects that might be the point. An attempt to foil her project, the first project that was going to come to fruition. Picking up a radish and attacking the ring of discoloration at its neck, Carol bites her lip. That's the foundation of her anger. Will has devised this Cathay Pacific scheme to block her bed-and-breakfast.

But why? she asks herself, moving her radish from the sink to the cutting board and taking up the knife. It's not as though there was going to be anything unpleasant about a bed-and-breakfast. It would give Will an excuse to putter around the farm and fix things up—the very thing he loves to do. Yet he has taken every possible excuse to stand in its way; and now, when it was actually going to take off, he has thrown up a giant barrier, stopping her dead in her tracks. It's as if he hated her plan from the start.

"Damn!" The word is out of her mouth before she realizes what has happened. There's a sharp feeling—not pain exactly, more of a shuddery recoil—in the tip of her thumb. Instinctively, she puts it in her mouth. On the cutting board, the tiny butt end of the radish rolls to a stop. The knife slipped off the end of it and into her own hand. She waits until the jittery feeling stops, then removes her thumb from her mouth to see how bad it is.

A little flap on the top gapes open. She bends her thumb back farther, and the cut opens more, the mouth of a stubby man getting ready to speak. Blood blooms up from the spongy inside and courses down in little rivulets. Carol puts the tip of her first finger on top of the flap, pushing it back into place. It throbs gently, and she can feel the beat of her heart in it, a tiny drumming.

"Damn," she says again. She isn't a swearer, but sometimes it helps. With her good hand, she runs water in the sink and moves the cutting board into it, washing off the splatter of blood. Then she rinses both hands under the stream, still holding the flap down with her index finger, and rubs them as best she can on the dish towel. The Band-Aids are in the bathroom.

Carol sits on the edge of the bathtub to wrap a large Band-Aid around her thumb, pinning the flap closed. It will slow her down. But at least it's her left hand. She holds it up and moves the thumb around. Stiff but workable. She can deal with this. The party is in four hours. A minor injury is not going to stop her.

Still, she sits there for a moment, heavily. Why should Will hate her bed-and-breakfast? Why, for that matter, should she want it so much?

"There's just no reason for it," she says out loud. She stands up to go back to work. She glimpses a darkness in the mirror, her body moving past, but she looks away.

"You bite your nails."

Margaret has Leanne's hand in her own, inspecting it. Her voice is less scolding than surprised.

Leanne looks down at her own hand. "Yeah, it's ugly," she says.

"Have you tried one of those polish things that tastes bad?"

Leanne tightens the corners of her mouth. "Oh, I don't know," she says. "Those remind me of things you spray on carpets to keep dogs from peeing on them."

"That would work, too."

There's a pause, and then Margaret smiles. It's not going to be a lecture after all.

"Okay, what do you want to do with them?" Margaret has dropped Leanne's hand and opened up their mother's bathroom cabinet. She pulls a bottle of nail polish off the shelf and frowns at it. "God, when did she buy this, 1978?" She unscrews the top and pulls the brush part of the way out. "Ick. It's completely gunked up." She closes it with two fingers and tosses it in the garbage. It lands with a shrill metallic thunk. "So what are we doing?"

Leanne holds her hand up next to her face, so she can see the back of it in the mirror. Her hands, she notices, are darker than her face, which is pale. Her forehead seems almost preternaturally white. "I don't know," she says. "I really don't care. Whatever you think would look good." Her eyes wander from her face, down her neck, to where her T-shirt tightens over her breasts. People always tell her she has a good body. She never knows what she's supposed to say to that. Sometimes she feels like a stranger in it.

Margaret stands next to her, surveying the cabinet. She's shorter than Leanne, with larger hips and a clearly defined waist. She's heavier but seems tighter and more compact. She might be considered pretty, except she always looks so intense. And her style of dressing always seems like a studied attempt to resist being seen as sexy: tailored pants, boxy jackets, understated jewelry. She sticks to a single style that suggests "elegant" and "unavailable" in the same breath. It's hard to get past that to see anything as ephemeral as beauty in her. Because that's sort of what beauty is, a lack of clear direction or shape. You can impose whatever you want on it.

"Well, you shouldn't do anything bright to draw attention to your nails when they're in that shape," Margaret tells her. "Let's just clean them up a bit and put on a nice matte pink." She rifles through the cabinet, picking up bottles and examining them before putting them back with a decisive clack.

"You don't have to do this," Leanne says. "I can do it myself."

"Yeah, I know," Margaret answers, her face still in the cabinet. "But this is some kind of fantasy of Mom's. A moment of sisterly bonding." She rolls her eyes and holds up two bottles. "Which one do you like best?"

The colors look exactly the same to Leanne. She starts to say so, then stops herself and points to the one on the left. "That one," she says.

Years ago their father installed a vanity in the master bathroom. Leanne sits on the small gold-painted stool, and Margaret perches on the edge of the vanity surface. She has found an emery board and starts filing Leanne's nails. Her stroke is regular and brisk, like that of women in nail salons. Leanne had a professional manicure once, at a salon in New York. It had been her friend Julie's idea for a fun Saturday outing. Leanne didn't find it fun. She felt weird sitting there, frozen like all the other white girls, while dutiful Asian workers hunched over their hands.

"Do you think Mom and Dad will move to Hong Kong?" Leanne asks.

Margaret snorts, not lifting her gaze from Leanne's hand. "Not in a million years."

"Why not?" Leanne is a little surprised at her sister's certainty, as well as at her scorn. Leanne was always her mother's baby, but Margaret and Carol would scheme together. They were the ones pushing to remodel the living room, deciding which private school the girls should attend, complaining about the paltry selection at local stores. Margaret absorbed their mother's dissatisfaction, and then she surpassed it.

"Dad might go," Margaret says, "if he can. But Mom won't. She's really into this bed-and-breakfast thing." Margaret says the words "bed-and-breakfast" reluctantly, as if they embarrass her.

"You think she's really going to do it?" Leanne hands over her first hand again as Margaret reaches for the polish.

"I don't know," Margaret says, the conviction in her voice lessening. She leans over to get a closer look at one of the nails as she paints. "I'm not sure I even understand why she wants to. But she seems pretty intent on it. She's already put an ad in the *Chicago Tribune*."

Leanne considers this. It's the first she's heard of an ad. It's not that surprising. What's surprising is that their mother confided in Margaret. It's Leanne she always used to share secrets with.

Margaret leans back, surveying the result so far. A small furrow of distaste creases her forehead, and she leans forward to correct something. Leanne has the feeling that they *are* having a moment of sisterly bonding, just as their mother intended. Probably, though, she didn't mean for it to be about her.

Maybe I could tell Margaret, Leanne thinks. But tell her what? That she has lied to Kit? That she doesn't want to go to Mexico? Except that wouldn't quite be true. That she doesn't really want to marry Kit, perhaps. Or doesn't know if she does. Margaret wouldn't understand that. Margaret has always known exactly what she wanted and proceeded methodically to get it. She'd never find herself in such a situation.

A still-unformed understanding of something is arriving in Leanne's head. It's like the moment when you're waiting for the subway to arrive: everything is darkness until, faintly, a dim light appears in the tunnel. Slowly, it grows brighter, but there's no sign of the train.

It's not just that they're different. Leanne and Margaret have never been particularly close. In grade school they played together, which meant Leanne agreed to do what Margaret wanted. When they got older, they grew even more different. They would do things together, but they never shared the kind of intimacy some sisters seemed to have. Margaret had more fun with Eddie, who was her age. Sometimes they let Leanne join them, but more often they told her she was a pain. That was where the nickname "Pester" came from. Occasionally, they were even meaner. Once they built a bike ramp out of a plank and cinder blocks. When it was Leanne's turn to go over it, one of them moved the plank to the edge of the blocks so that when she went up it, the plank slipped off and she crashed. Neither of them would admit to doing it, but she could tell by how they laughed that they had intended to make her fall. She didn't cry. She had learned very early that the best way to avoid more teasing was refusing to get upset.

Even when they fed her dog food, she didn't let on that she was upset. It was a warm September Saturday sometime in junior high. They were watching the Michigan game when Margaret said she wanted a snack. Eddie and Margaret went into the kitchen, and Leanne could hear the blender. When she went in to see what they were making, ice cream and Hershey's syrup were on the counter, and the two of them were holding jumbo plastic cups from 7-Eleven. Margaret was sucking the straw on hers, but the shake was thick, and her cheeks were caving in with the effort. As Leanne came in, Margaret gave up, pulled out her straw, and lifted the cup to her lips. When she took it away, a slash of chocolate was across her top lip. She smeared the back of her hand against it.

"What do you want?" she asked, and Leanne said, "Can I have one?"

Margaret was about to say something, but Eddie slipped down off the countertop where he had been sitting.

"I'll make you a shake," he said to Leanne. "Go watch the game. Call us if Michigan scores." Margaret shrugged and looked bored, so Leanne went.

When the two of them came back into the TV room, Margaret handed Leanne a plastic cup, her eyes on the game.

"What's going on?" Eddie asked, throwing himself into the arm-chair. Margaret went to the other end of the couch and curled up, feet tucked under. Leanne took the proffered cup and let the first gulp slide, shockingly cold, down her throat.

"How is it?" Eddie asked.

"Okay," she said. The two of them shrieked with laughter.

"Oh my God, you ate *dog food*!" Margaret gasped, and Leanne's throat constricted. *I will not throw up,* she told herself. *I will not cry.* She set the cup down on the coffee table. *I will not take that to the kitchen,* she thought. *They can do that.* And the cup sat there, sweating circles onto the table, through the afternoon, through Margaret and Eddie's spontaneous bursts of laughter, through Michigan's pathetic loss, until their mother came and said, "Time to go." Then Margaret silently picked up the cup and carried it to the kitchen, and Leanne felt that something, no matter how small, had been won back.

"There," Margaret says. She holds Leanne's hand up in front of her, as if she's incapable of lifting it herself. "What do you think? Do you want another coat?"

Leanne looks at her nails. They're still stubby and gnawed at, but Margaret has smoothed the edges to a nice curve, and the pink gives them a finished quality.

"They look great. Thanks," Leanne tells her.

"The thing is," Margaret says, "Mom has always wanted to go somewhere else. But that was before. I'm not sure she wants that anymore. I think she wants something of her own."

"Something of her own?"

"You know, like a business."

"But she's always said she wanted that," Leanne says, waving her hands in the air to dry them, "and she's never followed through on it."

"Well," Margaret says, "she got pretty close, with the children's clothing store." She stops suddenly, turning to put nail polish bottles back in the cabinet. There's something too deliberate in the set of her shoulders.

Leanne looks down at her hand. "Dad didn't give me my seed money, did he?" she says. "It was Mom's. For her store."

Margaret turns back, and from the honest misgiving on her face, Leanne can see that she didn't make this revelation on purpose.

"You didn't know that?" she says.

Leanne shakes her head. She doesn't trust herself to speak. She crosses her arms in front of her.

"Watch out for your nails," Margaret says, pointing.

Leanne extracts her hands gently and examines them for damage. "They're okay," she says.

They both stand there. They should turn and walk out, head downstairs to help out. But something unsaid hangs in the air. Leanne blows on her fingernails again, lightly, with pursed lips, so the thin stream of air tickles her fingers. She waits for Margaret to say something. She can feel Margaret waiting as well.

"Girls!" Their mother must be at the bottom of the stairs, yelling up. "I could use your help with the deviled eggs!"

"Eggs." Margaret raises her eyebrows and the corners of her mouth in a mirthless grin, then sighs herself into motion. Leanne finds herself nodding, even though Margaret has said nothing that might require agreement. Margaret points at Leanne's nails one more time before heading out the door.

"Don't knock them against anything for two hours," she says.

Someone must need Will somewhere. Party setup is in full swing, and he has already done the one job he was assigned: to deliver Kit's mother, Bernice, from the Grand Rapids airport. She's not quite what he expected. He had in mind a plump, gray-haired matron in a dress and jacket, perhaps sporting a hat or a hairnet—someone like David's mother—but Bernice is nothing like that. For starters, she's tall—not just tall but statuesque—and she has blond hair cut in a fashionable chin-length style. She wears a pantsuit with a large scarf draped across it, adding to the impression of height and giving her a vaguely bohemian aspect. Magnifying the effect is her attitude of uninhibited, uncomplicated warmth for everyone and everything around her. She behaves like a movie star turning on the charm for her fans.

"So Leanne tells me you're a pilot," she said to Will in the car. Kit was in the backseat. "And also of your attachment to your farm. I must say, I find that very humanizing." Will was unsure how to respond. What did it mean to call someone humanized? Bernice has a distinct British accent. He's sure Kit said his mother has lived in the States for over thirty years. That's often true of English people. It's as if they hang on to their accents on purpose. Will didn't say much for the rest of drive, just nodded and gave short answers to her questions.

Now they're home, and Bernice has met everyone and been shown to her room to "freshen up," as Carol puts it. Kit has gone outside to deal with the birdcage. Will roams around downstairs, looking for something to do. He passes Leanne on her way to the dining room, a stack of table linens balanced on two flattened palms.

"What are you doing?" he asks.

"This is all they'll let me do," she says, moving past. She betrayed him this morning, and now she won't answer a simple question. She's holding out on him, they're all holding out on him, angry about the Cathay Pacific revelation. He's officially the villain now. He listens to her rustling in the dining room. It makes him feel helpless and somehow bereft. He puts a hand on his neck and rolls his head right and left, cracking it.

In the kitchen, Carol is peeling eggs and passing them to Margaret, who is slicing them in two and popping the yolks in a metal bowl. Both of them are frowning, intent on their tasks, and

Will pauses in the doorway, surprised at how alike they look from behind.

"What can I do?" he asks. He senses a stiffening in Carol as he speaks. So she's going to continue with the cold treatment. Her voice is level, the tone that offers him nothing.

"Probably you should just stay out of the way," she says.

Margaret glances up. There's something edgy in the way she's moving—it's been there since she arrived, but it's clear she's going to acknowledge nothing, at least not to him. Her eyes meet his briefly, her expression carefully blank, before she goes back to her task.

"So David's not coming for the ceremony, either?" Will asks.

She looks up again, and this time there's a flash of something, perhaps anger, perhaps fear. "He just couldn't," she says. "He's completely swamped."

Carol moves a step closer to Margaret. "I think we should use the large blue plate for these," she says. "You finish the eggs. I'm going to get going on those garnishes."

"We'll have to make space in the fridge." Margaret turns away to look at the fridge, and Will fears he's overstepped the line and made her cry. He stands there, unsure whether to retreat or try to contain the damage.

"You know what you could do, Dad," Margaret says, turning around. She is not crying. She looks as composed and determined as ever. "You could go help Kit paint the other birdcage. It's sitting out in the garage."

"Oh yes, get it, please," Carol adds. "Help him take it out to the barn, so he doesn't get paint all over everything."

"He already went to the barn with it," Margaret tells her. "I saw him heading out there about an hour ago."

"Oh." The two of them pause, coming to an agreement without language. Will feels stupid as he waits. A transaction has occurred, but he has missed its import. Clearly, they're casting about for reasons to dismiss him, but he can't point that out because both of them would feign innocence and ask him what on earth he could mean. He would then be accused of bothering them with silly distractions and making trouble when there was work to do.

"Why don't you go entertain Trevor for a little while?" Carol says. "He's in the basement, right?" She looks quickly at Margaret.

"Is he? I didn't take him down there." Margaret stops what she's doing. "I thought he was upstairs." She wipes her hands hastily on a dish towel. "I'll go and check on him." She hurries out of the room.

It's Trevor. Whatever is bothering her has something to do with Trevor.

"I'm sure he's just playing somewhere," Carol says, more to herself than to Will. She glances up at him and sighs, obviously finding it harder to ignore him with Margaret gone.

"How long are you going to be mad at me?" he asks. Immediately, he regrets saying it. She'll take it as provocation and be even madder.

To his surprise, she merely presses her lips into a thin line.

"I'm not . . ." She shakes her head. "I don't know what to say."

"I kept meaning to tell you about the job. But I wasn't sure it would come through. I thought it would be a nice surprise." Even he can hear the false edge in his voice. He kept his secret because he was afraid of her anger; both of them know that. He lifts his hands in a helpless gesture. "I don't have to take it," he says.

Carol leans back against the counter. "Yes, you do," she says. "You do and you will." Her voice has some of its angry edge back, but its dominant note is resignation.

"It would be fun," he says, sensing an opening and unable to resist aiming for it. "You've always wanted to live abroad." He wants this. He's surprised at the strength of his desire.

"It would have been fun," she says. "It would have." He can't tell if she's giving him something or taking something away. She turns away from him and starts fussing with a bowl of radishes, taking them out one at a time and examining them. Will sees that her thumb is bandaged.

"What'd you do to your thumb?" he asks.

Carol moves it slightly, pulling it toward herself as if embarrassed by it. "It's just a little cut," she says. He can hear the barrier dropping down in her voice, like a garage door closing on the day. Conversation over. He's discharged, whether honorably or dishonorably, he can't tell.

"I guess I'll go help Kit with that cage," he says. "Like you wanted." He stands there for a moment, watching his wife's back. It offers him nothing.

fourteen

AT FIVE O'CLOCK, CAROL AND MARGARET START TAK-
ing things out of the fridge and carrying them to the dining room
table. Leanne is upstairs showering. She and Kit took a walk in the
late afternoon, showing Bernice around the farm. Carol felt an odd
flash of displeasure when Leanne suggested it.

"Why would you want to do that?" she asked.

"It's a treat for me," Bernice answered. Her voice hummed like
a well-tuned car. Her smile seemed genuine and unforced. Carol
was unaccountably annoyed by her. "I don't get many country
walks down in Atlanta."

"Well, the flowers are thriving, but they're a bit bedraggled
after all this rain," Carol replied. Later, she saw the three of them
standing outside the barn. Leanne was waving her hand and talking as the other two gazed up at it, seemingly fascinated. *I might
as well get used to it,* Carol thought. That's what her guests would
be like: entranced with country life, or at least a fantasy of it—rustic old barns, chickens scratching in the yard, attractively rusting
farm tools. Her guests' enthusiasm annoys her already. She's surprised at the strength of her disdain. *So, rustic is what you want?
Here it is.*

"I think we should put the cheese ball closer to the edge of the
table," Margaret says, "so people can get at it easier. The crudités
can go in the middle." She draws one plate forward and slides the
other back, then steps back to examine the result. "Something looks
not quite right. Did we bring everything?"

"We forgot the eggs!" Carol heads for the kitchen. Behind her,
she can hear Margaret rearranging things again.

In the kitchen, she finds Will leaning into the fridge, one arm on
the door. "What are you doing?" she asks. She keeps her voice even.
He's sweaty and still in his grubby work clothes. There are small

dark specks splattered all over his face and shirt. It can't be from the cage—she told them to paint it white.

"I'm starving," he says.

"We're having a huge spread in under an hour. Can you wait?"

"Don't we have any of that salsa left?"

"What salsa? Move, please." She avoids touching him as she moves around him to get the tray of deviled eggs. He eyes them covetously as they go by, but doesn't grab one. Out of habit, she pauses for the slightest second, waiting for him to try.

"I'll just have some cottage cheese," he says, turning back to the fridge.

"Okay, but then would you please get cleaned up and dressed?" She would prefer to avoid this particular argument, but if she doesn't get him in and out of the bathroom, she won't have time to get ready herself.

"As soon as I've had a snack." He pulls a fork from the drawer. Carol stands there as he peels the lid off the blue tub and sets it on the counter.

"I'll need the bathroom in fifteen minutes," she says, turning away.

In the dining room, Leanne has replaced Margaret.

"Margaret's in the shower," she says as Carol arrives. She's wearing a blue dress that looks like underwear. It flatters her angular figure, but some of the relatives will definitely think she forgot to put something on over her slip.

"Is that what you're wearing?" Carol asks. She can see from how Leanne's grimace quickly melts into patient blankness that she anticipated disapproval.

"I wish this was all over with," Leanne says. Her voice rasps a bit, as if her mouth is too dry. Carol swallows hard, bidding the annoyance rising in her throat to dissipate. She has been working nonstop for weeks to make this weekend as nice as possible, and Leanne wants it behind her.

"You're just nervous," she tells her. Leanne moves away from the table, and Carol notes how different her movements are from

Margaret's. Margaret moves with purpose and direction, but Leanne drifts. Now she is floating toward the window, her feet paddling along the carpet like the string on a day-old helium balloon.

Margaret has left a space on the table for the eggs. Carol puts them down and surveys the effect. The flowers she gathered from the garden this morning set it all off beautifully.

"Margaret did a nice job with the flowers," she tells Leanne, gesturing toward them. Carol had wanted to make traditional arrangements: a bunch of roses here, a gathering of daisies there. But Margaret had insisted they use the biggest container they could find, which turned out to be an old butter churn, and pile everything in. At first it looked like a jumble, but as the churn filled with flowers, it took on stature and beauty, its chaos transmuting to an order of its own.

I can use that idea in the bed-and-breakfast, Carol thinks. The butter churn is just the right touch.

"It's nice." Leanne doesn't sound enthusiastic, and Carol feels that prick of frustration at her daughter's vagueness.

"I don't think you appreciate Margaret's efforts to help you," she says. "She's been doing a lot."

Leanne looks away, like she did when chastised as a child, not denying the error but not owning it, either.

"It's not easy for her," Carol says, pushing. "Her life is quite difficult right now." That sounds stupid, and Leanne gives only a faint nod, the smallest possible sign of acquiescence to Carol's words.

"I think we're all a little on edge," Leanne says. "Things being what they are in the world."

"Well, we all haven't just left our husbands," Carol says. Leanne looks up in surprise. That got her attention. Carol's satisfaction at reaching her is quickly replaced with misgiving. "Now, don't say anything," she cautions. "It's a secret."

"I won't." Leanne looks away again, and as quickly as it vanished, her disconnection returns. "I'm not that surprised, actually."

Carol flicks one hand, dismissing the comment, unwilling to contradict it with so little time left. Besides, she's not surprised herself. But there's no time for that conversation, either.

She looks at her watch. In half an hour, guests will start arriving. She looks at the table and ticks things off her mental checklist. *Eggs. Crab dip. Cheese ball and crackers. Crudités. Trout rounds. Napkins.* The toast squares are on baking sheets, waiting to be heated up after the first guests have arrived. Everything is ready, waiting. She will shower, dress, and come downstairs, and then it will start.

They've done it. Surveying the dining room table, the flowers commandeering the center, the neat stacks of cocktail napkins in coordinating colors, Margaret experiences the first real sense of pleasure she has felt since arriving. In spite of the awfulness behind her, of David trying to make her life miserable, of Leanne's odd behavior and the fact that her parents are now barely speaking to each other, they have put together a party worthy of a wedding. She adjusts a plate, suffused with a feeling of possibility. If they can do this, perhaps she can make things work out in her own life. Perhaps the world tends not toward chaos and despair, but toward order and celebration.

As if to confirm the thought, Trevor appears in the doorway. He's wearing the neat pants and a polo shirt she helped him into, and his hair has been freshly combed.

"Look at you!" she says. "Come give Mom a hug."

"Grandma combed my hair," he says, "and the comb was wet." His face is drawn into the half pout that indicates he could break into laughter or sulks, depending on what happens in the next few moments.

"Silly Grandma," Margaret says, crouching to get her arms around him. "Doesn't she know that water is poison to little boys?" He pauses, deciding, and then she can feel the small shudder of a giggle. He moves his head from side to side against her cheek, maximizing contact.

"Is it true," he says, stopping, "that you picked up a real skunk in the barn?"

"Who told you that?"

"Grandma. I mean, Grandpa."

Margaret stands up again and then leans over to kiss the top of her son's head. Nothing in her life has been so pure, so complete and perfect, as her love for Trevor. Anything she does in its name has to be right.

"It's true," she tells him. "But I didn't really do it on purpose. I saw a tiny skunk scurrying along the floor by the spelts bin, and I just grabbed it without thinking."

His eyes wide, he stares at her. Slowly he crinkles his face into a rodent squint. He giggles again. Eyes bright with his own joke, he turns tail and darts out of the room.

"You can't hide from me, little skunk!" she calls. She turns back and looks at the table again. She feels calm, prepared, in control.

The feeling continues as the doorbell rings. Everyone else is still upstairs, so she answers it. It's Eddie, looking awkward at the front door, an entrance he has rarely used. Behind him, his twin seven-year-old boys stop shoving each other long enough to size up Margaret. He has also brought a date. Since he and his wife split up six years ago, he rarely has a girlfriend for longer than a few months, at least as Carol reports it. Tonight's date looks at least ten years younger than he is. She's short and wears the hairstyle Margaret dubbed "the Ryville Roll" in high school—one long curling-ironed roll encircling her face, perfect flatness everywhere else. Margaret smiles at Eddie's introduction, then promptly forgets the girl's name. Mentally, she christens her Roll.

"This is a real nice house," Roll says, although she's barely inside it.

"Thank you," Margaret says. "Come on, Eddie, you can help me set out the champagne." Eddie follows Margaret downstairs to the basement fridge, and Roll comes along, too. The twins trail after, clearly cognizant of the basement's stash of toys. Trevor follows with a proprietary air. As the twins start rummaging through the toy box under his watchful eye, Margaret leads the others to the fridge. She grabs two bottles of champagne and lodges one under each arm, then grabs two more in her hands. The others follow her lead, and they head upstairs.

"We're using the kitchen table for the bar," Margaret says. "There's an old washbasin full of ice there. We'll put these bottles in that." The washbasin had been Carol's idea, another item purchased in anticipation of the bed-and-breakfast.

The doorbell rings again, and Margaret stops in her tracks, arms full of champagne bottles. Consternation threatens her sense of well-being.

"Damn this rural promptness," she mutters. Fortunately, Carol can be heard clattering down the stairs.

"I've got it," she calls out. "Oh no, we forgot all about the champagne. Thank you, Margaret. If your father were helping at all, things like that might be a little easier."

Margaret leads the way to the kitchen. More relatives can be heard arriving, a large crowd of them, from the sound of it. Margaret takes the bottles from Eddie and Roll and arranges them artfully in the ice. Champagne flutes and other glasses are lined up on the counter.

"We may as well inaugurate this batch," Margaret says. She holds a bottle under one arm to steady it while she slowly works the cork.

"I hate them corks," Roll says. "I always get scared one's going to come flying out and hit me in the face."

"It won't if you stay out of its way." Margaret moves slowly and deliberately, offering her competence as an example. She eases the cork out gently so that it makes only the mildest pop. The champagne fizzes slightly, but not enough to overflow. No locker-room antics for her. She holds up the bottle for Roll, proof that there's a right way and a wrong way to do anything. Then she pours three glasses.

"Cheers," she and Eddie say in unison. Roll forces a smile, still struggling to appear at ease. Margaret tries to banish the ungenerous conviction that her attempt at edification has been wasted. Beyond the other two, she can see a gaggle of female relatives moving in their direction. They're slowed down by the need to stop and fondle Trevor, who has made the dire mistake of emerging from the basement.

"Incoming," Margaret says, gesturing with her glass.

"Margaret!" cries Aunt Janice. Eddie's mother has always been demonstrative to the point of brashness. Eddie skirts her deftly, leading Roll out of the kitchen and toward the living room. Loyalty under fire was never his strong suit. Margaret is trapped in the kitchen by the advance of her aunt.

"Hello, Aunt Janice," Margaret says. She walks forward and leans in, allowing Janice to hug her. She tilts her head, avoiding the wiry texture of her aunt's much-dyed hair, and holds her glass carefully to the side so as not to spill anything on herself. Beneath the scent of hair spray, faint undertones of honeysuckle and vitamins emanate from her aunt's skin.

"It's too bad David couldn't make it," Janice says in a low, meaningful tone. "Your mother told me all about it." Margaret stiffens. The hug is lasting too long. Over Janice's shoulder, she sees a tall man come in the door and lean over to kiss Carol on the cheek. It's Doug. Another man hovers behind him, someone Margaret doesn't know.

She pulls back from Janice and runs one hand down the front of her black dress, smoothing it back into place after the vehemence of familial affection. The feel of the dress calms her, returns her to herself. It's an expensive dress, silk and linen, bought at Nordstrom for the delivery of a particularly complicated conference paper: "Tacitus and Teleology." It worked then, and it will work now. She smiles brightly at another relative coming at her, carefully avoiding looking Doug's way. She draws back her shoulders and lifts her chin.

It's not that she wants to flirt with Doug. But there's a stirring in her stomach at the prospect of feeling attractive. She's not old and done for. Her life is full of possibility. Vasant made her see that. Now, standing in her parents' kitchen greeting relatives and family friends, she summons the exhilaration she felt at the gas station on the way to Michigan.

After Janice, most of the others settle for graceful pecks on the cheek or happy clasps of the hand. Margaret stands a bit taller on her heels, grateful for her dress, for having taken the extra time to blow her hair dry. After a few moments, she allows herself to look back at the door. Doug is no longer there, nor is he on his way toward her. Smiling all the way, laying her hand on the arms of relatives, Margaret makes her way across the kitchen to the foyer. He's not there, either. She hears a laugh, and there he is, in the living room, standing with Eddie and Roll. Roll is saying something, and Doug is laughing loudly. The party seems to be in full swing, so his laughter isn't out of place. He looks comfortable, at ease. Not like he's looking for Margaret or even thinking about her presence.

Beyond him, the living room's sliding glass doors are open, and a few people have spilled out onto the deck. She can see the twins there, and then Trevor, following them as they embark on some plot. Trevor looks awed by his older cousins. Watching him follow them, his face an unguarded portrait of longing, she is struck by his innocence. Up until now, his life has been perfect, with no cause for angst or sadness beyond the usual bumps and scrapes of childhood. What will he think about his parents getting divorced? About seeing his father on weekends and holidays, as a court-ordered schedule decrees? *The divorce:* it will become a physical fact in his life, a thing to live with rather than a way of life.

The darkness of everything swirls beneath Margaret, threatening to suck her down. She takes a deep breath.

"Trevor!" someone shouts on the deck. "Look how big you've got!"

Of course he's bigger, she thinks without letting the smile leave her face. *That's how it works. Time passes, and things change.*

"Doug," she says, walking toward him.

Upstairs, Leanne hears yet another person squealing over Trevor as she looks at herself in the mirror. The party has begun. This is it, except it feels unreal. All these people are arriving and standing around chatting, eating and drinking on her behalf, hers and Kit's. She should be down there hugging aunts, kissing old family friends on the cheek and remarking on how much their children have grown. Margaret is surely doing just that, helping Carol steer the party like a large ship while Leanne dawdles upstairs, acting like an adolescent.

She has always enjoyed the moments right before something happens. At home, with her store, it's when she arrives, unlocking the door and firing up the coffeemaker she keeps for customers and employees alike. There's something exquisite about that quiet time before the day has truly begun, before the first person walks through the door asking for pure wool yarn or an embroidery hoop. In those moments, the possibilities are limitless. The day could go in any direction, just as now the party could go in any direction. It's like the beauty of a canvas before the first mark has been made.

Her life is like that, she thinks. It's still a blank canvas, and marrying Kit is like drawing a line on it. It's not irreversible—married people split up all the time—but once you've been married, you can never be truly unmarried again, only divorced. It sets a mark on your life that can't be erased. She has never done anything that indelible.

Marriage should feel like a beginning, not an end. But every beginning requires there be an end to something else. Leanne looks at herself in the mirror. All at once she's sick of seeing herself. The same straight brown hair, the same brown eyes, the same nose with a minuscule, almost unnoticeable bump on the left side. She's not unattractive; she's just bored. She pulls her hair back and twists it around, lifting it to the back of her head. Perhaps she should put it up.

"Hey there." It's Kit. She sees him behind her in the mirror, standing in the door of the bathroom in navy pants and a pale brown linen shirt. He looks nice. "Are you ready to go and face the crowd?"

"I'm sick of me," Leanne says. "I want to be someone else."

Kit smiles as he leans against the doorframe. "Do you want to be me?" he asks. "We could trade."

Leanne considers. She looks from Kit to herself in the mirror. Would she want to be Kit? When she was little, she used to wish she were a boy. She used to imagine how nice it would be to run that fast, to move so carelessly and lightly through the world. But in other ways, being a boy seemed like the worst thing possible. All that activity, all that compulsion to compete. Now she's not so sure. Sometimes when she's having sex with Kit, she tries to imagine that she's the man and he's the woman. It's almost impossible to do.

"No," she says slowly, as if it's a real option. "I guess I don't want to be you."

"Why not?" He gives her an expression of mock injury. Leanne turns her back on the mirror and leans against the dresser, facing him. He has mirth in his eyes, and she tries to make her face match his.

"Because I'd still be stuck with me!"

Will emerges from his bedroom as Kit and Leanne are coming out of the bathroom. He steps aside to let them pass, then follows them down the stairs.

"Oh, here's the happy couple!" someone cries.

Things are well under way. From the staircase, Will can see a cluster of relatives near the door. The front door is open, and Carol is nearby, chatting with a group of people who recently arrived. There's another cluster in the doorway to the kitchen, and voices coming from the living room.

"Well, Will." His brother, George, shakes his hand, which seems strange and vaguely awkward. "You're finally getting rid of the last one."

"That's right." Will nods and chuckles, as he will undoubtedly have to do a hundred more times tonight. Getting rid of his last one. He senses somebody standing next to him and thinks it's going to be Carol. He's surprised when he turns and sees Bernice.

"George, this is Kit's mother, Bernice Lewiston," Will says, "Bernice, this is my brother, George."

"How lovely to meet you." Bernice's voice is a hard toffee, sweet but somehow unpalatable. She is wearing something wispy and colorful, and has fastened her hair with a sparkly rhinestoned barrette. Will can't help but keep glancing at the barrette. It seems wrong. It seems like something a little girl would wear, or a flirty coed, not an English woman of Bernice's age and stature.

"You done flying yet?" George asks, and out of the corner of his eye, Will can see Bernice turning toward him with an expectant smile. "Gracious," that's the word he would use to describe her. But it's a studied graciousness. He shifts his weight and scratches one arm with the other hand. She makes him nervous, standing there waiting patiently for his answer. It's as if she expects something from him.

"Well," Will says, looking around the room. "I don't know about that. I don't know if I'll ever be done flying."

Walking by him, Leanne hears him say it. *No, he won't,* she tells herself. She and Kit work their way through the foyer. Leanne greets people, introduces Kit, thanks everyone for coming. People address her as she passes.

"Are you excited?"

"Oh, yes." When she's faking friendliness, her voice develops a false ring that sounds incredibly obvious to her. She hates hearing it. She clears her throat, trying to make her voice sound normal. She's shaking the hand of one of her mother's friends, and the woman's hand feels damp and slightly too warm, like something rotten. Leanne resists the overwhelming urge to drop it, to pull away from the woman and go wash her own hands.

"Hey, Pester!" Eddie says. He turns around as she reaches the edge of the foyer, drawing her into the living room. Grateful, she walks toward her cousin. Surely things will be better there. Kit stays at her side.

"God," she says quietly to Eddie. "It's quite the turnout, isn't it?"

Eddie smirks toward the foyer. "Just wait till my mom gets her hands on you."

Leanne shivers a little. The living room door is open, and after a day of muggy heat, there seems to be a cool breeze coming in. She tightens her grip on the glass of soda someone handed her.

"Kind of makes you wish you'd eloped, don't it?" Eddie says. He drains the glass in his hand, watching Leanne over the top of it. When Leanne and Margaret were young, he seemed like the height of cool. He taught them to smoke, to identify car models, to listen to the Clash, to use the latest curse words. He introduced Margaret to Doug, and once or twice he took Leanne to Kalamazoo to play minigolf. Now he seems like a far less glamorous character, divorced, working in a factory, living in a Ryville apartment as he slides toward middle age. He sees his boys on weekends, probably taking them to monster-truck rallies or the local double-A baseball game with all the other divorced dads.

"You look a little sick," he says to Leanne. "You need a drink."

When they were little, Rem and Aunt Janice used to hang around on Sunday afternoons, drinking Jim Beam and eating chips. Sometimes Carol, Leanne, and Margaret would visit when Will was away on a trip. There was something incredibly comforting about Rem and Janice's house. Margaret was always trying to get everyone to go do something—a movie or a walk to the nearby lake—and even their mother would sometimes shake her head on the way home. "What a waste of a Sunday," she would say, but to Leanne it seemed ideal. Everyone was content there, willing to take the afternoon as it came. She wished they could go there all the time.

"You're right," she tells her cousin. "A drink is exactly what I need."

"I'll get us some champagne," Kit says, surprising her with his presence. He puts a hand on Leanne's arm and squeezes lightly. It's a squeeze meant to speak volumes, but whether to reassure Leanne or to warn her isn't clear. Leanne turns her head partly toward him as he moves off, so it's in her peripheral vision that he leaves.

Eddie is watching her, his eyes sparkling. "Forget the champagne," he says. "What you need is some of this." He takes a bottle from his jacket pocket and holds it up. The familiar gold-rimmed label spurs a sense of longing Leanne hasn't felt in years. She sees

Hoyt's apartment, the shelves full of cassette tapes, the bare floor where they used to sit in silence for hours.

"That," she says, "is what's so great about men. Interior pockets."

"Here," he says, holding out a hand. "Give me your Coke. No one will know the difference."

Carol looks over in time to see Leanne handing something to Eddie. She looks away, surveying the room without really seeing it, then looks back. Eddie and his date and Leanne are chatting. Everything looks quite normal.

"Excuse me," she says to her friend Sylvia. "I just want to check on the food."

A vague fear nags her as she heads for the dining room, like a large, hovering bumblebee. If she ignores it, it will fly away on its own. Lashing out at it or trying to shoo it off will only make it sting.

She stands in the door of the dining room and assesses the situation. As always, the deviled eggs are disappearing fast. The bowl of crab dip is half empty. The nuts are ebbing, and the cheese ball has a good hunk hacked out of it. Cracker levels are low. The crudité platter is far less disturbed, the stacked vegetables still looking pristine and orderly, only the smallest inroads visible in the dressing. And the cucumber rounds with trout salad appear to be untouched.

"More crackers," she says to herself. Cloaked in purpose, she threads her way around the people chatting between the kitchen and dining room. Once she has the cracker box, it's even easier. People smile and nod, and she moves by them, clearly on a hostessing mission.

It's going well, she tells herself as she refills the platters with crackers, arranging them in a neat half circle around the cheese ball, and lining them up in perfect overlapping rows next to the crab dip. Everyone seems to have arrived—the doorbell is no longer ringing. General movement has distributed people throughout the living room and dining room, filling both spaces with the ebb and flow of conversation. They have even spilled out onto the deck. Thank goodness she made Will move that hideous post-hole digger.

She glances nervously out the window. There has been a darkening in the light, and it's too early for the sun to be setting. She still refuses to allow that it might rain tomorrow. But she's worried about more rain tonight, which could make the lawn at the country club soggy, complicating Leanne's high-heeled walk down the grass aisle. The weatherman said rain, but he's always wrong. Probably it's clouding over a bit, the way it often does on Michigan evenings.

If only Leanne had agreed to have her wedding indoors, as Margaret did. Margaret never would have planned an outdoor wedding. Weather brings an element of uncertainty into planning, and Margaret hates uncertainty. But Leanne—it isn't that Leanne likes uncertainty, but she always seems to surround herself with it. It's her natural element, the way some people tend toward depression and others seem constitutionally cheery. Leanne's disposition is watery, blurred, unfixed.

Marrying Kit will change that. There will be another pole in her life, holding her steady even as she drifts along her own unplanned path. And if she has kids—Carol hardly allows herself the hope that Leanne will give her more grandchildren, since Margaret seems less likely than ever to do so—then that will ground her even further, tie her to the world in a way she seems reluctant to allow on her own. It's not that Carol wants her daughters tied down. But it would do Leanne good to have some stability in her life, something to give her a sense of progress.

"Things are really going well, Carol. You must be so pleased." It's Bernice, moving toward Carol and standing a little too close for comfort. She smiles benevolently at the table. "You really have gone to a lot of trouble," she says. "I'm sure the children are grateful."

Carol can't think of a reply. Bernice puts her off, makes her nervous and tongue-tied, not through any standoffishness or offense but because of her excessive good grace. Bernice is just too perfect.

"Well," Carol answers, taking the smallest step back to regularize the distance between them, "hostessing is something I'll be doing a lot of after this, with the bed-and-breakfast going!"

"There she is!" someone sings out in the next room, and for a split second Carol thinks they're referring to her. But then she hears Leanne's high-pitched "Hello, Aunt Janice!" Carol recognizes the artificial edge in Leanne's tone. She never could disguise her discomfort in social situations.

"I'd better just check on the living room and see that things are going well out there," she says, embarrassed by the intensity of her desire to escape Kit's mother. After all, the woman is soon to be a member of the family, even if an honorary one.

I'll make it up to her later, Carol tells herself as she moves decisively away. She hovers in the archway that separates the dining room from the foyer. It feels as if there's a small cloud hovering around her head. It's holding her back, this tiny darkness, urging her to turn around and say something kind in parting. *Don't be silly,* she tells herself. She has no reason to feel guilty. It's not as if she's shirking some pressing duty—she's just going about her business. Her daughter is getting married tomorrow, and she has a party to run. Pressing herself into motion, she sweeps out through the arch and into the foyer, where her guests are gathered in groups of three or four, waiting for her.

fifteen

EDDIE'S BOTTLE HAS SAVED LEANNE'S LIFE. SUD-
denly, it all seems bearable. Not only bearable but almost fun, in a
vaguely sickening way. The party is like swimming in the ocean
when the surf is high. Waves of it surround her, lift her up until her
feet aren't touching the ground, then set her down again, to get her
bearings and regain her balance. Every now and then one crashes
over her head, so that she tumbles without knowing where she is for
a while, but then her feet find the ground and she's back, preparing
for the next one.

She takes a sip of her drink. Eddie has abandoned her, letting her
be drawn into the exclamations and congratulations of others, but
before he left, he took her glass and topped it off from his bottle.
The whiskey, after she has gone so long without drinking, has taken
effect instantly. She's enjoying the feeling of looseness, the ease with
which she laughs and says hello to people, the slightly dizzy sensation when she moves quickly.

"Leanne, look at you, all grown up and getting married!"

For a moment she falters. She could fall into a trap here and consider the remark's significance. Here she is, all grown up. Grown up
and getting married. Next will come kids, then middle age, then old
age and the long slow slide into nothing. That's how it goes.
Somehow they're all delighted to see she has joined them on the
path. The one true way.

She flicks the thought aside and holds her glass a little tighter.

"Uncle Rem!" she says. He holds out his arms, and she lets
Eddie's stepfather hug her. He's her aunt Janice's second husband.
Eddie's real father disappeared when Eddie was only four. After
that, Eddie heard from him only at Christmas and on his birthday.
On each of those occasions, his father would send Eddie a gift,
something unremarkable like a basketball, wrapped in drugstore

paper. Poor Eddie. It's good he had Rem, who was more of a father than his real one. The thought fills her with affection for Rem. What a wonderful man he is.

"This is my uncle Rem," she tells Kit, taking her uncle's arm a little vigorously. Rem nods at Kit, then sheepishly takes the hand Kit has offered and shakes it awkwardly.

"Uncle Rem saved me from living my *entire* life in the hayloft," Leanne tells Kit. She waves an arm expansively. "The first time I went up, I was too scared to step on the ladder to climb back down. He came up and carried me down like a sack of potatoes."

"More like a goat, really," Rem says. "Front legs over here, back ones here."

"That's right, a goat!" Leanne giggles. "A goat who was bad."

"I'll remember that," Kit says, "in case I ever need to get her down from somewhere." He and Rem draw their mouths into smiles, looking at each other, not her.

Leanne takes a sip from her glass. The dark liquid is disappearing quickly, leaving ice cubes stranded like boats. She glances around the room, looking for Eddie.

"The kids were always up to something," Rem says, still focusing his attention on Kit. "The girls—they were okay, but Eddie was always in trouble."

"I'm sure Leanne could cause some trouble of her own," Kit says, falling in with the light tone. "She certainly does now."

He glances at Leanne. She presses her lips into the look of mock-upset required by his banter, but the desire to find Eddie and replenish her drink is sucking her attention from the conversation. She sees him across the room, and in a moment of pure divine intervention, he looks up and meets her eye. She raises her eyebrows and her glass slightly, a gentle request. He nods, then turns to the people beside him, making his excuses to leave. Eddie, Eddie, Eddie. She's always loved him.

Help is on the way. Leanne turns back to Rem and Kit. One of them must have asked her something, because both of them are looking at her, waiting for a reply.

"Sorry," she says. "I was distracted for a second." She gives them an apologetic smile, and the happy knowledge that Eddie is on his way imbues it with real warmth. She takes a deep breath. *Focus,* she orders herself, and it helps. Her head clears.

"I said," Rem repeats, "remember when you kids found that deer in the creek?"

"Deer in the creek?" In her peripheral vision, Eddie is moving toward her but has gotten tangled in a cluster of family friends.

"Yeah, the deer you found in the frozen creek."

"Oh, the frozen deer!" Leanne turns eagerly to Kit. "It was amazing! We found a deer in the middle of winter, frozen into the creek."

Kit looks puzzled. "You mean sticking out of the ice?"

Leanne shakes her head. "No, no, it was in the creek—right in it. In a deep part. And it was frozen right into the ice, underneath the surface."

"The creek froze over a dead deer?"

Leanne shakes her head again. Is Kit slow on the uptake, or is he testing her clarity? "No, it wasn't dead when it fell in. That was the weird part. It was standing up. It was like a fake deer, but it was real, just standing there, frozen. Frozen, you know, in the ice. *Down* in the creek." She stops. She's using too many words.

"I see," Kit says. "That is weird."

"You see some strange stuff around here," Rem says. "My brother once found a toad with two heads."

"Pollution, that probably was," Leanne says, her voice cheerful again. "Pesticide runoff, or something from the paper mills. But the deer—no one could explain that!"

"Maybe it fell in and drowned and froze at the same time," Kit offers. "Maybe the two things happened in tandem."

"That's what Margaret said," Leanne tells him. "When we found it. And Eddie said maybe it fell in and drowned and the currents pushed it into an upright position. But that's not what happened." They wait for her to explain, but she's lost. Explaining is too difficult. She remembers looking down at the deer, standing there like a huge, waterlogged stuffed animal. From the way it stood, it was obvious that the deer had dropped into the water right there. It had walked out and fallen through the ice and frozen instantly. It wasn't even a real dead thing. It was a frozen thing. When spring came, the ice would melt and that deer might clamber right out of the creek, scramble up the opposite bank and take up life where it left off. Water would be flowing and trees would be blooming and everything would be starting anew.

"Come here and you can see better," she remembers Eddie telling her. He was standing on the creek bank, holding on to a tree with one hand so he could lean out over the ice. His BB gun was crooked in his other arm. He leaned his gun against the tree and took Leanne's hand with his free one. She held on while she leaned out over the creek to see the deer better, letting all her weight hang from his hand. After a moment, Eddie pulled her slightly toward him, then opened his hand for a second so she started to fall, before quickly grabbing her again. She screamed.

"Chicken," he said.

But she leaned out over the creek again. She remembers thinking she could see the fur on the deer lifting slightly in a current beneath the ice. She could see its ears. She thought of horses' ears, firm on the outside, soft fuzz on the inside. A horse would stand perfectly still like that, ears alert, eyes wide, ready to burst into breathtaking motion. When it happened, it happened so fast you didn't even see it start.

I wish I was it, she thought. *I wish I was the frozen deer.*

"Hey, Leanne!" Eddie has arrived. "Hi, Rem." He has always called his stepfather Rem. Rem, Remy. Rémy Martin.

"Give me your glass," he tells Leanne. "I'll get you some more Coke."

Margaret is on her fourth glass of champagne, and her cheerful attitude is degrading quickly. People keep coming up to her to say hello, or to enthuse about tomorrow's festivities, and every time she has to give her standard answers to the question "Where's David?"

"He's crushed he couldn't make it. His department is a mess right now, and he just couldn't leave."

"He's completely swamped with work. We're both so sorry he couldn't be here."

"Even he can't believe how busy he's been."

She's said it so many times, she almost believes it herself. It's as if there's an alternate reality, one in which Margaret never went to a Shostakovich concert with Vasant, Vasant never invited her up to his place for a cup of tea, David never got angry and threatened her, no one ever called the police, and lawyers were never required. The funny thing is, that alternate reality is the only version of Margaret's life anyone in Michigan has ever known. It's Carol's version, the version in which Margaret's husband is a loyal and charming intellectual, Margaret is a dedicated and energetic wife, and their son is the crowning joy of their lives. Trevor. She looks around the room for him. There he is, on the deck, being handed some sort of snack by her uncle George. Undoubtedly, he'll go to sleep overfed tonight, hopped up on too much sugar. Eddie's twins are nowhere in sight. They must have abandoned the younger boy. Margaret wonders if she should find them and tell them to be nice to Trevor. That might be rude.

Doug is standing by the fireplace. Her cheerfulness abrades further as she catches sight of him. He chatted pleasantly with her when she broke in upon him, Eddie and Roll, but he seemed to be treading carefully, choosing his words and keeping the conversation general. After only a short time, he excused himself and went to congratulate Leanne. Now he's talking with the man who came in with him, a nice-looking guy in a striped shirt who obviously isn't from Ryville. They appear to know each other well. It's easy to forget, in Evanston, what small-town life is like. Here, strangers stick out like sore thumbs, because everyone knows everyone else. And everything about them, too.

Margaret always hated that. Even now she hates the idea of people talking about her, as they inevitably will, discussing the failure of her marriage. In a university community, that's bad, but in a small town, it's even worse.

Too big for her britches. That's a phrase people use in a place like Ryville—people who have always considered Carol and her daughters snobs, with their private schools and summer camps, their clothes from Chicago and their lessons in music and ballet. It's usually said of a girl—a girl who wants something more than a husband and kids and enough money to go the mall on weekends to buy a polyester blouse at Kohl's.

"Margaret, I can't believe how Trevor's grown!" One of her mother's friends grabs her arm. "So David couldn't make it, huh?" She's a short, stout woman, with wide eyes surrounded by spiky mascaraed lashes that make her look permanently surprised. Margaret can't remember her name.

"No, he couldn't come." It's one of those names starting in L and ending in a—Laura, Lisa, Lana. But more unusual.

"Well, I'm sure he's real disappointed." Lena. Layla. Luna.

"He is." Margaret has run out of things to say about David. She's tired of discussing it—or of not discussing it, rather.

"Lila!" Carol appears magically at her side. Margaret has never been so happy to see her. "Did you get a glass of champagne and something to nibble on? So how is Martin?" Carol takes Lila's arm as the other woman launches into a long story, something about surgery and physical therapy and hospital bills. Margaret tries not to let her interested expression fade. When Trevor wanders back into the house, looking around, she sees her chance. Quickly, she excuses herself.

"How you doing, peanut?" she asks him. "I see you've had lots of snacks."

"Where did those others go?"

"Who?" Margaret's heart aches.

"Those other boys."

"I don't know. Shall we check and see if they're in the basement?" Trevor nods. Margaret takes his hand. Eddie's twins are seven, she tells herself. They're old enough to behave civilly. They can't go around ignoring another kid just because he's a couple years younger. At least they'd better not while she's around.

She takes Trevor down the stairs, preparing her speech in her head. But when they arrive at the play area, Eddie's boys are engrossed in setting up a ramp to send cars over. Trevor heads right for them, and they make room for him without a squawk. Her lecture isn't required.

She goes up the stairs slowly, reluctant to return to the party. She can't stand the thought of talking to one more person. Her face feels tight from smiling, and welling up in her chest is a funny urge to cry. She has to take a break and pull herself together. But where can she go? She heads for the hall bathroom.

The door is closed. Margaret stands in the hallway. She can hear someone moving around inside, but she listens in vain for the running water that would herald an imminent emergence. She could go to one of the upstairs bathrooms, which will almost surely be empty, but that means negotiating the foyer—impossible to do without stopping to talk to at least three people. She leans her head against the hallway wall and stands there, taking deep breaths, glancing occasionally toward the living room. After only a minute or two, she hears footsteps moving in her direction. Someone else is also looking for the bathroom. Without thinking, she retreats to the end of the hallway. As fleetly and quietly as possible, she opens the door to the garage and slips outside, easing it shut behind her. With any luck, she hasn't been seen.

There's a nervous rustling in the gloom. Margaret turns on the light. The doves regard her from their cage. The larger one is huddled near the floor. The smaller one gets to its feet defensively when Margaret comes near.

"How are you?" she asks them softly.

The door from the house opens, and light spills in. Margaret starts upright, guilty.

"Margaret?" Doug says.

"I'm right here." Margaret can't keep a slight unfriendly edge from her voice.

"I saw you go out to the garage," Doug says. "I thought I'd check to see if you were okay."

"I'm fine." Margaret jerks a hand toward the cage. "I was just checking on the doves."

He closes the door behind him. "Doves?" Undeterred by her terseness, he comes closer.

"For the wedding ceremony." Margaret feels unwilling to explain the gesture Leanne has planned. But Doug nods, stopping a few feet away.

"The bigger one has been looking lethargic." Margaret softens her voice, relenting somewhat. It's nice of Doug to be concerned. She never showed much concern for him. She looks away as if he might guess her thoughts.

Doug leans over and opens the door of the cage. He reaches in and, so quickly and softly no one has time to get ruffled, he catches the larger dove. He pulls it out and holds it in both hands, its head sticking up and feet sticking down from his grasp. His thumbs stroke the bird gently but firmly as he examines its head, rolling it to one side and then the other. It tries to flap its wings once, when he takes his left hand off it, but for the most part, it goes still, fixing him with eyes like tiny bright beads.

"Looks fine to me," Doug says. "A little inactive, maybe. But there's not anything clearly wrong with it." He holds the dove against his chest in order to open the cage again, then eases it gently in. "The eyes and feathers look fine."

"Maybe it's just depressed," Margaret says.

Doug turns to her. "So how have you been?" he says.

Margaret flushes. "I've been fine," she says. She raises one arm out to her side, following its progress upward with her eyes, as if it weren't hers. Realizing this must look strange, she stops. "How about you?"

"Okay, I guess," Doug says. "Mother's tired a lot of the time. And she doesn't walk well. But she's doing great."

"I'm sorry to hear that." Doug's mother was never very well, but sometime in the last ten years, she was diagnosed with lupus. Carol heard about it from a friend and told Margaret.

"I always wanted to send you a letter or a card," Margaret says, her heart filling with the sense of her own inadequacy as a friend. "I'm really sorry I didn't."

Doug looks at her simply, with no malice. "I'm sorry, too," he says. "It would have been nice to hear from you."

It's the sort of thing David would have said. But David would have been aware that it was the right thing to say.

Margaret looks down at her black pumps. She has a familiar longing to tell Doug everything—about David, their marriage, driving up to Michigan in the rain. *I'm afraid the police will come to claim my child,* she wants to say. She could break down and cry, ask him what she ought to do. Go ahead with this horrible divorce, a custody battle fought in courts and adjudicated by complete strangers? Or go back to Evanston and take her chances on being able to sort out something more amicable with David? That's the riskier route, because it isn't clear what could happen.

"I wanted you to meet my friend Louis," Doug says. "Your mother said it would be okay for me to bring someone."

"Oh . . ." Margaret feels confused. So he brought someone—as in a date? She looks at Doug, standing there across from her, and it's clear that she knows nothing about his life. It's been over ten years since she saw him. Or since she was in the same place with him, rather. She doubts very much that she ever really saw Doug. She remembers standing outside her dorm at night, Doug casting about for words to tell her something about himself. Something he wasn't sure about. Maybe he was hoping she would help him. But she wasn't willing. She wasn't much of a friend.

Doug turns toward the doves. "I'm sure they're going to be great," he says. "I don't think there's anything wrong with that big one."

"He's probably faking," Margaret says, relieved. "To get more food."

"She," Doug says. "It's a female. They both are."

"They're both girls? Are you sure?" She stares at the birds. Two females! That would definitely shock her mother.

"You don't expect me to get that wrong, do you?" Doug says.

"I'm a farmer. I ought to know birds." He smiles as if there's a private joke between them. But there isn't. She doesn't even know this man, and he doesn't know her. The urge to tell him everything seems silly. What could he say? He can't help her any more than she could help him in Chicago all those years ago. Besides, she's made her choice.

Margaret nods. "So they're girls," she says. "It doesn't matter." She moves toward the door, but he's standing between her and it. "It doesn't mean a thing."

She inclines her head slightly toward him, and Doug steps back to let her pass. She slips by him quickly. The first thing she's going to do is have another glass of champagne to celebrate her newfound certainty. She can hear Doug following her as she moves forward, in control again, out of the garage and back to the party.

Carol is on the deck. The sun is setting and the wind has risen, but that doesn't necessarily mean rain. Perhaps a little shower passing over before midnight, leaving time for the water to soak into the ground and the grass to dry out.

There's a sting on her arm, and she slaps quickly—too late. Mosquitoes are out. The house will be full of them now, what with everyone going in and out, leaving the screen door open. She'll have to get Will to go around with the Raid before they go to bed. Even that won't get rid of them all. She'll do Trevor's room with extra care and shut the door. She doesn't want him itching and miserable all day tomorrow.

She looks around for Trevor. She's seen Margaret doing it, too, keeping track of where he is, not wanting to let too much distance get between them. She doesn't see Margaret, either; she must be wherever Trevor is.

She picks up her champagne glass off the deck railing. It's frosty with condensation, and the bubbles are few and far between. She likes it this way—it doesn't fizz in her nose so much, or make her want to hiccup. She takes a gulp, and the remaining bubbles burn in her throat as the liquid goes down. She must be thirsty. *I should get some water instead,* she tells herself, but she doesn't feel like walking across the deck and into the house to get it. Tiredness is starting to dog her.

"Hey, Will!" someone booms.

There's a general perking up as Will appears on the deck. From where she stands in the darkness at the edge, Carol can see him outlined in light from the living room. When he was young, he had a classic fighter-pilot physique—hard and lean, daring the world to resist him. His body is wider and more settled now, but he still has an electrical charge, an energy that lights him up from within.

"Will, word is you're going to keep flying." Janice's husband, Rem, is the speaker. He was always a fan, encouraging Will to tell flying stories at family gatherings. Everyone loves Will's stories: the passenger who gets drunk and causes trouble, the uppity flight attendant, the practical jokes played by pilots on each other. He always used to have one in reserve. Lately, he doesn't talk about the airline as much.

"Guess those Japs don't care how old you are, do they?" Will's brother, George, says. Typical: prejudice and ignorance combined. How did Will's secret application to Cathay become common party gossip? "Cathay is Chinese," Carol says, draining her glass with a jerk of annoyance. She turns away, looking for the happy couple, but they, like Margaret, seem to have disappeared. Maybe they're finally getting something to eat.

"What do you think, Carol? You going to like living in Hong Kong and eating Chinese food all the time?" It's Rem again, making what he thinks is jolly conversation.

"Oh, I don't think it will come to that," she says. She holds up her glass, gesturing her desire to get a new one.

Rem ignores the gesture. "What do you mean? You think he won't go?"

There are other people watching her as well. Carol shrugs, not looking in Will's direction. "Maybe he won't pass the physical," she says.

There's a small explosion of laughter, as if she's said something hilarious.

George steps over to Will and pats the slight paunch on him with a proprietary air. "What do you mean?" he chides. "Look at the man! He's the picture of physical fitness. A real George Foreman." He points to Will's head. "Sharp as a tack, too! And eyesight like a hawk!" It's true. Even now, nearing sixty, Will doesn't need glasses.

"Yeah," Carol says without thinking. "But can he hear?"

The laughter is a smaller noise this time, and Carol looks at Will. He's staring at her, eyes wide. She's hit the mark. And he's surprised—it must not have occurred to him yet. She's a little surprised herself. It's been a slow decline; she never really noted it consciously.

The breeze flutters up again, feeling even cooler this time. Carol wraps her arms across her body and looks around, wanting to say something to dispel the dampening of cheer her remark has caused. She gives a hesitant, exploratory laugh, a foot in the door of mirth as it edges shut.

"Besides," she says, "Will needs to be here and be a full-time farmer boy. We've got bed-and-breakfast guests coming, and they expect the real thing!" That does it—people laugh, and the conversation starts up again. But Will's face, even as he joins in the laughter, is edged with sadness.

Clutching her glass, Carol goes inside, closing the screen door tightly behind her. *Mosquitoes out, Carol in,* she thinks. *Will love, Carol fifteen.* She shakes her head, trying to clear it. She must be getting drunk.

People have consolidated in the living room and the kitchen. She's crossing the empty foyer, trying to erase the image of Will's eyes, when she gets the feeling she's not alone. She stops and turns around. Leanne is sitting at the top of the stairs. She sees Carol looking and waves a hand. Actually, she just holds a hand up, fingers spread, as if to say *Stop.* Carol halts, unsure whether to go upstairs. Then she sees Kit coming from the kitchen with a glass of water.

"Hey there," he says, smiling carefully, and Carol nods to him, reversing her mental course. Whatever is going on with Leanne, it's for Kit to handle now. She turns and heads for the kitchen.

Kit climbs the stairs slowly, deliberately, holding a glass of water in his hand. He stops a few stairs below Leanne and squats down, leaning his back against the wall.

"Here." He holds out the water. Grudgingly, Leanne takes it. She feels dizzy, as if she might pitch forward down the stairs. She knows she should drink the water, but it's the last thing she feels like doing. She wants to lie down, right there, and go to sleep.

"Drink," he says.

"Kit," Leanne says, leaning her face toward the glass (where did he find such a huge plastic glass?), "I've been trying to tell you."

"Come on, drink," he says. Leanne puts her mouth on the edge of the glass, and some of the water sloshes against her upper lip. Maybe she can absorb it that way. Kit continues to watch her, so she lifts her lip and lets some of the water slide into her mouth. She forces herself to swallow.

She has to finish what she started. She has been sitting here, looking down on people at the party, surprised by how easily it went on without her. *It's okay,* she's been telling herself. *It's really okay.* No one will mind having come to a cocktail party if the wedding doesn't take place. The party was for Carol anyway, and for Will. It was a chance for them to see all their friends, to show off their grown daughters and Trevor. And that has gone fine. Everyone saw Leanne. There's no need for them to see her getting married.

"Kit," she says. He puts a hand on hers and pushes the cup toward her again. Dutifully, she drinks. This time she takes a big gulp, and it feels good, icy water going down her throat. She gulps and gulps until it seems that the glass must be empty. When she moves it away from her face, she's surprised to see that it's only half gone. She gasps for air.

"Kit," she says, "I can't go to Mexico with you. I'm drunk."

"That you are," Kit says, nodding solemnly.

"No, I mean, I'm *a* drunk. *A* drunk." She wonders if he gets it. Perhaps she should say it again, more clearly. "*A* . . ."

"I know," Kit says. "Drink some more water. Your father's going to make a toast."

Leanne's heart fills with happiness. She's told him. He admits that she's right. They won't get married after all. He must have known it all along. He's just been waiting for her to make up her mind. They're in it together.

Kit stands up and reaches out a hand. Leanne gives him her cup, then her hand, so he can pull her slowly to her feet. He puts her hand on his arm and starts down the stairs, supporting her with one arm, carrying her water with the other. Nice, nice Kit. Her steps are wobbly. She pauses once, and he senses her hesitation and stops, so she can guzzle some more water. Then they move forward. By the time they reach the bottom of the stairs, she's doing okay. She's steady enough on her feet, with Kit's support. She leans into him and walks. Her sense of relief keeps her legs moving. They didn't have to fight. He understands.

Guests have gathered in the living room. Margaret is standing in the center, next to Will. Leanne doesn't see Carol, but she must be somewhere close by. People step aside for Kit as he leads Leanne to the front.

"Thank you all for coming tonight," Will is saying. "I want to say how glad I am to have all my family and friends here to help us celebrate."

Standing next to her father, Margaret can feel his hesitation. He hasn't planned in advance what to say. That's so typical of him. She's always thought she was like her father, a mover, a doer, but really, they're different. She's a planner, and he charges ahead blind.

Will turns to Kit. "Kit is a great guy," he says. "He's the kind of person you can talk to. I admire that. I couldn't have picked a better husband for Leanne myself."

Margaret can see Leanne swaying slightly on Kit's arm. She looks happy, happier than she has looked all night.

"And so," Will is saying in conclusion, raising his glass, "here's to the happy couple. May they be as happy . . ."

Margaret's eyes widen. Will he say it? She looks around the room for her mother. There she is, standing next to Aunt Janice, a fake smile plastered to her face.

"May they be as happy as they deserve," Will finishes. Margaret sees, suddenly, Doug standing in the crowd, as relaxed as a benign king. The stranger, Louis, is at his side. Quickly, she steps forward before people can start talking again.

"I'd like to make a toast, too," she says. A hard knot has formed in her stomach, the bitter offspring of her resolve.

"They say now that one in two marriages ends in divorce," she says, smiling at the crowd. "I know this worries my father. But I'd like to say to him that, given those odds, I'm sure my sister's marriage will be a long and happy one."

"Hear, hear," shouts Uncle Rem, and others join in, raising their glasses. Margaret looks at Leanne over her glass as she drinks. Leanne is still leaning on Kit, smiling as people lean forward to speak to her. She looks like she's not hearing a thing. Margaret's eyes turn to Carol. Carol is staring back at her, shocked.

At least someone got it, Margaret thinks. She drains her glass.

"Nice toast, Dad," she says.

"Thanks," he says. "You, too."

Will is distracted. He can hardly answer Margaret. He wants nothing so much as for all these people to be gone. And he may get his wish. The toasts, oddly enough, seem to have provided some kind of sign for the party to end. Already, a few people are gathered around Carol, saying their goodbyes. Kit and Leanne have moved to the couch, exhausted, no doubt.

It occurs to Will that he's starving. He hasn't eaten a thing since he finished off the tub of cottage cheese. Maybe there's something left on the food table. He ambles toward the dining room, stopped several times by people congratulating him and saying goodbye. He shakes hands and kisses cheeks. Finally, he gets to the dining room.

As he expected, it's empty. He surveys the damage. There's some kind of dip that's nearly gone, and a few scattered crumbs of cheese. Empty bowls dot the table, giving no sign of what they might have contained. There's still a big pile of vegetables, though, and quite a few small cucumber rounds with some kind of salad on them. He picks one up and bites into it. Fish.

He eats the rest of the cucumber things, and then he starts in on the vegetables. There's a lot of dip left, something creamy, and when he loads that on, even the summer squash isn't bad. From the foyer, he can hear the sounds of departing guests. He should be out there, saying goodbye with Carol, but right now food is more important.

"Hi, Dad." He turns. It's Leanne, standing in the doorway. She looks a little wobbly on her feet, and slightly pale. She probably hasn't eaten anything, either.

"Hey," he says. "Come and have a snack." Leanne walks toward the table as if intending to do just that. But when she gets there, she leans heavily against it, looking down at her hands. He sees a thin layer of moisture clinging to her upper lip.

"I don't know what to do," she says.

Will stops chewing a pepper long enough to take a good look at her. Her shoulders are hunched, and her lip is trembling. "What's wrong?" he asks. One of Carol's phrases comes to mind: "an attack of nerves." Or maybe Leanne ate something bad. The possibility that she's drunk crosses his mind, but he doesn't want to think it. He never saw her with any champagne, and that's all they were serving.

Leanne stares at her hands. "Nothing's wrong," she says. She looks up at him and laughs, a short, loud exhalation, as if trying to make a joke. The effect is gruesome.

"You proposed to Mom on the third date," she says. "How did you know you wanted to get married?"

Will looks down at the veggie plate. There aren't many red peppers left, but there's lots of broccoli and cauliflower, and a whole pile of scallion lengths.

"Sometimes you arrive in a place and you know it's the right place," he says. "Or sometimes you just take the leap of faith. It's like flying. Sometimes you can see it. You look out the window and there it is, the place you're going."

"But not all the time?"

"No, not all the time."

"How do you know when you've gotten where you're going if you can't tell you're there?" Her expression has gone from light-hearted to quizzical, as if she's having a hard time putting his sentences together in her head. She's certainly acting drunk.

"It's called dead reckoning," he says. "You fly in the right direction at the right speed for a certain length of time, and when that time has passed, you're there."

"You don't know you're there?"

Will tilts his head. "You *do* know you're there. You must be there, because you've reckoned it that way."

Leanne looks at the red pepper in his hand. Her face is quizzical, the way it used to be when she was a baby. He's not sure what they've been talking about, but he longs to embrace her. The memory of everyone's coolness toward him earlier in the day stops him. He stands, frozen, unsure what to do.

"I need to go to bed," Leanne says. She starts for the door. He watches the back of her. In the archway, she stops and turns her head. "Good night, Dad," she says, an afterthought. She doesn't look at him.

"Good night, Leanne."

Half an hour later, it's over. The last guests are gone, and Kit has followed Leanne into the room they're sharing. Margaret put Trevor to bed and helped clear the dining room table and load glassware into the dishwasher before Carol urged her to go to bed herself. Margaret swayed slightly on her heels, considering, and then for once, did as she was told. Now it's just the two of them, Will and Carol, in the bright kitchen. Lights are still blazing in the rest of the house, and Will thinks of the electricity bill, ticking higher every second. He should go turn them all off. But something compels him to stay, to continue drying platters and trays as Carol washes them. He stacks them gently on the other counter, careful not to chip the edges or bang them against one another. Carol will have to put them away. He's not sure where they belong.

Carol is atypically silent. Normally, she would be going over every event from the party, analyzing comments, quizzing him about what people said to him. Instead, she washes steadily, a small sad frown on her face.

Leanne is getting married tomorrow. And then he'll join Cathay Pacific. Or maybe he won't. Maybe his body has tricked him for real this time, not just aging but decaying. He thinks of how quiet the television has seemed lately, how he missed air-traffic control hailing him. Decadence, decline, conclusion. The great trajectory.

Outside, there's a flash of light. A few seconds later, there's a long low growl, then a short clap.

"Damn," Carol says to herself.

Will pauses, dish towel in hand. "I heard it, too," he says softly.

Carol moves at the sink, but not toward him. She stops, her hands plunged into the water halfway to her elbows, as if looking for something.

"You'll probably pass the physical," she says, not looking at him. "But you know I can't go to Hong Kong."

"I just thought . . ." He has no idea what to say. Worse, he has no desire to protest. She's telling the truth.

"I know you'll go." Her voice is oddly gentle. She's not trying to start an argument or convince him of his mistake. She's nudging him gently, as she used to nudge the girls, toward understanding some simple, unchangeable thing.

"I will if they let me," he says dully. The dish towel hangs limp at his side. He can't say anything else. Something is driving him to go, something inside him that it's too late to change. "I'll go," he says, "but I'll come back. After a year or two."

She nods. His words don't surprise her. When she answers, she sounds tired, more than anything else.

"It will be a trial separation," she says. "And then we'll have to see."

When he was younger and they fought so often, he used to imagine the end of their marriage. He'd imagine getting fed up and walking out, suitcase in hand, or coming home to a house with the locks changed. Sometimes he'd make up speeches and imagine himself delivering them. He envisioned crying, fights, protests, broken dishes. Not this. This is like takeoff, something you know is going to happen but still yanks your stomach out when it does.

The first time he ever flew supersonic was on the T-38 in flight school. It was like nothing he ever knew. It was just a gee-whiz flight, a little go-around to give you the feel of it, and Will hadn't expected anything special. He'd been on the T-37 for months, and the planes didn't look all that different. But when they took off and started climbing at ten thousand feet a minute, he felt something drop in him. Instinctively, he grabbed his harness. The base was vanishing behind him so fast it seemed irretrievable, a stone dropped from a bridge. This was movement, he realized, real forward motion, no time to think back or second-guess. As he watched the ground drop away, the future clicked into place, and he felt an overwhelming joy. Now he was doing it. Now he was really going somewhere.

sixteen

IT'S EITHER LEANNE OR THE RAIN THAT WAKES
Margaret, although neither has made a sound. The room is lit with
even, gray light, and Leanne is standing inside the door. Margaret
squints at her. She's pale and biting her lip. It's so silent in the room
that Margaret can hear the long, smooth rustles of Trevor breathing
from across the hall. Last night she put him to bed and, on impulse,
climbed in with him. She lay there, one arm over his warm self, until
she was almost asleep. Then she slipped out from under the covers
and quickly, arms clutched around her body as if to hold in the calm
she had borrowed, slipped across the hall.

"Sorry, Margaret." Leanne comes forward to kneel by the side of
the bed. Her face moves into view right in front of Margaret's. "I
hate to wake you."

"I'm not sure you did wake me," Margaret says, putting a fist to
her eye. She's becoming aware of a distinct throbbing in her right
temple. Champagne. She hoists herself up on one elbow.

"Margaret, I'm sorry to hear about you . . . about you and
David." Leanne takes a deep breath after speaking. Looking at her
sister's moist face and red-rimmed eyes, Margaret realizes that
whatever hangover pain she feels, it's only a fraction of Leanne's.

"Oh, well . . ." Margaret drops back on the bed, rolling over to
stare at the ceiling. "Whatever. What's done is done."

"What are you going to do?" They are still whispering. It must
be before six.

"I'm going to sue him for divorce and custody." Margaret closes
her eyes. The words sound so sure, so final. They have the quality of
fixing whatever happened between her and David, freezing it into
one interpretation. That's a relief. She rolls over onto her side and
leans on her elbow once more, this time resting her head on her fist.

It's as if she and Leanne are exchanging confidences at a slumber party: who likes whom, who got kissed at the dance.

"I'm going to do whatever it takes to sort out my life," Margaret says, again using words to organize the mess of her life into a clearly defined narrative. It's the pre-set language of divorce she's using, she realizes, the discourse of the spurned wife. She'll get a small apartment with a nice room for Trevor, and she'll become one of those busy divorced mothers, budgeting carefully, rushing to get her dry cleaning on the way home from work, showing up alone for parent/teacher conferences. There are worse things to be.

"Are you sure that's what you want to do?" Leanne is frowning, her eyebrows drawing together as if contemplation is an effort.

"What other way is there?" Margaret says. It's not an entirely rhetorical question. If there is another clear path, she's willing to hear about it.

"I guess that's the only path." Leanne's voice is losing force. "But there might be ways of going without a path."

"Like what?"

Leanne shrugs. "I don't know. It just seems . . ." She raises a hand and waves it from one side to the other. "It's such a road map. Once you put all that machinery in motion, it's just going to . . . to go of its own accord."

Now Margaret frowns. It's funny, but Leanne has put her finger on the very thing that seems so horrifying about the whole process.

"I know what you mean," Margaret says. "But the question is, where else can I go?" She puts her hand, the one she's not leaning on, against the side of her cheek. Her face is cool in the morning air. Her words seem to have galvanized Leanne.

"Actually," Leanne whispers, "that's why I came to see you. I wanted to use your car. I need to go."

"Go where?"

Leanne shakes her head slightly in a vague, involuntary motion. "Just . . . go," she says.

Margaret sits up. "You don't want to get married."

Leanne clutches one wrist in the fingers of her other hand, hunching her shoulders together. She puffs her cheeks as she breathes out. "He wants me to go to Mexico with him," she says.

"And you don't want to?"

"Well, yes and no."

"Yes and no?"

Leanne looks at her with the expression of a teacher who has gone to great pains to explain something and now realizes that it has fallen on completely deaf ears. "How can I know what I want?" she says. "I don't. That's the whole point. That's what getting married is—being sure. Well, I'm not."

Margaret takes this in. "Does Kit know you're leaving?"

Now Leanne's head drops, and Margaret sees tears coming into her eyes.

"No."

"Leanne." Margaret touches her sister once, on the shoulder, feeling an unusual desire to reach out and comfort her. They've never been close that way. "Leanne, are you sure you want to leave?"

Leanne bites her lip, but she nods, the most vigorously assertive gesture she's made yet.

"Okay, then." Margaret swings her feet out of bed. "I'll get you the keys."

Leanne shudders slightly, from fear or relief. "I'm so sorry about this."

Margaret shakes her head firmly. "There's no reason to be sorry about any of it." She takes the keys from the dresser, where she has left them on top of a pair of socks, so they won't scratch the dresser.

"Everyone is all set for the wedding. Mom's going to be so disappointed. And Dad . . ." Leanne stops, frowning at the keys as Margaret puts them in her hand.

"It's your family, Leanne," Margaret says. "You get a free pass."

"But not with Kit." Leanne looks Margaret in the eye, projecting gratefulness but also fear. "I don't get a free pass with Kit. He'll never want to see me again."

Margaret looks out the window. The day couldn't be more miserable. Another pathetic fallacy. "No," she tells Leanne. "Probably not."

Leanne nods. She closes her fist on the keys. She moves forward, a little impulsive jerk, as if to hug Margaret, but then turns instead and slips out the door. She makes no sound as she leaves.

Margaret stands in the bedroom. It occurs to her, vaguely, that she ought to be annoyed. Her sister has done what she has always done, shirked all responsibility, leaving Margaret to do the dirty work of breaking the news to Kit and trying to console their parents. One of them will have to drive Margaret to Chicago while Leanne, vague and self-centered as ever, will be zipping off in Margaret's Rabbit, not even sure where she's going or how she'll give the car back.

But Margaret isn't angry. Her predominant feeling is pity. Pity for Leanne, who can't put her hands on one single thing she knows for sure; for Kit, who wants something Leanne can't give; even for Will and Carol, who want only to do the right thing and will be faced with a situation where the right thing is unclear. She's sorry for herself, too, not now, but years ago, when she should have done what Leanne did but couldn't, because she can't commit to uncertainty the way Leanne can. She chose certainty instead, a certainty that turned out to be wrong.

What should she do now? It's unlikely she'll be able to sleep anymore. Still, she could use some more rest. Her head is throbbing, and her stomach feels off kilter. She climbs back into bed, pulling the sheet and blankets tight to her chin. She's tense, waiting for something. She's not even aware of what, until she hears the sound of her car starting up. There's a pause after the motor starts, as if Leanne is considering. Then there's a thud and the sound of wheels moving forward. Margaret can hear the wet sound of the pavement sucking against the tires. The motor revs, then quiets at the edge of the driveway, waiting. A truck roars past with a high-pitched whine. As it fades away, Margaret hears her car's engine revving again as Leanne pulls out onto the road. It slows down, then speeds up and zooms off, growing fainter as it moves out of hearing.

It's before seven when Will wakes up. No one else is stirring. Beside him, Carol's chest is rising and falling with a heavy rhythm that means she's in a deep sleep. One hand is thrown over her face.

Everything is off balance. The house feels like a plane out of trim, pulling in too many directions at once, subject to every bump and bubble in the air. Will thinks of Leanne last night, her vaguely hysterical laugh, her wobbliness on her high heels. He thinks of the toast Margaret made, the bomb Carol dropped last night. Nothing is going to work out as he expected.

Gently, so as not to disturb Carol, he climbs out of the bed. The worst thing is to lie still when he feels like this. He puts one hand on the door while turning the knob, easing it slowly open and slipping out. It has already closed behind him when he remembers there are guests in the house, and he should probably be wearing a robe over his bare chest. It was too muggy to sleep with a T-shirt on. But no one is up yet. He'll go downstairs and have a snack, maybe a cup of tea, then come back up and get dressed.

He takes the stairs softly and walks silently across the foyer, his right ankle snapping once in the still house. When he gets to the kitchen, he's shocked to see that he's not alone. Bernice is sitting at the kitchen table, a mug of tea in one hand. Steam rises toward her face, which is turned to the sliding door, looking out. She turns and smiles as he freezes in the doorway.

"It's okay," she whispers. "I've seen a man in pajama bottoms before."

Will hadn't even thought of that—he was just taken aback at having his solitude disturbed. He glances down at himself, embarrassed, and turns to go back upstairs.

"Shhh," she says, making a fed up expression and waving one hand dismissively. "Don't bother. Really, what do you think I am, an ingenue?"

Will isn't sure of her tone, but he steps tentatively back into the kitchen. He's aware of a slight tension in himself. He's sucking in his gut. "I just thought I'd have a cup of tea," he says.

"The water's already hot," she answers, gesturing at it. "And I'd be glad of the company."

Will gets himself a tea bag and a mug, setting it on the stove and sloshing the hot water in. He goes to the table, still feeling self-conscious about his bare chest. Bernice looks much as he would have expected her to. She's wearing a pastel-flowered kimono, and her hair is loose at the sides of her face, free of sparkly barrettes. One on one, in the morning light, she looks pretty. He glances away.

"Well," he says. "Carol's not going to like this day."

Bernice turns to regard the gray drizzle, falling steadily to the ground. "I think it's perfect," she says. "It lets you know what to expect."

Will can't help but be surprised. He hadn't taken her for bitter. "What, lousy weather?" he asks.

She smiles. "No, not that. Just surprises. Things you didn't expect or plan for. But you go on. That's what marriage is."

"Ah." Will buries his nose in his tea.

She nods, watching him. "It's different when you live alone," she says. "Then everything can be kept how you want it. Most of it, any-way."

"Or at least the things you have control over," Will says, surpris-ing himself by speaking.

"Oh yes, well, you're right about that." Bernice sets her mug down on the table, placing it very carefully in what seems like a des-ignated space. "And the world is allowing us less and less control now, isn't it?"

"I'll say." Will eyes the cupboard, wondering whether there's anything good left after the party. With Bernice sitting there, he feels a bit shy about rummaging bare-chested through the cup-boards. Again he resists the impulse to glance down at his own chest, to see how saggy and aged it looks.

"You must feel like you have a lot less control than you used to," Bernice says softly, fixing him with that expectant look. Will won-ders what she's talking about—control over his family? Over his marriage ending and his daughters going their own ways? Or his career—his pension fund, his investments, his status at the airline. All those are things he thought he had control over once but have now slipped from his grasp.

"I mean"—Bernice takes a sip of tea—"you must feel as though you have less control over the airplane. After September eleventh."

"Oh, that." He traces a circle on the table with his mug. "Yeah. I guess so. I fly a lot of the transcontinental routes, you know. That could easily have been me up there. But TWA and American weren't integrated yet. And that American flight—that was a Boston crew." He pauses, but she seems interested. "The captain was a few years younger than I am. I didn't know him. But we had a lot in common—air force pilot, tour of duty in Vietnam, then the airlines. He had three daughters, not two." He glances at her quickly, embarrassed to reveal how much he knows. The airline newsletter did a long profile of the guy. Will carried it in his suitcase for a month, reading and rereading it when he was alone in his hotel room.

"The funny thing is," he says, "I didn't feel like I'd gotten lucky when I heard about it. I felt guilty." He leans forward. "I guess that's a pretty common feeling. Like in war."

Bernice nods. "I would think so," she says. She hesitates, then hiccups, a small noise, and places one hand over her mouth. In that gesture, Will sees through the graciousness and the calm to the real Bernice, and his heart clenches in sympathy for her. She's alone. She's a quiet, aging lady who has organized her life with great precision to downplay its central fact—loneliness. For her, sitting downstairs alone in the silence of morning is not a hard-earned treat, or even a quietly stolen pleasure. It's how she starts her day.

He looks at her, wishing he could think of something to say to show he sympathizes with her situation.

"Are you expecting someone?" she says.

"What?"

"Someone just pulled into the driveway."

A stone drops in Will's stomach. He didn't hear it.

"I'll go check it out," he says. He glances at the clock as he passes the stove. It's 7:20.

He knows who it is when he opens the door, because then he does hear something: the distinctively heavy idling of a police cruiser. What could they want? Stepping out on the porch, he automatically pulls the door shut behind him. The cruiser idles for a moment longer, and then the engine switches off. Will stands on the porch and waits.

A noise complaint from last night—that's all he can think of. The last time the police came to his house, it was to tell him that one of their horses had leaped the fence and been hit by a car. The car had sheared the horse's leg cleanly off, and the state trooper called to the accident scene had shot it in the head. But there are no animals on the farm now, with the exception of a few barn cats who come and go periodically. Carol had been encouraging him to get a flock of chickens or a couple of goats. Something kids who stay at the bed-and-breakfast can pet. It will add to the authenticity, she said. Will she do that alone, with him in Hong Kong?

"Mr. Gruen?" The sheriff walks toward him, his boots and sunglasses—in the rain, no less—making him imposing, even though he's the same height as Will. He doesn't look familiar.

"That's me." Will looks at the second officer. He does know him: Jim Kovacs, the son of a friend of his father's from way back. Old Jan Kovacs is dead now, from cancer of the mouth. Chewing tobacco, people said.

"Hello, Jim," he says, and the man nods.

"Will."

The sheriff looks down the highway, putting his hands in his back pockets as if regretting what he has to say. Will realizes that he's standing there in his pajama bottoms. He puts one arm across his chest, hanging it from his shoulder. The rain, he notices idly, seems to be tailing off.

"Mr. Gruen, we're looking for your daughter Margaret."

There's nothing Will has been expecting less. Still, he doesn't blink, just stands there, his face blank. A pair of barn swallows is swooping and diving in the sky above the road. It looks as if they're making perfect circles, circles that intersect at two exact points. Could they be doing it on purpose?

"She's not here," Will says. He holds himself perfectly still, so that his thought waves will beam themselves into the house. *Nobody come to the door.*

Jim clears his throat. "We understand she came up here for your younger one's wedding," he says. "With her son."

Will looks up at the swallows. Swoop and dive, swoop and dive. No one can tell him they don't do that for fun.

"Nope," he says. "Too busy. She's a professor, you know. Down to Chicago."

The two cops glance at each other.

"Well," Jim says—the sheriff seems to be letting him do the dirty work—"we drove by here last night and ran into a car in your driveway with Illinois plates. It was hers." He shuffles a little and glances at his superior. "We didn't come in then. We didn't want to ruin your party."

Will's gut runs cold. The car. Involuntarily, he looks out over the driveway. The Rabbit is gone. It's providence. Or maybe he's missing it in his eagerness to make it gone. His mind races. Did Margaret pull it into the barn? Did she foresee this and leave? She must have. But what on earth could she have done to make the police come after her? As soon as the question forms, it fades to a small footnote at the back of his mind. He glances once more, but the car really is gone. Maybe he made it disappear by wishing it would.

"Well," he says, sweeping a hand toward the driveway, "it's not there now, as you can see."

The sheriff follows Will's hand. It's clear the Rabbit isn't there, or they couldn't have pulled into the driveway themselves.

"Mind if we look around a bit," the sheriff says in a voice that suggests it's not a question.

Will takes a deep breath and looks up again. The swallows are gone. It's probably not that much fun after all, flying around in the rain.

"As a matter of fact, I do," he says. "Unless you can show me a warrant."

Jim makes a reflexive gesture. "Now, I think we're all reasonable people here," he says. He glances at the sheriff, but the other man nods, once, slowly.

"Okay, then," the sheriff says. "We'll let them know."

Who's them? Will wants to ask. But he knows better than to say a word. The cops turn around and walk back to the car. He can see Jim glancing surreptitiously at the house windows, but the sheriff walks with his face forward, his arms stiff at his sides. He doesn't look back at Will as they climb into their car.

Will thinks of Carol, asleep behind him. Leanne and Kit, too. Is Margaret there as well? And Trevor? He knew something was up. No one told him anything. They're going to have to tell him now.

He stands on the porch, unmoving, as the cops start the car. They sit there for a moment, the sheriff talking into the radio. The other one—Jim—glances over at Will, then back to his superior officer. Finally, the sheriff puts down the radio, and they move forward. They don't pause at the end of the driveway, just pull right onto the road. It's a good thing no one is coming. Will waits until the cruiser has sped up and disappeared, obscured by the Peddets' tree line. Then he turns around, wipes his palms on his pajama bottoms, and steps back into his house.

The rain patters against the windshield. When Leanne hits the lever, the wipers drag themselves across the window, driving silvery rivulets before them and toward the hood. This is no day to get married, even if she were sure it was the right thing to do.

She doesn't know where she's going. But as she gets away from the house, her mind grows clearer. Her stomach feels sick, and her head is killing her; she should have thought to take some aspirin before leaving. Even her hands on the steering wheel are shaky.

She's as hungover as a college kid. It seems to be getting hotter in the car—the windows are steaming over. She cracks hers. A little rain sprays in, but it feels okay, as refreshing as anything could feel right now.

She's ruined everything. She might have made it through last night if she hadn't started drinking. But even then she would be facing the same problem. Kit, she knows in the cold light of day, is still expecting to marry her. He has known about her drinking all along.

Tears fill her eyes, and instinctively, she bats the wiper lever. Things are still blurry, and she sniffs, rubbing the back of each hand in turn against one eye. How could he still want to marry her? How could he have known and never mentioned it? Didn't he worry about being married to someone so weak and feckless?

She takes a deep breath and steps on the gas. She's doing the right thing. It will be hard for Kit, but it's better this way. He deserves someone more solid, someone sure of what she wants.

She slows down to drive through Ryville. After Ryville, she'll come to the expressway, and there she'll have to make a decision: east or west. It seems clear. She'll go Chicago. Maybe she can stay with one of Margaret's friends and help her sister find a new place. Things in Cold Spring will be okay without her for a while. She has already lined up her best assistant manager to take charge of things for a week. She and Kit were supposed to be honeymooning, flying back to Atlanta with his mother, then renting a car and driving down to the Keys. She has at least a week before she has to decide whether to go back to Cold Spring.

The streets of Ryville are deserted. She drives by the Dairy Queen, the Friday-night hot spot. There's the insurance office where her aunt Janice works, and the turnoff to the factory where Eddie was recently made line manager. There's a small diner where she and Margaret used to go sometimes, and, as she gets to the edge of town, the high school they never attended because, as their mother put it, a diploma from there and fifty cents would get you a cup of coffee.

Leanne brakes at the town's single stoplight. There are no other cars, and after a minute, she's so eager to be on her way that she eases through the red light. She makes the turn toward the expressway and speeds up, putting the town behind her.

She hasn't gotten far when she sees the red lights in her rearview mirror. She wipes her eyes. "Damn." To think there was actually a cop sitting in downtown Ryville at seven o'clock on a Saturday morning. Who was he hoping to catch? He must have seen her pull through the light.

She pulls over and turns the car off, watching in her mirror as he glides in behind her. She keeps her hands on the steering wheel. With any luck, the ticket won't be expensive. If she's going to give up her store, she should watch her expenses. A knot catches in her throat.

The cop climbs out of his car and walks slowly toward her. Leanne thinks of the conversation with her father from the night before. She was blurry and tired, and what he was saying barely made sense. Dead reckoning. You might arrive somewhere without knowing it.

The cop leans toward her window, and she rolls it down.

"Officer," she begins, "there wasn't anyone at the light—"

He cuts her off. "Are you Margaret Gruen?" he asks.

Leanne looks at his hand, puzzled. He doesn't have his ticket book in it. "No," she says. "I'm her sister."

He bares his teeth once, not really a smile. He doesn't believe her. "I'll need to see some ID," he says. He looks into the backseat as if expecting to find something there.

Leanne takes her purse off the passenger seat. She reaches in and finds her wallet. The cop shifts nervously, his hand moving toward his gun. He's young, clearly younger than she is, and anxious about being alone with her. Since when has Margaret become a dangerous outlaw?

"Here you are," she says, holding out her New York State driver's license. He holds it up, scrutinizing it, then looks back at Leanne. Light rain is falling on the license, and he flicks it to clear it off so he can peer at it some more. She glances at his badge. *Terhune.*

"Is there a problem?" she asks.

"This is Margaret Gruen's car, isn't it?" he asks.

Leanne nods. "Yes," she says. "She lent it to me." It occurs to her that Margaret could have reported the car stolen to bring her back. That's the kind of thing Margaret might do if she thought Leanne was making a mistake. But her sister had supported Leanne's desire to leave. Maybe Kit reported the car stolen. But he wouldn't know the plates.

"I'd like to see the registration," the cop says, and Leanne hopes Margaret is as organized about her car as she is about everything else. She pops the glove compartment open and almost smiles. How could she have doubted her sister? On top of a box of tissues is a small folder with Margaret's handwriting on the front: *Car Documents*.

"Here it is," Leanne says, handing the whole thing to the cop. He flips it open to the first page and reads. After a moment, he hands it back to her.

"Where is your sister?" he asks.

Leanne's stomach flips. This is really happening. *Dead reckoning,* she thinks. Suddenly, it seems clear what her father was trying to tell her. Your life doesn't happen somewhere in the future. You can't wait to arrive at it. You're already there.

"I don't know," she says.

"You don't know?"

"No."

"Why do you have her car?"

Leanne grips the steering wheel harder. Her stomach felt sick already; now she's almost certain she's going to throw up. She wonders if she can get the cop out of the way so she can step out of the car.

"I told you, she lent it to me." She takes a deep breath. "For my wedding. I flew to Chicago, and we were supposed to drive up together, but she didn't come. I drove up to Michigan alone." Her sudden flow of speech seems to relax the cop.

He rests one arm on the top of the car window. "So where is she now?"

Leanne shakes her head. "Like I said, I don't know."

"You're getting married?"

She nods. "That's right, today."

"So where are you going?"

There's a spill of freckles across his nose. His chin is nice, and his eyes are dark but not cruel. One ear sticks out more than the other. To her great frustration, Leanne's eyes fill with tears.

"I don't know," she says, looking down at the steering wheel. "I was just . . . I just couldn't sleep, so I went out for a drive." She sniffs, trying to get control of her tears, and looks back at the cop.

Amazingly, the tears seem to have exactly the right effect. He leans back, unsure of himself, clearly wanting to put distance between them.

"Well, all right, then," he says. "But watch yourself. You were going a little fast through town."

Leanne nods, shocked by how quickly things have turned around. He swivels on his heels and moves back toward his car, adjusting his hat in the rain. Leanne watches in the rearview mirror as he climbs back into the cruiser.

He hits his blinker once and, without waiting for her, moves out onto the road and passes her. He lifts one hand stiffly, dismissing her.

Leanne sits in the car. The rain has gotten harder. She can hear it drumming on the roof like tiny fingertips. The police want Margaret. Undoubtedly, it's a mistake, a misunderstanding. She turns the key in the ignition, but the car wheezes grindingly. She started it already. Leaning forward to squint through the windshield, she checks to see that the cop has truly gone. Then she looks behind. No one. Smoothly, in one easy curve, she does a U-turn. The light turns green as she approaches, and she speeds up. She wants to be home.

seventeen

MARGARET WAKES FOR THE SECOND TIME WHEN the phone rings. She sits bolt upright. Who would call on the morning of the wedding? It might be David. Or Leanne. Maybe she's having trouble with the car. Whichever it is, there's no doubt in Margaret's mind that she's the one being hailed.

She hurries to the kitchen and grabs the receiver.

"Hello. I'm trying to reach Margaret?" It's the last voice on earth she expected to hear.

"Vasant?"

"Oh, Margaret, I'm very glad it's you." Warmth floods Margaret's body. One of the things that drew her to Vasant was his calm, melodious voice. Just hearing him speak was somehow sensual. Now his voice has manifested itself when she most needed to hear it. He sounds relieved to hear her, too. Perhaps the separation has been unbearable for him.

"I think we have a problem." His voice is stilted by anxiety. Margaret looks at the clock: 7:40. Under four and a half hours to the wedding. Except there won't be a wedding; the bride has fled. And Margaret has to explain it to everyone.

"What's going on?"

"I was going to ask you about that. I've been quite concerned the past few days. About David, I mean."

"David?" Margaret's heart thuds. He wouldn't have done anything self-destructive. She's sure of it. Or at least she used to be, when she knew him.

"Yes, David has been acting . . . a little unhinged." He says it reluctantly, with his characteristically Indian good manners. Vasant is nothing if not gracious. She liked that, too, the strict propriety masking a passionate sensibility.

"Unhinged?" Margaret can hear shuffling coming from her

father's study. He must be up, too. She lowers her voice almost to a whisper. "What do you mean, 'unhinged'?"

"Well, he challenged me to a duel."

"What?" Margaret forgets to be quiet and gives a short, hysterical bark of laughter. The way Vasant says "du-el," with two syllables, makes it sound as if people actually conduct them.

"Yes, I was coming into the department after teaching my afternoon lecture, and David was there, lying in wait, as it were—"

"Lying in wait?" Margaret suppresses an almost overwhelming urge to giggle. She had no idea Vasant could be so dramatic.

"Yes, and he handed me this, uh, note that he had printed up . . ."

"A note? He challenged you to a duel in a *note?"*

"It appears so, yes." Vasant's voice drops, and now he sounds less dramatic than simply morose.

"Oh God." Margaret takes a deep breath. The effort not to laugh is making her feel as though she's going to hyperventilate.

"I can only assume"—and here Vasant's voice takes a cooler, more formal tone, as if he's treading cautiously—"he is aware of things transpiring between you and me."

"Oh my God," Margaret says again. It's too much, too many levels of misunderstanding and missed connections. Poor Vasant—he's like a dramatic character who turned up in the wrong play. "Yes," she says, "of course he knows. I told him myself."

"I see." It's clear from Vasant's tone that he doesn't see. In the play he comes from, a nineteenth-century melodrama, perhaps, infidelity is always secret. Margaret sighs. If only she could join him in that play. Suddenly, she's exhausted with the prospect of everything she has to do. Here and now, with her family, there's too much, and now this ridiculous farce going on in Chicago without her. She's going to be the laughingstock of Evanston.

"Look, Vasant," Margaret says, "I'm really sorry you were dragged into this. David has cracked somehow. It was not our arrangement. This was not supposed to happen."

"Your arrangement?" For the first time, an angry note creeps into Vasant's euphonic voice. "You had an arrangement concerning me? Perhaps I could be privy to it?"

"Not about you." Margaret puts a hand over her eyes. Her head is aching. "About us. David and me. We were supposed to be free. You know, both of us, free to . . ." What was it her lawyer said? *Open marriage.* She isn't going to be able to describe and justify something she never truly wanted.

"You know what?" she says. "It doesn't matter. What does matter is that David's behaving crazily. But I'm going to work it out. What did you . . . How did you leave it with him?"

"I did nothing. I thought the best thing would be to pretend it never happened. After all, I don't think it would be good for people in the department to know he's acting . . . as you say, crazily."

"No, you're right, of course. Thank you. Maybe you could avoid him for a while?"

"He has given me one week to respond, in any case."

Margaret squeezes her lips together in order not to laugh again. She takes a deep breath through her nose. "That's good," she says. "I'll be back there before then, and I'll try to sort it out with him."

"I just thought you should know." Vasant sounds uncertain.

"Thank you, Vasant. Really. I mean it."

"You're welcome." There's an awkward pause. "And things there? Does your sister's wedding progress well?"

Margaret can't stifle the laugh this time. "Oh, yes, as well as can be expected," she manages to get out. "Thanks again. I'll let you know how things are going."

"Yes, thank you, that would be nice."

Margaret hangs up the phone and leans her forehead against it. She doesn't cry. Her soon-to-be-ex-husband has gone completely mad, her sister has taken her car and ditched her own groom at the altar, and her mother is about to come downstairs and keel over when she finds out, but Margaret feels slightly better. It's as if the insanity has finally gotten out of hand. There's no telling what will happen next.

The whole thing with Vasant seems childish and somehow desperate. Margaret is sorry she got him involved. As for her flights of fancy about a future together—she pushes away the vague sense of embarrassment. There's no time for that now.

Her marriage to David has no future, either. But there's an odd comfort in the fact that David loved her enough to be jealous. For years, she secretly suspected that his issues with fidelity were not, as he claimed, intellectual, but about not loving her enough. She stifled her doubts and went along with his idea not because she wanted it but because she wanted to be the kind of person who did. She wasn't—and neither, in the end, was he. She rocks gently from side to side, her forehead rolling back and forth on the telephone's smooth plastic surface.

The front door opens. Startled out of her thoughts, Margaret straightens up. *Get a grip,* she tells herself. The phone leaves a tactile impression on her forehead. She goes out into the hall.

"Margaret?" Leanne is dripping in the foyer, whispering and looking pale. She's holding out a cupped palm. "Here are your car keys. I decided to come back."

The phone wakes Carol. One ring, then half a ring stopped short. Her eyes open, and she's not sure if she heard it or dreamed it. She looks at the clock. Wedding day.

And marriage-ending day. *Trial separation.* She hadn't thought about the words before they came out. But then they were there, a fact, living and breathing like a third person in the room. She stares at the ceiling and considers how she feels. Strangely, she's not distraught.

Sometimes, when she was a young housewife, she would lose control of her checkbook. Little errors would creep in here and there, and then they would add up to bigger errors, and by the time she sat down to untangle the numbers, the account log would be an impenetrable web of confusion. Will would get annoyed with her. *Just figure it out,* he would say. *Just sit down and do the math and sort it all out.* And she would shake her head. *I can't,* she would tell him. *There is no sorting it out.* She would call the bank, get the new balance, draw a line under the entries so far, and start over.

That's how she feels now. It's almost a relief to acknowledge it—yes, it's a mess, but she doesn't have to wade into it, she can turn her back and move forward.

Irresponsible, she tells herself. She's being irresponsible. A responsible wife would sit down and start talking, go back to the origin, the moment where things went wrong, and set it right. But what moment would that be? Marrying Will? Then she wouldn't have the girls. Moving to Michigan with him? What part of her life would she lose by erasing that?

Slowly, she becomes aware of a low murmur downstairs. Maybe someone really is on the phone. She sits up. No matter what happened last night, today is the wedding day. Time to get things going.

She catches sight of herself in the mirror as she stands, but turns her back on the image to make the bed. She doesn't spend much time in front of the mirror anymore. When she was young, she liked how she looked, spending a lot of time perfecting her hair and makeup. These days she looks in the mirror out of necessity, to make sure her hair is done right, her mascara not blotching onto her eyelids, but there's no pleasure in it. It's not her, the lined face, the thinning hair, any more than the young girl with the dark eyes and elegant nose was her, although she tried to believe it was.

She turns from the neatly made bed and contemplates herself, standing still, her arms at her sides. The face in the mirror gazes blankly back at her, refusing to give up its secrets. She picks up the decorative pillows off the floor and arranges them neatly on the bed. Her robe is on the back of the door. If people are already up, she should probably make some breakfast. They're all going to need it.

From the hallway, she can hear that the voice on the phone is Margaret's. She moves quickly to the bathroom and pushes the half-open door aside. She nearly jumps out of her skin to see someone there.

"I'm sorry," she says quickly. It's Kit, sitting on the edge of the tub, his chin on his clasped hands. He gives her a wan smile.

"That's okay. I'm just sitting here." He stands, offering to leave, holding up a hand to prevent her from backing out the door. "I'll let you have it." He's tall, she realizes as he draws himself upright, taller than Will. Funny that Leanne should have a husband taller than hers.

"No, stay, I just . . ." She feels awkward. Something about him conveys an intensity, as if she interrupted something very private. He holds something in his hand.

"What's that?" The words are out before she can consider them. He stops, frozen, and holds his hand out to her, palm up. In it is the ring, the tiny antique sapphire set in old-fashioned silver scrollwork that Leanne was wearing yesterday.

"It's Leanne's ring," he says. The words seem to wilt him, and he plops back down on the edge of the bathtub. His voice is quiet but direct. "She told me last night she doesn't want to go to Mexico. But it looks like that's not all she doesn't want."

In spite of her confusion—Mexico? Who's going to Mexico?—Carol finds herself moving forward, her hand reaching out to Kit's. She closes his fist around the ring.

"Don't say it," she says. "It isn't true." She's surprised by the conviction in her voice. It's Leanne's day. Margaret's marriage is ending, and Carol's, too perhaps, but Leanne's is just beginning.

Kit bites his lip, looking up at her. He wears the expression children get when they want to believe in something they're starting to doubt, like the tooth fairy.

"She's not here," he says. "She left."

"She'll come back," Carol says. "She's just clearing her head."

Kit looks down at his closed fist, as if willing the ring to disappear inside it.

"You know"—Carol is taken over by an impulse to fill the silence with words—"I hope you and Leanne will come back here and visit a lot. You should think of this as your country home. There's plenty of room. And I'm going to set it all up as a bed-and-breakfast, you know, so it will be easy as anything to have guests." She's babbling, but it seems to have the right effect. His shoulders loosen slightly. He lifts his head and looks at her, and she stops talking. He holds his hand out, the empty one, palm up, in that funny way he has when he asks a question.

"Was it like living someone else's dream?" he asks. "Coming here?"

Carol regards the young man before her. All her life, she has imagined the day when she could tell her grown girls exactly what she suffered, how much anger she held in and how much love for them it took for her to keep going on, as she felt it was her duty to do. She has imagined them putting their arms around her and saying, *Thank you. We understand.* Now is the first time anyone has asked her to tell this story.

Kit looks back at her. He's not handsome, really. There's something too soft about his lips. And he could use a haircut.

She shakes her head. "No," she says. "It was my dream, too."

His eyebrows rise, and there's a slam from below. They both start and look toward the hall. It sounded like the front door.

Will has been in his study. After the police left, he thought of a photograph. It's a picture of the girls, sharing the seat of his father's tractor when they were about six and four. As soon as he thought of it, he felt certain he needed to find it and give it to Leanne on her wedding day.

Margaret has been talking on the phone. After the police left, he looked in her room and saw her lying there, asleep with a little frown on her face, a look so worried he couldn't bear to wake her with more questions and problems. He went instead to his study, and began rifling through the family photo albums.

When the front door opens, his first thought is that the cops have come back with a warrant. He goes quickly to the foyer.

"Leanne!" he says, stopped short by the miserable specimen standing there, dripping on the carpet. "I thought you were the cops!"

"The cops?" Margaret is there, too, standing in the hallway from the kitchen. She turns as pale as her sister.

"They were here. I sent them away," Will says.

"They stopped me, too," Leanne says. "They were looking for you."

"Fucking hell." Margaret sits down, right there at the edge of the foyer. Leanne immediately lowers herself onto the floor as well. Will feels tall and distant all of a sudden. He goes over to the staircase and sits down on the fourth stair.

"What did you tell them?" Margaret asks.

"That I didn't know where you were," Leanne says.

"Me, too," Will puts in. "I told them they couldn't search the house."

"Oh my God." Margaret closes her eyes and opens them again. "You guys did the right thing," she says. "They would have taken Trevor."

"What?" Will is shocked by the anger that spikes through him.

"It's David," Margaret says. "He's reported Trevor kidnapped. Apparently, one parent is not supposed to take a child across state lines with the intent to deprive the other parent of access. Or something like that."

"That asshole!" Leanne says. She stretches out on her side and puts her head on her arm, speaking with her eyes closed. The relaxed position jars oddly with the anger in her voice. "How could he do that to you?"

Margaret clutches her knees to her chest. Will thinks he has never seen her look so knowing and so like a scared child all at once.

"How could I do it to him?" she says. "We've both made a huge mess of things." She rubs the carpet with her hand. "I've got to go back and try to sort something out with him," she says. "It's the only thing to do." She rubs the back of her hand against her nose, then sneezes.

"Carpet dust," Will says.

Margaret's eyes are watery from the sneeze. "You guys didn't even know," she says. "But you lied anyway." Her face twists, and she looks like she wants to say more, but Leanne interrupts.

"I came back to sort things out with Kit," she says. "I don't want to go forward without him."

"What about Mexico?" Margaret says, rubbing her pajama sleeve against her nose.

"I want to go," Leanne says. "I'm just scared." She opens her eyes. "It's his dream, not mine. I don't want to end up . . ." She stops and closes her eyes again. "Crap, I feel sick," she says.

"What will you do?" Margaret is looking at Leanne with a new interest. Leanne doesn't move, and for a second Will wonders if she's fallen asleep.

"Get a dog," Leanne finally says. "Go to Mexico. Or not. Get a villa. A shack somewhere. One of those islands off the coast of Africa. What are they called? The Seychelles. I have no idea."

"I have no idea, either," Margaret says. "I mean, about me. What's going to happen for me." Neither of them moves.

"I wanted to find a picture," Will says. "But I couldn't. I'm sure it's in there somewhere. It's a picture of you girls on your grandfather's old yellow tractor. It's the happiest you've ever looked. I wanted you to have it, Leanne."

"On Granddad's tractor?" Margaret says, frowning at him. "Wasn't his tractor green?"

"He had an old one that was yellow, but that was before we were big enough to go on it," Leanne says, eyes still closed. "Are you sure it was us?"

"Who else could it be?" Will asks. "It was the two of you, sharing the seat, with your hands on the steering wheel. It was yellow. I can see it like it was right here in front of me."

Margaret lies down on her side. "You know," she says, "we're going to have to pull ourselves together and go through with this thing now."

"I'm not sure I can," Leanne says. "Is there any way to just skip it?"

"I can't believe neither of you can remember that shot," Will says. "It was classic. The way that yellow tractor gleamed in the sun." They both ignore him. "Maybe it fell out of one of the albums and got behind the shelves or something." He stands up to go back and look some more.

"Don't go," Margaret says without moving.

"No, stay," Leanne says. "This is almost bearable like this." Slowly, Will lowers himself back onto the step.

"You see?" Carol's voice floats down from above. Will looks up and sees her gliding toward the top of the stairs. Behind her is Kit, a look of wonder on his face. Carol's eyes meet Will's, and for the first time this weekend, he feels like the two of them are in on something, working together. She gestures at the foyer below. "There she is, Kit, lying like a lump, with under four hours to go. Leanne!" Her voice takes a level of command Will hasn't heard her use on the girls in years. "Come upstairs right now and talk to your husband!"

eighteen

THE RAIN HASN'T EVEN HAD THE DECENCY TO COME down decisively, forcing them inside, but has throttled back to an off-and-on drizzle, misting down from a grayish sky. It makes the edges of everything look fuzzy, as if the world is in soft focus.

"Look how green and lush the plants are," Margaret says close to Carol's ear. "This weather has been great for them." It's an almost laughable attempt at optimism. Carol wants to respond to Margaret's gesture of support. She bites her lip, trying not to feel as if some malevolent god has arranged everything to disappoint her.

"Dad's enjoying playing host." Margaret's voice is slightly forced, hinting at her own anxiety. Carol has noticed her glancing around nervously. Will is holding Trevor's hand in his as he greets people, and Carol can feel Margaret's attention stretching taut with every move Trevor makes. She reaches a hand out to brush her daughter's side. They're standing in the door of the Green Lake Country Club. Carol should be out there, too, greeting guests with Will, but she can't. She needs some time to pull herself together.

"Oh, God," Leanne says behind them. "I think I'm going to be sick." There's rustling as she turns around and heads back to the ladies' room. Margaret watches her go. The look on her face is inscrutable.

"I've never seen anyone have such bad nerves," Carol says. "It's just awful."

"It's not nerves, Mom," Margaret says dryly. "It's a hangover."

Carol presses her lips together and gives Margaret a *no more nonsense* look. Things are bad enough without Margaret spreading tales of bridal debauchery.

"Just give her these," she says, taking a box of mints from her purse. Margaret takes them silently and follows her sister into the ladies' room.

Carol stands, watching guests arrive with umbrellas, raincoats covering up their dress clothes, plastic bonnets tied to their heads. This is not how it was supposed to be. It was supposed to be a gorgeous day, sun lighting joyful faces, Leanne stunning against the greenery, a blue sky whispering to them of infinity. Instead, it's Will chasing off the police, Margaret weeping at the breakfast table, Leanne not even able to eat anything. She'd been out driving around—to calm her nerves, she said. When she returned, she acted more like a prisoner being led to execution than a bride about to marry the man she loved. She went upstairs, and for two hours the sound of earnest conversation came from the room she and Kit were sharing. Just as Carol was about to panic, Leanne emerged, already in her dress, holding Kit's arm in one hand, a wad of Kleenex in the other.

"But it's bad luck to see the bride in her dress!" Carol cried, and Kit smiled at her, shaking his head.

"I'm not looking yet," he said.

The justice of the peace arrives, and Will pumps his hand. He's acting the way he acted when the girls were born: beaming, goofy, inflated with his own importance. He places a hand on the other man's shoulder and juts his chin at the sky. The two of them laugh. Then Will draws Trevor toward the justice and says something, indicating him with his other hand.

Of all of them, Will is the only one who seems, if anything, to have gained something from what happened. Even right after the incident with the police—what lies must David have told them to send the sheriff to kidnap Trevor?—Will has seemed more hearty and booming than he has in days. He's acting like a man who has just dodged a bullet, not a man who has lied to agents of the law and seen his daughter transformed into a fugitive. Not like a man embarking on a trial separation. Now he's striding around like Trevor's guardian angel. Anger swirls in Carol's stomach, but it's not at Will. How dare David do this to Margaret, to all of them, on Leanne's wedding day, too. He deserves every punishment Margaret's lawyer can dole out.

And yet that's the worst part: Margaret has taken the whole thing very strangely. She'll change her mind later, when she comes to her senses, but for now she's insisting on dropping the lawyer. Instead, she says she's leaving for Evanston tomorrow morning, with Trevor, to talk to David.

"How can you do that?" Carol cried. "How can you go back there with him acting this way?" Margaret had not countered that she had thought it through, had not explained point by point how this was clearly the best strategy or declared that Carol just couldn't understand.

"I don't know," she said, shaking her head. "I don't know what's going to happen. That's the point." She had pulled Trevor onto her lap and smoothed his hair over and over, until the boy got fed up and climbed down. Then, as he headed for the playroom, Margaret sat there, her arms at her sides.

"I think she's over the worst of it." Margaret lifts her feet as she returns, checking her shoes for scraps of toilet paper. She runs her hands absently down her dress, a beautiful sheath made of green silk shantung. It looks like something Carol might have made for herself in the sixties. "Am I all in place?" she asks.

"You look absolutely gorgeous," Carol says. "I only hate to see it spoiled by this miserable rain."

Margaret comes to the door and surveys the scene, letting her eyes linger on Trevor. "It won't spoil it entirely," she says. "It's just something we didn't plan for."

There's a rustling behind them, and Carol turns, expecting Leanne. But it's only the doves scrabbling around in their cage.

"You should take them and put them under your seat soon," Margaret says. "Unless you want to make them part of the procession."

Carol leans over to peer down at the birds. "The male one is feeling better, I think." She glances up in time to see Margaret smile and look away. "What?"

Margaret shakes her head. "I think you're right" is all she says.

The door to the ladies' room opens, and Leanne appears, pale and wispy.

"I love Kit," she says, her voice wavering on the verge of tears. "I really do. But this is awful."

Margaret laughs. "You are so right," she says. She goes to Leanne. "Here, have another mint."

Leanne looks like a child who doesn't know whether to laugh or cry, and then her face rearranges itself and she's an adult again, taking a mint from the proffered box.

What's going to happen with her bed-and-breakfast? Carol isn't so certain anymore. In the last few days, the idea has come to seem like it was as much about lashing out as it was an attempt to do something. A pretend farm. Its original impulse was meanness. She feels vaguely embarrassed about it. *You want rustic—here it is.*

"You girls will always have a home here," Carol says. "I'm not leaving the farm." They look at her, Margaret with a small smile, Leanne considering.

Margaret puts a hand on Carol's arm. "I'm glad," she says. "I might need a place to get away."

"And no matter what happens"—Carol speaks quickly to get past the lump in her throat—"no matter what happens, we'll always be a family."

And then Leanne is moving forward in her beautiful dress, her arms held out, her face scared but somehow serene. She puts her arms around Carol and hugs her, and Carol can feel the smooth solidity of the satin bodice, which looks so light and airy but is constructed like a suit of armor.

"Thanks, Mom," Leanne says.

After a moment, Carol draws back and regards her daughter. She wants to say something, to offer some final piece of wisdom and ask some final question: *Are you sure about this? Do you think you'll be happy? Do you need anything from me?* But none of them seems right.

"You're perfect," she says. She looks at Leanne's face, then sweeps her eyes down the length of the dress. She stops in horror. "Leanne," she breathes. "You didn't finish the hem."

Leanne's face goes, if possible, a bit paler. She leans forward to see. "Oh damn," she says. "You're right."

The three of them stand there for a moment, frozen in surprise. Then Carol shakes her head. "I've got a sewing kit," she says. "The little one in my purse." She'll get her keys from Will, retrieve her purse from the car, and then they can quickly stitch in something, anything. Everyone will have to wait.

"Wait," Margaret says, stepping forward. "It's too late for that. It's too late to sew anything." She rummages in her own purse.

"What do you mean?" Carol demands. "Leanne's fast."

"Not fast enough." Margaret seems to have a ton of stuff in her bag.

"Well, what do you propose we do, then?"

Margaret stops rummaging and holds up a small item in triumph. "The bride's best friend," she says happily. "Scotch tape!"

And then Leanne actually laughs, and Margaret is smiling and squatting down to tape up the hem, and Carol looks out to see that most of the seats have been filled and it's time for her to go sit down. She goes to the metal cage and wonders, for the fifteenth time, whatever possessed Kit to paint it green. Is it a joke on their last name? That doesn't seem very nice. Maybe it's a tribute to Michigan, to the lush greenness around them, which would be funny, since the green is the result of all this rain. She notices Leanne looking at the cage, too, with a small, private smile.

Carol picks it up. "I'm going to go take my place," she says, and both girls look at her. With their faces at the same angle, they look alike, more so than they did as kids.

"Okay, Mom, thanks," Leanne says. "See you after."

Will is walking his daughter down the aisle. There's no music, just the soft sound of the rain, a small lapping from the lake, the rustle of people adjusting themselves on damp chairs. He hears it all. He can see Leanne in his peripheral vision, her chin held high. Earlier she seemed nervous, distraught even, but now she is calm. Her face is pale, but there's a small smile in the corners of her mouth, and her eyes are soft with what must be happiness. Her dress rustles as she walks. Tiny pearls dangle from her ears.

Those are the pearls that were his eyes.

There are familiar faces on both sides of the aisle. It's traditional for the bride's people to be on one side and the groom's on the other. But Leanne has never been weighed down by tradition. She has always wanted to do things her own way. She takes after him in at least that one thing.

The man his daughter will marry is standing next to the justice of the peace, in front of a white trellis. His hair is limp from the rain. In spite of the weather, Will is glad they're outside. The air is clean and fresh. Carol might have preferred a church, for the tradition of it. Then again, maybe not. Since yesterday, he has the feeling he barely knows Carol. But this ceremony seems right for Leanne: simple, still, with one graceful gesture at the end.

On his arm, Will can feel Leanne struggling to walk on the uneven lawn. She clutches his elbow, and he stops while she pulls her heel out of a boggy clump of grass. She smiles at him, her eyes laughing. Then she straightens up and they start out again. He is walking his daughter down the aisle. This is a day all fathers look forward to living. A lot of them never will. He was one of the lucky ones. The Air Force ordered 833 Thuds for Operation Rolling Thunder. Almost half of them were shot down. Not everyone had his luck on reentry.

Margaret is standing near the trellis, watching her sister. She was five months old the first time Will saw her. She could already sit up. She was a determined baby with piercing eyes, such a deep blue they looked black. She had learned to smile and laugh and roll over and reach out to grab a toy before he ever met her.

Now she's a grown woman, with a marriage disintegrating around her, and for the first time ever, she seems unsure where life is taking her next. For some reason, he doesn't feel sad about that. He's almost happy for her, odd as that seems. She'll make her own way now.

Will and Leanne stop walking. They have reached the end of the aisle. He kisses his daughter on the cheek. He has tears in his eyes.

He turns and walks awkwardly toward the chair next to Carol, his part in the ceremony over. His part in Leanne's life is over in some sense, or at least changed forever. That's something he's grown used to, the constant back-and-forth of family life. Even now that the girls are grown, things keep changing all the time.

"I don't know what's going to happen," Carol said to him that morning. "But I think it will be good for us both to be apart." He was knotting his tie at the mirror. When he was a young man, Carol used to do it for him. She said he always got it too loose.

"Do you want the bed-and-breakfast that bad?" he asked, and was surprised at the silence that followed. When he turned, she was shaking her head, her expression almost apologetic.

"No," she said. "It's not that. It's just that I've made you the reason for my unhappiness for too long." She looked up at him, frowning. "It's too easy."

Will looked back in the mirror. He couldn't tell if his tie looked good or not. He could see Carol over his shoulder in the mirror. She was still, gazing out the window.

"Okay, then," he said. "I'm ready to go."

The justice of the peace is speaking to Leanne and Kit. The back of Leanne's head looks like Carol's. Next to him, he can sense Carol, a new Carol, one he recognizes less than the one he sees in his daughter. A separation. The conversation hovers between them, complete and faceted, like a gem. It's irreversible, but oddly, it doesn't change the pure joy he feels, looking at the back of Leanne's head.

He might be making a mistake. How many mistakes has he made already? Signing on for the Air Force—was that a mistake? Joining TWA instead of Delta or United, moving the family back to the farm. Somehow none of his mistakes has turned out to be fatal. Is that luck, or fate, or something else entirely?

In war there are two main questions. The first is *Why me?* The answer to that is simple: *I was there. I was in the wrong place at the wrong time.* The second question is *Why not me?* That should be just as easy to answer—*I wasn't there. I was in the right place instead.* But somehow that's not satisfactory.

The justice of the peace is smiling. Kit leans over to kiss Leanne. She puts her hands on his shoulders, her arms resting on top of his. Her eyes are closed, and it's clear that in this moment, she's happy. They step apart, and Will realizes it's over. She's married. She's leaving the family and yet she's still here, part of it in a new way. Everything is spinning apart, transforming itself yet again into something rich and strange. His eyes blur and he can't see. He feels transported, lifted above everything in his life, ethereal. He feels as if he's floating above the heads of the guests, an airy spirit, looking down on it all.

The bride and groom turn to Carol, who has pulled the birdcage from under her seat. She stands up and struggles with the door. Leanne moves to her mother and unlatches it. She reaches her hands inside and takes a bird. Kit steps forward to take the second one. He seems a little taken aback by how it feels. The two of them look at each other, Leanne calmer than she's looked all day, Kit raising his eyebrows with wonder. Leanne's lips move as she silently counts: *One, two three.* Together, they draw the birds toward themselves, then toss them lightly upward. The justice looks up in surprise. Margaret takes a step back, laughing. There's a shuffling of wings and flapping, and the birds hang there for a moment. Then one of them shoots upward and the other follows. The heads of all the guests turn up, following their flight. Kit and Leanne stand close together, their faces growing shiny in the rain. Will, too, raises his face to the sky and watches them go.

acknowledgments

I would like to thank David Hamilton at *The Iowa Review*, where a version of material from *Flight* appeared as "Name of the Game." Thanks also to Yaddo, the Virginia Center for the Creative Arts, and the Sewanee Writers' Conference for help and encouragement. My agent, Nat Sobel, deserves boundless gratitude for having seen what this book could be even before I could. Jenni Lapidus and Anna Bliss at Sobel Weber were astute and generous. And my editor, Sydny Miner, was somehow rigorous and nurturing at the same time. Their unflagging help made this a better book.

Michael Cunningham set me on this path by saying exactly the right thing at exactly the right time, and Romulus Linney kept me moving down it with his wisdom and his friendship. I can never thank either of them enough. I owe my reader friends for their insight and even more for tolerating me: special thanks to Susan Aasen, Maura Hogan, Elise Mac Adam, Paula Morris, James Wallenstein, Amy Weldon, Sarah Zimmerman, and especially Allan Hepburn and Lisa Lerner, my blue-eyed boy and my brown-eyed girl. I also owe much gratitude to the Vietnam veterans whose writings about the war helped me envision some small fraction of it, in particular G. I. Basil, Jack Broughten, Ed Rasimus, and Dick Rutan.

The greatest debt of support is owed to my family: Fred, Sallie, Heidi, Bob, and Miranda, my bunny, my best one.